SING DOWN
THE STARS

L.J. HATTON

SING DOWN THE STARS

SKYSCAPE

SKYSCAPE

Published by Skyscape, New York

www.apub.com

Amazon, the Amazon logo, and Skyscape are trademarks of Amazon.com, Inc., or its affiliates.

ISBN-13: 9781503946569
ISBN-10: 1503946568

Cover illustration by Chris Gibbs

Cover design by Kristin Smith

Printed in the United States of America

When they came, it wasn't with flying saucers or rockets. They weren't hulking monsters or Roswell Greys. They were more like jellyfish—bioluminescent blobs of goo that spread out across the sky.

They brought the rain . . .

CHAPTER 1

The Show opened at twilight, when anything was possible.

It was the time of not quite day or night when the promise of something unexpected shimmered in the wonder light, and the mundane turned to magic, if wielded by a master's hand. Magnus Roma was a master; The Show was his dominion. He was my father, and it was my home.

Forecasts had called for storms that night. We held our breath, but they never came.

My father said that people once danced in the rain, that they chased lightning and rode the wind, but not anymore. Not where others might see and suspect, and not since the Great Illusion made rain a bad omen. The only weather that crowds would tolerate now was the kind that came with the price of admission, and *that* we were happy to provide.

Lightning struck the apex of a fence around our circus grounds, brilliant against the darkening sky. Nothing but Tesla coils and a large-scale Faraday cage, but the effect was mesmerizing. Blue current swirled the lines, touching the earth as another bolt crackled off the fence peaks, illuminating our field with St. Elmo's fire. So many people were used to looking up in fear of what they might find among the clouds that it took a while for them to do anything other than startle, but eventually, those who had crowded the gates forgot they were in a hurry. They shed their worries and watched, awe flickering in their eyes like candles lit with ideas they'd never dared dream.

The Show was a mad scientist's paradise: Creatures long extinct zipped overhead, and wire-walkers lilted along live cables that should have electrocuted them. Jugglers tossed metal rods pulsing with energy, while swarms of mechanical sprites filled the air with bubbles and glitter and the scent of hope. High above it all rose our magnificent big top, an explosion of quilted color held aloft by suspension wires attached to balloons, rather than posts. The largest, at the center peak, caught the fading daylight so that sunset turned it rosy at the gathers, and metal bands forced the balloon into its shape. It drifted slightly with each change in the wind, clinking tiny bells along the bottom hem. A song of The Show that could only be heard if you were close enough to listen.

Pay attention, not merely admission, read a sign above the gate.

"Mommy, look!" a child squealed and pointed to a pair of hand-built unicorns milling between the props of a radiant tent maze inside the electric field. She ran forward, giving chase when the creatures shied away.

At The Show, fantasy and reality shared common ground, and technology served to dazzle and delight. Danger was as much an illusion as a magician's card trick.

But then the warden came.

Most people didn't recognize wardens on sight. The Commission wasn't like the military; they weren't even police with conventional uniforms. Theirs was a civilian operation, with offices in every capital of the industrialized world, plus outposts in places that didn't have words to translate as "industry." This warden wore his insignia—an ankh crafted from a splitting double helix—embroidered on the pocket of a black shirt, like a company logo. There was another on his ball cap, speared through with a clover-shaped pin that marked him as a survivor of the riots that engulfed Brick Street before I was born.

He was taking in the sights same as everyone else, smiling at the right things and meandering through the exhibitions. It was possible that he was there for nothing beyond the obvious, but, living in a circus, you get accustomed to not taking things at face value. Menace trailed him like cologne. His applause and smile were as fake as my Y chromosome. This man was both a warden and trouble, and I didn't like the way he was looking at me. Of all the things meant to draw scrutiny and dare people to figure out their secrets, I wasn't one of them. The Show had been built for me to hide behind.

An angry shout drew my attention from the warden to a star-encrusted tent belonging to Zavel the Mystic, our magician. The backmost corner began to twitch, and the tiny, dark-skinned face of Birdie Jesek wriggled out from under the muslin. She smiled brightly as she ran past me, a fresh pair of nicked sparklers in one hand. Close behind came Jermay, Zavel's son and apprentice, determined to get them back.

He snatched at Birdie as she scampered, barefoot, up one side of a tall tent-prop and ran along the lantern strings to another, hopping sparks as she went. She crossed the entire tent village out of reach, snapping the ends off her sparkler wands to stick in her hair.

Watching Jermay was dangerous, because I was supposed to take precautions. Playing it safe meant keeping up the appearance of a boy who didn't stare at other boys, or find their frustrated scowls endearing. But I wasn't always cautious when it came to Jermay; I liked to watch him.

I had his features memorized—olive skin like mine, with the dark hair common to most who lived the traveler's life. But unlike my sisters' brown eyes, or my green ones, his were a startling blue that looked painted on. They were an anomaly so extreme that passing strangers stopped for a second look.

Jermay had been my best friend for as far back as I could remember. Long enough to say that if there was any real magic in the world, he was where it hid, pretending to be a sixteen-year-old boy who refused to accept that he couldn't catch a little girl half his age.

Birdie was the youngest member of the Flying Jeseks, our acrobats, and even though she'd only been with them for two years, she'd taken to the high wire like she was born to it. Mother Jesek insisted that Birdie only stole Zavel's sparklers because she wanted to shine.

My oldest sister, Evie, shined; it never did her any favors.

Beyond beautiful, Evie's skin didn't just reflect light—she glowed, like a lantern drawing moths. A young man had her cornered near the train, by the exterior paddocks used to house the exhibits that were too large to contain inside. He was the sort one might find handsome, but otherwise unremarkable, except for a tingling suspicion at the back of my head. He was *too* unremarkable. More than nondescript, he was literally *unnoticeable*. The harder I tried to get a look at him, the more out of focus and distant he appeared, like watercolors running in the rain.

He was one of *them*, and that was worse than a warden. He shouldn't have been real, even at a circus, and especially not at The Show.

Unnoticeables, and the stories about them, were supposed to be urban legends. A fanciful fringe tacked on to the end of things said about the Medusae and the Great Illusion.

Maybe I should back up and start there—everything else did.

"Back then," people are fond of saying, as though speaking vaguely is safer than saying it plain, but everyone knows they mean *that year*. One single year in which the world both ended and began again.

The clouds came first, pressing through the atmosphere on every continent, like a massive storm system had covered the planet. It rained—everywhere. Death Valley. The Sahara. The Gobi. Even

Antarctica. Science called it atmospheric agitation; humanity called it a miracle. Soon, details came from the international space stations: hysterical screaming about things they called "space nettles" because there *was* no word for what had settled above us. They weren't ships the way we'd been taught to think of flying saucers. They were organic. *Alive.* These nettles floated on solar currents like Portuguese men-o'-war on the tides, stretching their tentacles into a grid cast over the Earth.

They sealed us off. Their presence interfered with nearly every satellite in orbit, causing communications to go dark in 90 percent of the world.

Then our visitors showed themselves, imprinting their images on our atmosphere.

That's all they ever did. They never communicated; they never attacked. They never even told us their names. Some newscaster started calling them Medusae because they looked like jellyfish, and it stuck. The Medusae hung in the sky while humanity went insane below. Riots and mass suicides, attempts to dislodge the ships with military force because the world was certain that silence equaled provocation. We almost choked ourselves with the aftermath of ordnance, and that was *before* the UN managed to coordinate a six-continent nuclear strike that included half the total payload of the United States, China, India, and the European Union. Russia, Pakistan, and a few countries that weren't even supposed to be nuclear capable agreed to be the second wave, but we didn't get that far.

Eerie, glowing tentacles dropped down and vaporized every warhead in midair, more than a mile from the Medusae themselves. That was the only move they ever made.

A year passed and the sky was never blue. It warped into pink and violet where the light passed through. No one understood how we survived without a "majority-species die-off" because of it, but the plants kept blooming, and the birds kept migrating. For that year, the Medusae watched, and then they left, leaving no evidence of their existence beyond the memories of those who lived through their time here. The news still broadcasts video of them on the anniversary. This is number twenty-four. I've heard next year, there'll be a parade.

Things stabilized, and after a while, people began to question if it had happened at all. There were fingers pointed, and a lot of talk about coronal eruptions, high-altitude radiation clouds, and mass hysteria brought on by aerial chemical tides. It wasn't a total denial, but most of the explanations left out any mention of off-worlders and gave people a pile of sand to hide their heads in. That year became the Great Illusion in our history books, but its legacy was very real, and despite their lack of willingness to speak the word aloud, most people still believed aliens had made contact.

Half the planet rebelled against technology, certain that satellites and space probes drew them to us in the first place. Like there's an entire alien race out there tuning into reruns of old sitcoms and chowing down on space junk like potato chips. People sought solace in the old ways and hid behind a Luddite banner of inconvenience.

The aerial view of the world changed. While Paris stayed the City of Lights, and there were still a few other bright spots, major cities the world over cut power, rationing it to blackout conditions at night, eager to believe that doing so would cloak us from outside interest. D.C. and Moscow moved their essential facilities underground. London and New Delhi turned Neo-Victorian, starting a domino effect of backpedaling pop culture that swept the world and created The Show. People wanted the old world, or at least a sanitized version of it with medicine and plumbing.

The wardens were commissioned to great fanfare, tasked with investigating alien life and safeguarding Earth, and at first, it seemed like that's what they had in mind. They started off with interviews, and tests on water and soil samples beneath the areas that'd had the highest concentration of alien presence. People slept better at night. But the thing about fanfare is that it's Carnie 101—the easiest form of distraction. Once you understand that, you know to start looking at things from more obscure angles, away from the flash and the noise. That's where you'll find the truth behind the trick.

Stories of more sinister things popped up, but as soon as they did, they were silenced. Unnoticeable strangers that no witnesses could ever quite remember. People who now had peculiar abilities. Vagrants and transients who disappeared from their usual haunts and stopped showing up at clinics and shelters, like they'd been snatched straight off the street and hardly missed by anyone. Families swept out of their houses in the middle of the night, leaving nothing behind but empty rooms and confused neighbors.

It was all very efficient. *Government* efficient. The kind of thing no one risks talking about in company.

Rumors, my father said—*bogeymen*—but in his eyes I saw something to worry about. He was scared, and that meant they were real.

Now an unnoticeable had come to The Show.

I had always pictured these strange out-of-focus people as puppets wearing dark suits, with vulture eyes behind tinted sunglasses—not as someone young vying for the attention of a pretty girl who couldn't be bothered. And I knew Evie would want me to keep my distance, but I crept closer while she pretended to listen to the man beside her, using our mechanical dragon, Bijou, as an excuse to ignore him.

She stroked Bijou's nose, igniting the switch behind his top horn that made him stand on his haunches. The waning sun caught the underside of his wings, burning across rows of jewels set into titanium alloy between the joints. Shafts of light cast off Bijou's jewels speared through the unnoticeable, so they came out on the other side of his body. He had no shadow.

I could see him, but he was no more than a whisper on the wind.

The unnoticeable ducked his head closer to my sister's ear and said something that made her look away; that's when she saw me. Our eyes met long enough for me to understand that I should leave, but without me she had no one to help her. If nothing else, I could claim Evie needed to get onto her mark before she was missed.

Another step closer, and I could hear Evie's voice.

"This is neither the time nor the place." She spoke with the rasp that developed when she was afraid.

"There are only a few minutes," the unnoticeable said.

He stepped forward, and so did I. Evie's eyes snapped back to mine as she arched her eyebrows. Another signal for me to move along, but this time he wanted to see what had taken her attention.

"Who—" he started, drawing himself up tall and straight, the way men do when they think they're being intimidating. "Who are you?"

He wrapped his hand around her arm, now solid enough that his fingers dented her skin, and pulled her back—but he still had no shadow. I felt the first flush of panic burn behind my ears, smelled the crackling ozone in the air around me as small pebbles began to vibrate at my feet. How could someone without substance touch anything?

"That's my *brother* being overprotective of the person who changed his diapers," Evie said lightly.

Brother. Right. I had to keep control of myself, watch my manners and my voice. Penelope had to remain Penn's secret.

"Off with you, Penn," Evie ordered, freeing herself from the unnoticeable's grasp. Annoyed, he pulled a cardboard pack from his jacket and took out a cigarette. "Keep your eyes on things that concern you."

And make sure official eyes have no reason to find you.

I finished the rest of our father's warning in my head. Silently, I asked his forgiveness for disobeying. I didn't trust myself to move; I was too angry.

"I'm already running behind, and I haven't even lit Bijou for the night," Evie said.

"Do you need a light?" the unnoticeable asked.

He struck a match.

"I can manage." Evie laughed nervously. She cupped her hand around the end and stole the flame, so it flourished in her open palm.

Using her gift outside our arena was dangerous for everyone who carried the Roma name. So long as our father was with us, we were protected, but he'd been gone for weeks, and without him . . .

I made her expose herself. To an unnoticeable.

The cigarette tumbled to the ground as he spluttered, "The rumors are true?"

I glanced down, to see if the cigarette was real, but it wasn't there, either. The ground was smooth dirt, undisturbed. This man was here and not here at the same time. He was as impossible as Evie stealing a flame she couldn't have touched.

"Never trust your eyes at The Show." Evie smiled at him coyly, but didn't quite pull it off. "They're in on the act, and we've convinced them to lie to you."

She blew across her fingers so the flame drifted off their tips into Bijou's snout. It was blown back out as a fire spurt that brought nearby children running and cheering for more.

By the time the sparks had faded, I was gone.

CHAPTER 2

Behind the big top, The Show's train sat braked on the tracks, swirling with reflected lantern light. No plain engine would do for my father—he'd created a three-level city on rails to accommodate our numbers. And then he'd fixed it so that we could travel anywhere, whether there were railways in place or not. The Show carried its own, laying track and picking it up as the train rolled. It was the perfect mix of old school and new age.

These wheels have tasted the air of a thousand towns, my father said, in the same way he claimed to have seen sunrise from every angle. Never sunset, though. Beginnings were far more interesting than endings. One held promise, the other only darkness.

We have mapped this world across the skies. Its boundaries are marked by the ebb and flow of smoke from our stack. For Magnus Roma, there was no meeting of strangers, only reunions with friends he'd once passed and promised to revisit.

I let myself in through the last car and made my way down the corridor. Under my breath, I counted steps, recited rhymes, did all the things my father had taught me to keep myself in check, but still the chandeliers rattled overhead.

"Stop it!" I shouted, and they did, but frustration kept breaking surface in my thoughts—the first bubbles in a pot about to boil. I brushed aside the curtains of beaded scarves to enter as always, ran my hands over the same carved wooden trunks, and threaded my fingers through the same meticulously crafted wigs, but there was no sense of "same."

Just before my sixteenth birthday, when Papa disappeared, I thought he'd gone on one of his deliveries. He bought our safety with the tech he developed for the Wardens' Commission, and several days a year were dedicated to demonstration and delivery, but this felt different. He'd been gone too long. Without him, the walls he'd built between our circus and the outside world would crumble. The cracks had already begun to show—the warden, and Evie's unnoticeable. Soon we wouldn't be able to pretend anymore. Everyone would know that my sisters' abilities weren't a matter of creative lighting and mechanics. They'd know that Penn was really Penelope. My family was *touched*— the kindest way of saying contaminated, though saying it wasn't kindness at all. Since the Great Illusion, anything different was in danger of being called alien. To be *touched* was to be more than human, but somehow less than human, too.

Blue sparks crackled between my fingers. I made a fist to cage them, but fear had started a chain reaction, and I wasn't sure I could stop it.

The official stories told us that the Medusae hadn't done anything other than watch, but there *were* changes. Pockets of people all over the world were suddenly blessed or cursed with abilities that had never been seen outside children's stories. The first gifted girl was born the day the Medusae disappeared. More followed, all girls. *Always* girls.

It began with fire, and crying infants who were inexplicably at the center of an inferno with no cause. Parents trying to save them would be burned by the flames, but the babies were not. There weren't many in the first wave, and they were spread out over the globe, so no one put it together, but others were born, and with them, more fires.

In families that survived one touched girl, their next child was another kind of nightmare. Rather than spawning flames, she would cry over a dirty diaper, and sprinklers would go off; showerheads would burst. Families would wake to find bubbling fountains had erupted in the night, even in the desert.

By this point, neighbors were talking and the families considered moving to stop the gossip, but things didn't get really strange until a few of them had their third daughter. This one, they would believe normal, or as the more desperate said, *human*, but that only lasted a few days. By then, the parents noticed that their floors were always dusty and their planters overflowing with earth. Lay the infant on the ground, and she'd soon be surrounded by rocks. Sometimes those rocks were diamonds. Her tantrums could shake the house, if not the block.

The Medusae had altered Earth's children, but only *some* of them. Everyone else was left mundane and scared.

Of course no one ever met a gifted girl, or saw one use her power in person. They were always tales from other towns, overheard and passed along by friends and distant relatives. Try to find one, and you'd discover that the girl in question had moved, at night—leaving no trail, almost like she'd never existed in the first place. There would always be a helpful warden on hand to assure the neighborhood that there was nothing to worry about.

If my sisters were discovered, we'd disappear, too—only our father refused to run. He built The Show to hide his girls in plain sight and prove to everyone who ever saw them that there was no need to be afraid. The plan had worked so well that we couldn't be blotted out of common memory. We had to be ruined. The Wardens' Commission would make sure our fall was seen, maybe even fatal. That night, there could be no mistakes. I absolutely *could not* lose my temper.

I set about readying my sisters' costumes.

Nieva—Evie—wore a heavy dress of glass and metal ribbon, gathered above her knees in the front. It had to be polished so her flames would make it shine.

Nim's was made from the stuff they use to build weather balloons. A gown that flowed like water, light and cool, but she called it cold as dead skin.

Anise hated her dirt-laden dust coat and high leather boots. She hated being on display, period, but she bore her part, as they all did.

That left only Vesper. I *always* left her for last.

So many people were terrified of having touched children that it was rare to have a third daughter in the same family. Girls like Vesper, who came fourth, seemed impossible. She could play the winds like a harp. Her costume was beautiful, bright white silk that floated around her when she moved. I could smell the sunshine trapped in the fibers, and it nearly made me cry.

Vesper and I were two years apart, but we could have passed for twins, aside from the color of our eyes. For me, she was a reminder of the life I would always be denied.

Fourth daughters were rare, but fifth were unheard of. If the Commission even suspected that I wasn't a boy, it wouldn't matter what my father offered them in exchange. They would stop turning a blind eye to our unnaturalness; all of his inventions combined weren't worth the oddity of me.

I lifted Vesper's wig reverently, and set it on my head in front of the mirror. Piles of gold ringlets covered the short chestnut tragedy of my own hair, while longer bits curled around my face. She was scared of the wig, fearing it would catch on something and drag her down, but without it, we looked too similar. She wouldn't risk me being mistaken for myself.

I slid my feet out of my boots and into her shining white heels, then slipped her dress from its hanger. Like this, I looked the way I was supposed to—like Penelope, youngest daughter of Magnus and

Iva Roma, rather than Penn, the son who was never born. Maybe my hair wasn't blonde, but I would let it grow as long as Vesper's wig. I could walk beside Jermay, even hold his hand or steal a kiss, and no one would care.

Penelope hated Penn.

"You can't do this, Penn. Not tonight," Evie said from the door. She'd entered quietly, but I heard her. She snatched at the wig, pulling it from my head so fast that I fell off Vesper's shoes.

"Can't you use my name when there's no one else here?" I asked.

When she reached down to help me up, there was another scent on her besides her apple shampoo. Bitter and sooty as a freshly doused campfire. Dealing with the unnoticeable had tried her temper, nearly to the point of flaming out.

"Penn *is* your name." Evie put her fingers in my hair and tried to smooth down the bits that had caught in the wig, then unceremoniously whisked the dress off my shoulders.

"I'm tired of hiding—I don't want to be a coward anymore!"

"Nim's been whispering in your ear again, hasn't she?"

"She's right."

"You walked away rather than doing something foolish, Chey-chey." Evie's voice softened. "If Papa doesn't return—"

"Don't say that!"

"I must say it." The whites of her eyes turned red with tears. "We create illusions for others, but cannot afford to believe them ourselves. If they come for us, Nagendra will be lucky to see a prison cell. Birdie would be homeless again, and you—" Evie placed her hands on my face. "It's too much to risk for a daydream. All right, *little brother?*"

I nodded, trying not to shiver in the chill air without Vesper's costume.

"We're leaving tomorrow, I swear. But for now, Penn Roma must prove himself to be his father's son."

The irony was that my parents *had* had a son. He was born the same night as I, only second rather than first. Had we been born in the opposite order, then he might still be alive and I might be Penelope proper—but I was impatient, and charged ahead. If there had been any doubt that I was touched, it died with my first cries, when my newborn temper shook the stars from the sky. Burning hail struck my brother dead.

No matter how important my father or his creations, my curse was something new. My mother christened it "singing down the stars" to make it sound like a gift, but what I could do was fearsome and dangerous and powerful, so my parents buried my brother nameless, claiming only one child had been born. For extra protection, they claimed that child was male. I became a ghost in my own body, hiding behind the boy I killed. They'd waited so long to have a son, and I stole him from them; the sorrow of it took my mother shortly after.

Evie opened a small case on the table and pulled out a roll of bandages to reinforce the ones I already wore.

"Arms up," she ordered, but her voice was no longer angry. "You should have been born with Nim's figure, then we wouldn't need these."

She winked at me, but I wasn't in the mood for jokes.

"Me with her figure, and her in my place."

"No." Evie shook her head.

She wrapped the bandages around my chest, over layers that the day's movement had loosened. She tugged them as tight as possible, until the pain of it made me forget how hard it was to breathe. When I was small, I thought getting to dress like my father made me special, but all that being special had ever won me was misery.

"We're all fortunate that you're our little sister, little brother," Evie said. "Were it Nim in your place, this family would have known only darker days. Her temper wouldn't stay so simply hidden."

True. If Nim could have done it, she would have called the heavens down at the first flash of a Commission patch, and likely burned us all before she realized what she'd done.

"And that's why you're not going to mention any unusual guests to Nim or anyone else until we know there's reason to worry. Say it, Penn."

"I won't tell anyone," I promised. But a forced promise was the kind I'd never had a problem breaking, if I had to.

Evie snapped her fingers to brighten the room by the strength of the glow she hid among outsiders. It was a parlor trick that had enchanted me as a child, when I was foolish enough to ask if I'd shine when I was grown. She said I was born brighter than she could ever hope to be, but no one could see their own light.

Such a lovely lie.

Tears hit and ran down my cheeks, but I didn't have the air to truly cry. Evie didn't stop wrapping until she had covered my entire torso, changing my silhouette against the wall, and burying Penelope deeper inside Penn. She reached for the lime trousers I had discarded. I fumbled with the buttons of my shirt, finding she'd wrapped me tighter than usual. She knocked my hands aside and finished for me, snapping our father's suspenders into place and straightening the ugly purple stripe on my trouser legs. My feet, which seemed so delicate inside Vesper's heels, disappeared into grotesque, flat boots, while Evie hung a pinstriped coat over my shoulders.

Everything was cut thick and sharp, creating the illusion of lines that didn't exist, and replacing the curves that belonged on a teenage girl with the straight planes of her twin. It didn't seem fair. He only had to die once; Penelope was murdered every night before The Show.

"There," Evie said, and tried to smile. "You look perfect."

"I look like a boy."

"Chey-chey . . ."

"I'm not a child! And I don't want to be . . . *this* . . . anymore!" I was shouting. She had squeezed too tight, and the pressure forced the words free.

"You can last these few hours." Evie plucked a scarf from its place draped over one of the wardrobe doors, used it to wipe my face dry, then folded it into my pocket. "Tonight, Penn will be so perfect a boy that the rich men and women will hide their daughters from him. Then we will get back on the train, and disappear. Once we're moving, Penelope can cry or put on a pretty dress or use a wig to make her hair longer, and I won't say a word. We'll go home to the Hollow and see if Papa isn't waiting as he promised."

"What if I make a mistake? It's more than the unnoticeable; there's a warden out there, Evie. I doubt he's here for entertainment."

"Take this," she said, reaching into the beaded bag slung across her chest to pull out a small jeweled lizard.

"You collapsed Bijou?"

The miniaturized dragon stretched himself out from snout to tail, shaking off the bits of string that had snagged on his scales inside the bag. Curls of smoke still wafted out of his nostrils, but he didn't blow fire. He beat his hummingbird wings to lift himself toward my shoulders.

"You need him more than The Show does."

Bijou tucked his wings against his body, curling his tail into a jeweled choker, which could barely be seen beneath my oversized cravat.

"If you feel yourself slipping, let Bijou's weight remind you to pull back. You will be strong, Chey-chey, because you are a child of Magnus Roma, and there is no weakness in you."

She held her palm up flat to mine, allowing hers to ignite against my skin. Fire never burned me when she held it.

"You have more strength than you know—enough to crush them. They don't need to see it for it to be true. You are Celestine, and they cannot hurt you."

But they could—*they had*—and there was no way to forget that. All I could do was nod and pretend to agree with her, adding one last lie to the pile of others balanced on my shoulders.

CHAPTER 3

I stepped off the train and into the night, half-expecting the warden to be waiting, but he was nowhere in sight. This was the last hour before the main event, and I had a tour to give.

"My phone's not working," a man was complaining when I arrived. He wore an expensive suit and shoes that had no place in an open field, and was likely in attendance only by force or obligation. "Does anyone have a signal?"

Most of the crowd gave him dirty looks. It was well after the designated time for personal tech to be turned off, though most people didn't bother to follow that regulation with phones.

A couple of teenagers checked their mobiles, but had no signal either. Unlike the businessman, who had a sleek metal unit that slipped easily in and out of a suit pocket, they wore clunky backpack units with dials and handsets that were part of the local fashion. The girl's corseted mini-hoop dress looked tighter than my bindings and stopped above her knees, grazing the tops of her boots. Her boyfriend was wearing formal tails with shorts. They both sported capes and a particular shade of aubergine eye shadow that made them look like oversized rag dolls someone had rescued from the trash.

I hopped up the short ladder onto the back of a ticket booth–slash–caravan wagon parked beside the tour's entrance, and tapped a sign bolted to the wall.

NO PHONES ~ NO CAMERAS ~ NO EXCEPTIONS

I could have told them that it was the Faraday cage interfering with their signals, but this was a matter of tradition. Crowds always entered the Caravan of Wonder without the benefit of lights or windows. Darkness set the spectators on edge, replacing the reality they knew with a formless void, easily molded by the right words spoken in the right tone. Screen lights would ruin that.

"Budge up and keep moving," I ordered in a practiced accent. The man grumbled and shoved his phone into his pocket. The teens stowed the handsets in their backpacks. "Keep your hands on your children, and nothing else. From this moment on, anything you touch may decide to return the favor."

The younger members of the audience fidgeted at my warning, while the rest rolled their eyes, acknowledging that this was all part of the act. But they were wrong—the danger was very real, and very close. The warden had joined us. He slipped into a space near the front without a word.

On with The Show.

By the time I'd led the crowd a few feet into blindness, with only a dismal lantern to guide their way, the tent had begun to rustle. A disembodied hiss threaded its way through, and all the whispers fell silent; the people bunched close.

A pair of women clutched at their children with one hand. With their other hand, they clung to each other. The two of them had been so eager that they'd pressed their way to the front, just so their kids could see the sights first, but now those same little ones had to be coaxed forward. One tried to hide herself behind the warden, and to my surprise, he obliged.

The lantern flickered, so I tapped the glass, but instead of rising, the flame cut out, plunging us into absolute pitch.

"Light the torch," a trembling voice begged.

"'Twon't do no good, Madam," I said, deepening my voice. "We've wandered into Erebus's territory. This is the World of Shadows; we'll get light when it's given. Keep up or get left back."

Hurried feet scratched the ground behind me as I carried on, leading them closer to the phantom hiss. We stopped, and an animated hanging light snapped on overhead, swaying slowly.

There's a very peculiar sound that comes from a person when they mean to cry out, but their voice dissolves in their throat. A strangled hitch, as though unseen fingers have wrapped around their mouth. That nameless, invisible something spread through my audience as they tried to scream from the revelation of the hiss's source.

"Nagendra," I announced with a flourish. "King of All Serpents."

He sat on a black chair inside his enclosure, his long, thin limbs stretched at odd angles. It wasn't the tattoos that covered his skin from the tips of his fingers to the top of his bald head that made the crowd gasp and back away in horror, and it wasn't the rows of pierced loops in his ears or the chains threaded across his face that they shrank from. Nagendra's enclosure was filled with dozens of live and writhing snakes. They coiled through his legs and dripped from his arms as living jewelry.

"Nagendra came to us from the East," I said. "Reared in a viper's nest, he cannot speak as a man, but prefers the company of snakes to those who cast him off."

Only the last part of that had any truth to it. Nagendra *did* prefer his snakes to most people, but he was an excellent speaker. He'd been educated at Oxford.

Nagendra stood, lifting a boa constrictor from the back of his chair to drape around his shoulders. Smaller snakes moved out of his path as he stalked the enclosure, pausing only to give a menacing hiss with a pierced tongue.

We both pretended it wasn't directed at the warden.

The group's allotted time ended, the light faded, and my lantern whooshed back to life.

"Moving on," I said, and ushered them into a tent containing a pebbled-glass tank. Inside, a girl my age lay sleeping with her head on her folded arms.

The crowd gasped.

Just below her navel, where human hips should flare to form the tops of human legs, she had a tail, and she was completely submerged in pond water. Rows of stacked and glittering scales attached to her torso, fin meeting flesh with a protruding dorsal skirt of translucent copper. The murky water gave her skin an inhuman tint, and patches of mosslike lichen and algae clustered over her arms.

"Behold Winifred Singh, the Siren of legend, captured on holiday in Greece."

Another half-truth. Her name *was* Winifred Singh, but she'd never been to Greece.

"She's asleep," whined the little girl who had taken to the warden.

"Be grateful," he said, inviting himself into my script in a way that suggested he'd heard it before. "Were she awake, her voice would steal your breath." Those should have been my words.

"Siren songs only work on boys," the girl protested.

Children always raised the first challenge to the boundaries we set. My father called that both a terrifying and hopeful observation.

"There were few women at sea for the ancients to speak of," I said. "But she's every bit as deadly to a girl as she is to a boy."

The warden smiled, and I felt a shiver all the way to my feet.

"That's hardly polite conversation." My sister Nimue appeared from behind the tank, flowing into view, as graceful as the water she could command. "And it's no way to talk in front of company."

Nim was twenty-three, a year younger than Evie, and two older than Anise. She stood tall and thin, with black hair piled high on her head, secured by glittering pins. Cool as a river, and just as able to adapt, she took notice of the warden and kept going.

"No need to let our Siren scare you, little brother," Nim said. "Fishy's hibernating."

"Then we should let her be, and not try our luck."

My words had two meanings: For the crowd, they were part of the act, but to my sister, I hoped they conveyed something more. It was her nature to beat against an obstacle until it broke or disappeared, but wardens weren't as easily removed from one's path as a dam from a stream, and she didn't know about the unnoticeable.

"Good idea," Nim said. "No need to make any of you *orphans* today, or turn your *mothers* into *mourners*."

Her answer came as layered as mine, and sharp as a knife in my back. Sometimes Nim wasn't just cool, she was cold. She was goading me, but I had a life's worth of lessons from my father to push her voice out of my ears:

Water is no match for earth, which soaks it up. Earth can be scattered by the wind. Wind gives itself to fuel the flames, which water will in turn consume. Balance, Penn. That's the key. Keep your balance and no one can knock you off your feet.

Each spiteful word Nim spoke became a balloon on a string. I could let them float away.

"Let's move along," I said.

But that one little girl wasn't ready to go. She dropped the warden's hand and tapped the glass with her finger.

Tap . . . tap . . . tap . . .

Angry, dark eyes popped open, and the little girl froze. On with The Show, it was.

"Get back!" I shouted, regaining the momentum of my performance. The warden grabbed the girl and yanked her away, while Winnie went into motion.

She flicked her metallic tail, so its tip struck the glass, then darted toward the front of the tank. Webbed fingers, draped with seaweed, pressed against the glass as she narrowed her eyes hatefully, churning the water with an incessant swish that swirled her hair like spilled ink. Her fists beat the tank's inner wall before she set her hands to clawing at an intricate metal plate fastened over her mouth.

The crowd took a collective step back. Parents swung their children into their arms, no longer certain that their eyes were lying to them. Several reached for phones, only to find that they still wouldn't work. Ragdoll-boy was shaking a camera furiously, but it refused to take a picture.

"Well, that's a lucky break," Nim said. "I guess she's done sleeping."

"Looks like," I said as the last of my sister's barbs drifted away.

"What are you playing at?" a woman in peach demanded. Like the teens, her style was pseudo-Victorian, but not as dramatic. She looked like a runway model dressed as a laced-up sofa cushion. "You said that thing would kill us." She gaped, ready to brandish the parasol-purse in her hand for protection.

On her collar was a tricolored pin in the shape of a cloverleaf, just like the one the warden wore on his cap.

Red for honor, the wiki-definition of the clover would say, just like it would tell you that the pins were mementoes for everyone who had lived through the Brick Street uprising. *White for peace. Gold for prosperity.* In theory these were the Commission's foundations, but there was another version everyone learned before they were out of grade school.

Red for the blood spilling into the streets. White for the bodies and grief no one speaks. Power is golden, but heavy as lead. Remember the brick street; remember the dead.

On dreary days, when he turned somber, Nagendra's mealtime recitations bled from Shakespeare into stories of the panic on Brick Street. These thrilled me when I thought they were no more real than the comics I tore apart for a wall collage, but when he told these tales, the adults went silent. Mother Jesek would glare at Bruno until he stood and ushered Nagendra from the room. I was too young to understand that his stories weren't bedtime adventures; they were memories.

He'd been there the day Brick Street disintegrated. He'd seen the riot and knew the secret things that the Commission had taken such care to eradicate from history. All that blood and destruction had actually happened; it changed and haunted him.

"What a horrible boy you are," said the woman in peach.

I smiled at that. I had to—thinking of Brick Street would have made me sick, otherwise.

"She'll kill you right quick," I said, "but that plate's special-made by my father. And no creature of this world or any other can best one of Magnus Roma's inventions. You're all wearing your earpieces—turn them on. Even if she screams, you won't hear it."

I toggled a switch on the bit of metal protruding from my ear, and a tiny light glowed orange against my skin. Throughout the audience, others did the same. Thin wires wrapped around to form mouthpieces for them, while I made a show of testing a large floral microphone clipped to my lapel.

"Everyone hear me?" I asked, and they nodded. "Good, then we're safe enough, so long as—"

"She's got it off!" Nim screamed, resigning herself to the script.

The crowd's attention shifted to the tank. Winnie had pried one side of the plate from her mouth.

"Lock it down!" The stagehands pulled a lever on the tank's side, activating a claw from the back. It hoisted Winnie to the top. Smaller manacles clamped her wrists tight to her sides.

"You folks got your money's worth today," I said, adding a fake laugh. "We'll just pull her out of the water a bit, so . . ."

As the claw topped the tank, the last of the metal plate slipped away. Winnie sucked in a deep breath, opened her mouth, and wailed.

Nim and the stagehands grabbed their ears, falling to the ground. The water boiled, and at just the right moment, when a few doubting souls allowed their hands to stray toward their earpieces, the glass façade shattered. A stampede started with the first trickle of water that wet the crowd's feet.

It didn't matter that in the three years she'd traveled with The Show, Winnie had never spoken a single word.

"Run," I shouted into my microphone. "Get out of here! Run!"

No one hung around to see the stagehands help Winnie from the tank, or watch them free her legs from the harness inside her phony tail. They didn't see anyone give her a towel or retrieve the rebreather that had been concealed inside her faceplate. And they didn't stay to watch the broken glass reseal itself or Nim raise her hands, conductor-style, to call the spilled water back into the tank.

That was the real magic of The Show. We were masters at making people see what wasn't there, and hiding things that really were. Our ways had always worked, so perhaps it's understandable that my stomach clenched at the sight of the warden passing through the curtain without the orange light that said he'd had his earpiece turned on. He tugged the brim of his cap as he passed me, and men don't tip their hats to boys.

The Caravan's final leg was the Mech-nagerie, a showcase of my father's most complex creations.

The children loved the smaller creatures like wind-up mice and ducks, and stayed at a cautious distance from Scorpius, a gargantuan scorpion, with his wicked tail that was as long as a man was tall.

"The Constrictus," I announced in another tent, pointing to a metal serpent whose body was thick as a tree. He circled himself thrice around the tent, moving along the floor at a slow crawl, occasionally lifting someone up along his back to make them shriek.

I'd seen the Constrictus tear tanks to scrap; he could easily crush a man if I told him to. The warden wasn't even that big . . .

No! Nim's aggravation was making me crazy. Thankfully, there was only one curtain left to open.

"Xerxes, Lord of the Sky."

Reactions to Xerxes were always unpredictable. Some would slip into an awed reverence. Some would hesitate, unable to decide if they wanted to continue on, passing dangerously close to claws the size of their head, or turn back and risk the Siren's wrath. Once, a man tried to scoot out from under the tent's side.

I laid my hand against Xerxes' front flank, where the lion's body blended seamlessly into the talons of a giant raptor. He was warm to the touch, and even seemed to breathe. His eyes blinked; his head turned, keeping watch over the crowd.

"It's an alien!" a boy shouted, and pulled his hood up to hide his face, but the boy behind him said, "Don't be stupid. Aliens are squishy."

"Is that a real mutation?" Ragdoll-girl asked.

"Can't be," said her friend. "Tech like that takes a lab and a whole lot of attention." He backed up a few steps, away from the warden.

"H-how much power does that thing draw?" The warden spoke again, addressing me for the first time with an unexpected stutter that belied his fear of my father's creation.

"The cage keeps the ambient current under wraps," I told him. "We look like a thunderstorm from overhead, nothing more, and Xerxes is a machine, like the others. Only a different gen."

That was only a fraction of his being; my father found a way to give Xerxes a piece of his soul.

When the gryphon glanced down at me, I didn't see the fierce, blazing eyes of a monster; I saw Magnus Roma. My sisters disagreed, but humored me because they thought I'd made it up to console myself over our father's disappearance. They just couldn't see it. Living things had a spark in their eyes that didn't exist in machines. Xerxes had that spark. He was self-aware, and there was no way to convince me otherwise.

"Now that we're here, choose your words carefully, if you mean to speak," I said. "You cannot lie in a gryphon's presence. If you open your mouth and no words come, everyone will know what sort of person you are."

"Surely that's not true if it's not real," someone said.

"Never doubt that one of Magnus Roma's creations will do exactly what it's designed to do."

Some of the crowd puffed up, but didn't risk opening their mouths to test or contradict me. The warden simply stared at Xerxes, his eyes raking from one end of the golem's body to the other, unable to contain the whole thing with a single glance.

It felt strange, as though I were witness to some ritual deciding supremacy between man and machine, or even this man and my father. Stranger still when the warden's expression shifted just enough for a brief grin and a dip of his head, like he was bowing out.

Xerxes took the cue. He fanned his wings, raised his head, and sent up a call that left the crowd shivering.

The warden tipped his cap to me again, before crossing in front of Xerxes to the exit. An electric current raised the hair across my neck, and I leaned closer into Xerxes' flank, like one of those children in the crowd who'd rushed to hide behind their fathers' legs when they needed shelter from their fears.

But my father wasn't there to protect me anymore.

CHAPTER 4

Inside the big top, half of the arena was filled with U-shaped riser-benches; the other half was a mirrored wall. The mirrors made the space look twice as big, so The Show was twice as grand. They also hid our preparation area from view.

After my tour, I hurried behind the mirrors to find Evie and Klok.

How to explain Klok . . .

Before I was born, the Wardens' Commission approached my father with an idea for a metal man who didn't bleed or question orders. A soldier no one would mourn. My father tried, but reported failure. Like everything else inside The Show, it was a half-truth; he'd not made a weapon, but he *had* created Klok.

Klok looked like a teenage boy, but beneath his gloves were metal braces that spanned his hands, dipping into the flesh at the joints, and around his neck was a metal band with a display screen to make up for my father's trouble synthesizing a voice. His fingers could tear through stone like wrapping tissue; his mind was pure computer, but he had a soul, along with the light in his eyes that marked him as more than a machine. And so he became another stray taken in by The Show. As much a son to Magnus Roma as Penn, and just as false.

He worked as a stagehand, and at present, he was winding Evie's brass corset shut while she hugged a mirror-prop for balance.

Vesper stood beside her, leaning against the prop with a scowl on her face. Her skin had been powdered white, making her look like a ghost with my face. Up close, the powder caked and cracked. Her image was a mockery of my own, and her foul mood had blown clouds in to cover the big top.

"There's a warden out there," she said.

"He's allowed, same as anyone," Evie replied. This argument must have been going on for some time.

"He took my tour, but the unnoticeable that cornered you hasn't shown his face again," I said. Mentioning him wasn't an accident.

"Unnoticeable? Where? When?" Vesper fumed.

Nim's temper was a quiet thing, patient and planned—a river following its set course until it overflowed its banks to cause a flood. Even then, it could be beaten back by better sense. But Vesper . . . Vesper was as unpredictable as a tornado and often left destruction in her wake. Even our father couldn't control her.

A tempest wind blows where it blows, he said. *One cannot steer a gale.*

There was a beep and a rat-tat-tat like a printer. Blue words rolled over what should have been Klok's voice box.

"Should I go and see?"

"Yes," Vesper and I said as Evie answered, "No."

Evie glanced over her shoulder. "He isn't—Ow! Not so tight, Klok."

She winced from the twist of her corset key. His display flashed.

"Sorry, Nieva."

"It's all right." Evie rubbed her hand across her stomach. "We're all on edge, but that's no excuse to go running after rumors."

"He's not—" I tried, but she wasn't listening.

"Vesper won't be having any accidents at the warden's expense, and you won't go seeking out people who can't be found. Understood?"

"I understand¬," Klok beeped.

"Understanding doesn't mean agreement," Vesper said sourly.

"And being discreet doesn't make him unnoticeable. Penn doesn't know what she saw. He was asking a question. That's it."

"He had no shadow." I was too full of pent-up energy to be reasonable; arguing with Evie burned some off. "And he put his hands on you. I saw you wince from across the field."

A gust of hot wind blasted through the backstage area, blowing Vesper's wig in all directions. The glass bits hanging from Evie's trim tinked together.

Klok beeped and produced a string of words on his display.

"That's not appropriate language," Evie scolded. "Especially not in front of a young lady."

"Penn is a boy. Boys use inappropriate words."

"Do they now?"

Beep . . .

"Yes."

"Which words?"

Rat-tat-tat . . .

A long string ran across his screen, so fast the words were nearly illegible. Evie made a face.

"Klok, Vesper, go check the animals. *Now!*" she ordered.

Vesper took Klok's arm, grinning. The wind died down as her snarling turned to snickers.

Klok gave me the confused look he always wore when he said something he shouldn't have, and he let my evil twin lead him away.

"You two are unfair punishment," Evie said once he and Vesper were gone. "Half those words were nonsense."

"He asked," I said. "If I hadn't given him a list, he'd have gone to Nagendra. Then you'd have taped over his screen."

"If you think you're actually in charge around here, you've let that top hat go to your head. Help me. I can't fit the skirt myself."

She held out the reflective wrapper that made her look like a burning candle during her act, and I hooked it into place along the eyelets that circled her waist.

"Get onto your mark before I tell Klok to replace you," she said.

"How *exactly* would he announce without a voice?"

"Klok's more resourceful than you give him credit for. And he's as stubborn as you."

She sounded like our father, insisting that Klok was more than the sum of his parts.

"Scoot. The cue's about to sound."

Jermay was waiting for me near the hidden arena door, which meant I'd been backstage through Zavel's magic act, and now the music said the Jeseks' was ending as well. A dramatic swell announced the climax of their acrobatics, and soon after came applause.

"Go." Evie shooed me toward the door in our mirrors.

"Be careful out there," Jermay said as I ran past him. "Warden's front and center." He let his hand fall to his side, hooking my little finger with his own—a way to say "good luck," and an empty promise that everything would be all right.

I made it to the mirror door just as Birdie led her family out of the arena. She was beaming. Bruno, their father, swung her up off the ground.

"This little bird may have arrived late, but she's a Jesek sure as life," he said.

"What's all this?" I asked.

"I flew," she squealed and flung herself at me.

Two years earlier the idea of her hugging anyone would have seemed impossible. When my father found her, Birdie was half-starved and squatting in an empty house. He gave her a sandwich and she followed him home.

She kept to the darkest storage cars. We all tried to coax her out, but no one could—except Bruno. Every night, he took a plate of food and a book, and sat on the floor to read aloud, as though he was tucking in one of his own children. Birdie would snatch up the food and run, until she got comfortable enough to sit with him. One day, he left his daughter's old costume with the food. He told Birdie she was expected at practice with the rest of the family.

An hour later, she appeared in the arena. Her hair was a mess, her face was dirty, and the costume didn't sit straight, but she was there. Birdie hadn't left the Jeseks since.

"I really did it," she squeaked. "I flew!"

"That's wonderful," I said.

"Come on," one of her brothers said. "I think Mama may have hidden a cake away to celebrate."

She grabbed her surrogate brothers by the hands and they walked off together, while she flipped between them.

The Show was family, and nobody was wiping the smile off Birdie's face when it had taken two years to put it there. I was not about to fail the people my father had promised to protect.

When my cue sounded, I marched to the podium with my head up high. I tromped whiny Penelope down to the bottom of Penn's boots and held her there. When I spoke my part, it was as Magnus Roma's son, with Magnus Roma's voice.

"I hope you've all enjoyed our introduction," I said.

The lights dimmed to a spot, and a ripple of apprehension surged through the night's excitement.

"But this is The Show, dear patrons. What serves as greatest entertainment elsewhere is merely the beginning here."

The spotlight raked across the crowd, and furtive glances followed in its wake.

"Do you hear something?"

"Not the snakes!" a voice cried out from the stands.

"Is that a crackle in the air?" I asked. Now people were craning their necks to find the source of the sound.

A small flame flared to life while Evie stood on her mark in the arena's darkened wings. The flame bounced in her hand, its light catching the glittering shards of her costume. She threw the flaming ball onto the ground, where it unrolled into a spindly thread.

"She's not human!" gasped a mundane from the stands. Others called out "Alien!" and "Touched!" *Monster. Freak.* One faceless onlooker managed to spit out the technical term of "pyrokinetic." I acted like the words didn't make my skin crawl. We were too close to the anniversary. Videos and photographs of the Medusae were everywhere, thanks to anniversary specials and rallies, and fresh enough in people's minds to cause an uproar.

"Turn the lights on!" the crowd demanded. There was a rush of stamping feet. "We can't see!"

"My apologies," I said. "Evie, these *fine people* need some light."

She pulled back sharply on the bit of burning string still in her hand, splitting the air with the crack of a flaming whip. Bright embers shook loose from the tip, falling slowly back to the dirt floor.

"Leaving so soon?" she asked. "Samson hasn't even gotten to show off yet."

Beside her, the shape of a large dog formed entirely out of fire, sitting at heel. The top of his head reached her shoulder.

The crowd stopped, uncertain which way to go. The warden was still in his seat.

"Always scaring off our customers, Nieva." Another spotlight snapped on, revealing Nim in the arena now. As she walked to the center, her costume flowing over her body like liquid metal, a pair of dolphins made from water swam in the open air, waist high, on either side of her.

It wasn't likely that anyone in the crowd had ever seen an elemental golem before, which was a good thing. The more impossible things seemed to be, the more they were accepted as part of the act. This was all some kind of trick. Only entertainment.

The audience began to calm and retake their seats as a bear grew out of the ground, rising in the form of dust and sand and pebbles with shiny black stones for eyes. It lumbered high on its back legs, but at Anise's bidding, it bent over, splitting into a litter of chubby cubs that ran to the edges of the arena, chasing the children back to their seats. Vesper floated down from above, accompanied by the owls she had summoned from air so thick it turned white.

I could see the concentration on the warden's face. Unlike those around him, he would know what my sisters' creations meant. It was one thing to build the unheard-of out of metal and polymer, like our father did, but to give life to fire, water, earth, and wind was more than science. These golems weren't built—they were summoned—and that was more than human.

The devastation I could have wrought with an ounce of their skill . . .

"I give you the daughters of Magnus Roma," I shouted, hoping to distract him.

The crowd broke into applause as Evie bent live flames to her will, unleashing them to swirl about the tent and light the arena for the others. Nim's water dolphins dove and leapt among the fire spurts as easily as real dolphins might through the ocean.

Anise ran from one upward-thrusting rock piston to another, making them rise and sink in a complicated pattern. And Vesper . . . Vesper flew. That beautiful wig spiraled out, free as a weed. Her gown fluttered around her feet while she walked on air and awe above their heads.

The warden counted my sisters as they circled the arena, unable to contain his interest, but he didn't stop at number four.

His eyes met mine.

The intensity of his focus cut against my skin until I could hardly stand it, but I wasn't so foolish as to look away, or give him reason to believe his curiosity was warranted. There were four elements—*only* four. Magnus Roma's son couldn't possibly be a fifth daughter. He couldn't be Celestine. Celestine wasn't even a proper word; it was a description my father came up with. The warden couldn't know something that didn't exist.

He smiled, and it was a horrible thing, hypnotic as one of Nagendra's pets mesmerizing its prey before a kill. I was so fixated on him that I lost track of which part of the routine was being carried out. One of Vesper's owls knocked me tails-over-top-hat. Samson reared back, to stop me from falling through his body, but I came close enough to light my sleeves on fire.

I knew better than to scream, even when the flames dipped down the seam. Screaming meant that something was wrong, and that would only cause a panic. Evie was close, and she'd never let me burn.

"Always trying to get into our act!" Nim was on me in a second, and I found myself surrounded by her water dolphins, each spouting spray from the top of its head. The crowd cheered while I fizzled, trying not to choke on the smell of melted fabric.

"Shameless," Vesper added. It was the owls' turn to circle, drying me off so my clothes wouldn't cling.

"Back to your place, Ringmaster," Anise said. She jerked her thumb toward the ceiling, and one of her bears picked me up by the collar of my shirt. It dropped me back on my podium. "Careless little boys don't get to play in the arena."

"You can sit in time-out until the grown-ups are done," Evie said. She made a circle with her finger. "Face the wall."

The audience was laughing now; they thought the whole thing was choreographed. In reality, Evie was telling me that I should stay slumped down, not giving the audience anything but my back to look at. And to make the point, Anise spun my podium, ground and all, so I had no choice but to comply.

The laughter got louder.

The final act lasted only twenty minutes, but it felt longer. When the end cue sounded, Bijou purred against my throat, reminding me that we were almost clear. All that remained was the bonfire, because no performance ever closed without Evie dancing in the flames.

After the bows were taken, the procession headed out, toward the cliffs that overlooked the river. Evie went first, shining through the night like a woodland elf headed for court, with Nim close behind in case something went amiss. Samson ran beside them, nipping at those who strayed too close. Vesper stayed back to secure the real animals in their pens. When Klok and I tried to join the winding line of lantern-bearing Show members leading the crowd, Anise slipped out of the group to stop us.

"Go back to the train," she said. "If anyone asks, tell them you're overseeing the packing of the tents. We're running behind, and must make up every minute we can find."

"But—" I stammered. "Is anyone else staying with the train?"

"Squint and Smolly. So you'd best hope there's no need to worry."

Squint was an engineer, the man who kept our train moving when my father was gone, but he only stood as high as Birdie's shoulder. His wife, Small Molly, was two inches taller, but she was still well under four feet. Over the years, the children of The Show had run the two names together. "Smolly" was all she had answered to in my lifetime.

Anise raised her dirt-encrusted goggles and perched them on her head to hold her bobbed hair off her face. "I know Evie believes the danger is lifting, but she's wrong, Chey-chey. You feel it, don't you?"

I did. The night had become kinetic. Static before an electric storm.

"Something's coming. Go back to the train, but if you feel the need, you run. *Don't* wait for us. Get yourself clear, and trust us to get to the Hollow. *Promise me.*"

Her hand came down heavy on my shoulder.

"I . . . I promise."

"Klok, make sure she keeps her word—by force, if you have to."

Anise wasn't as trusting as Evie when it came to my word, so she made sure I didn't have any loopholes to jump through. Klok was twice my size, and half as willing to go against my sisters' wishes.

"I will keep Penn safe," his display read.

"If it comes to a run, then it's Penelope you'll have to watch over," Anise said.

She wasn't like Evie, who tried to make things seem as bright as possible, or Vesper, given to fits of drama; Anise grounded the rest of us. It was part of her *touch*. She didn't raise alarm without cause, and now she was shaken. Klok looked from me to her and back again. He bit his lip, faltering for the first time and looking the most human I'd ever seen him.

"Go on," she said, nudging us toward the train. Birdie's moonlit outline was already headed that way, illuminated by strands of colored lanterns in the trees as Jermay swung her up onto his shoulders to carry her. "And Klok?"

He turned around, inclining his head.

"Don't forget to watch out for yourself, too."

I went to bed, chanting a silent mantra against my fears. *It's almost time. It's almost over. They're almost back.* Over and over I repeated words that rang hollow, telling myself that once the bonfire was doused, my sisters would return, and the train would be laying track by daybreak. Those whispered promises lulled me into a half-sleeping haze. One moment I was trying to convince myself not to panic, and the next, I was being shaken awake.

"Back already?" I asked, expecting Anise, but when I opened my eyes, the pair staring back at me were wide and dark, and framed by long hair.

Winnie leaned over me. Then the girl I'd only ever known as mute opened her mouth and said, "They're coming."

CHAPTER 5

My train car pitched sideways, knocking me, Winnie, and everything else to the floor, while smoke rose from beneath my door to fill the room.

"We derailed," Winnie said, but that shouldn't have been possible. There was no proper track beneath us. "The door is blocked," she said. The wardrobe had toppled against it.

"The window too," I added. The car had fallen with the glass to the ground.

"Help us!" we screamed, and beat against the wall.

"No one can hear us." Winnie kicked the wardrobe in frustration. Her hair hung in tangled knots from the tumble.

"How long have you been able to talk?"

"As long as you, more or less. Can't *you* get us out of here?"

"It doesn't work like that." I'd spent too much time fettering the Celestine. I couldn't call her up at will.

Winnie flung the wardrobe open, and began throwing armfuls of my stuff over her head. My whole life, and every dream I'd ever held, amounted to an ankle-deep heap.

"Help me," she said. "If I lighten it, we might be able to move it."
I squeezed into the space between the wardrobe and the wall.
Pressing my feet against the wall, I braced my back against the wardrobe's side and shoved; my reward was the scrape of wood against the floor. Winnie jammed herself into the gap beside me, and we worked the door wide enough to crawl through under the smoke.

"What's going on?" I asked.

"We're being boarded. They brought in the hounds."

Suddenly the threat of suffocation wasn't the scariest thing about the night. If unnoticeables were the Commission's unseen secret, hounds were the unspoken. They were the ghosts of all those gifted girls who vanished into memories. Some were studied, to see if the Medusae's secrets could be unlocked, but most were made hounds, the common name for trained hunters. Hounds were touched like my sisters, dispatched by the wardens to capture or neutralize their own kind.

There was no use hoping that this was a freak accident, or a dream brought on by Anise's warnings. The Commission had *attacked* the train. My father had fallen out of favor, and we were being collected.

Winnie and I darted from car to car so fast I didn't know whose space we were in. Through the windows, there was pandemonium, as those who'd been at the bonfire scattered, most with their lanterns still in hand, like clumps of fireflies fleeing across the cliffs.

"He brought in military," I said, taking in the drab green and stenciled numbers on each rumbling vehicle that had surrounded the train.

"I didn't hear any choppers," Winnie said. "They came from close by—probably the reserve base in the next county."

Calling up reserve troops was a warden's privilege, if circumstances warranted it. The man who had attended our performance would know he was dealing with four exceptionally strong elementals who had precision control over their abilities. He'd know how smart my father was, and if he wasn't a complete idiot, he'd know my sisters were as clever. He'd come prepared for anything, but hopefully, he was concentrating on the crowd and wouldn't notice a couple of girls in their pajamas sneaking out under his nose.

All my hopes of escaping undetected vanished with a young girl's scream.

"What was—*umph!*"

One hand covered my mouth and another covered Winnie's. I had opened my mouth to bite its owner before I smelled machine oil on his fingers.

"Klok?" I tried to ask.

He pulled us backward until a wooden plank slammed over our heads. We'd crossed into Zavel's car and were cowering in the secret compartment of a magician's disappearing cabinet.

While we watched through a narrow gap between slats, a reserve soldier held Birdie by the back of her nightshirt. Obviously taken from her bed, she'd been caught off guard and was in a disheveled state similar to the feral look she'd had when she first boarded the train. She tried to kick him, but he raised her off the ground, out of range.

"We have to help her," I whispered.

"We can't help anyone if we're caught," Winnie said.

Another man joined the first and demanded details.

"This is the only girl I've seen," the first man said while Birdie did her best to free herself.

"Too young and wrong color," the second said. "Warden says our target's all knees and elbows, passing herself off as Roma's boy."

My stomach dropped. The first guard had thought she was me. They'd wrecked the train to find *me*.

"Hey!" I recognized Jermay's voice, and my stomach lurched back to where it belonged. "You really need body armor to handle one little girl?"

I was about to call out, hoping the reserves would let the others go to chase me, but as the man holding Birdie turned, a flash powder explosion went off. Jermay had ignited one of his father's prop bags on a side table.

Birdie finally landed her kick. Her captor howled, dropping her, and she scrambled away.

"That one boy enough for you?" the injured man snarled at his partner.

His partner jerked him to his feet, and their heavy boots stomped off down the hall. Klok waited for a five count before removing the back exit from the cabinet so we could escape. Another glance through the window showed Jermay and Birdie running together toward the open field that had previously held the circus's tent city. They must have found one of Zavel's rabbit holes and gotten out that way.

"We need Squint," I said and headed for the front of the train.

Klok shook his head; he opened his palm to show me his secondary display as we ran. It flashed: **"Squint and Small Molly have left the train. I assisted."**

That was no surprise. My memories of Squint and Smolly went as far back as my memories of Klok. They'd joined our circus when he was a boy, and despite his being bigger than both of them put together, he'd followed the pair like they were his parents. No one bothered to correct him, least of all Squint and Smolly.

"If they're out, then there's no one to wait for," Winnie said.

There was, however, another problem. The next car was on its side, like my room, and completely impassable.

Beep.

"Squint has rerouted the exhaust into the cooling system. Pressure will increase without ventilation. Once it has exceeded capacity—"

"He set the train to blow?"

Years of my father's work were caught up in our engine and magnificent gilded cars, and generations of our family's memories were spread across the rooms and walls.

"Our future's worth more than the past," Winnie said. "We have to get out of here."

It made me sick, but she was right. I glanced around, desperately seeking something I could take for a memento stronger than a memory. The only thing small enough to carry was my father's red leather work coat, which had fallen from its peg. He'd worn that coat forever, and I was responsible for half the soda stains on it.

I slipped it on and belted it around my pajamas to keep it from falling off. My father's a lot bigger than me.

"Right, then." I climbed up a pile of toppled furniture and pushed one of the now overhead windows open. "Up and over."

I had an idea.

The sky blazed red and orange, with smoke trails weaving from all directions. The train had been sliced in pieces by eruptions of rock. The ground below rumbled, with shallow cracks radiating from the feet of a woman in a black uniform. She was terrakinetic, an earth-mover, like Anise. At the right angle, her uniform took on a greenish sheen.

The reserves held back and let her work, watching her bring down what remained of the tents in the field. Thankfully, none of them seemed to notice the three of us running along the top of the train.

In the distance, the Jeseks' silhouettes scaled the cables from the central balloon that held the big top aloft. The basket below it was big enough to hold thirty people, and everyone knew that if it came to a raid, we were to use it to get to the Hollow, a safe haven that belonged to my parents. The balloon's guidance system could find it from anywhere in less than a day.

Once the last Jesek was in the balloon, two of the others detached the cables and let them fall on whichever unfortunate members of the raiding party happened to be inside the big top. Bruno steered the balloon toward the open field where Jermay and Birdie would be waiting along with the rest of our Show family.

I dropped back into the train on the other side of the wrecked cars, and took off, pounding the floor with my bare feet. Winnie landed lightly behind me; Klok shook the entire car.

"Penn, what are you doing?" Winnie asked. "Get back outside."

Klok reached over her, likely to make good on his promise to Anise. I jumped back, out of reach, but his arm kept coming. Sometimes it was easy to forget his body wasn't human, and then he'd do something to remind me—like letting his telescopic arm grow an extra two, three, four feet. I flattened out on the ground and let his hand fly over me.

"Stop it," I snapped. His arm retracted in my direction. "We'll go, but first, we can increase our odds."

If it was my father's legacy the warden was after, I'd give him more than he could handle.

CHAPTER 6

We approached the metal door that kept my father's golems secured. If it had been only the reserve unit outside, I would have risked making a run for it, but not with hounds, and especially not with hounds strong enough to topple a multistory train like a set of blocks. We needed something to cover our escape.

"Open it," I said.

Klok ripped the door from its frame with the locking pins still attached.

In their pen, our unicorn herd pawed at the ground; their eyes snapped on, glowing an ominous red instead of their usual gold. Bijou lifted his head and trumpeted out a shriek. I'd never seen any of them act this way—as though they could sense the danger we were in.

"Grab what you can. We'll go out through the overhead release."

Beep.

Another message streamed across Klok's display: **"No power. No hatch release."**

"Winch it by hand," I shouted over the growing noise through the walls. My understanding of the train's construction was vague, and I hoped the engine wasn't ready to blow.

Klok leapt from crate to crate, toward the ceiling, pushing the hydraulics in his legs to their limit. Winnie took the backpack that held her tail and rebreather from its hook on the wall.

"We can share the breather," she said, hoisting the bag onto her shoulders. In the water, only the hydrokinetic hounds could follow. "I'd rather outrun one than all of them."

Klok dropped from the ceiling, landing hard enough to dent the floor. His face had taken on a stony resolve that made me shiver. It was a look I'd seen on my father's face a hundred times.

"The hatch is open⌐" he said.

"Loose the Constrictus, and turn out the herd," I told them. "Let Scorpius run free, but get out of his way. I'm going after Xerxes."

Winnie hit the master switch for the unicorns' paddock; they swarmed out into the car while the great snake oozed along below their hooves, lifting them as he passed.

Klok helped her onto Bijou's back, and they rose into the air as Scorpius went on a rampage. He slashed his tail along the walls of the car, bashing his head and claws against everything he touched.

In his enclosure, Xerxes' head rested on his paws with his wings tucked against his back. Even inert, the effect of breathing was there, making his body rise and fall. I climbed up near his neck and laid my hand against the control plate to activate him. He stretched, pulling back on his forepaws, then tilting forward, before deploying razor-edged wings. His head whipped around, so we met eye to furious eye and nose to beak.

"We've been boarded," I said. The whole train shuddered. "Help me."

There was no question of comprehension, and no hesitation. One powerful beat of his wings, and Xerxes launched us through the hatch.

The side of the golem car crumpled below us as Scorpius burst free. Behind him came the rush of unicorns and the slithering clink of the Constrictus in search of something to crush.

After that, only bedlam.

The clearing was now a nightmare of everything that made The Show thrilling. Too much action to see everything at once. A frenetic swirl of lights and smoke with strange sounds coming from places no one could find. But we weren't losing, and that was what mattered.

The Constrictus made straight for the nearest truck, crushing it small, then dragging it off. Scorpius attacked like a thing possessed, whipping his tail for a bludgeon in ways his programming shouldn't have allowed. Our little mice went after the vehicles, scurrying up into the casings. As the trucks passed on, they dropped bits of their engines and froze useless in the field.

Across the field, shining figures appeared everywhere there was resistance—unnoticeables, but they didn't engage.

This was the final stand of Magnus Roma. My father had been prepared for this day, even if we hadn't, and he'd set his creations to protect what he couldn't. Wherever he'd gone, it must have been an attempt to stave off this collapse, but he'd failed.

Our unicorns became a line of unbreachable rage. Shoulder to shoulder with their horns pointed outward, they created a blockade between the reserves and the train, defying anyone to test their resolve. Each man foolish enough to try was met by rampant feet, or the slash of honed metal seeking an artery to sever. And then suddenly, the unicorns were swept aside by a blast of wind, as easily as someone sweeping clutter off a table.

I'd forgotten the hounds.

A girl appeared in a uniform identical to the one worn by the woman who'd flipped the train, only hers was tinted violet. I wasn't sure if that was just the light, or if the wardens sorted the hounds like any other tool, and I had to shake the image of Vesper confined to a purple suit out of my head. Around the field were other girls, some Birdie's age and size. Flashes of red and blue signaled pyro- and hydrokinetics.

At first, I thought it was their clothes giving off the color, but then I realized the tint rose from their skin like an aura. My sisters had never given off such colors. No one else even seemed to notice the effect. Was it a consequence of captivity?

The aerokinetic hound walked on wind toward the train. She moved with a puppeteer's jerk, prying at a metal-and-glass collar around her neck. Similar bands at her wrists and ankles began to glow. Her body seized; she opened her mouth to scream, but nothing came out. Then she fell to the dirt, covering her uniform with dust as her body convulsed. When she stood up, she was calm; her eyes were glassy and distant. She flicked her hand and another gust cleared the few remaining unicorns to make an entrance to our train and allow the warden's men to ransack it.

I thought about calling out to her, warning her that the train was going to explode, but held my tongue because she held hers. She looked right at me, and instead of turning me in, she didn't say a word.

I shook my head, but she nodded with a sad smile and let herself drift inside, pulled along by the influence of her bands. She was giving me a chance, and shackled as she was, maybe boarding the train was the only kind of chance she had left. I couldn't even thank her for letting us go.

I didn't want to live in a world where death was the only mercy I could show.

There was another rumble and I looked for the terrakinetic woman, but this wasn't her, nor was it the Constrictus returning for seconds.

From the back of the train, and through the pulsing wall of smoke created by so many foundering machines, came screeches and roars from the menagerie that my sisters had released to save them from the train's destruction. Horses and zebras stampeded into the open, followed by the graceful lope of a pair of giraffes. Performing dogs shot between the legs of men in their way, while screaming chimps and small monkeys made for the trees. Unstoppable in their momentum, but slower for their size, our elephants brought up the rear.

In the lead sailed Vesper, still in her white dress and the shoes that Evie had scared me out of. A storm at her side, her blonde hair streaming, Vesper became our avenging angel. This was the tempest in full fury, and she was both terrifying and magnificent to behold. I couldn't imagine her reined in by collars and manacles that forced her to do some warden's bidding.

A piercing V-shaped flock of wind birds flew ahead of her, clearing her path as they went. The warden's men stared until the last possible moment, then scattered as live animals trampled their motorcade. The herd reached the unnoticeables and ran straight through without stopping. *Straight through their bodies.* Some of the unnoticeables flinched, some didn't, but none fell. They were ghosts.

Evie's flaming dog, Samson, ran headlong into the troops trying to regroup, swiping the air with fiery paws. Anise's looming Kodiak and Vesper's raptors struck from opposite sides. Nim's dolphins carried the rubble away over the side of the cliffs to ease everyone's escape.

After all their talk of not staying behind, my sisters did exactly that, to make sure the rest of us got out alive.

We weren't losing . . .

As a soldier reached for Nagendra, a cobra struck from inside the sleeve of his coat.

Near the tree line, our lion master and his wife stood their ground with whips in hand, protecting their beloved cats as they tore into body armor like tins of potted meat.

Zavel whisked off his top hat and threw it at the men chasing him. It hovered in the air behind him, spinning faster and faster without falling, captivating them until they stood still and watched it twirl. When the hat's timer ran out, and the flashing lights on its brim turned from blue to red, it exploded in a cloud of smoke and sparklers.

We were winning . . .

The balloon reached the first of our escapees. Nagendra climbed to the top of the ladder, and Zavel grabbed the rungs as they skimmed past. He made sure Birdie and Jermay were on the ladder below him before he began to climb. The extended Show family was safe and on its way.

"Get on the ground," a voice ordered behind me. When I turned, Evie's unnoticeable was hovering in midair.

"Y-you're a hologram!"

"Penelope, listen to me—land. He doesn't care about the rest of them, and you'll never make it by air. They'll target this signal. If you don't land—"

"Get away!" I screamed. He knew my name. My *real* name. How did he know? Evie wouldn't have told him, so who did?

I pulled Xerxes around to face the unnoticeable. He struck out with his wing, but it went right through.

"Is your entire family this bullheaded?" he asked. "I'm trying to help you! Get your friends on the ground, before—Down! Get down! Now!"

Something tiny streaked past my face, another tore into my shoulder, and for the second time that night, I heard Winnie warning me.

"Hummers!" she screamed.

Scorpius crashed snout first into the dirt. His tail went limp at his side, and the next instant he had shrunk down to the size of a spinning top. One by one the lights went out in the unicorns' eyes. The Constrictus arched up off the ground, thrashing from one end of his massive body to the other.

"Higher," I ordered. "Get above them!"

But it was too late.

My father had created the hummers to incapacitate dangerous or malfunctioning machines for repairs. They were a safety measure meant to aid in healing, and the Commission had corrupted them into this *obscenity*.

Bijou, with Klok and Winnie still atop, peeled sideways into a spin. Klok wrapped his arms around Winnie's body, tucking her head under his chin so she was protected as they fell. Another unnoticeable remained in the air where they'd been. She blinked out of view at the same time as Evie's man, and I swear he mouthed *I'm sorry* to me as he faded.

Something struck Xerxes' flank near my leg, and I glanced down, praying that I wouldn't see what I knew it had to be. A metal hornet, the size of a walnut, protruded from Xerxes' false flesh, spitting sparks. He roared, bucking uncontrollably as his systems were rewired and his power cells drained.

Another hummer struck, and another, and another, until Xerxes began to go dormant. The thrumming through his limbs stopped; that odd effect of breathing ceased, but he fought death until it brought him down. His eyes went dim, and it felt as if I was watching my father being killed—pulled out of my reach because I wasn't strong enough to hold on to him.

I expected to crash against the rocks below—just as Xerxes had tumbled over the edge, toward the river—but I stayed in the air. The wind pressed itself against my skin, forming a cushion. I couldn't rise or fall, but hung suspended in the grip of some new horror I had no name for.

A tingle came, and heat, causing my insides to churn with sudden familiarity. I couldn't remember the night my brother died, but that moment had imprinted on my subconscious. What happened then was happening now. Burning rain fell around my body on its way to the ground, knocking the infantry off their feet.

I heard a shrill, terrified screech, and turned my head in time to see a flaming trail bisect the rope ladder from the balloon's basket. Flames caught the cords, and the ladder fell with Birdie and Jermay still clinging to it. They'd been almost to the top. I could only watch and be thankful for the splash that told me they'd hit water rather than dry ground.

I'd been so careful for so long, and kept my abilities crushed beneath layers of makeup and bandages and self-control, but my focus had shattered. The only home I'd ever known was in flames, I couldn't see my sisters, and the last link I had to my father had gone down with Xerxes. Birdie couldn't swim, and I wasn't sure Klok's mass allowed him to do anything other than sink. Even if Jermay or Winnie were able to help them, where could they go without the balloon? All the power I'd tried to contain inside me leaked out through the cracks. I couldn't control it.

I swear I tried.

I imagined pouring water on the raging fire in my soul and tying my hands so they couldn't move. I pictured myself small, and reined myself in so hard that I thought my bones would break from the compression, but nothing worked. The sky was falling . . . and then it got worse.

The moon glowed brighter, bigger, as though it were drawing nearer. Beneath me, the river started to move. Ripples, then swells, then waves.

"Nim, run!" I cried, knowing only my sister could have done such a thing.

The water rained up, into a vertical wall. I looked down on the sister who was so often my nemesis and saw her standing on one side, while a blue-tinged hound stood on the other, with the static wave between them. Two women who didn't look like they could lift a barbell, and they were holding up a river like it was nothing.

Finally, Nim shoved her hand forward, creating a cascading arc of watery dolphins. They drenched the hound and washed her away. Nim fell to her knees, exhausted, and let the wave crash on top of her.

I still couldn't free myself from whatever held me aloft.

More burning rocks streaked through the sky, smashing everything they touched, and leaving only craters behind.

"Stop," I begged, but they kept coming. This was what had happened the night I was born, and now I was in danger of killing my sisters the same way I'd murdered my brother. "Stop it!"

For an answer, one of the stones slammed into my shoulder, spinning me downward into free fall. Another hit the back of my head. I lost count of those battering my arms and legs.

I was *so* tired.

I saw the train explode, but never heard it. And as the dark water broke my fall, drawing me deeper into oblivion, my last thought was that we'd lost.

I'd lost.

I'd lost everything.

CHAPTER 7

People were talking. They sounded far away, as though I were still under water, but I was flat on my back, with rocks for a pillow. Nearby, popping flames from a campfire vied with the dusk sky above. I'd lost hours, and felt every one of them as a separate point of pain that made it hard to move.

"Evie?" I croaked, not realizing how ravaged my throat was until I tried to speak. "Nim?"

I reached a hand toward the fire, but it wasn't their shadows I saw. It wasn't Vesper or Anise . . . brave, stoic, stupid Anise, who went to the bonfire knowing something was coming, but refusing to abandon the others.

"Who's there?" I asked, louder.

"She's coming around," said the voice I now knew as Winnie's. "Penn? Can you hear me?"

"Penelope," I rasped. Anise had said to leave Penn behind. "Help me up."

Wherever I was, it wasn't near the train. Winnie and Klok appeared first as a small blur and a large one. I blinked and caught sight of Jermay. He raised his little finger, and bent it.

Everything's okay, without the words.

As far up as he'd been when the ladder fell, his body could have broken on the water's surface, but he was fine, and Birdie was, too. She knelt beside me with a cup of water.

"Where are we?" I asked.

"Downriver," Winnie said. "It's not even a proper town, just an unincorporated area the locals call Inshore."

The riverbank was on my left, close enough to hear and smell. Other scents and sounds came from the bridge we were hiding beneath. From the rattle, no one official had bothered to keep the place up in a long while.

Klok dropped onto his haunches and flashed me a message.

"Thought you drowned."

"Not me," I said. "I'm buoyant as a bilge rat."

He gave me a stiff pat on the shoulder and an eerie not-quite-human grin.

"Makes me glad," he said, then added, **"Making supper,"** in what would have been the same breath, if he'd actually spoken.

It was best not to try to figure out Klok's thought processes. As near as I could tell, he could have several running simultaneously. Sometimes they came out in tragically awkward collisions, and the result was that not drowning was as important as supper.

"Are we all that's left?" I asked.

"The others tried to turn around for us," Winnie said. "But the fail-safes took over. They're at the Hollow, I'd imagine."

I nodded, as though knowing that my father's precautions had protected the others made things better, but it didn't.

"Did you see what happened to my sisters?"

"We didn't surface for over three miles, then drifted another five or six," Jermay said. "Winnie and Birdie shared the breather, and Klok breathed for me and you. Hopefully the warden thinks we drowned."

"So you don't know if they were taken?"

I jumped up too fast, and found myself back on the ground. Dark spots crept into my eyes.

"The balloon went above the clouds," Birdie said. "No one followed."

"Why would they? He wasn't after carnies!" Evie's unnoticeable had said as much. "They don't send hounds to collect acrobats and magicians!"

"Penn, calm down," Jermay said, kneeling in the grimy rocks beside me.

His hands on mine felt weighted, and hot. I pulled loose, trying to gain my feet, but my legs had turned to useless lumps of jelly.

"You were down for a long time," he said. "And you went pretty deep before Klok found you."

My next attempt to walk went no better than the first; it didn't help that Jermay was there to catch me again. He should have let me hit the ground, but instead, he sat with me so I wouldn't tip over, and picked up the cup of water.

"Drink it," he ordered. His eyes turned stormy. Their unnatural hue darkened, so he hardly looked like the boy I knew. I was already losing myself. I didn't want him to change, too. "You haven't had water in hours; you need it. Klok got us some decent fish, and Birdie rummaged up some clothes that won't get us pegged as a carnie crew on sight. Don't ask where she got them. You're better off not knowing."

She must have stolen them. Poor kid, she swore to Bruno that she'd never steal again, now that she had a family to take care of her.

"Get yourself together, then we'll figure out what comes next," Jermay said.

But the only life I'd ever known was over. There was no next.

I sat at the river's edge, the water splashing the toes of my boots. A twisted version of my dream blinked back with teary eyes. There I was, reflected in the dark water, with my hair sticking out in all directions. I dragged my foot through a pile of pebbles and watched the rings destroy the image with a silt plume.

No matter how hard I strained my eyes toward the sky, there was no smoke over the moon. Only the river told me the direction of the train's remains.

When I couldn't stand the stars anymore, I let my eyes fall back to the stilled water. The dress Birdie had stolen for me was cotton, with stripes that had probably been white when it was new. I was fairly certain the pink parts had started off as a shade of red, but had been beaten dull by use and washing. The hem was frayed, and there were patches in the skirt. Two of the buttons were broken. It had probably been someone's favorite, and Birdie must have raided a laundry line to get it, but it wasn't the kind of thing I had wished to put on when I dreamed of wearing dresses. I'd always thought being my true self would mean freedom, but this was another disguise.

Sitting alone gave me time to wonder about my sisters and their fate, and to decide on the questions I wanted to ask Winnie about why she'd pretended to be mute when she wasn't. I knew she'd had a run-in with the authorities before my father found her, and Evie told me that whatever the Commission had done to Winnie was why Winnie couldn't talk, but did my sister know not talking was a choice?

I was still sitting there when I heard footsteps along the shore.

"I brought you some supper," Jermay said. "It's a little burnt, but at least it's food."

He held out a charred, skewered fish. The river had washed away most of the scent of exploding powder that normally clung to his skin after his act, and the stranger's clothes got rid of the rest.

"If you were any sort of real magician, you'd turn this into something appetizing," I said. Klok had cooked the fish with the heads still on, and mine was staring at me.

"If I were a real magician, we'd be at the Hollow before you could take a bite." He sat just close enough that our knees touched, skirt to blue jeans.

My legs were thin and ash pale everywhere they weren't bruised by the meteorites that had knocked me from the sky. I could feel the same soreness under my sleeves.

"You look . . ." Jermay began, but faltered. He glanced from my face to the dress that Birdie had stolen for me, lingering on the hand that was playing with the belt cinched around my waist. "Like Penelope."

I'd felt cold all night, but now my face was flaming hot and my stomach was burning.

"You can tell me I look stupid. I won't stab you with my fish-kabob."

I shook it at him and the head lolled sideways.

"You look the way I pictured," he said.

He'd thought of how I would look as a girl?

"I'm half-drowned, covered in sand, and wearing a torn, stolen dress."

"Pretty Penelope at the shore," he insisted stubbornly.

So this was life without The Show. Burnt fish that was raw on the inside, and nerves that were raw inside me.

"Tell me this doesn't feel weird," I said.

"It's definitely different. If I look up too fast, I wonder where Penn went."

Why shouldn't he miss Penn? At least Penn was useful.

I chewed through my piece of fish without tasting it, only swallowing. If I kept my mouth full, there wouldn't be room for my feet in there.

"Please say something," Jermay begged. "Don't tell me I lost my best friend just because she lost her trousers."

What good were words?

Should I mention the frailty of his father? Or the trucks with blacked-out windows and no plates that rumbled over the bridge? Should I mention the most likely outcome for us?

"I don't know what to say," I told him.

I barely knew who I was, or which of the dozen voices I'd used for The Show actually belonged to me. I looked like Penelope, but still felt like the boy who didn't exist.

"I watched you fall," Jermay said after a long silence. "I tried to find you, but the water was too dark. I . . . I thought you were dead. If Klok hadn't kept going under . . ."

He was looking at me again, in a way he wouldn't have dared while I lived my life as Penn.

"I didn't like thinking that," he said.

"I-I didn't like seeing you fall, either."

I couldn't picture a time without Jermay in it. Without his voice to tell me a joke or aggravate me. When I thought about the brother whose life I had usurped, Jermay was the only one who could cheer me up, though he never knew why I was sad. That's how I knew how worried he was now—normally, he'd be juggling seashells or using my fish for a hand puppet to get me to laugh.

"I don't care what you look like, Penn. I just want you around to be seen. So don't almost die on me anymore, and I won't almost die on you. Deal?" He stuck his hand out.

It's rare to know you're at the moment you've dreamed of your entire life, but I was there. *Penelope* was there, and I felt as if I could do anything, including the one thing I'd never been allowed.

"Deal," I said. "But it only counts if it's sealed with a kiss." I yanked him forward, and this time, Jermay was the one spluttering.

Sitting down, we were nearly the same height—nearly perfect. I made myself keep my eyes open so I'd never convince myself this was a dream. Close, which was all we'd ever been allowed, became closer and closer until it turned into a single space we shared. And finally—

Balance.

We stayed like that until we had to breathe.

"Next time, we should try that when I'm not eating something awful," I said.

Jermay grinned, stretching his lips tight across his teeth in the way he only did if he was embarrassed. Most of my life, he'd always looked the same, but out here in the green shirt and jeans that Birdie had given him, the magical quality that usually simmered beneath his skin broke surface, making him less real and more fantasy. My face grew hotter the longer he stared at me. To distract him, I changed the subject.

"Did you manage to save anything we can use?" I asked, afraid his next words would be calling me an idiot.

"You could say that. I have a surprise for you."

He put two fingers in his mouth, blowing through them with a sharp, shrill whistle. Something shook itself free of the sand. It trotted in our direction, picking up the fire's shine on its small metal body.

"Xerxes!"

"You were too out of it for me to show you sooner. He landed near me in the water. The crazy thing was trying to swim, hummers and all."

Jermay set his hands on the ground, allowing the shrunken golem to climb into his palms. "Klok got his basic systems running, but he's stuck small."

Shrinking had done nothing to dull the ferocity of his gaze or the menacing click of his claws against the rocks. I hugged him, relieved to feel the vibration from his mechanical heart beneath feathers so soft I barely believed they were metal. He blinked at me, and I could almost hear him call my name.

"It's me," I said, ruffling his head.

Xerxes stretched out his forepaws and went right back to sleep, curled up on my lap.

Later, when the others were sleeping and clouds had covered most of the moon, I was still lying awake, watching Xerxes breathe. A trilling vibration tingled my skin from Bijou's spot on my arm. He'd coiled around me like the serpentine bracelet of an ancient Egyptian queen, and I'd managed to convince myself that if he and Xerxes were still alive, then maybe the rest of my father was out there, waiting to be found.

How did I know we were the only refugees?

Vesper had the skies, and Nim could have hidden underwater just as we did. Anise and Evie were far from helpless. There was a chance they were still free and on their way home to the Hollow.

But there was a better one that they'd been caught and collared.

My whole life, someone had given me directions, told me where to stand, what to say, and how to act. Without that, I was a spinning compass with no idea how to find north.

"Tell me what to do," I said to the sky.

The words left my mouth, and a meteor streaked across the night, matching the path we'd taken via the river. Coincidence, surely . . .

"Should I go back for them?" I tried again.

The stars twinkled. Another two meteors shot across the sky, their tails marking the crash with a crude *X* before they sputtered out.

That settled it. As I gathered up Xerxes and Winnie's pack, I composed my good-bye.

Jermay would be the hardest to face, and Klok the most difficult to convince, but my reasoning was sound—my sisters needed me, and Birdie was too young to be left on her own. She was a child who wanted her mother and father; they had to get her home.

"What's wrong?" Winnie sat up quickly when I jostled her shoulder, as though she'd been hovering near consciousness for fear of what would happen in her sleep.

"Can the rebreather handle another marathon?" I asked.

"Magnus knows his stuff," she said through a gaping yawn. "But the roads are faster."

"Not for me. I'm going back to the train."

"There *is* no train, Penn." I hadn't heard Jermay stir. Maybe he hadn't been sleeping, either. "And your sisters wouldn't want you doubling back. I *won't* let you throw their effort in a ditch." He jerked Winnie's pack out of my hands and passed it to her.

"What makes you think I'm asking permission?" I lost the fragile control I had on myself. Birdie and Klok startled from sleep. "*I'm* the reason the warden boarded the train—that unnoticeable came for *me*. *I'm* the reason you fell. I'm—"

The river began to churn at its nearest point, with pebbles bouncing below the surface until they gained enough momentum to break free and soar into the air. My blood turned scalding in my veins.

"Penn, stop." Winnie was beside me as I held my head to end the pounding. Her voice drowned in the whoosh filling my ears.

Something pulled me up, and I felt my body grow lighter in the last moments before it tried to leave the ground. The effect ended sharply with a bucket of cold water dumped over my head, shocking me out of my daze.

"Look at yourself," Jermay ordered. I breathed in, and the sting of inhaled water made my eyes tear. "They *saw* you, Penn, and no one could miss that." He pointed to the stars that were blinking in time with my pulse. "If we go back, we'll never make it out."

"I have to try."

"No!" Birdie cried. "I won't go back!"

She tore off toward the main road.

"Birdie, wait!" Winnie called. "We can't let her go alone."

"She's not alone," Jermay said. "We're going with her—*all* of us."

"Get her to Bruno and Mother Jesek," I said. "I'll be careful."

"Penn—"

"Keep them safe for me, Klok," I continued.

"I protect Penelope," he rat-tatted.

"You protect *our family*. They need you."

"Penelope needs me."

"You're too big to hide."

"I want to go with you."

He was disturbingly difficult to argue with. His face was too earnest and his eyes too pleading. Somehow, he found a way to emphasize the "want," even in writing.

"I'll be okay—I've got Xerxes," I told him.

"And me," Winnie added. Xerxes poked his beak out over the top of the pack that rested on her shoulders, a glimmer of excitement in his glass eyes as he opened and closed his beak with a loud *snap*.

"Winnie!" Jermay shouted. "You're supposed to help me talk her out of this."

"You've got family waiting at the Hollow—I don't. The Romas are as close as I've got."

"You should go," I told Jermay. "Catch Birdie before she's out of sight. You'll never find her if she gets it in her head to hide." Mother Jesek often said that her little bird was part ghost, because if Birdie didn't want to be seen, she wouldn't be.

Klok beeped out one last note for me: **"Nieva will say: Find Penelope and bring her home."**

"If Evie's at the Hollow, then I'm happy to be found," I said, and finally Klok clanged off.

I held my pinkie up for Jermay, but his hands stayed in rigid fists at his sides as he walked away. I watched him and Klok until I couldn't see them anymore. He never looked back.

CHAPTER 8

Going into a town or village for The Show meant fanfare. We'd be decked out in our costumes, nailing up notices, while the inevitable line of children tried to wrangle tickets. Entering Inshore with Winnie was clandestine and claustrophobic. The night was no longer merely an absence of sun and heat; it had a personality, with habits I didn't know.

I pulled out a fistful of fabric at the neck of my dress, trying to obscure my silhouette. Being female had been a danger for so long, I couldn't make myself believe those rules had changed.

To make it worse, the hair on my arms twitched under the influence of a stray current. I cast a panicked look at the night sky, but the moon stayed fixed. It wasn't responding to my nerves the way it had at the train. I let go of my dress and tried to relax.

"Control it, Penn," Winnie warned as the nearest streetlights flared when we passed. "You'll draw attention to us."

Carnie 101, back to haunt me. Drawing attention was all I knew how to do. I was skilled at misdirection, not avoidance, but since I lost the train, none of my usual sleight of hand worked.

"Control it, or I'll have to leave you here." Winnie stopped in the shelter of an old shed with a broken door. She transferred her backpack to my shoulders, so Xerxes' weight could remind me that he was with me.

Something sharp stung my earlobe, just before Xerxes butted the back of my head with his own. He'd nipped me with his beak, calling up memories of my father tugging my ear before a performance.

"Thanks," I whispered. Xerxes dropped down in the pack. His forepaws kneaded into my back, trying to find a comfortable spot.

"We can't go asking about wardens and unnoticeables," Winnie said. "We'll do best finding someplace where things are already being said and listening in."

"Like where? This place is barely a town. It's not like there's a pancake house on every corner."

"You're such a train-head." Winnie rolled her eyes. "Not everything comes with a sign you can read from the tracks."

She left the deserted square, and I followed onto a side street with enough light to mean someone still had their place open, only it wasn't what you'd call a restaurant. Mismatched tables and chairs had been set outside, creating a makeshift café. People who were near our age talked and laughed in small groups.

"A charity stop?"

"Friday always means free food."

One table was a tangled mob wearing the colors of the local university. Elsewhere, people drifted in the spaces between, all gaunt faces and hollow eyes. A large sandwich board on the corner read "Hot Coffee ~ Sandwiches ~ Cookies."

"You want news, this is the best place to get it."

In this case, unincorporated meant Inshore was unregulated. While the nearest towns were in blackout during the night hours, here there was no one to enforce such ordinances. Animated creeper lights strolled the lane, toting lanterns on their spindly legs, while climbing lights like the ones we used to light tour exhibits at The Show converted over-door placards into makeshift lampposts.

We were only a few miles from the train's destruction, but everything was different here. Victorian brass and copper had been replaced by chrome and silver. The designs were sleeker; the machinery quieter and styled from old black-and-white B movies. A guy at one of the tables we passed was hunched over a tablet that had been outfitted with retro-glass, so his display was holographic 3-D, but also monochrome. A stick-on magnet between his eyebrows held a pair of glasses on his face without the need for earpieces.

"There," Winnie said, and started toward a young man in an apron who had emerged from the nearest building with a tray full of steaming coffee cups. We didn't get very far before he was swarmed.

Another door opened farther down the street, and another guy emerged carrying a tray, but his was full of food. Most of the people who had flocked to the first tray rushed the second. Winnie and I were the only ones left.

"Is there anything to spare?" I asked the guy with the coffee. He was the definition of mundane, basically a brown-skinned, brown-eyed, brown-haired paper doll printed in 3-D.

He looked up and met my eye, then did the same with Winnie. Whoever he was, he made a habit of noticing people, and that could prove problematic.

"You're new," he said.

"Only around here," Winnie said bitterly. "If there's not enough for strangers, we'll go somewhere else."

"I'm sorry," the guy said. "I didn't mean to run you off." He put the last four mugs of coffee on a table. "Sit down."

He tucked the tray under the table and took a seat himself.

"Might as well," I told Winnie, though it was obvious he'd made a bad impression. "Got nowhere else to be."

"You don't have to be afraid here," he said. "Most folks call me C. B., for Coffee Bean."

He slid one of the mugs across the table to me. I'd never liked the taste of coffee, but I liked the smell, and the warm mug felt good in my hands.

Winnie sat, and C. B. slid her a cup, too. The Asian guy who'd been handing out sandwiches joined us with a cheerful "New people! What's your name, sister?"

You're not my brother, I wanted to say. That kind of casual familiarity creeped me out.

"This one they call Rye, on account of the sandwiches," C. B. said, grinning. "He also answers to Idiot."

"We're Jenny," Winnie told them.

"Both of you?"

"It's a common name."

One of the creeper lights skittered onto our table. It danced around the edges while I drummed my fingers, and the creeper imitated my pattern with its feet.

"Never seen one do that before," Rye said. He beat out a rhythm with his hands, but the creeper had lost interest. It took a roll around the table.

Those machines were a sight tied so strongly to the life I'd just lost that I could feel tears forming. I reached up to wipe my eyes.

"You okay?" C. B. asked.

"She's been acting off since we saw that black smoke," Winnie said, cutting me off before I could answer. "Now she mostly stares and cries."

I shifted my feet uncomfortably. I'd been numb since I woke up near the river, and had done plenty of staring, but I wasn't sure about the crying.

"No mystery in the smoke, sister, just a derailed train," Rye said.

"I've told her the smoke was nothing, but—" Winnie was interrupted when another creeper light joined the first, so they twirled in an awkward ballet—vying for attention, like untrained puppies. The climbing lantern from the nearest placard dropped down from its post to watch.

Retro-glass guy had his tablet held toward us now, taking a video that he'd probably post online. If the warden was running a face-recognition search, we were already found.

Another pair of spidery creepers tripped toward our table. C. B. and Rye shared a look; Winnie glared at me as though I'd summoned them on purpose.

I turned my mug in my hands, absently tracing a looped image etched into the side. When I realized what it was, I nearly threw the coffee across the table. I glanced at Winnie's mug and saw the same design—an ankh formed from a DNA helix.

"Where do you get this stuff?" I asked. C. B. and Rye were watching us, probably wondering why a couple of wandering kids hadn't devoured the free meal already.

"Our sponsor donates it every week," C. B. said.

"Which sponsor?"

"A generous one. Why?"

Good question. Why would the Wardens' Commission supply food to random strangers? That wasn't part of their job, so what did they get out of it?

More importantly, what did they put *in* it?

"We should keep moving." Winnie brushed the creepers from the table and gestured back toward the road. "Thanks for the eats." She stuffed a cookie into her pocket, because hungry girls wouldn't leave food behind.

When we stood, others were watching us, and more of them were filming us. It wasn't surprising considering nearly every lantern in the alley had migrated to our end.

"Stop! Shoo!" I waved my hands at the lights, and they scattered back to where they'd been before we arrived.

"Hey!" retro-glass guy yelped. "My screen went dark."

He started shaking his tablet, like that would help.

"How'd you do that, sister?" Rye asked.

"I didn't do anything. I just—"

I was tripping over excuses when a commotion drew his attention to the other end of the street.

"Not again," C. B. grumbled as the noise came closer.

More teens, marching in lines of three across. The ones in front were wearing rubber masks shaped like the Greys—what people thought aliens looked like before the Medusae came and showed us that they didn't have triangular heads or giant black eyes. The teens had foam hands with long fingers and were wearing shirts emblazoned with the tricolored cloverleaf, only the leaves were made of words from the Brick Street rhyme.

Displays like this weren't uncommon near the anniversary, but this one was certainly an unwelcome surprise. They marched right through the café to the cheers of the group from the university. Everyone at that table had removed their sweatshirts to display more cloverleaves.

"What's happening?" I asked.

"Flash mob," Rye whispered. "They film themselves to get attention. We've been the target of choice for the last three months. Don't know why."

I did. The Commission was using them for something; they were using the people, while pretending to help, and these guys had figured it out.

"Get out of here," C. B said, trying to intercept one of the "aliens."

"I thought everyone was welcome," the alien spoke back, voice muffled by his mask.

"Yeah," said the alien beside him. "Play nice, or we'll zap you with our powers." He shot C. B. in the face with a water pistol.

"We've already had to move the canteen twice because of you, and I won't do it again. Leave!" Rye snapped.

"I came to eat, and I won't leave until I've been served." The first alien plopped into a chair and propped his feet on the table, waving his foam hand dismissively. "Brains, if you please. Human. Don't bother cooking them."

"You're going to scare off the people who really need this place."

If I hadn't seen the coffee cup, I would have believed C. B. was sincere.

"No one needs what you're offering." The second alien climbed up onto the table and removed his foam head. Underneath, he was mundane like the rest of them, but he was furious.

One of the cloverleaves handed him a tablet and a microphone, and he began to shout about how people were blinded to the truth of the world. He declared C. B. and Rye to be Commission puppets. He spoke of the anniversary, then held up one of the coffee mugs and demanded to know what the wardens wanted with the local homeless.

"We're trying to help, brother," Rye said, but the unmasked alien kept shouting.

A girl shouted the Brick Street rhyme over him; others turned it into a round.

Remember the brick street.

Remember the dead.

The main speaker started calling out names, and as he did, the people with him held up enlarged pictures of the homeless, each marked with a name. All missing. All regulars at C. B. and Rye's charity stop.

Someone at the university table reached into a bag. She slung her hand at C. B., and a sticky toy jellyfish slid down his shirt, leaving a slime trail. That triggered the others at the table, and everyone who had been marching. One of the toys landed square on my head. Another stuck to Winnie's neck.

The university group jumped up and started taking pictures, hooting and laughing. C. B. grabbed the seated alien's head and tried to pull it off, while Rye tried to drag the speaker off the table. Most of the crowd fled.

They had the right idea. Unincorporated or not, this kind of commotion would draw the police. I grabbed Winnie's arm and ran.

The walk back up the incline toward the shed felt longer than our descent. Coiling fog rose off the night's frost. It wrapped around my ankles, stealing what little warmth was left in my body as it curled toward my knees. After life aboard the train, a town was a filthy thing. Even the streetlamps cast dirty color to pollute the night.

Lights flickered along the bridge—ghosts or fairies keeping watch in somber silence. Never once, in all my years with The Show, had I truly understood the fear that piqued in those who followed me into the Caravan of Wonder, but I felt it there.

People like me . . . we were *jokes*. Maybe the guy with the list of missing people had a good reason for what he was doing, but for the rest, it was nothing but an excuse to cause mayhem.

They wouldn't have kept laughing if they'd seen the Celestine emerge, and the disturbing part was that I didn't hold her back to keep from obliterating the charity stop or the street behind it. I did it because I knew the fake aliens were filming, and I would have been seen.

There was a part of me, a very dark and terrifying part, that wanted to show them exactly what they were mocking. I was ashamed to admit it was getting harder to tamp that part down.

Xerxes poked his head out of my pack, resting it on my shoulder. I reached for Bijou, wrapped heavy and warm around my arm, and patted him.

Winnie and I stopped at the shed, kicking the nailed-up boards on the broken door until we found one loose enough to pry up and slip through.

"Not exactly a sleeper car, but it'll do till morning," she said. "It's not safe on the street if that lot draws police. We can head off at first light and follow the riverbank until we've got no choice but to go into the water."

We settled in among a pile of musty canvas bags, pretending not to hear the scritch and squeak of nesting rats, but didn't turn off our lantern. It was small, and not warm, but we'd both lived with The Show long enough to take comfort in illusion.

I imagined the clatter of wheels outside was the sound of the train laying track. The wind meant speed, and the promise of a new town up ahead; we were only cold because Squint was repairing furnaces. My sisters were down the corridor, as always.

Eventually, I must have bought the lie, because I was woken when someone else's hands rattled the boards across the door. My eyes met Winnie's; I hit the switch to turn the lantern off.

A brighter light bobbed beyond the door.

"Gimme a go," a man ordered. "I'll get us in."

There was a shuffling of feet as a second man replaced the first. Either he was stronger or more stubborn, because soon cracking wood and popping nails had me and Winnie scooting into the shadows with the rats. The boards gave way, and two large shapes backed in through the door.

"Must've warped in the weather," one said.

The other one turned. He swung his torch high and wide, flooding the tiny building with light. Winnie and I held on to each other, shaking in a way that had nothing to do with damp or chill.

"Lookie here, Bull." The man with the torch smiled. Bull turned slowly, then straightened with a startle as his buddy said, "We hit the mother lode."

CHAPTER 9

"Back away." Winnie stood up, facing the two men.

"No need to worry, dolly, ol' Tuck ain't gonna hurt you."

Tuck was the most strangely shaped person I'd ever seen. He had thin legs and wiry arms, but he was all bloated around the middle. He looked like a spider in a hand-me-down coat.

"Are you deaf?" Winnie snapped. She stood taller and straighter, her eyes fixed on them. "Turn around and leave!"

Bull did exactly that, but he was hesitant and confused, like he didn't know why he was doing it. Tuck didn't move at all.

"We'll scream," I said, standing beside Winnie.

"Holler to high heaven out here, and only the devil will hear, princess."

Winnie's fingers pulsed at her side, readying a five-count the way we did to cue an act. I knew exactly what she was thinking. When she hit one, we were going to run. Tuck couldn't chase us both, and from his size, even following one of us would be a chore.

I reached for my pack, and Xerxes with it.

Winnie's little finger folded down, followed by the one next to it, and the next . . .

"Why don't you be good girls and come along," Tuck said. "No sense arguing with your elders, eh?"

I don't think he realized his friend was gone.

Winnie's thumb tucked into her fist, and—

"Cue!" I shouted.

She swung her pack straight at Tuck's face. Mine caught him in the gut, where his flesh met Xerxes' metal hide, and he fell to his knees. We were off and out the door, passing Bull, who didn't pay us any mind at all.

"Wha—" I began.

"Questions later," Winnie insisted. She yanked my wrist.

The streets had been given over to nighttime vermin scavenging trash and scraps by moonlight. Dogs with their ribs showing under mangy fur patrolled the bridge. Cats chased rats that were nearly their own size.

There was no one out here to help us.

Behind us, someone ran with heavy steps, moving much quicker than I would have thought Tuck capable.

"I'd say it's a good time to find out how well my father made that rebreather," I said. "Get back to the river!"

We slid down the sloped bank toward the water. I made the mistake of looking back and saw Tuck skidding clumsily down the path we'd taken, towing Bull along with him.

The river took my breath away. It had been cold before, but now a thin crust of ice had formed near the shore. The freeze crept up the stripes on my dress; my father's coat turned cumbersome, making each step more difficult.

"D-d-deeper," Winnie chattered. Her sweater was full of water, dragging her down. "We need—"

She was choked off when she was grabbed from behind; I was lifted in the next instant.

"That wasn't very smart." Tuck let go, and I fell shivering onto the ground. Winnie landed beside me. "And bad things happen to stupid dolly girls who wander where they don't belong."

"Do something," Winnie rasped.

"I'm trying," I whispered back, but all I got was one pitiful, short-lived flare in the sky that would be used for wishing if anyone saw it.

"Let go!" Winnie shouted when Tuck reached to pull her off the ground. She turned her attention to Bull. "Don't let him hurt us. Stop—"

Tuck slapped her sideways so hard he split her lip. "You two are more trouble than you're worth. I think we ought to right the balance."

We were on a warehouse floor with our hands tied to a central beam behind us. We'd been blindfolded and hadn't seen where Bull and Tuck took us, but it had to be the water district. I could hear boat bells as they rang in the narrows.

The men must have been squatters. A burning pile of trash on a clear patch of cement floor was as close as they had to a furnace. The way Tuck kept looking at us made my insides squirm.

"You little lovelies are going to more than make up for what Bull 'n' me lost these last months," he said.

He reached for my leg, and Winnie kicked him in the side of the head, where his ear had already swelled up like a piece of cauliflower. He fell, cursing as dark spittle ran from the corner of his mouth. He drew back to hit her, but Bull caught his arm.

"Don't go damaging the merchandise. One of these little bits has a rich daddy somewhere, and black-and-blue ain't the image we want him to see." Bull didn't speak often, but he was obviously the one with more authority. Tuck didn't have the patience to think things through.

Tuck spat out a mouthful of thick spit and blood.

"We're not rich," I said, desperately trying to convince them we weren't worth keeping.

"Nice try, princess," Bull said. "But hardscrabbles don't carry the kind of tech you girls have. Where'd it ship from? The Sundowns in Seoul? Helsinki? Ah—doesn't matter. I know where it's going."

Of course he'd want to sell it. My father's inventions were unique; each piece was worth a fortune.

"We stole all of that," I said. "I'm a carnie girl. We both are."

"You're a quick thinker, I'll give you that, but you've no part here. Soon as I figure out who you belong to, I'll sell you back to your poor mother to ease her mind."

"My mother's dead," I said.

"Good to know." Bull smiled. The three teeth that weren't green were missing. "Makes you worth more to your old man, I'm sure. Me and Tuck'll be much obliged for the pay—obliged enough to slip through the mountains and out of this backward pit for good."

"Through the mountains" was a common goal for people who thought life was easier on the other side of the ridge, where the tech restrictions were lighter. There were glass towers there, and buildings that rose above the clouds. There were companies that made components for my father, and implemented his designs as practical devices. I'd been there—it was where the wardens came from. That's why we lived on the train.

A loud metal clang sounded from the table in the center of the room where the men had piled the things they took from us, and then more cursing as Tuck jumped, shaking his hand, with Xerxes' beak clamped around his fingers.

Knowing how powerful Xerxes was at any size, I was surprised Tuck could still use the hand at all. Xerxes sprang backward into the air and hovered, growling as loudly as his reduced mass allowed.

Tuck took a swipe with a pry bar; Xerxes slapped him with a wing, leaving him with a gash above his eye. The golem swiveled his head, taking in the whole room and pausing on me and Winnie, before rocketing through one of the many holes in the ceiling that he was small enough to fit through.

Tuck stormed across the room, pry bar in hand, and raised it like a bludgeon. Bull plucked it out of his grip before he could bring it down.

"They're no good dead."

"What about that one?" Tuck asked, pointing at Winnie. He had a look in his eye, a dark, hungry want.

"If Daddy's not interested, she's worth her weight in the Chapels, but the Abbess don't pay if you break her."

My stomach flipped.

An abbess was what people around here called a madam. Bull's backup plan was to sell us in the red-light district. Such things were illegal, of course, but the kind of illegal that shouldn't be seen more than shouldn't be done. Those who could stop it were more concerned with watching the skies for ships than watching the streets for trouble.

The fire went out in Winnie's eyes. When she opened her mouth, no sound came out, not even a sob. She drew her feet up and leaned closer to me, so I shifted as near as my tied hands would let me, until I wanted to scream from the ropes burning my skin.

"Leave her alone!" I snapped, but Tuck lumbered forward. He ripped Winnie's sleeve, revealing scars I'd never seen. She wore long sleeves when she wasn't in costume, and inside the tank, her skin was covered in moss and makeup. The more severe marks passed out of sight around the back of her shoulder.

Tuck wasn't fazed in the least. He reached for the neck of her sweater, and she balled herself up tighter.

"There's a warden after us! If he finds us, he'll find *you*!" It was a gamble that either man believed the Commission was a danger to them, but I was desperate—and it worked. Tuck released Winnie's sweater; he stood up, crouching over us.

"What's that?"

"You want to know who we're running from? Too bad. You'll never see them coming, and you know why, but you'll see the hounds. Same as we did. You know The Show?"

"Course."

"*We're carnie girls.* We got boarded, so we grabbed what we could carry, and ran."

"Leave off," Bull said. His piggy little eyes narrowed, and his face turned very serious, as he pulled Tuck away.

"She's lyin'," Tuck spat.

"I'm not! They're searching for anyone who made it off the train before she blew. We heard what happens to people who get found, so we hid."

"And what're a couple of Kewpie dolls worth to a warden?"

"Roma's my father. Leave my friend alone, or when the one chasing me asks why I won't talk, I'll tell him it's because of you, and you can try and convince him otherwise."

Bull shoved Tuck to get him away from us.

"I said leave off. If these little bits are who and what she claims, you don't want nobody finding your prints on either one of 'em." Bull set Winnie upright, then put his filthy coat around her shoulders.

"See for yourself. My father's marks are on the tech you took."

Bull dragged Tuck to the table, where they continued to argue. Tuck was still nursing his sore head, but Bull had one of my father's inventions in his hands, pointing to something on the side.

"I don't care what you think those scratches mean! I'm *not* listening to fairy tales about people who can fly over the countryside and call up earthquakes or fire spouts on a wish. I found 'em. I'm owed one of the pair!"

If it was as easy as wishing, I'd have been rewarded with some small show of power to scare them into letting us go. I held my breath and pulled as hard as I could, imagining a firestorm beating down upon the warehouse roof, but no stars fell. A door in the back blew open, slamming against the inner wall as a random gust of wind swirled through the room, but I was powerless.

"There's unnatural happenings 'round The Show and those who call it home," Bull said, shuddering when the door slammed shut again. "If anyone can attract trouble, it's that lot. I'm heading for the station house. You fetch the Abbess. If no one knows this mark, then princess or not, we'll chuck both over for the trouble, but I'm not risking my neck if this one's telling the truth. Fair?"

"Fair," Tuck said, but he didn't seem too happy about it.

He unwound his scarf, came toward us, and grabbed me by my hair, pulling up until I tried to scream. Once my mouth was open, he stuffed the scarf inside, then tied the ends off tight around the back of my head.

Bull tied a rag around Winnie's mouth, but I doubted she'd be saying much anyway. She'd gone back to being mute, and I didn't want to think about why. I had never imagined she'd experienced anything that could leave scars like those.

"Douse the lights, and get gone," Bull said.

Winnie and I were left in the dark, with no way to call for help and no way out.

CHAPTER 10

My arm fell numb from Winnie leaning against it, and it stayed that way while the rats came out of the walls to investigate our presence. They were better company than Bull and Tuck, but they were also more skittish. Eventually the back door creaked, and a parade of lights rolled into the room, scattering the rats.

Creeper lights.

Specifically, the creepers from the backstreet café. Uneven, glowing cords dripped down from the ceiling as the placard-climbers dropped in through the roof. We were miles from the shops—there was no way the lights could have found us, and no reason they would have tried.

I nudged Winnie with my shoulder.

One of the creepers butted my leg to get my attention. Creepers were dedicated entertainment machines, but this one raised its front legs and brought them in front of its lantern-face to tell me: *Shield your eyes.*

They weren't real words, or at least there wasn't a voice speaking them. The warning was a thought put into my mind from outside.

I looked at Winnie and squeezed my eyes shut, to cue her to do the same. A second later, there was a flash of heat; the ropes around my wrists disintegrated.

"Did you do that?" I asked the creeper, once I'd opened my eyes and removed my gag. It put its front legs down and danced with its companions. There were two patches of ash on the ground from the ropes.

"Penn, what's going on?" Winnie was talking again, and rubbing her raw wrists.

"I have no idea."

The creepers were acting so out of character that I would have believed my father sent them if we hadn't been so close to danger. Had he known where we were, my father wouldn't have left us alone in that warehouse, with the threat of Tuck and Bull returning at any moment.

Even that moment.

The door creaked again, and the creepers fled, dousing their lights as they went. The climbers retreated into the rafters.

With a group approaching, the best odds would be for me and Winnie to abandon our tech and hide, but there wasn't enough racket for a group. If it was only Tuck and Bull, we had a better chance letting them think nothing had changed. We could find out if someone from the Commission was on the way, and I had a chance to save Bijou and the rest of my father's work from the table.

We sat down, with our hands behind our backs and the rags around our faces.

"Got two here for you," said Tuck's voice. "One belongs to Bull, but he ain't here."

"Well?" A woman's gravelly voice. "Let's see them. Wasting my time don't raise their value."

The closest lamp turned on. I blinked up toward the light and saw a woman with spindly arms and splotchy skin. She stood with a hunch, wearing rags that barely qualified as clothes. There was a strange quality to her skin, like a candle flame cast through colored scarves to form unnatural shadows.

"Those scars'll drop the price," she said, taking Winnie's chin in her hand. "What's the other one's tale?"

"Runaway with a dead family," Tuck said.

"That true?" the woman asked me, with a sharp tug on my hair to pull my face into the light.

I shook my head as fast as I could, but found myself unable to look away from the Abbess's surprisingly clear eyes. Memories of The Show swirled through me, dragging up names and faces to go with them—everyone from my father and sisters to the stagehands. Something was pulling them out like a magnet pulls iron. The experience lasted seconds, but I felt drained by the end, and the whole time the Abbess's eyes moved from side to side at REM speed.

"Nasty little liar, that one," Tuck said, and slapped me, sparking lights behind my eyes.

When I looked back up, the Abbess sort of flickered, creating the illusion of a second face beneath the first.

"No one's gonna miss 'er, Abbess."

The ghostly second face disappeared, leaving only the horrible, dispassionate one.

"She'll need a scrub to get the dust off, but we can deal." The Abbess nodded absently.

They moved to the far side of the warehouse to settle on a price.

Winnie and I crawled off, not wanting to risk casting our shadows if we stood up too close to the lamp that Tuck had lit. As we neared my father's tech, the creepers came out of hiding. They swarmed the table, putting everything back into our bags.

"Tell me I'm not dreaming this," Winnie said.

"If you are, then so am I."

The machines were efficient. The one that had been their spokesman came forward again. It tapped my arm, then jabbed its front leg upward.

Klok waved at us from the rafters, where he and Jermay both sat straddling the beams. Jermay raised his hand, bending his little finger toward me. The peculiar blue tint to his eyes was heightened in the shadows, sparking off with frozen lightning that made me wonder if there wasn't actually a bit of magic trapped inside them. We could certainly use it.

I wiggled my pinkie back at him.

Birdie ran across to join them, sure-footed as only someone accustomed to the Jeseks' high wire could be. Klok took her hands and lowered her on his hydraulic arms until she was close enough to the table to drop onto it. She didn't make a sound.

"How'd you find us?" I whispered to Birdie.

"Xerxes homed in on Klok, then these guys showed up. We followed," she said, passing our bags to a tangle of climbing lights beside her. "Let's go."

Jermay took the bags from the climbers, letting Xerxes wriggle back into my pack before he slung it over his shoulders, and started for the vented window they'd used to sneak in.

Birdie grabbed Klok's wrists. A bundle of climbers reached for Winnie, wrapping tight around her, then they zipped up into the ceiling, hoisting her onto the rafter behind Jermay. When Klok returned for me, the oddly communicative creeper raised its leg to wave good-bye.

From overhead, I could see how much hair the Abbess was missing, and the way that the wisps hardly covered her scabby scalp heightened the flickering outline around her edges. Up there, it was clear how truly buglike Tuck's body was. It was also from midair that I saw lights flood in through the windows. Two here-but-not holograms appeared, neither of which was Evie's man. One was much older; the other looked a lot like Rye, only he'd traded his apron for a silver jacket.

"Five on high," he said. "No one on the . . . *Jenny?* How . . . What happened to you?"

He stared, shocked at Winnie's disheveled appearance. He even sounded concerned.

Someone must have reprimanded him on his end of the transmission because Rye looked off to the side, then continued. "Take the building," he said.

"What's that?" The Abbess startled. Floodlights cut through her thin dress, casting the shape of her skeletal body against the cloth.

A low rumbling shook the whole building with the impact of machine-tread on stone.

"I thought she was lyin'," Tuck said.

The Abbess threw her arms up to hide her face and made for the door farthest from the lights, hissing like an angry cat.

Tuck stood still while bits of metal and wood smashed around him. Some flew straight through Rye, who was floating near us.

"You need to run, sister," he said, cordial again. "They're coming, and it won't matter what's in their way."

Shelves knocked over, shattering glass as they fell, and I was still dangling from Klok's hands. He held tight, but the vibrations passed through his arms. Jermay had reached the vent and was propping it open when something large hit the main warehouse door. The jolt knocked Birdie sideways. She screamed as our guardian climber lights shot out to catch her. Klok pulled me up quick, and we slipped away. Jermay and Winnie dropped out onto the roof of the adjacent building.

"Run!" I shouted.

"Which way?" Winnie asked.

Good question.

We were in a dodgy part of town with nothing familiar, and all the warehouse roofs looked alike. The creeper lights and climbers hadn't come out with us, so there'd be no more help from them. I could see blurred shapes in the streets where more unnoticeables had been dispatched.

"Are you all right?" Jermay asked, pulling me close when we paused to get our bearings. Klok rat-tatted the same thing.

"None of us will be all right for long," I said. "That unnoticeable knows us."

"The warehouses are no cover," Winnie said. Their walls were too thin, threatening to collapse under our feet from the rumble alone. More roofs spread out in all directions, stacked dominoes ready to fall. Dark gaps between them were the only indication of streets below us as we ran toward the hanging moon. "If they bring in air support—"

"Don't even think that," I snapped. For sky-eyes, picking a person off a roof was as simple as scooping fish off a boat with a net.

"They're on the roof," a voice announced. An unnoticeable was with us. Another new face—how many of these things were there?

"This way," Birdie shouted and spun right, hopping onto another roof. She scrambled across and climbed up a ladder that connected to another building.

"They're headed south," the unnoticeable said, appearing on the next roof, too. Birdie ran through him; the rest of us followed.

"Where are we going?" I asked.

Jermay and Winnie shrugged. Birdie stood on the higher roof, searching for something, while Klok brought up the rear. "There! Follow the flame. It leads to help!" Birdie pointed to a distant glow that leapt suddenly higher in the night.

Then she was off again, flitting from one building to the next, hardly touching down. Each roof we hit came with another flickering unnoticeable.

I had no idea who Birdie's "they" were, but she'd survived a long time before my father found her. The idea that she knew someone with a mind to help wasn't something to argue with.

Follow the flame, nudged a voice in my head. *Follow the flame. The door's open.*

As we drew nearer, I could see that the light was actual fire wrapping around a bronze crucifix in a giant bowl below the words *Cathedral of the True Flame.* The flame leapt again, and again the voice said: *Follow.*

"Smart kid." Rye was with us now. After urging us on, he shouted, "They're headed for the church!"

Birdie shimmied down a post beside the last building, then hurried us across the narrow road and up the stairs to a pair of imposing wood doors. The law said no one could force their way into a holy house without permission.

She ran through Rye and into the building.

"I can't go in there," Jermay said nervously. He stopped running so quickly that dust settled over his shoes.

"Get moving before they switch to tactile transmissions," Rye said, then he yelled, "Stop!"

"Penn—it's a church. I can't."

It was true enough that there were people who cited prayer books as reasons to call us worse than carnies. Sometimes they gathered outside the circus grounds and tried to turn people away, claiming the flash and shine of The Show was merely a veneer of gold over garbage. But I didn't see many alternatives. More unnoticeables were blinking in around us.

Birdie was already inside, and Winnie had gone after her.

"Don't!" an unnoticeable ordered.

The others crowded us, making a vain grab for Klok, who shuffled Jermay the rest of the way over the threshold. This time, I didn't just see them; I felt their hands.

Holograms with hands. How was this possible?

Klok shut the doors behind us. Jermay winced at the thud, drawing himself up tight for several seconds before cracking an eyelid to survey our surroundings.

"We're okay?" he asked, as though it was a shock we hadn't turned to salt as soon as we set our shoes against the rugs.

"Over there," Birdie whispered, ducking low between carved wooden benches. She led us, crouching through the rows until we reached a closet with two doors. "Inside. Hide under the seats."

We wouldn't all fit in one door, so Klok and Jermay went to the other side while Birdie, Winnie, and I smushed ourselves into a space that should have barely fit one of us. A bell clinked overhead.

"That's the call to let them know the box is full," Birdie said.

I heard another door click open, and the sound of feet across the wooden floor. Whoever answered the bell stopped at the other side of the closet, jiggling the handle when it wouldn't give.

"This is the Father's side, dear," said a woman's voice. "It'll be a few moments. He was in bed."

I flattened out on the floor. Through a grate near the bottom of the divider, I could see that Jermay was in the same position. I reached my fingers through, and we lay there with our hands hooked together as if contact could keep us from being discovered.

"There's an order to these things," said the woman. "I really must insist."

She turned the knob on our door.

Birdie grabbed our side of the knob with both hands, and Winnie pulled against her until her muscles shook. I tugged Birdie's belt with the hand that wasn't holding Jermay's. When the woman tried our door, it lurched, but didn't open all the way before Birdie slammed it shut, making the bell *tink* again.

"What on earth?"

This time, the woman peeked through the crack. When our eyes met I forgot how to breathe. She let go of the door and retreated a step.

"Shove her over and run out the back," Jermay whispered through the grate.

"No," I said. "Stay put."

By now, we'd be surrounded.

Maybe things would have happened differently if she'd kept at it, or called us out and demanded we leave, but there was a knock against the church's front door, and the woman went to answer it.

"What do you mean, making that kind of racket at this hour?" Her kind tone disappeared.

"We're looking for someone."

I'd heard that voice before. I peeked out, but all I could see was the woman, in a long gray dress, holding her hand on the outer door so whoever was on the other side couldn't open it.

"And you think they're here?" she asked.

"They were seen entering," he insisted.

"Of course they were," she said dismissively. "I don't suppose your miscreants are a mob of university kids running around in fright masks?"

"Three girls; one tall and gangly, with short hair. The other two are dark skinned. One of the boys is a real monster, hulking huge, and the other's a slippery rat of a thief."

It wasn't unusual for people to think poorly of those of us who lived on the train, but it was worse hearing it said.

"I don't see anyone like that."

"You're sure?"

"I'm a nun, Warden. We're always sure. If you don't trust my eyes, then use your own—but stay on that side of the door."

Warden.

The one who'd followed my tour and stolen my lines. The man who destroyed my life. He was here.

The woman stepped back to let him poke his head into the sanctuary. He bent to take a look beneath the empty seats. He glanced toward our box, but looked away just as quickly.

"Satisfied?" the woman asked.

"If you see them—"

"Then it's my business. And yours is done here."

"You aren't as hospitable as I'd expect someone in those clothes to be."

"And you aren't as stupid as I'd expect someone in that uniform to be. Are we finished with the veiled insults, or shall I fetch a chair and some tea?"

"Good night, Sister," the warden said.

"Wait . . ." The woman sighed, and I thought surely she was giving us up. "Try the alley, past the old churchyard. We've had trouble lately—could be kids, or something else entirely."

"Thank you," he said earnestly, then left, shouting orders for those with him to head to the churchyard.

"Idiot."

The woman slammed the door.

"You can come out now," she said. "He's gone."

No one moved more than a shrug of my shoulders. Birdie mouthed, *What do we do?*

"Hmm," the woman said. "If there's no one holding the doors closed, they must be stuck. I'll have to ask that nice warden to get them open for me. Can't very well have a confessional no one can get into . . ."

"No!" Jermay burst out of his side of the box.

"Please don't," I said, coming from my side with Birdie and Winnie. Klok planted himself in front of us.

"Oh good, someone *was* in there. For a moment, I thought I might have lost my mind." She looked us over. "You really *are* children, aren't you?"

"Yes, ma'am," Jermay said.

"Human?"

"One hundred percent, ma'am."

"No need for hyperbole; I'm not sure anyone's one hundred percent anything these days. There's always room for improvement, or I'd be out of a job. Now follow me before they start snooping through windows."

She started toward a door at the back of the sanctuary.

"You lied . . ." Birdie announced, hurrying after the woman, ". . . in a church."

"That wasn't a lie, dear." The woman led us into the back hall, and farther into a simply furnished house with a small table and a roaring fire. "A lie would have been 'I have never seen those children, not even once.' I couldn't see you very well at all. Therefore, it was not a lie, just a carefully worded truth. Besides, it's still Friday, and I'm fairly certain that well-intentioned slips of the tongue are forgivable on Fridays."

She went to a cupboard and brought out a stack of dishes.

"I don't have enough plates, but if you don't mind eating from bowls and saucers, you're welcome to join me for a very early breakfast. Then I need to figure out where our priest has wandered off to. By now he's gone looking for the person who was supposed to be in the confessional. The last time that happened, we found him in the garden, trying to give penance to a bush he'd mistaken for a parishioner."

I took a saucer and handed the bowls to Klok and Jermay, but Jermay wouldn't take his. He kept scuffing the tip of his boot into a worn patch on the sister's rug.

"Does Friday make it all right for me to be here?" he asked.

"And why would you need a Friday for that? Are you really a thief?"

"No, ma'am . . . I mean . . . My father says we aren't welcome in churches. People like you think he's evil, so I'll burn up."

"Hmm . . . we haven't had an evil burning in a while. Might be due for one at that." The sister winked at the rest of us over the top of Jermay's bowed head. "But I suppose I need to know what sort of evil thing you are. Just to keep the books straight, you understand."

"My father does magic for the circus," Jermay said softly.

"In that case, I need your word that you won't go changing into anything unnatural and smashing down the walls. I hate a mess."

"I can't turn into anything!" Jermay's head shot up.

"Well, then, do you promise not to go eating any small children while you're here?"

"I don't eat children."

"Are you sure you're evil? Where are your horns?" The sister turned his head to check behind his ears.

"I don't—"

The sister sighed, as though this was all very irritating.

"And you call yourself evil. No horns, no scales—I bet you don't even have a tail."

She paused, and Jermay shook his head.

"Just as I thought. You don't need a Friday edict. Sit down and drink your tea."

CHAPTER 11

Our rescuer's name was Sister Mary Alban. It was almost an hour, between heating up oatmeal and double-checking the door locks, before she actually told us. She said other things were more important.

Klok picked through our salvaged bags, intent to take advantage of a real workspace while we had it. He was on the floor with all of the pieces he needed spread out on Bull's coat. Birdie stuck close to Jermay, until she fell asleep, curled into a ball the way she used to hide in the train's back cars.

Winnie emerged from the bathroom. She'd combed out her hair and was wearing donation-bin jeans and a sweater that covered her scars, but her eyes carried the haunted sadness from the years that she was mute. She walked toward the fire and unceremoniously tossed in her old clothes, then sat down to watch them burn, hunched over with her hands holding her feet. I should have made sure she was okay, or even asked who it was that had hurt her—anything—but I kept drifting to whichever side of the room had the fewest people. I couldn't shake the notion that they'd be safer if they were a greater distance from me.

After a while, Jermay joined me at the table, which sat directly in front of the stove. He was clicking his fingernails with his thumb, so I knew there was something more than the obvious eating at him.

"Worried about Zavel?" I asked, pushing a cup toward him. Wisps of mint wafted up from mine, reminding me of the tea my father made to help me sleep. He said nightmares hated mint, because it took away upset stomachs and replaced them with happy dreams. But a few ounces of dead leaves and hot water didn't feel very formidable against machines that could flatten buildings.

"He's too old, Penn," Jermay said. "What if he forgets to eat?"

I put my hand over his to stop the clicking.

"What are the chances of Mother Jesek or Smolly letting anyone starve? Smolly would kick him in the shin, and Mother would stuff his mouth with sandwiches when he opened it to yell."

The joke wasn't worth laughing at, but I'd hoped for a smile.

"If he thinks something's happened to me . . ." Those unnatural blue eyes sparkled with tears. They were the sky and the sea stretching out along the horizon. Something I could stare at forever and never find an end. "I'm all he's got, and he's—"

He took one of his hands out from under mine, shifting it so that mine was now trapped between his two.

"Can't we just be happy we're safe for now?" I asked. Sitting at the table with Jermay felt normal. I wanted a few moments where I could simply breathe.

"But it's too easy," he whispered. "Why would she hide us?"

"We're all hiding from one thing or another." Sister Mary Alban had stepped up behind us, silent on her bare feet.

She clasped her hands together, and they began to glow with a soft bluish light that quickly became a crackling cage of lightning. When she opened her fingers, the energy hung in midair, swirling into a sphere that flexed and stretched until it formed wings, finally settling on the shape of a dragonfly the size of a peach, which perched on her knuckle.

"How did you do that?"

I was out of my seat and a foot from the table without even knowing when I decided to move. Jermay had done the same; he was holding his breath like I was, too.

Klok lifted his head for a look, but he seemed uninterested. He went back to fiddling with Xerxes' components.

Winnie and Birdie stayed as they were: one staring into the fire, one sleeping.

"How?" I asked again. The sister blew out a puff of air that scattered her dragonfly to glowing bits.

She was too old to be one of the touched, and I'd never seen anyone other than my sisters have enough control over their abilities to create a golem, even a small one.

"I thought you might be more comfortable sharing your secrets if you knew mine." Sister Mary Alban sat down and reached for another cup of tea.

"I didn't ask why; I asked how!" Electric currents weren't elemental. Heavenly fire belonged to Celestine. Was this one of her careful truths, when she said one thing while hiding its real meaning in the pauses between words?

"The reasons why people do the things they do are infinitely more informative than the mechanics of how they get them done," she said. "*How* is the simple part—I did it with practice. As for the *why*—I know a warden when I see one. There are very few reasons for someone of his occupation to be chasing someone your age. In my experience, none of those reasons were sufficient to turn you over to men with guns."

The way she said it made me curious to know her experience with men and guns. When she opened the door to the warden, she'd stayed partially hidden behind it, and she never left the building. Maybe we weren't the only ones who had sought refuge in that sanctuary over the years.

"Are you afraid of me?" she asked.

"You're unexpected," I said. "That doesn't happen very often."

Not growing up in a world of manufactured dreams, where wishes could be granted with the turn of a wrench, and ingenuity was as effective as fairy dust.

I took the seat that had been Jermay's, and he took that as his excuse to go sit with Winnie. He didn't even touch her, but I couldn't stop watching them. The clothes she wore were much nicer than the ones Birdie had found for me.

It was a horrible, petty thought, made worse by the fact that I couldn't stop it from repeating itself. Winnie had saved my life more than once since she spoke her first words on the train, and I was begrudging her sleeves long enough to cover her scars, all because she looked more like the me I wanted to be, sitting next to Jermay, than I ever had.

"Were you injured, too?" Sister Mary Alban's voice surprised and shamed me. I shook my head, wondering if she could see my jealous thoughts on my face.

"Winnie wasn't injured, she's—"

"Scarred and scared. I know. What about you?"

I shook my head again. Was this how Winnie had felt those silent years? Maybe there'd been things she wanted to say or share, but the words wouldn't come. Mine felt stuck in my teeth.

"Head shaking I can work with," the sister said; I swirled the mint leaves around my cup before I took a sip. "You're from The Show, aren't you?"

Cold fear poured down my back, at odds with the tea scalding my throat. The woman unnerved me. The way she moved her hands when she spoke was very much like Nim, and her habit of cutting through layers to get straight to the truth of a thing reminded me of Anise, but her eyes were the worst. They were the precise shape and color of mine and my father's—and Evie's. Having this person in whom I could see so much of my family sit beside me—and ask the kinds of questions people were supposed to be afraid to voice—was too much.

"Your friend with the remarkable eyes said his father was part of a circus," she explained. "It wasn't hard to narrow the possibilities."

"The warden can't come in here, but what about other things?" I asked.

"You mean things that are a little harder to notice?"

"Yeah. Things like that."

Holograms didn't need to bypass locks; they could bypass walls. And hounds . . . Well, they could just knock them down.

"These walls are old and thick," the sister said. "We often get complaints from parishioners because their phones won't work with the doors closed."

"Unnoticeables are a bit more advanced than a mobile signal."

"So is this." The sister reached up and took a chain from around her neck. The medallion on the end was warm when she placed it in my hand, and heavier than its delicate appearance hinted at. "It was given to me by someone who wanted to keep me safe in his absence. It's worked rather well, I think."

She slipped the chain over my head.

"I can't," I said, and tried to hand the necklace back, but she curled my fingers around it.

"St. Christopher is the patron of travelers. He'll see you home."

I opened my hand for a better look at the medallion. It was small and brassy from age; the man engraved on the front carried a walking stick. An etched halo circled his body, and he looked a bit like Jermay's father—too old to do much protecting.

"It's vibrating," I said.

"It recognizes your father in you."

I flipped it over, and found a maker's mark, worn smooth and shallow by time as someone had worried the design over and over. I would have known it in my sleep. In fact, I felt like I was dreaming, sitting at that stranger's table and staring at her familiar eyes while tracing the braided *M* and *R* my father left on every piece he crafted.

"Your tea's gone cold." Sister Mary Alban grinned slyly as she plucked my cup from the table. She turned to the stove, putting her back to me.

"This is my *father's* mark. Where did you get it?"

"It was a gift," she said, distracted by adding new kindling to the stove. There wasn't enough of a fire left for the new wood to catch, only embers that were quickly buried when the pile inside the stove shifted.

"From who?" I pressed.

"Someone I've not seen in a long time." She started rifling shelves, I assumed in search of something to light the wood. "Keep the medal close. It may not look like much, but appearance is rarely the defining factor of a thing's usefulness."

She gave up her search. "Someone's taken my matches. I guess I'll have to do this the fun way." She flicked her wrist in the air, summoning another dragonfly. This time it flew toward the stove, landed on the tinder inside, and rekindled the fire.

"Who are you?" I asked her.

"Someone who would appreciate your not mentioning that little trick. This is a very basic order. The less complicated an adherent's life, the better."

"Then no one else here knows what you can do?"

"That *is* the definition of a secret, dear. It's not as though I go around calling myself Mary Elmo or Mary Erasmus—a bit on the nose given the blue lightning, don't you think?"

"Is that what the 'true flame' on the front of the building means?" I asked, hoping she'd oblige in telling me more about herself and where she came from. "Simplicity, and nothing else? No machines. Nothing . . . um . . . special?"

"Now that is a hard question," Sister Mary Alban said. "There are flames of fire, but there are also flames of compassion and kindness, flames of spirit, even love. I'd say they're all true." She paused, glancing between me and Jermay, who was rubbing Winnie's hands to warm them up. "Most in this order would say that technology and that which runs on new and strange power sources are the temptations which nearly cost us the world, and so—*evil.*"

"And what about people with new and strange powers?"

I looked away from her, uncomfortable with having Evie's eyes bearing down on me from a stranger's face. And I already knew the answer. My first act in life was murder. What good is there in that?

"Evil requires intent. It's not—"

Someone jiggled the door latch, ending our conversation. When the door didn't open, the person in the hall pulled harder, and when that still yielded no results, they knocked. *Impatiently.*

Sister Mary Alban motioned for us to stay put, despite the instant urge to run and hide.

"You might want to put that on," she told Klok, and pointed at Bull's coat on the floor. "No need showing more than you intend to be seen."

Thankfully, Bull had long arms, and the cuffs went nearly to the ends of Klok's fingers. Once his metal parts were hidden, and after another knock, the sister opened the door.

Another woman entered, wearing a brown dress and dressing gown. She was much younger than Mary Alban, closer to twenty than fifty.

"I expected you to come and tell me what this ruckus has been—" This new woman faltered when she took notice of us scattered around the room.

"It was a minor issue, and it's been handled," Mary Alban said.

"From the look of things, it was at least *five* issues, and that's more than minor." The woman set her hands on her hips and a scowl on her face, which aged her fifteen years in as many seconds. "Who are these children?"

"They're guests. Children, this is Dorcas. She's a novice in our order."

Dorcas didn't indulge the introduction.

"What are you thinking, bringing in strays off the street?" she hissed.

"I think the technical term is 'aiding and abetting,' but 'granting sanctuary' sounds more pleasant."

The sister backed Dorcas toward the door.

"They could run out of here with everything we have." Dorcas stepped sideways, snatching up Winnie's pack from beside the door. She shook it, gasping when the top flap jostled open to reveal the tech inside.

"Running is hardly the way to avoid the people outside, which is their main goal at present," Mary Alban said.

"Did you know about this?" Dorcas shook the pack again.

Her question didn't require an answer. While Klok had covered himself, he'd done nothing about Xerxes, lying on the floor with his inner workings exposed. Too late, Klok snapped the casing shut, which earned a squawk from Xerxes' beak.

"They're children, and strangers. I took the name of St. Alban—what do you expect me to do?"

"Let the children in, but cast this wickedness out before it brings darkness to our door."

The longer Dorcas was there, the hotter my face and hands grew, until I hid my arms behind my back for fear that they might glow. She was speaking about my father's work as though it were a contagion. That fury compounded what I'd felt for the loss of the train, the loss of our family, even having Tuck manhandle Winnie while I was unable to stop it, and I was too tired to push down the emotion. It matched the raging burn of the fire from the stove as it flared through the top grates, and the howl of the wind down the chimney.

Sister Mary Alban's attention shifted to me, but she didn't say a word.

Unlike the times before, I felt a spark inside my chest in response to the unpleasantness. This was a new presence that was trying to help me. It was a solid thing, awaiting the order to rise and knock the stars from the sky. There were no windows. If the stars sang down, we'd never know unless they pierced the roof. I clenched my fists to hold them back.

Birdie was awake now, and like Winnie, she was staring at me from across the room. While Jermay seemed to be considering whether he should leave the fire, a hand took hold of mine. That was when I realized that Klok had joined me. He squeezed my fingers.

There and then, it wasn't hard to see my father's want for his dead son in Klok's construction. Klok had the same coloring as me and my sisters, save for the paler scarlike patches serving as entry points for his wires. His eyes were near-perfect duplicates of my father's, and my father had incorporated more of his own features into Klok over the years.

Klok squeezed my hand again, and suddenly I wasn't afraid. I took a deep breath, filled my senses with the mint-flavored steam from Sister Mary Alban's kettle, and told the stars to wait. To my amazement, they listened.

Winnie stomped across the room to wrench her pack from Dorcas's hands.

"This is mine," she said. "And it saved my life, so I'll thank you not to speak poorly of the man who made it."

"Men aren't my concern," Dorcas said. "Mechanical aberration puts us all in danger. Every bit of this could be *alien* for all we know."

It seemed the only flame that burned in Dorcas was one of fear and suspicion.

"The Medusae will return, or they won't," Mary Alban said. "And they will do so without a care for what a group of scared children carry in their backpacks."

"Look at that thing!" Dorcas jabbed a finger toward Xerxes, now sitting at heel between me and Klok. He fixed her with an unflinching stare that was so much like my father's, I expected to hear his voice come from Xerxes' beak. A ridge of fine metallic hair stood up along his spine. "It's *breathing*. What arrogance does it take to usurp the divine and give life to that which was never meant to walk the earth?"

"Xerxes makes people smile," I said. Both women stopped their argument to stare at me. "My father made him to entertain people, and show them what's possible if you dare to dream it's so."

How was that a bad thing?

"We'll leave as soon as we're able, but for now, we can't." Jermay made his move across the room, stopping at my other shoulder. Our hands brushed together at our sides, and our fingers spoke their silent wishes for good luck.

"If you send us away, we won't be able to outrun them," I said.

"Help us," Winnie added, followed by Birdie's "Please."

Dorcas wanted to argue—every tense line across her brow said it—but she backed down, just as Bull had done when Winnie and I were cornered in that shed.

"I won't stand in the way of charitable ambition, but find your solution quickly. And don't leave those *things* lying around where people can see them. You'll scare our priest to his death."

CHAPTER 12

An adrenaline crash hit hard after Dorcas left, making sleep a necessity, but no one wanted to venture far from the first room we'd felt safe in since the train.

Winnie and Birdie shared the room's two-person sofa. Jermay and I pushed a couple of fireside chairs together so that they faced each other. We each sat in one and stretched our legs out into the other. Klok was too big to fit anywhere but the floor, and every time I opened my eyes to change position, I found him sitting up, hard at work repairing Bijou. Xerxes was still small, but moving well. His soft clanging about the room became our lullaby.

I think Birdie was the only one who slept more than twenty minutes at a clip, and she did it while under Winnie's arm, hanging on to her hand. I had Winnie's other one, so that with my legs hooked to Jermay's we were all in contact.

I was on my seventh or eighth attempt to find a position that didn't result in the chair biting me in the spine when I realized Sister Mary Alban had come back from trying to calm Dorcas elsewhere. She was bent down and pulling Xerxes out from between the cupboards with both hands. Klok's reset had started Xerxes cycling through his complexity programs. The first was imitating a house cat, and he'd been chasing mice.

Carefully, I slipped my fingers out of Winnie's and pulled my hand away. I had one leg disentangled and was working on the other when Jermay bolted up in his seat. He grabbed his back where a muscle must have spasmed. I held a hand up to remind him not to yelp.

Show life had gifted us with languages that didn't require spoken words; Jermay understood my makeshift signing perfectly. I pointed to the sister, then pressed the air with my hands to tell him to stay put—I wanted to talk to her alone. He nodded and rolled his shoulder, trying to get comfortable again.

I crossed the room, telling myself that it wasn't sneaking just because the sister's back was to me.

"This is your fault," she said, but not to me. She was speaking to Xerxes. "I hope you know that. Everything's gone completely out of hand."

Once she'd freed him from the cupboards, Xerxes snapped at her.

"Don't be sour. You know it's true."

This was stranger than watching the warden interact with Xerxes during my tour. She sounded like she actually expected an answer.

"Was all this worth it?"

She released Xerxes into the room. He coasted over to Klok, then pointedly turned his back on the sister.

"I've not forgotten the last time you did that to me," she called out to him. "I *did* forgive you, though." Then quieter, "I wonder if you've managed to do the same."

I decided to take a chance.

"Why do you look like my father?" I asked her. "You have his eyes."

"Because he's my brother, and not in the ecclesiastical sense."

"He's never mentioned a sister."

He never mentioned family of any kind, other than the one we built on the road.

"Magnus made a choice a long time ago, and it wasn't me. So I came here to protect the ones I cared about—including myself."

The sister laid her hand palm up on the table, allowing electricity to seep from her skin. It filled in the shape of her dragonfly like someone carving an inscription with a laser beam, and the golem sat there, beating its wings. She clenched her fist, and it vanished.

"He was actually working on that traveling coat you're wearing the last time we spoke—for your mother—but it wasn't going well. He said the rhythm was off." She grew suddenly uncomfortable and motioned toward the hallway door. "May I show you something?"

I followed her from the kitchen, back into the sanctuary. We'd barely cleared the door when a woman came rushing at us out of nowhere.

"Did she make it?" the woman asked. "I tried to direct them, but I don't think any of them possess—"

Sister Mary Alban cleared her throat, then stepped aside so I was out in the open. The woman's sudden approach had startled me, and the sister was the closest thing to hide behind.

"Penn, this is Beryl. Beryl, meet Magnus's youngest: Penelope."

"You said I needed to see some*thing*, not someone."

Beryl wore dark pants and a shirt, similar in color to a reserve uniform without the camo or patches. She was tall and stocky, reminding me of Bruno Jesek with her fierce expressions, and she was familiar in another way I couldn't quite pinpoint. Her voice, or the way she moved—something hit a chord.

"I thought we'd lost you, girl!"

She swept me up off the ground and swung me in a circle like Bruno would with Birdie.

"Do you have any idea the scare you gave us when word of the train's fate spread? And then to find you and Winifred in the state you were in . . . Never thought I'd be happy to see a Commission sweep-up in my life."

When she put me down, she kissed my cheek and hugged me again. I felt like a three-year-old being introduced to an overbearing aunt who might pinch me at any moment.

"Sorry for shouting out there, but it's always difficult to get through when no one's got the gift. Oh, what does it matter? You heard me and now you're here."

I backed up a few steps because it looked as if she might try to swing me again.

"Who *are* you?" I asked. "And what are you talking about?"

Beryl looked genuinely surprised. Her eyes shot to Sister Mary Alban, then me, then back.

"Don't take it too hard," the sister said. "She didn't know me, either."

Beryl sank onto the nearest bench.

"I thought Magnus had told *all* of his girls. When he said he'd asked for a meeting to discuss—" Her attention came back to me and she stopped. I was branded the child who'd wandered in on a delicate conversation. "I thought surely he would have prepared you before he left."

"Prepared me for what?" I asked. "Why did he want a meeting with you?"

"Not me, kid. There were hounds sniffing around, and a lot of chatter about The Show and its untapped assets. Your dad refused to listen to sense; he said he still had a card or two to play in negotiation, so he kept the train rolling."

"Negotiate? With who? For what?"

"The Commission, honey." Beryl patted my hand. I didn't know why she insisted on treating me like I was a toddler. "He had some secret he'd kept in his back pocket for years, and he hoped it would be enough to buy him more time. Obviously, it wasn't."

My father didn't have any secrets that I knew of. Xerxes was the last major build he'd done that wasn't specifically on Commission order. The only thing I could think of that he was keeping secret besides me was Klok. He knew what the wardens would do to Klok; my father would never let him face that.

"Is my father alive?" I asked. "Did you see him after he left us?"

Beryl shook her head, like I was speaking a language she didn't understand.

"Magnus said you'd lived a shielded life on the train, but I had no idea," she said to the floor.

"Actually, I think he meant 'shielded' in the literal sense," Mary Alban said. She took a seat on the bench in front of Beryl so she could turn sideways and face her. "I finally understand why he built his circus inside a cage."

"Set dressing," I said, wondering how that was possibly relevant. "People like the light show."

"Maybe, but Magnus used it as a dampening field to suppress your touch. It's how he kept you under wraps, and it's why you're so worried about your abilities now."

"Suppress? He didn't train you?" Beryl asked, shocked.

You couldn't train a Celestine. I was a sparking wildfire wrapped up in a flood fueled by hurricanes and earthquakes. No one could tame that, certainly not me.

"If my father had to suppress my abilities, it's only because I can't control them."

"Your power is raw, but judging by the control you showed tonight when Dorcas was trying your temper—" Sister Mary Alban started, but I cut her off.

"I couldn't control it; I could only stop it."

"Which is harder—firing a gun, or stopping the bullet once it's in flight?"

"Stopping it, but—"

"But nothing. You channeled the momentum and dissipated the force. Your problem isn't control, Penn. You need practice, and now that we've found you, Beryl can—"

"No! My abilities are too dangerous. *I'm* dangerous." And I wasn't about to pass that danger on to someone else. "That's why there was chatter, wasn't it? They saw. I messed up, and he tried to fix it."

"Absolutely not," Beryl said. She reached for my hand, but I pulled it out of reach.

"One of you tell me what's going on. No more half answers. No more secret looks," I demanded. I didn't bother to tell them that I was a breath away from screaming for Klok, or that he was under direct orders from my sister to protect me.

"Show her," Sister Mary Alban said.

Beryl nodded solemnly. She rose and stepped into the aisle.

"I don't see anything," I said, but once the words left my lips, they were a lie.

Beryl's skin changed, losing its color and turning pallid and sickly. Her hair thinned into scraggles. She shrank, losing mass as fast as a collapsing golem until she wasn't herself anymore. A chillingly familiar hag had replaced her.

"What's your tale, girl?" the Abbess from the warehouse asked.

"Wh-what is this?" I stammered.

I had nowhere to hide, and I couldn't escape. The benches where Mary Alban sat blocked one door, and the Abbess blocked the other. I couldn't go out the front for fear of the warden.

Which monster should I choose?

"Penn, calm down," Sister Mary Alban said. She'd promised the church was safe; she wasn't supposed to usher danger in the front door and arrange a private meeting. "She's not what you think."

"Stay away from me," I warned, ready to bring the building down on top of us, if I could. A corpse couldn't be sold and it couldn't be made into a hound—problem solved.

"It's me," said the Abbess's mouth with Beryl's voice. The fractures in her appearance returned, chasing the pasty color from her skin and revealing her true face underneath. "It's really me."

"*What* are you?"

"Someone like your father, and your aunt, and untold others who were either lucky or unfortunate enough to be touched at the inception of the Great Illusion."

"My father was an adult then," I argued. "So were you."

It was only the children who were touched; you had to be born that way.

"People say the Medusae covered the whole planet, but not at first contact. Do you know what an antipode is?" Mary Alban asked.

"Should I?"

"It's a spot on the globe that's connected to a reciprocal location on the other side. You could drill a hole from one to the other, through the core, and have a straight line."

"Like the poles?" I asked.

"Exactly. There were tiny gaps between Medusae bodies all over the world, less than a quarter mile wide, and every one had an antipode that was also a gap. Our skies didn't turn pink for days."

"We thought we were lucky, that they were safe zones." Here, Beryl took over the story. "But they were channels that the Medusae used to get a closer look at our planet."

"How close?" I asked.

"Close enough to *touch*—if you don't mind the pun. Most points have land on one side and water on the other, so they could get wide-spectrum results."

"You mean they actually landed?"

There were no pictures of *that* during the anniversary. The whole mystique of the Medusae was that they were passive observers. If people knew otherwise, it would change everything.

"I wouldn't call it landing," Beryl said. "It was more like sentient luminescence. Lights that filtered through the clouds and moved from person to person. *Through* people, in some cases. They were sampling our environment—and us."

There were definitely no pictures of that, either.

"I think they only meant to get a closer look at us," Sister Mary Alban said. "But there was a reaction in everyone they came into contact with. It seemed short-lived at first, with the only side effect being a bit of extra life to the eyes—much like your magician friend."

"Jermay's normal."

"Isn't everyone in their own way?" the sister asked. "The glittering effect only lasted hours, but when that faded, the other changes kicked in."

Jermay's only abilities were the kind his father taught him, and I would have said the same of my father. If he'd been touched like Sister Mary Alban, then what was his gift? I'd never seen him do anything more spectacular than build exhibits for The Show. Was it just him, or had my mother been affected, too?

"Being touched is why you can throw sparks?" I asked Mary Alban, then I turned to Beryl and added, "And how you can change your face?"

"I can make you *believe* I have," she corrected. "Which comes in handy when one is trying to locate and secure scared runaway children who often run straight into trouble."

"You save them!"

As the Abbess, all she had to do was put out word that she'd pay for any kid taken in off the street, and scum like Tuck did the legwork for her. Paying more for the uninjured kept them safe. And with someone like Sister Mary Alban to help, she could relocate touched kids to new families who didn't know their backstories, and who wouldn't be under Commission surveillance.

"Wait . . . How did I know all that?"

"Because what I *do* is project thoughts," Beryl said, grinning. "That's how I got you here."

Follow the flame . . .

She grinned again.

"It can go the other way, too—pulling them out. I had to see if you were who you appeared to be when I saw you in that warehouse."

"That was you pulling up my memories of The Show?"

"It was, and now that we've got you here safe, I can pick up the slack your father never should have left you with. How many of you made it?"

"All five of us, and we're going home," I told them. I didn't need a new family or a new life. Mine was waiting at the Hollow. "My father has a safe house. Hopefully he's there, and even if he's not, the others will be."

"That warden's well on his way to sealing the block. *I* barely made it inside, even projecting a uniform," Beryl said.

"Which is exactly why you can't walk us out, but I was thinking that maybe someone else could. Several someones."

I had it worked out in my head. Come Sunday morning, the church would be packed with parishioners and people seeking first-Sunday charity. No way could the warden screen everyone going in or out, not with people rushing back to their cars, and kids running around to burn off the energy they'd pent up during services.

"On Sunday morning, we could each leave with different groups of people. You can watch our backs unseen, and the five of us can meet up at the edge of town."

Neither Sister Mary Alban nor Beryl was thrilled with the idea of us splitting up, or continuing down the road unescorted, but it was the lesser risk. There was nowhere in the town or surrounding area that Beryl could hide us that the warden wouldn't search. We were too big a target, and that put her and every child under her protection in danger.

The two women remained behind in the sanctuary, conspiring to find a plan B, or at least to strengthen plan A. I went back to the little house with its fire and cramped spaces. Klok looked up, but once he was satisfied that it was only me, he went right back to work. It was the first time I'd ever thought about him having to sleep, though I knew he had a bedroom on the train. I didn't think he'd taken so much as a catnap the whole time we were in the church.

I returned to my chair to find Jermay had adjusted it so he could lie down on his chair with his feet hanging through the space in the back of mine. Instead of waking him up, I slipped in beside him so that he was lying at my back. A moment's hesitation, and I reached for his hand, which had already chased away so many bad thoughts on our journey. I threaded my fingers through his, pulling his arm around me without a word; he moved a bit, settling his chin on top of my head.

It was as close to home as I could get until we reached the Hollow. I closed my eyes, and hoped to dream of anything other than falling stars and wishes that never came true.

CHAPTER 13

Saturday passed in lurches of hours that were separated by dragging lulls. I'd ask Sister Mary Alban every question I could think of at once, then my brain would try to digest what she'd said. By the time Sunday arrived, I'd convinced and unconvinced myself that we might actually escape. I was a wreck.

The sister raided some donation bins so we could change our clothes, and others' perceptions of us. Winnie and Birdie would wear the white and brown uniform of parochial schoolchildren. Klok stood tall in dingy workman's jeans and a shirt with no coat. The sleeves were long enough to cover his arms, and leather gloves kept his hands out of sight.

Jermay and I drew what could be called Sunday best. A regretful tide churned inside me when Mary Alban brought in my clothes, draping them over a chair, and I wondered if somehow she'd guessed the thoughts I'd harbored about Winnie on Friday night. My suit was beautiful: satin and lace, with a long-tailed bustle-blouse and fancy trousers fit for the pampered princess that Bull had accused me of being.

I wanted to retch.

"We will make it to the Hollow," Klok assured me. "And you look pretty. I like blue."

Because, of course, compliments and color preferences were of equal importance to escaping with our lives.

He meant well, but there was a new earnestness to Klok's expression that made me squirm. In a way, he was becoming *too* human to me. Too real, and too much like the surrogate brother that my father had always treated him as. Brothers didn't fare well in my family.

"Don't look so grim," Sister Mary Alban warned me as I worried my sleeve.

I'd taken to chanting "Don't fall" under my breath to make sure the stars didn't answer a call I never meant to give. The mumbling must have sounded like "Don't fail," because Mary Alban assured me we wouldn't.

"I won't say this will be easy, but it's doable," she said, when she'd gathered us all together in the last hours before our escape.

"They're here," I said. "I can feel it."

The night the warden took the train was terrifying, but what I felt in that room was a quiet fear—one that had built up without my notice until it was dense enough to flatten my lungs.

"I need some air," I said. I had to move, or else I was going to pass out.

"Should I come with you?" Klok asked. He looked almost hopeful, but he looked at me with my eyes and that was too much. Why couldn't my father have used brown instead of green?

"I'll be okay," I said, instead of the "absolutely not" I wanted to throw at him.

I had a vague memory of being inside a church when I was small, but the details had worn away, like a dream too many hours past waking. The sweet mix of incense and candle wax was familiar, but the wooden floor felt odd and too hard under my feet. I liked the color of the rising sun through the glass panes, but for the most part, it was the antithesis of the train. No machines, no technology, no ambient sounds beyond the wind against the outer walls.

A pair of boys in gold robes came in early to light the hundreds of candles that would burn throughout the service. Each tiny flame changed the appearance of the sanctuary by a degree. Together, they gave the room and the moment a sense of mystery, and a weight that would have been missed had the church allowed electric lights.

Against the wall, there stood a tiered table with rows of other candles unlike the tapers the boys had lit. These had been used and snuffed for years, their wax forming a deep seal as it melted down the sides in layers. I had asked Sister Mary Alban why most of them were dark, and she said they only burned when someone wanted to send up a special thought or prayer for a loved one. I chose five in a row, one for my father and each of my sisters, then a sixth for everyone else I hoped had escaped the train, and I finally felt like I'd accomplished something.

I sat on one of the carved benches and lay down to watch the candle smoke trail to the rafters. Everything mingled into clouds that had darkened the ceiling nearly black, and it was easy to imagine that all the years the church had seen still lived there. All the breath and songs and prayers hung over the people who would soon fill the room and add to the mix.

The church was built from history, where every sound and scent mixed with textured wood and paper to create something that couldn't be copied by metal or circuitry. I liked it. I felt safe, and it was a feeling I was loath to give up, but there were footsteps crossing the floor. A hesitant tap of shoe against wood.

"You've been gone a long time," Jermay said. He stopped near my feet; I didn't sit up.

"I needed to think."

"You usually think faster."

"Blame the hat." Sister Mary Alban had pinned a ridiculously undersized piece of silver to the side of my head, claiming it was all the rage with local girls. It looked like an upside-down teacup. "I can't think straight in a crooked hat."

"Does lying down help?" Jermay asked. He lay down at the opposite end of my bench, stretching his legs out so our shoes were sole-to-sole. "What are we looking at?"

"Nothing." I tapped my foot against his. "And everything."

"Really? Because all I see are filthy tiles that Mother Jesek would break her neck trying to reach."

He tapped my foot back. I'd hoped to be given a pair of magnificent heels, like Vesper's, but instead I was wearing boots. They were beautiful, with silver laces and metallic thread embroidered along the sides, but they still reminded me of my ringmaster boots.

"I'll be sure to tell her how little you think of her acrobatic skills."

Jermay pulled his foot back and kicked the bottom of my boot.

"You do, and you're dead."

Neither of us bothered to say the obvious where our deaths were concerned.

"Now I have another reason to make it to the Hollow," I said. "I want to see Mother sic Birdie on you."

Tap.

Jermay's turn.

"Won't happen. Little Bird's my new best friend."

Tap.

I sat up.

"Good, then you don't have to worry about replacing Penn."

"You're not serious." Jermay sat up and faced me, cross-legged.

"I don't know what I am. I think I lost myself under all the makeup and costumes and lies, and this is just another one." I shook my blouse hem. "We're a great big lie sitting in the middle of a place where people are supposed to tell the truth."

"The truth is that you're Penelope Roma. The truth is that no matter the clothes or the voice or the face, you're the person who marched out in front of a warden and stared him down."

"The person who almost killed you, and Winnie, and—"

"And so what? Even trained soldiers misfire now and then."

"Weapons don't have memories. I have to live with it."

"*Good*—keep living. You *survived*, Penn. That's it. And the truth is that I can't stand watching you flounder around like this because you think you were wrong to do it. Stop trying to convince yourself that you're a monster because the *truth* is—you're not. And the person I grew up with knows that. That person, *this girl*"—he leaned over and tugged my lace sleeve—"knows what she has to do."

He stood and offered me his arm.

"On with the show, yeah?"

"On with the show."

Too bad The Show was gone.

Soon enough, I was smushed onto a bench between Jermay and the outer arm. My shirt was too small, but the feeling was so much like the bindings that turned me from Penelope to Penn that I welcomed the pressure. The ornate tails tucked under my legs reminded me of my performance coat.

Birdie and Winnie lingered near the door, folded into the company of local students. Klok stood behind the back row, nearly indistinguishable from the people on either side of him.

At the priest's signal, we all stood—though he required assistance from two others. He raised his hands and spoke a long series of things from memory; at each pause, the people around us answered back in the same manner. I moved my mouth, but I didn't know the words.

The comfort I'd found in the silent emptiness of the building was gone; even the highest balconies had people in them now. I couldn't find the sense of peace that had come with watching smoke paint the ceiling. There were too many faces looking down, obscuring my view. Any one of them could have been searching for me. I reached for Jermay's hand and held it tight. He tapped his foot against my boot.

"Almost there," he whispered.

I tried to convince myself he was right, but "almost" had never seemed so far away. I held his hand tighter, until the benches were dismissed.

Winnie and Birdie slipped out first, with the group headed to the schoolrooms in the back of the church. Once they made it outside, they'd sneak away.

Klok would go last. Sister Mary Alban said it was customary for the workmen in attendance to stay and help with renovations in lieu of putting money in the offering box. Klok would remain with them, and find his way to the road alone as soon as the rest of us were safely gone. He'd carry Xerxes and Bijou, since the golems' weight wouldn't slow him down like it would the rest of us.

That left me and Jermay.

I took my father's coat from the arm of the bench and put it on, snapping the clasps. Suddenly, the sleeves shrunk in, so the cuffs rested against the back of my hands; the bottom hem rose to my ankles. Around my waist, the whole thing cinched tight, as though wrapped with iron bands; each clasp fused shut.

Sister Mary Alban had said my father made the coat, but it didn't click that she meant it was a machine, or a thing as wondrous as any he had created. It had never moved like this when my father wore it.

"What did you do?" Jermay asked.

"I only fastened it." The entire contraption hummed against my skin, and I couldn't find a way to take it off. "Did anyone see?"

"I don't think so, but let's get out of here before we find out different."

Jermay and I stepped into the exit line, and the crowd surged, pushing us along until we hit a bottleneck at the door.

"It won't come off," I whispered. The clasps had flattened out; I couldn't get a fingernail under any of them. "I think the river water shorted it."

"If you keep fidgeting, someone's going to notice us."

I dropped my hands and waited for the crowd to dissipate, but we were still stuck near the doors with the people who were chatting and shaking hands. We moved forward by tiny steps, slipping into gaps as they opened.

"What's that sound?" Jermay asked.

"Wind?" I guessed. The trees I could glimpse through the doors were definitely blowing hard. "Maybe a storm's coming in."

That was the last thing we needed.

"That's rotor force," an older man behind us said. "Been a while since I've seen a chopper holding over town. She must be an airlift from emergency services."

"Emergencies are painted orange and white," said someone ahead of us. "And this one's got no call letters for a hospital. She's solid black with silver runners."

I stood on my toes to find a clear view of the black helicopter overhead. "It's a sky-eye."

The man behind us chuckled and shook his head, probably thinking I was a silly teenager who'd heard too many ghost stories. Sky-eyes were no more real than unnoticeables . . .

"We've rich folks up this way," he said. "It's probably an executive. If there was trouble brewing, you'd see uniforms on every corner. That's how it was when *they* were overhead."

"We can't." I stepped out of line.

"If we don't leave now, we're stuck," Jermay said, but he followed me. I returned to the alcove full of candles I'd lit for my family. Fear convinced me that leaving them for all to see was the same as exposing the ones I wanted to protect.

As I reached for the thin gold candle snuffer, Jermay licked his thumb and forefinger, then made the quick-pass hand motion his father used to put out table lights during their act; half the stand went dark.

"They're out. Now let's go." Jermay tugged on my arm. "We can get out the back way, near the charity bins. There'll be a crowd."

"Wait. Listen."

In the near-empty sanctuary, it was easy to hear the sound of an opening door. Jermay shuffled us into the alcove's farthest corner.

"Who is it?" I asked. "Can you see?"

"It's someone headed for the confession closet."

I heard the clink of the bell, and allowed myself a breath.

Another door opened from the direction of the rectory, and more footsteps came.

"Hello, Sister." The warden, and I didn't believe he'd come inside to speak to the priest. "Oh. You aren't the one I spoke to before," he said.

"Services are over, please go—unless you'd like to unburden your soul, in which case, God be with you."

It was Beryl, wearing clothes like Sister Mary Alban's, and a new face that was fine-featured beneath a spray of blonde bangs. She tried to leave, but he stopped her by the arm.

"I can understand your friend wanting to help a group of children being chased by armed men, but she should ask herself if such measures would be necessary if they were what they appeared to be. So should you. They've no place with decent folk."

"Then they sound like half the people who come through these doors seeking help. If you think another sister has secrets hidden away, then you'll have to ask *her* how to find them, and let me get back to my own concerns." There was no fear in her voice. "I've got hungry children who need herding, and a wandering pair of layabouts who need to be found and set to task. I don't have time to talk." She left him where he stood, sweeping out of the room.

"What do we do?" I asked. I tried counting heartbeats to gauge the time we spent waiting, but mine kept leaping about inside my chest.

"I'll distract him. You run," Jermay whispered.

"Forget it. He'd leave you to chase me, anyway."

"Not if he's got an eyeful of hot wax." Jermay nodded toward the candles. "I said I'd distract him, not let him catch me."

"Maybe he's gone."

"Trying to escape, are you?" The warden's voice filled the alcove just before his body appeared at the entrance.

Jermay's arm tightened around my waist, while I put one foot behind me, ready to bolt.

"Something tells me this particular sister isn't so easily put off." He stepped closer. "Whatever punishment got you assigned to this place, I think worse might be waiting if you get caught hiding in here."

"Then maybe we should turn ourselves in," Jermay said.

"It would probably be easier," the warden agreed. Every word he spoke felt like it had two meanings.

One of the candles leapt back to life. It caught another, and another, until the entire row that I'd wanted extinguished was lit again. The light wasn't bright, but its meaning was clear enough—I wasn't alone. Somehow, Evie was with me.

"You two haven't seen anything *strange*, have you?" The warden startled, shifting focus to the candles as though deciding whether or not the flames had been lit the whole time.

"I saw someone wearing a green dress with blue shoes—that's strange, isn't it?" I asked, mimicking the bubbly voice of a woman I'd heard in the crowd.

"I guess it is." The warden chuckled. "Off you go."

"Yessir," Jermay said, his words nervously slurred and thick.

We walked in slow motion until we'd reached the door to the hall behind the sanctuary and were on the other side. With the door shut tight behind us, it felt safe enough to risk breathing again.

CHAPTER 14

"Is he gone?"

The pale blonde version of Beryl was waiting for us in the hall.

"He didn't know us," I said.

"You're sure?"

"He's only ever seen us in costumes and makeup. Dressed like this, he didn't know us."

Before, I'd *hoped* our escape would work, but now I believed it.

"I'm not so sure," Jermay said. "There's something strange about that man."

"Only the fact that he's a warden," I insisted.

"Come on," Beryl said. "Out the back, and let them think you're a pair of spoiled kids who didn't want to get their hands dirty."

If Winnie and Birdie had gotten away without trouble, and Klok stayed on schedule, we'd make it home to the Hollow in a day. Then we could disappear someplace Penn would never exist again. I could be Penelope proper—maybe even Penelope *with* Jermay.

We made our way down the hall to the outer door, pushing it open into the sun. Long lines of people waiting for food and clothing stretched to the churchyard fence from a row of tables. We headed for a table at the front where other teens were handing out bags of provisions, and took places at one of the soup stations. Things were going smoothly until a boy beside me sloshed his ladle and splashed the boy next to him. The second boy took a swing at the first.

The sisters who had been supervising hurried over to separate them, but didn't get there fast enough to stop them from turning over the entire pot in their scuffle. Seeing it go over, the younger children began to cry.

"Go," Beryl whispered. "While they're occupied."

She wasn't the only one with that idea. The girl who had been assigned the end spot at the clothing table slipped off, unseen by the supervisors. An impatient few from the line rushed the bins, tearing through them, which made others do the same for fear they'd be left out. They were happy to fill the spaces that Jermay and I vacated.

"Hurry," I said. "If this gets any worse, the police will come."

"What about Klok?"

Jermay nodded across the courtyard to Klok and a handful of others who were carrying large wooden seats and erecting some sort of stand, while doing their best not to hear what was going on behind them. Trouble was usually better ignored than stopped. Those who got too observant were often expected to name names.

"Klok," I said, under my breath. Klok inclined his head, still walking backward with his half of the load. "Follow us."

He finished what he was doing, then headed for our satchels, which he'd hung from a tree to collect on his way out. He crossed the bags over his chest and went to help with the next load. Once that one was in place, he'd be able to walk away behind us, without it looking like we'd left together.

As Jermay and I neared the gates, the rumble of chaos got louder. Looking back to see what had happened wasn't even a choice; it was a reflex.

The altercation started between those two boys had turned into a full-scale riot. Men and women pushed their way to the front of one line; children darted between their legs to snatch whatever they could carry. The sisters ran from side to side, in an attempt to contain everything.

"This isn't necessary," Sister Mary Alban said.

No one heard her. Even if they'd been listening, they couldn't have heard. They didn't even hear the cracking of boards that said the staging area that Klok and the others were shoring up had taken too many hits from jostled bodies. The stops fell away, causing the piers to sway, and when the structure took one blow beyond its strength, it gave out altogether. A beam, taller than the men trying to catch it, dropped like a felled tree, racing its own shadow across the yard toward the tables.

And then it stopped.

Hundreds of pounds of oak, and the metal braces attached to it, ground to a flat and nearly horizontal stop two feet from Sister Mary Alban and the people who were huddled under the tables to escape the violence.

The shouts ended, and the fighting ceased. Jermay and I quit running. Everyone's attention shifted to the beam resting firmly in Klok's grip on the end of his telescopic arm. He wasn't wired to let someone be crushed; his job with The Show was to prevent exactly that sort of thing from happening.

Klok set the beam down, carefully and slowly. He knew something hadn't gone the way he intended, but looked confused about the details. As his arm retracted, his speech screen activated, flashing blue through the scarf tied around his neck. The readout beeped. While there was no way to read it, I was certain it was an apology.

I was just as certain that it didn't matter.

"He's not human!" Dorcas shouted into the silence.

"Dorcas . . ." Sister Mary Alban protested. "That young man just saved many lives. The nature of his body is beside the point."

Run, Beryl pushed into my head. *Don't stand there and stare—run!* The crowd was buzzing with suspicion and fear, but unlike my tour, I had no control here. There were no curtains to draw or script to follow.

"Nature!" Dorcas spat. Every tiny motion on her face registered as a separate mental image, like a movie flipping frame by frame. Each was another shredded piece of hope. Dorcas kept backing up, scrambling past the tables without turning around. "There's nothing natural about that . . . *thing.* It's *alien.* It has to be."

Alien was the worst word she could have used; it jump-started the panic a second time. She, and most of the people in the yard, ran shrieking for the church doors.

RUN! Beryl ordered.

"Hurry now." Sister Mary Alban ran toward us, shooing Klok along. "We'll have to risk the side way and get you into the alley."

She herded us around the courtyard to a small and dingy door that led to what had to be the oldest parts of the structure. We ran through a crumbling breezeway with crumbling walls that she warned us not to touch, stopping at a rusted gate. I heard Klok's display rat-tat another message.

"No need to apologize, dear," the sister said. "I'm certainly not going to complain that I don't have a piece of oak stuck in my skull." She turned the lock on the gate, lifting the lever to open it. "Penn, you have the medallion?"

"Yes."

"Keep it close."

Jermay and Klok slipped out. Sister Mary Alban reached over and hugged me tight.

"Good luck, Chey-chey," she whispered, then shoved me through.

The church's gate crashed off its hinges. I kept moving, trying not to trip over the lace and satin I'd coveted for so long. I twisted mid-stride to look back. The stone walls and high buildings were enough to block the signal that the unnoticeables used, but the riot had given the authorities an excuse to send people into the yard. One of them grabbed Sister Mary Alban and spun her to the wall, as if they were going to arrest her.

"Run," she shouted, with startling calm. She pressed her palm flat to the damp stone, and suddenly it was alive with blue current that burst off in a swarm of electric bees. They spread across the alley into a barrier to guard our retreat.

"Stop!" shouted the men caught in her electric field, and I picked up my pace, sprinting after Jermay as fast as I could. My horrendous hat slid forward so the silver ribbons fell into my eye. I ripped it off and threw it behind me, wishing it would explode like Zavel's whirling top hat.

Klok dropped back. His hands shot out, pulling down railings and overturning rubbish bins to create a gauntlet for those behind us.

"It's not enough," Jermay said. He broke Mary Alban's order and looked back, too. "They'll circle around and cut us off. We have to risk Dad's rabbit holes while we've got the chance to do it."

Rabbit holes were what Zavel called "short-range come-and-go gadgets." My father called them quantum headaches. He didn't like transportational technologies, as they were all based on schematics he said no human mind could have developed, but Zavel talked him into making a few small disks to use in his act. They didn't cover much ground, but they could move just about anything up to a mile. Using one was as easy as thinking of a destination, but only when they hadn't been submerged in river water and soaked through.

Klok dug into one of the satchels and pulled out three black disks. Jermay turned his over to check for damage.

"Cross your fingers," he said, and threw it on the ground. It hit the pavement and began to swirl. Mine did the same right beside it.

I pictured the next town on the map and called out: "Take me to Winnie and Birdie." Jermay did the same. Klok beeped.

I leapt into what felt like a strong wind. I came apart traveling through a kind of between-space one cell at a time. For a second, I felt the molecules in my body bumping against each other, settling into their rightful places, and then it all stopped, leaving me standing at the base of a hill. It wasn't a perfect landing, but close enough.

Jermay stumbled out of thin air beside me.

"Where's Klok?" I glanced side to side, and up onto the bridge, but didn't see him anywhere. "Didn't he make it?"

"He was right behind me," Jermay said. "I saw him activate his disk."

If the disks were damaged enough to skew our landing, then Klok's might not have been able to register his commands at all. If the warden caught him, then the Commission would know my father lied to them. They'd pull Klok apart to duplicate him. I couldn't let that happen . . . *I wouldn't.*

"There!" Jermay pointed to the over-street where a hulking figure was running our way. I never thought I'd feel so happy to see Klok's fake face.

"You made it!" I leapt up and grabbed his neck.

Dorcas's fears were founded; my father *had* created a life in Klok. I could hear a heartbeat; he breathed in and out. The Commission would have murdered him.

"Continuing to run would be better than stopping to hug. But thank you."

He hugged me back.

"You are so *you*," I told him, then ran, with Jermay at my side.

We hit the main road and pushed harder, until my ankles screamed for mercy inside boots that barely let them bend. I put my focus there, leaping off the pain to propel myself forward. I ignored the weight of my coat, and the blouse with its dragging tails that picked up stones with every step.

Fear swelled, only to be confined by the coat and crushed to powder with the next agonizing impact of my heel against stone. This was a performance, like any other, and I had to see it through. Pain was an ally; pain was applause. The kind that came as our feats escalated, and this was our Grand Escape. It seemed impossible, so the payoff would be more spectacular in the end . . . so long as everyone kept clapping, and I could convince myself the distant whoosh was something other than the sky-eye overhead.

I had no idea if we were even going in the right direction until a pair of figures appeared up ahead, wearing brown coats over white dresses and holding hands as they kept up a deliberate pace toward the horizon. Winnie and Birdie didn't know there was reason to do more than walk, yet.

"Run," I tried to shout, but swallowed a mouthful of dust.

I was falling farther back, the illusion of applause broken by stuttering steps and a hacking cough. One of Klok's arms caught me, dragging me along like a toy on a string.

Winnie and Birdie whipped around, responding to something in Jermay's voice, which I only half heard through the din of rumbling metal. The same sound from the night we lost the train.

This was no act. There was no Show. The Show was dead, and so were we.

The sky-eye swooped by, leveling out over our heads. It didn't matter how fast we moved now; we couldn't shake it on foot. It seemed a cruel and taunting fate to fail after so long, but hope is like that. You hang on with both hands, and then one, and then your fingertips, until you're clinging by the nails, feeling them burn and splinter. In the end, you don't give up on hope; it's ripped out of your grasp while you try, in vain, to get another grip.

We were overtaken, surrounded by bodies in camouflage so the world became a wall of brown and tan, with plumes of sand pitching over the top from the sky-eye's rotors. The five of us ended up in a circle back-to-back, shrinking in because "closer together" was the only direction we had. Arms linked, hands and fingers intertwined, determined never to let go.

If there had ever been a time for Birdie to prove Mother Jesek right, and disappear, this was it, but she was only a little girl with a knack for hiding in tight spaces. We were trapped in the wide open.

"We'll be okay," Jermay whispered to me. "Somehow . . . you'll see." He squeezed his little finger around mine, breaking our rule that the promise was supposed to go unspoken, and insidious hope wound its way back inside me, threading through my organs like a fast-spreading disease.

A blast of wind swept the road when the sky-eye finally set down, blowing dirt into the sweat on my face. Its side panel slid open; the row of uniforms inside split to allow someone through—the warden. *My* warden, as he seemed a personal plague. He'd removed his coat, and stood before us wearing a smile that might have passed for amicable if there hadn't been something sinister behind it.

"Hello, Celestine."

CHAPTER 15

With his hair blowing wild, and the oncoming trucks churning out charred exhaust behind his head, the warden looked like a creature from one of the stories my father told me as a child, only more terrible for the fact that he was real. I didn't glance away. Nagendra always said that the moment you blink at a snake is when it strikes.

"The name's Penelope, if you don't mind," I said.

"And if I do?"

I didn't answer him.

"Thought as much." He tapped me under the chin before pacing back toward the others.

"Let them go, and I'll come with you," I said.

I could save them. I could repay Winnie, and protect Klok, and make my father proud. Four for one was a good trade.

"Penn, no!" Jermay shouted. "You can't trust—"

"Now that, I take exception to," the warden broke in. "The value of my word is absolute—I do *not* lie, young man."

Heat built in my face, threatening tears I wouldn't give the warden the satisfaction of seeing. My hands burned, igniting my wrists, then my elbows and on up my arms. I was dancing in the bonfire with Evie. If I could dance with fire, what threat was a man with no name?

I was the daughter of Magnus Roma.

I was the *fifth* daughter of Magnus Roma.

I was Celestine.

Fall, fall, fall. I chanted silently to the skies.

"Let them go," I warned.

Fall, fall, fall . . .

The heat set a blaze inside my chest. Gone was that feeling of a cord connecting me to the heavens. They were burning me up, instead.

Just one, I begged. *Give us a diversion. Give us a chance.*

After that, they could crush me with the warden and his men, and I would leave this life happier than I'd ever been while living it.

Fall, fall, fall . . .

"I suppose you're—*technically*—the only one I need *alive,*" the warden taunted, pretending to consider it. "It might be less hassle, at that."

"No!"

"Markesan, your weapon," the warden said. He held out his hand, and someone stepped forward.

"Stop baiting her before she brings the sky down on our heads," a woman said, as she slapped the gun from her hip into the warden's palm.

"And here I thought you weren't a believer," the warden said.

"Because she's not supposed to be possible," Markesan answered. "But I saw what happened at the train, and so did you."

"It was a circus; I saw a lot of things. It's time to separate the parlor trick from reality." The warden gestured for Markesan to return to the line. "I should probably start with the little one. No sense making someone so young witness something so messy." He pointed the weapon at the position I assumed Birdie occupied behind me.

"Please don't!" I begged.

"Then stop me." He shrugged. "Show me what you're worth without your sisters holding your hands and your father tacking your feet to the ground."

The fire hit my knees and burned my strength away, knocking me to the dirt.

Fall, fall, fall . . .

I kept the chant going, praying that, if nothing else, I'd burn so bright I'd take the warden with me into the ashes.

But the Sunday morning sky stayed blue and perfect.

Right up to the point it turned gold, and the fire turned to freeze.

Ozone and ice, a whisper of power building to a roar that stopped the world. I was going to fly off the Earth and shatter against the horizon.

The warden's people looked up, searching the sky for burning rain, while my attention went to Sister Mary Alban's medallion, now glowing bright. It floated up and out of my father's coat, hovering around my neck as though someone had lifted it with invisible fingers.

"What are you doing?" demanded the warden.

A thrum, not unlike the artificial beat of a golem heart, matched pace with my pulse. I felt strength returning to my body by degrees the longer I rested in the medallion's light.

"Penn, is this you?" Jermay asked.

I shook my head, pulling up against his and Winnie's hands. Behind me, Klok was rat-tatting something. Beside me, Winnie jerked on my hand, and I heard a sobbing cry that could only have come from Birdie, frantic in the wake of the warden's casual threat to kill her.

"Don't let her go, Winnie," I shouted. "Don't let her break the chain!"

The power flowing from the medallion wasn't my doing, but I knew it was meant to help. It was the same phenomenon I'd experienced with the creeper light inside that awful warehouse. The medal was trying to explain itself.

Current raced across our chain of hands. I heard Jermay's yelp and Winnie's squeak, followed by another cry from Birdie, then Klok's frantic beeping as it hit them each in turn. The golden hue that had coated the world when I was on my knees became a wall of amber light, curving around us at the precise distance required to contain us all. To the warden, we must have looked like the man on the medallion, surrounded by a halo.

"Stop this!" The warden tried to reach through the barrier; a power surge threw him backward.

"Birdie, don't you dare run," I called when she jerked on Winnie's arm again.

I had no idea what to do next. Even if we pressed our way through, using the barrier to split the blockade, the warden would follow until fatigue made us drop. A shield wasn't enough. We needed an escape.

"How many rabbit holes are left?" I asked Jermay.

"Three."

And there were five of us.

"Klok can carry Birdie," Winnie said.

"And you and Jermay can share one. Leave me the last one. The medallion can guard our retreat, but only as long as I'm here."

I shifted my hand to Jermay's shoulder to keep our circle intact while he ripped into his pack. So far, the force field was holding, flinging off each attacker who came too close.

"Klok has too much mass to carry a passenger," Jermay said, handing out the remaining disks.

"I'll take Birdie," Winnie said, still holding her hand.

"What about you?" I asked Jermay.

"You and me, like always," he said, holding up the last rabbit hole.

"Don't let your mind stray, or your body will follow," I told Winnie.

"They won't get us to the next town, but they're a head start," Jermay added. "Get as far as you can, and keep running!"

Winnie threw the first disk onto the ground; Birdie hopped onto her back. The disk swirled to life, and they jumped in, disappearing from sight. Our shield shrunk in to make up the difference.

"Stop!"

The warden's gun was no longer lowered, but raised and pointed straight at my head.

"Your turn," I told Klok. "We're right behind you."

The warden twitched his wrist sideways and fired his gun as Klok leapt into the rabbit hole's vortex.

Jermay and I hit the ground, but the medallion held. A ripple started at the point of impact against the shield, flickering like rings in a pond. All of the slack rushed out, and once it had processed the bullet's momentum, a shock wave flew in all directions. In its wake, everyone outside was laid flat. The trucks and sky-eye were still intact, but most of the people weren't even conscious.

"Hurry," I said to Jermay. "We can be gone before they're moving."

He threw the last disk on the ground. It did nothing but lie there like an actual hole. He picked it up and threw it again.

"The water must have choked it," he said. "It's dead. We've got to get off the road and hide." He threw his satchel's strap over his head.

The medallion's field began to weaken as we moved. We found a ditch and squeezed in beneath the bushes as it fizzled.

"Tell me that thing's got another trick or two in it," Jermay whispered, nodding to the medallion.

It was unresponsive, laying flat against my coat.

"I think we killed it," I said, and struck it with my palm.

The warden's followers jostled branches, shoving the ends of rifles into the bushes to poke around. One skimmed my shoulder as it jutted between me and Jermay, others sliced the air above our heads. Boots stopped close enough that I could have tied the laces together.

Shadows from the leaves around us blocked most of the light, but I was able to see Jermay's eyes widen as the rifles came again and again.

He leaned forward, closer, until I expected him to fold in two, but instead he put his hands on either side of my face and kissed me so quick that he breathed in my surprised squeak.

"I should have done that when we were talking at the river, and if we're dead, I'm not losing my last chance."

I would have answered, if my flummoxed brain could have figured out what to say, but another rifle nearly smashed us both in the head.

"This can't be our last chance," I said. "There has to be something. Try the rabbit hole again."

"Penn—"

"Try it! What can it cost us?"

He set the disk down, but it was still inert.

The warden's men switched to a new tactic, ripping the bushes up out of the ground, and they were coming our way.

"What's wrong with you?" I shook the disk as hard as I could. "Work!"

I felt a shock. The disk wobbled in my hand, flopping onto the ground, and began to spin.

"It's working!" Jermay laughed, but I didn't. I stared at my hands, wondering if the rabbit hole had recognized me as my father's daughter the way Mary Alban claimed her medallion had. Maybe it worked for his sake.

Jermay stepped into the vortex as the bushes around us were ripped away. A branch knocked us apart.

"Penn!"

His fingers dissolved before I could grab them. The rabbit hole closed over his head, leaving the blank disk behind with me.

I was alone—well and truly alone. I didn't even have the golems anymore.

"We've got her!" someone shouted. "The boy disappeared."

A foot came down heavy between my shoulders, holding me to the ground with a grown man's weight.

Keep running, Jermay. Don't you dare double back.

I kissed the tips of my fingers and laid them to the ground over the circle that had carried him away.

"Where'd he go?" The man standing on me snatched the rabbit hole off the ground. He kicked me with the toe of his boot. "What's this? What's it do?"

"Manhandle that girl again, and you'll be more concerned with what *I* do." The warden approached from the side and pushed him off.

"She's one of *them*. We have standing orders about—"

"She's one of *mine*, as are you—according to your orders. Leave her be."

He offered me his hand, but I stayed in the tucked curl I'd assumed when I was kicked.

"Did he hurt you?" the warden asked. He knelt down to pry my arms away from my stomach; he was a lot stronger than I'd anticipated.

"I barely touched her," the man protested. He started to say something else, but before he could, the warden was on him. His forearm had the man pinned to a tree and turning colors from fear and lack of air.

"If she's damaged, I'll be holding you responsible."

Everyone was watching them, and that gave me my chance, slim as it was. I shot to my feet and through the nearest gap between bodies, passing close enough that I knocked two of them down as I went.

I was caught almost immediately.

Hands grabbed for me, and I was shoved back to the ground. I tasted blood in my mouth and wiped it away, in case the warden planned on keeping up this weird compassionate act and tried to do it himself.

"I guess I'll have to keep a closer eye on you, won't I, pet?" he asked, smiling down at me.

"I'm not your pet."

"Better mine than someone else's."

I couldn't catch the air to answer back. Something clamped around my body, a tight restraint I couldn't see or reach, and despite myself I winced.

"Your tricks only work once," the warden said.

"It wasn't a trick, I—Ahhh!"

Whatever had me, it cinched tighter, biting into my flesh below my ribs. My back bowed off the ground.

"What's wrong with her?" I heard one of the uniforms ready a rifle, then several others followed suit, whispering about my being possessed by aliens or worse.

"Arms down!" the warden ordered. "What's happening? Penelope, talk to me."

"Falling apart . . ." I think I said.

I was being scattered by the wind. It was exactly the feeling I'd had when I used the rabbit hole.

"Jermay?" I struggled to say his name out loud.

"The boy's gone."

Yes, he'd gone, but maybe he was coming back.

Was it possible? Had he found a way to return for me?

The invisible something kept squeezing. One of Nagendra's snakes. It had wrapped around me, and now it wouldn't let go.

No . . . that didn't make any sense. Nothing made sense.

I was fading.

"Is this Magnus's coat?" The warden was on his knees again, and frantic. He turned my head, so I was looking him in the eye. "Is it? Did the coat belong to your father?"

Maybe I nodded, because he started pulling the edges, trying to find a seam or a clasp.

"Fell in the river." I either said it, or thought it, but either way, he understood.

"The water damaged it?"

What did it matter? It was just a pretty coat that smelled like my father, and now it was giving me a hug because he wasn't there to do it. It was wrapping me tight, trying to protect me from this horrible man, and soon Jermay would reappear and we'd be at the Hollow.

I felt myself fall. Odd, since I didn't remember getting up.

"Take me home," I whispered.

The world turned to a wall of light, drawing me in, and I tumbled happily into the abyss as the warden screamed behind me.

CHAPTER 16

I thought I was dead.

The rabbit hole had torn me to atoms this time, and it was impossible to breathe without lungs. My mind drifted out of the pain into a beautiful place where the train and The Show still existed. A string of paper lanterns was the last thing I saw.

It was also the first.

As I opened my eyes, the lanterns blurred into a smudge of vibrant dots, made of hues not possible in the real world. I was out of the warden's reach. I could go looking for my mother the way Zavel spoke of seeing his late wife again in death—but then I heard a voice.

"Are you magic?"

It was a child's voice, young and female, and dripping with the curiosity of a Show patron longing for proof that our illusions were real.

If this was the afterlife, why was it a stranger who greeted me? Why did I hurt? My ribs clenched, aching like I'd embraced the Constrictus; pain crackled down my arms. My head was a stone soldered to my neck.

Something had gone wrong.

"Are you?" the child asked again. Her excitement curdled with impatience.

"I'm Penn," I said, sitting up from death in the middle of an empty field.

It was dusk. My mouth was dry, as though I'd slept long hours without waking for a drink. Overhead, that line of lanterns hung bright and round.

"You appeared out of nowhere. You *have* to be magic," the girl insisted.

Now that I could see her, she appeared to be the mix of clean and dirty that came from a mother who insisted her children wash their hands and face, no matter how stained their clothes had become. She was Birdie's size, and she had absolutely no business being in a field alone.

"Stop talking and start climbing," a voice called down from a tree. "Who cares where she came from so long as she ain't a cop? You're not, are you?"

Where the branches met the trunk was a boy of ten or eleven who had gotten his last pair of jeans at eight. He was trying to cut one of the lanterns down, and having no luck at all.

"I'm no cop," I told him, and he nodded.

"Didn't think so. They don't usually show up bleeding."

"Bleeding?"

"Unless that's your brain leaking out of your skull."

I reached for my brow line and found a ridge of dry blood from cutting myself in the scuffle.

The boy put his knife between his teeth and scooted out along a branch, shaking the lantern with both hands. It still refused to budge, but began to glow along with the others, inverse to the darkening sky.

My body was tingling in the aftermath of panic, and my hands shook so badly that I had to hide them in fists. I wasn't dead at all.

On the ground, something caught my eye. It would have been easy to take for a stick, but bits of metal were still visible. It was one of Birdie's burnt-out sparklers. A breeze moved through the field, lifting fallen leaves to expose other debris mixed among the mulch. The corner of a torn flier, and half an admission ticket for the Caravan of Wonder. Confetti paper, trampled and dulled by the elements.

"Is this where The Show stopped last?" I asked, crumbling bits of confetti off my fingers. Most of it was singed from the explosion. Somehow I'd overlooked the charred swath of grass.

"Where you been, you don't know that?" the boy asked. "Up a tree, like me?"

"Under a bush, actually."

"Oh. Well, yeah." The boy was now trying to free the lantern by hacking away at the branches to see what held it in place. "Commission lifted the train right off the tracks, then lifted the tracks, too. Nobody bothers with paper, so they left the lanterns."

If they truly thought those lanterns were plain paper, they deserved to lose them.

"Of course, the way this lot's going, there might be no taking them down without taking the tree!" He laughed.

"Then why not leave them?" I asked.

"People buy Show stuff," the girl said. "A couple of those shiny balls knocked loose in the fight; each one was worth two days' eats. A whole string, and we're rich!"

"Shut it, Lizzie!" the boy hissed. "Keep spilling our business, and you can thank yourself for your empty stomach."

"What'd I spill?" Lizzie set her hands on her hips. "*You* told her my name. *She* can see you're up that tree, and you sure didn't climb it hunting squirrel meat and jay eggs." Now she crossed her arms, looking sadly at the ground. "Don't matter anyway. You still can't cut none that didn't fall."

No one could who wasn't Show-born. Our lanterns were like everything else in my father's repertoire. They responded only to those who knew the trick.

They were such a tiny thing compared to all I'd lost, but seeing them was an omen. The Show had survived in some small capacity.

"Let me," I said.

The boy looked at me like I was crazy, but he'd been at it long enough that he was willing to take a break. I whistled the sound cue for the lanterns' release, and the branches began to move.

"Whazzat?" the boy cried, hanging on to his perch as tight as he could.

"I told you she was magic!" The girl clapped.

The leaves near the boy's head rustled, parting to allow a string to drop. A mechanical spider slid down to my eye level.

"Pack it up," I instructed.

The spider zipped back into the tree and unceremoniously clipped the tie to each lantern, dropping them like overripe fruit. When the spider was done, it returned to the string, and transferred to my shoulder.

Lizzie gathered as many lanterns as she could carry, but the boy was more cautious as he lowered himself from the tree.

"That ain't magic, and it ain't human. What's that make you?" he asked.

"Someone who'd rather see you trade 'em for eats than some tosspot trade 'em for worse. Just mind who you sell to. Word of The Show brings trouble."

"Then I guess I'd best not mention you, eh?"

"Best not."

"Done deal." The boy snatched up the lanterns and ran with a hasty "Come on, Lizzie" shouted over his shoulder as he made for a pair of bicycles, one with a wagon tied to it.

I sat beneath the tree, letting the spider crawl from the back of one hand to the other while I tried to piece together what had happened.

One second I was at the mercy of a man who couldn't decide if he wanted to defend or shoot me. The next, my body had followed my wandering mind. If not for the persistent ache in my chest and creeping current along my arms, I'd have thought myself unconscious, and dreaming.

The space between The Show's final performance and the road was miles and cities. No rabbit hole had that kind of range. Even at a full sprint, and with assistance from the river, it took hours to cross on foot. So, how had I returned in a blink and a flash?

"I don't suppose you have any ideas?" I asked the spider.

It crawled up to my neck and spun a thread to hang there like a pendant.

"Not what I was hoping for," I grumbled.

I patted my coat for pockets to see if my father had stashed anything in them, but there was nothing, not even dust or grime to say I'd walked a single step. I'd gone from there to here, literally on a wish and a prayer.

And then, like the clearing of fog with the rising sun, clarity came.

A *traveling* coat, Sister Mary Alban had called it, and then explained its flaw. The rhythm was off.

The coat's purpose solidified as a fact I must have known my whole life, but let slip. I suddenly understood, as if the coat were explaining itself to me the same way the creeper lights had. My father had been building this coat for my mother—it was a contingency plan, a quick exit to anywhere if he couldn't protect her anymore.

"Take me to the Hollow!" I cried hopefully.

I shook the coat's hem.

"Put me on the road with Jermay!"

Still nothing.

"They need my help," I cried, but the coat refused my logic. "I need them! I need . . . I need to not panic."

I picked up Mary Alban's medallion, closed it between my hands, and thought of the sanctuary with its rows of benches. The ceiling with its centuries of smoke and soot. The candles I'd lit for my family.

In my mind, they flared to life again, the way I wished I could get a response out of the coat.

"Help me," I whispered. "I am the daughter of Magnus Roma, and I need your help. *Please*—help me."

A familiar tightening squeezed my chest; the coat's pattern of circuits and wires blazed, searing into my skin. Spots and streaks replaced the branches over my head. Then the world went dark.

CHAPTER 17

The coat became as unforgiving as Evie's brass corset. Breathing was only a wish and memory until the mechanism eased, leaving me bruised to my lungs. I landed on my back, arms limp, with hands too weak to reach for anything. I couldn't turn my head, but staring at the ceiling was enough to prove my last thought had brought me to the church.

What had been a safe haven now felt like a tomb.

Determination became both my fuel and my distraction, allowing me to limp down the aisle to the stand that people could use to wash their hands as they entered the building. I used the cloth beneath the bowl to wet my head and clean the blood off my face.

It was too dark, and the light through the windows was the wrong color, far past twilight. The coat didn't just skip miles, it seemed. It skipped time, as well, and I made a mental note to ask my father if it was sewn from the same material as rabbit holes.

If I ever found him, that is.

I was overcome with the desire to light another candle and leave something shining here like the lanterns in that field, but the vestibule had changed, too. Candle stands and tables lay toppled. Wax had splashed the walls. Dried rivers of it ran along the floor, joining the fallen one-to-another where they'd made their final stand arm-in-arm.

I reached for a candle. The wax sealing it to the floor snapped beneath my fingers, and a similar sensation splintered through my body, rattling veins and bone. My last scrap of control died shrieking in an inferno that gave birth to a rage stronger than any I'd ever felt. It seared through my hands until I would have sworn my fingers were shafts of light in place of skin.

A flame appeared atop the candle's wick, reminding me of Samson, burning bright. It was the light missing from Evie's eyes the night we lost the train. It was the worry on Jermay's face, and even Klok's, when they came to save me and Winnie, and it was Birdie's scream for fear that the warden would execute her on a lonely road. The heat notched higher, burning through my better judgment, and the candle turned to a molten lake inside my palm.

Shaking, I brushed my hand clean and stared at it. I pried another candle from the floor, held it up, and thought of fire.

Nothing happened.

"Come on, burn!"

I clenched my fist tight enough to drive the imprint of my fingernails into the soft skin, ran through every foul emotion I could muster, and imagined the warden's horrible, smiling face, but it seemed I was only a flare—one quick flash that extinguished itself as soon as it formed. I didn't have time to waste figuring out why.

I tossed the candle aside, and focused all of my concentration on a destination.

"Take me to the Hollow," I told my coat—but I didn't move.

I stomped my foot and tried jumping in place. I only landed back on my feet.

Why wouldn't it work?

When I'd asked for home, the coat took me to the train's final stop; when I thought of the church candles, it took me to the sanctuary, so what—

Of course. I had no touchstones of sight or sound to guide the mechanism inside the coat. I didn't know what the Hollow looked like. I knew how to find the door, but there was no image on a map to mark it. I'd not been inside the actual house since I was a newborn. I couldn't remember it.

So where did that leave me? Alone, and confined to locations I could picture in my head?

Most everywhere I'd been was seen from the train's window while we were in motion. Those towns were distant and in the wrong direction. My mind drifted to places I was only allowed to visit in the company of my father or sisters—like the building with the ankh on the side that my father refused to let me enter because I was too young.

He had left me and Vesper outside with Nim, but took Anise and Evie with him. I remember Vesper crying because Nim told us that if we were bad children, she'd shove us through the door and they'd never let us leave—this building was the place where touched children were collected and sequestered. My father said she made it up to be cruel, but when he'd emerged from that building, he was running, and so was Evie. He was carrying Anise, though she was too big.

Anise had her hands over her ears, and her face was stricken. She was hiccuping from trying to swallow her tears; every time she did, the building's stones cracked. One great rumble sent the ankh crashing to the sidewalk. I'd never seen metal break like glass, but the symbol ended up as a pile of pieces.

Nim and Vesper ran after our father, but I was more curious than smart. I looked through the door.

I saw faces with eyes that turned dark and hollow while I watched; once they faded, they never blinked. It took a long time and many over-heard whispers to understand that I had seen death—the aftermath of a botched escape, maybe a rescue gone wrong. I never asked, but from that point, I was a very good child. I didn't want to be sent back.

That building stayed with me like Brick Street stayed with Nagendra, and for weeks, I woke screaming, rocking in bed until my father came to calm me down. I could hear monsters clanging in the halls and feel their breath on my neck. They shook my room with their giant hands, and tried to drown me in a fiery river.

That was the image that came to me in the church. Death exploded into full view inside my head. That building came into ultraclear focus. Time and nightmares added details I wasn't sure I ever actually saw: individual blades of grass beneath security lights, vermin sneaking through the fences to see what they could scavenge.

My arms began to burn.

"No!" I cried out loud when the coat clenched. "Not there. Don't take me there!"

I tried to hold on, grasping at the wall stones for an anchor, but it was too late; I was already on the move.

A line of green appeared in place of the vestibule, giving me barely enough warning to close my eyes before I fell, tasting dirt.

There'd been a point, between here and there, where everything stopped, pain included. For that brief moment, I was a creature of air, with all the substance of one of Vesper's owls, listing through the atmosphere. But that respite was over. One by one, my nerves reattached, bounded on all sides by prickly leaves. I was at the base of a holly hedge. The coat's effects were getting worse, pressing my already bruised ribs beyond where I thought they would break, to where I welcomed the relief of tension that would come if they did.

I placed my hands palm down, testing my arms to make sure I hadn't impaled them as I fell. A snout pushed through the hedge, snuffling my fingers and face with hot puffs of breath that left my cheek damp. Dark fur around the animal's nose and mouth was visible only because of the contrast with its teeth, which I had a clear view of once it began to growl.

It whined, pulling back to make room for tan front paws with pointed nails it used to dig a trench. The snout came back, growling again. I slid sideways under the bush, but hit the side of a building. I tightened my right hand on a rock, ready to smash the dog in the face.

"Baxter!"

I'd been breathing shallow, fighting the instinct to gulp air now that I was able, for fear of making noise, but at the sound of the man's shout, I stopped breathing at all. The gravity of my predicament was worse than I'd allowed myself to think.

I was in my childhood nightmare.

This was an official building—if there were dogs, there had to be guards to go with them.

"Baxter!"

The dog ignored the call, digging deeper until enough dirt gave way beneath his feet that he could slide into the tunnel he'd created, and I found myself inches from his snarling yap.

"Go away," I whispered as he growled. Apparently, to Baxter this sounded like "Grab my arm and pull." He clamped his jaws around the sleeve, near my wrist. His teeth sunk just deep enough to hit current, and he jumped back, yelping.

"Hopper bit back this time, did she?" the guard asked in a familiar voice. "Serves you right."

Carefully, I leaned into the trench that Baxter had made to get a look at the person who had him by the collar. So this was what Coffee Bean did on the nights he wasn't dosing random strangers who came looking for a meal.

Baxter lunged against his hold.

"No you don't," he said, snapping a leash on the collar and winding it around his hand. "You dig up one more bush, and I'll catch fire for it." C. B. dropped to his knees, so he and the dog were roughly the same height. "You're lucky I like you, you worthless mutt," he said, ruffling Baxter's fur.

How could someone who sounded so genuinely friendly have a job like this?

"What's that?" C. B. asked; he pulled something from the dog's teeth.

A piece of trim and torn leather from my coat, and it definitely didn't look like anything that belonged on a rabbit.

Baxter whined again and stretched his paw out as best he could. C. B. moved forward, still on his knees, and I leaned back, pressed into the wall.

Fall, I chanted to the stars. *Catch his attention. Fall.*

All I needed was something bright enough to make him turn around and lose interest in rabbits hiding in the garden hedge.

Fall—please.

I was too tired for this. The coat had packed extra hours into the space of what should have been a single day, and after the vestibule burnout, even adrenaline had its limits.

C. B. reached into the trench, groping blindly. My right hand tightened on the rock. Smashing a man in the head wouldn't be as easy as beaning a dog, but if I had to, I had to.

He grabbed my left hand, and I felt surprise shake through his arm. C. B. shifted position so that we were looking each other straight in the face. It took a minute, but he recognized me. I thought he was going to call me out, but someone called him, first.

"Problem?"

This voice was older, more authoritative.

C. B.'s fingers flexed with a startled jolt, and he pulled away, mouthing *keep quiet* as he climbed quickly to his feet. Baxter took his place.

"No problem, sir," C. B. said. He dropped the piece of torn trim into the dirt and covered it with his heel, pretending to stumble back when he gave Baxter some extra leash.

"Your dog seems to disagree."

No, his dog seemed to want to tear my arm off for proof that I was under the hedge. And thanks to my coffee buddy, I was now leaning on the arm I needed to throw my rock.

"Shoo," I ordered in the loudest volume I dared.

"Rabbit, sir, but it's gone now. I checked."

C. B. tugged on the leash, but Baxter wasn't ready to give up.

I tried blowing in the dog's face, but that was about as effective as it sounds.

"Move, you stupid mutt. Move!"

Awkwardly, I swung my forearm down toward Baxter's face. C. B. pulled hard at the same time, so that I missed the dog and hit the ground.

Loose dirt and gravel sprayed right into Baxter's nose. He ran and hid behind his master's legs. "Sir" moved toward the hedge, tapping the dirt at the mouth of Baxter's trench with his toe.

"Fill this in before Admin sees it, or you'll be filling in landscaping reports instead," he said, and walked away.

"Yes, sir. I'll do it right now, sir," C. B. stammered. "Come on, you." He tugged Baxter away with him. "Now I've got to leave my post, and repair the damage you did to the flower bed. Didn't think about that when you were chasing rabbits, did you? Didn't think of me, or how the yard will be empty all the way to the fence. If someone escapes, it's your fault, too. You're just lucky I . . ."

His rant kept going until he was too far away for me to hear, but he'd made his message clear enough. If I could get to the fence, I could escape. He was the only one on ground patrol.

I crawled out of Baxter's trench and took a look around. The stars were twinkling to my pulse again.

The building was much as I remembered it, made mostly of rock and occupying a wide yard. In the distance was the glowing haze of a city skyline, but here there were metal fences on wooden posts—the kind that belonged around prisons. It looked like a farm, but my long-ago fears told me there was more to this place than I could see.

No!

I needed to calm my mind enough that I could control my next landing, or else some stray thought was going to carry me off to places that should only exist in ghost stories.

Everything has boundaries, Penn, my father had taught me. *When things get too big for you, make them shrink.*

There was always something to anchor myself to, and I could find it, so long as I didn't allow my fears to outgrow the rest of me.

Steady the gale, and the wind can't blow your thoughts into chaos. Still the maelstrom, and nothing can scatter your resolve. Confine the fire, or your fear will consume you. A boulder blocking your path is a pebble grown beyond its station; crush it under your heel.

I seized on the scent of dirt that was still in my nose, and held tight, reaching into myself for the echo of a familiar voice and the steadying presence that came with it.

Anise.

Condensing my worry for everyone to a single thought of a single person was a step in the right direction. My legs grew strong on solid earth, unmovable as a mountain's shadow. My self-control grew roots, leaving me unshakable. Even when we were separated, Anise was my grounding wire.

"Thank you," I whispered, and set off to find my escape.

CHAPTER 18

A chime sounded, announcing the hour as two in the morning, only there was no indication of *which* morning. Were Jermay and the others already at the Hollow?

At present, the coat seemed to be taking a rest, so I'd have to wait to find out. Wait and not panic, in the middle of the sort of Commission facility my father swore existed only as a fable, where the stones of the building cried out from the pain they had witnessed. The lights flickered bright and dim in their own language, meant to impart what had happened unseen by the outside world.

The dread of that fear spawned embers in the grass around my feet. I stamped them out, and a jutting rock popped out of the ground in response. It caught my boot and snarled my next step. I was beginning to think I'd be better off if I just stayed on the ground so I couldn't fall.

"How did you escape?" a voice whispered.

I raised myself up on hands and knees until I was eye level with a low, barred window with the glass broken out.

"Who's there?" I leaned closer.

A pair of hands latched on to the bars. They were caked with blood; a boy's face appeared between them, strained from holding himself up to see out the window. He couldn't have been thirteen.

"Take me with you," he begged.

"Who are you?"

"My name's Wren. I've been here for days, but I don't know why. I didn't do anything wrong, I swear."

Wren. Another lost birdie. If that wasn't Providence, nothing was.

"They keep taking people from our room, but no one comes back. I want to go home."

I wondered if he was once a hungry runaway who accepted an offer of a meal from someone like C. B. or Rye. What did the Commission want with mundanes off the street? Boys, at that.

"Please, help me."

My better sense said I had no loyalty to a stranger in a hole in the ground; springing Wren would lower my chances of a successful run at the fence, but half my Show-family wouldn't exist if my father hadn't taken a few extra risks for them.

I told my better sense to go hang itself.

"Step away from the bars," I warned him.

This wasn't likely to be pretty—or precise. Calling down fire by accident in the middle of an onslaught was one thing, but I'd never aimed before. This was cracking walnuts with boulders.

I used Anise's voice to remind me that our gifts weren't all that different. She dredged rocks out of the dirt; I pulled them from the sky. A rock was a rock, and what could be more common than that?

Common is good. Common is effortless. Common is possible.

"Common," I whispered. "Not special. Not difficult. Common as dirt. Common as rocks."

"What are you doing?" Wren asked. He was shouting, but his voice barely breached the rumble in my ears.

"Stay away from the wall!"

Power passed through my body, feet to hands and back around, until the only thing I felt was trembling.

"Help me up," Wren called out of the dungeon. "I can't reach."

Alarms were going off. People were screaming. Lights swept the yard from all directions. Every indication said the sky was falling . . . Only, it wasn't. I hadn't sung down the stars, but thoughts of Anise had brought me an earthquake.

At the building's base, a fissure split the ground beside my boots, dislodging the bars so they fell inside, leaving the window open. People were fleeing side buildings as the foundations rumbled; they stumbled over fresh cracks and piles of rock that burst from under their feet. One of the guard towers shook to pieces.

I leaned into the hole. Wren jumped, and together we struggled back out.

We'd just cleared the window when someone else appeared at the sill, hoisting himself into the night.

"Out of the way," he ordered gruffly, as he turned and pulled someone up behind him. The next person brought someone else. On and on until there were at least thirty—all male.

Another alarm sounded, and this time, when the remaining tower lights moved, they all converged on our window and the people clambering out of it.

"It's him," Wren said, terrified and staring at something behind me. "The warden."

I turned and saw a man descending the stairs of the main building. His features were impossible to see with the light behind him, but I could tell he wasn't the same warden I'd seen before. This one stood shorter, and broader. His clothes cut sharp angles at his shoulders and waist. He was a gargoyle, but not my monster.

"Don't let him catch you," Wren insisted. He sounded suddenly younger.

"Did he hurt you?" I asked.

"Just run!"

Wren took off for the fence with everyone else, but the warden didn't go ten steps beyond his building. He raised a radio to his mouth.

"Secure the source and relocate it to diagnostics," he said. There was no emotion in his voice, not even a change in volume or pitch, but the words were as clear as if they'd been written in the sky. He thought one of the prisoners caused the quake. He still didn't realize their break-out had begun with a break-in.

A melee started at the fence. The first few escapees had reached the wires, but found them running with enough electricity to kill. Some were thrown back, smoking and twitching. Others turned on the guards who had been dispatched to bring them back into the prison. It was either fight or surrender, and that was no real choice at all.

Fall, fall, fall . . .

I was pleading with the stars to strike. If I'd known what to call out, I would have begged for another quake on top of it—anything to crack the fence so that we could run through.

Anise could have done it. She'd have plowed the fence posts under with a stray thought and a snap of her fingers. I took a deep breath, and prayed she'd lend me her tenacity.

"Turn out the hounds," the warden ordered, and still he didn't move.

Another alarm came, backed by the buzzing of an electric lock. Five people emerged, all female and all wearing tight, one-piece uniforms that made them look like something out of a comic book. Stray light glinted off bands of glass and metal at their wrists, ankles, and throats.

"Clean this up," the warden shouted at them.

A couple of the women frowned or tried to dig their heels in, but disobedience didn't last long once the bands activated. One twitched in the aftermath of shocks worse than what the fence doled out, lurching forward against her will. Tiny fires formed and died on her fingertips as she fought for control of herself and her ability, but she was forced into the fight.

"Fall!" I shouted to the sky. The warden expected this to be easy, but I'd bring the sky down on his head, moon and all. "Fall!"

I stomped my foot. If it took a tantrum to make this work, I'd put a toddler to shame.

Pale streaks came into view between the stars as tremors returned to the ground. A mound of sand and stone formed at my feet. The mound became a wave rushing toward the yard's boundary, growing larger in the shape of a sailfish breaking the surface of the earth. By the time it reached the fence, it was taller than the posts and rolled right over the top of them, leaving us a hill of dirt for a ladder.

"There!" the warden called. "Contain the aberration!"

The idiot thought I was one of his boys.

"You're a hound!" Wren stammered when I met him on the run.

That word and everything it represented crawled under my skin and burrowed in. It pressed all the buttons on my temper at once, and in so doing, it unlocked something.

"No I'm not."

"But you're . . . you're . . ."

"I'm getting us out of here."

The feeling of that connecting string returned, accompanied by what I could only think of as music. Notes, clear and pure, trilled along the line, growing louder and more intense. They piled on top of one another in a furious rhythm.

Penn stepped aside, and the Celestine Penelope came roaring into existence.

An aerokinetic hound left the ground, headed for me. This time, I didn't pull back or beg the stars to keep their place. I *wanted* them to come. A flaming stone slammed her straight back to earth. The final piece of my control clicked, and I painted the sky black with rage, streaking fire down in bursts to rip the night wide.

Life and death sat perched in my palm, a bird awaiting its cue to fly. All I had to do was give the word. *One breath.* It was too easy to give myself over to the power surge. This would *not* end like the fight for the train. I would *not* lose another soul. I wouldn't lose at all.

A hydrokinetic hound split the ground with a geyser. A twitch of my wrist, and I filled it in again, altering the angle of the water so it hit the hound, whose skin glowed blue. Impossible or not, my sisters' gifts were mine to use, and the Celestine refused to squander them.

My father assumed that I wouldn't be able to control my true nature if I set it free, but I was stronger like this. Trails of burning rock cut the sky to ribbons. Vehicles exploded as every falling star hit its mark with deadly precision. The building we had just cleared collapsed, ensuring it would never be used again.

"Impossible," Wren said, but that was a word losing meaning by the second.

On the warden's face I saw a hatred that matched the one I felt. Shattering falls of rock and fire drove a line straight toward him. He stepped sideways to miss a direct hit; once he was in motion, he broke into a full sprint.

"Time to go," I told Wren.

I'd distracted the hounds long enough for most of the escapees to overrun the fence; it was our turn. The dirt wasn't packed like a natural hill, so we dug in with our hands and feet. Unfortunately, those ahead of us were having the same problem, resulting in rivers of gravel and earth cascading down.

"Don't wait for me," I told Wren when he looked back to see if I needed help. "Go on!" We were nearly to the top; the air should have been clearing, but I still couldn't breathe. The heat of anger, which had fueled my attack, was replaced with the uncomfortable burn of another impending skip with my coat.

There were no words for the strangeness that overtook me, other than to say energy replaced flesh. I had presence, but no substance.

I blew apart, so that bits of myself detached and floated off, but the sensation didn't last long enough to truly feel it. For that brilliant and terrible moment, I understood. *Everything.* I held out my tongue to taste the ashes like they were winter's first snow.

Time slowed down. I was buzzing. Electricity danced like the blazes from our Faraday cage, leaping with a snap of blue fire. It spiraled down my arms and wove itself around my wrists. It lashed out at the warden and his men, bursting dirt and gravel into the air and robbing them of their handholds, lilting with the laughter of a mischievous child.

Each snapping, fiery tendril bridged a connection between me and the yard's fence. If I pushed against them, they pulled, leaving me to float in a state of equilibrium.

Words like *conduit* and *capacitor* swirled through my head, coaxing out memories of sitting on my father's workstation as a child.

"Careful. Don't touch," he had warned when I tried to stick my finger into live current. But was he protecting me from the shock, or the reality that it wouldn't have hurt me?

I thrust my stinging palms into the dirt and released the current I had absorbed, to do as it pleased. The ground boiled, belching gravel into the night as it disintegrated from under the warden and his guards. And then I was falling, too.

I closed my eyes, tilted backward when I felt the coat activate, and welcomed oblivion when it came.

CHAPTER 19

I was no longer falling, but the darkness never left me. I didn't have the strength to open my eyes.

The coat had shrunk to the point that I could have worn it for skin, burning so hot I thought it was trying to remove the flesh that was actually mine. I'd pushed too hard, channeled too much energy through a body not meant to handle it. Every bone felt brittle and every muscle sprained; my blood had dried in my veins, leaving me a husk.

I could believe this was death. I could even believe it was better than being taken alive, but my ears told me I'd not made it through whatever mystic slip the coat could open and close at will.

"Stop her!" several someones chanted, ominously.

They were the same voices I'd heard behind me on the hill, but louder.

Band by agonizing band, the coat released, breaking loose like an overtight spring. Explosions of pain painted the back of my eyelids with stars that didn't exist.

"Bring her down!"

The gargoyle-warden's voice. And I had no way to hide myself or flinch away. I expected hands to snatch me up, but no one touched me. I opened my eyes enough to know that I was near a light.

There was a stream of harsh, meaningless sounds, followed by more angry shouts of "Stop her!"

"Bring her down!" the warden repeated. The last syllables were overtaken by that same garbled oddity before the loop replayed itself. I tried to think of Anise, but could only picture her moving backward, away from me. The harmonized exchange I'd shared with the electric fence was gone.

"Stop her!" The voices.

"Bring her down!"

I'd been condemned to an existence of mere seconds, in which each iteration was marked by a gap of gibberish before it began all over.

"Stop her!"

"Bring her down!"

"Go on!"

The pattern changed abruptly, and the new voice was mine—the authoritative one I adopted for The Show. I was hearing myself urge Wren farther up the hill so that I could make my stand alone.

What was happening?

I directed all of my strength to my eyes, prying them open. The light was still there, stark and hot as cinders blown across my face. I blinked and found my hand—palm down, with the fingers bent, still covered in dirt.

Another blink, and I knew what lay beneath my fingers was blue, thicker than grass, and tall enough that it touched my nose. I was lying on someone's rug.

I'd landed in a cluttered room. Boxes were stacked on the floor and most of the furniture was still covered with muslin from being freshly moved. I'd been deposited beneath a side table next to a couch. The table was draped with a cloth that reached almost to the ground, but gave me about a foot of clear view.

"What have you done, Magnus?" someone whispered, and the loop replayed again. "What is she?"

This voice chilled me, even more than the gargoyle's had. Wherever I was, I was in the presence of the warden who had taken the train.

He spoke so easily, sitting with his back to me, unaware of my presence and facing a screen that took up his entire wall. The image was of those final moments on the hill atop the fence line. He'd frozen the playback on a frame of my face, which was odd to see without color and streaked with electrical chaos.

"And what were you up to, pet? Why go there?"

The warden clicked his remote and the screen dissolved, leaving a life-size holographic projection. Color seeped back into it as he rotated the frozen frame with a swipe of his fingers. When it stopped, he stood up, face-to-face with the gargoyle.

The warden was taller by several inches. He had blue unit patches on his shoulder, while the gargoyle had maroon ones, and he very clearly hated the other man.

I still couldn't stand up. I'd progressed to moving my arms and legs, but with the efficiency of someone trying to swim without water.

I heard a sort of defective buzz, then static.

"Yes?" the warden called into thin air.

I dragged myself a few inches closer, moving the muslin by a fraction, but the coat objected to the movement, spitting heat along its seams until I had to put my hands over my mouth to stop the sob. A jolt near my knee triggered a spasm that sent my leg kicking dangerously close to the table's leg.

"I found them." A voice came through an intercom. "You'll want to come down here."

Evie's unnoticeable. His voice was distorted by popping feedback through the intercom system, but I knew it too well. All the anger and indignation came back twice as strong as it had been in the moment I'd seen him with his hands on my sister. Had I not been weighed down by my father's insufferable contraption, I would have given myself away.

"Five minutes," the warden said sternly. He chucked his remote at his desk, through the gargoyle's holographic head, and left the room.

Carefully, with one arm wrapped around my ribs, I used the table leg to pull myself into the open. This time, shocks hit my arms, causing them to shake. I bit my cheek, but I didn't make a sound.

The chronicle of my previous escape had gone into motion when the warden threw his remote. It ran in reverse, so that everyone on the hill charged backward down, and the mound itself sifted through a sieve into the ground. The guard towers shook themselves into place, against gravity. I took the remote and started the recording moving forward again. It had backed up to well before the quakes, so that everything was static, except for the wind. Unlike the screen, the hologram had no sound.

The warden had said it would take five minutes to reach the unnoticeable's position, so I had at least ten, if he was coming back. They'd be minutes well spent if that recording caught any secrets that would teach me how to make my abilities cooperate again, and I needed the time to find some indication of where I was. If this office was somewhere I'd been before, it was a subconscious memory.

The boxes on the desk were mostly supplies like paper fasteners and tape, nothing interesting or useful, not even a photograph or a nameplate to prove the man was more than a monster who'd crawled out of my nightmares. He had a box filled with Show memorabilia—tickets and fliers, an empty, flattened soda cup—him studying his target, or maybe a trophy. Near the bottom of that box, things got creepy when I found a poster of The Show troupe all together. My sisters' faces had been circled with colored pens corresponding to their abilities. Red for Evie, blue for Nim, green for Anise, and purple for Vesper, all matching the auras I'd seen around the colored hounds. He'd outlined me head-to-toe in a halo of gold.

I glanced up at the security recording to see how much time I had left. The first earthquake had just hit. Holographic debris fell and disappeared as it passed out of frame.

What would I unpack first in a new office? I asked myself. There were no file cabinets. The only computer I could see was disassembled and in a chair.

A warden would need files and reports. This one was actively tracking me and my family, which meant he was in contact with local law enforcement. Some of that he could do on his phone, but he had to have a tablet, or at least a document reader that he could use to keep up with things until his office had been set up.

I scanned the room for anything that didn't look like a sealed box.

On the replay, the gargoyle had just emerged from the main building. Guard tower lights were tracking escapees, but with the image in three dimensions, those lights did more than brighten the room I was in. They crisscrossed, highlighting sections at random.

"Jackpot."

A chair on the far wall had the muslin peeled back. There was a pile of small notebooks and a coffee cup on the table beside it. A leather bag was propped against the leg, and poking out was a slim plastic-and-glass tablet.

PASSWORD, the screen prompted when I turned it on.

I flipped open the top notebook on the off-chance that he kept his passwords written down, but there were only scribblings about chromosomal tripling and genetic studies on fraternal twins. I knew twins were used in a lot of studies because they were natural control pairs, but I didn't even want to think about what the Commission wanted with them.

I snapped the book shut and moved on. Below the notebooks was a file with detailed images of the Medusae put through different filters for x-rays and infrared light, world maps with color-coded markings, then more notes written in a language I didn't understand.

I went back to the tablet and entered MEDUSAE, thinking that was a logical password for a warden, but it didn't work.

What else was the warden involved with?

I tried THE SHOW, and MAGNUS. I cringed as I typed both PENN and PENELOPE, but neither of those worked, either.

I glanced back at the replay. Fire was falling from the sky, destroying everything in its path, and so real that I flinched away from a meteorite that passed harmlessly through the floor. Then I was running for the fence. I hadn't noticed the current take point on my hair, but the short strands reached skyward, oscillating as power jumped from one to another. My eyes were rimmed in light, but devoid of it across the lenses. Electricity from the fence enveloped my arms and hands, giving me wings. *Actual wings.* I raised my hand, mimicking the hologram, so I was palm-to-palm with myself.

Maybe . . .

C-E-L-E-S-T-I-N-E. I entered the word that the warden shouldn't have known, but did.

I tapped "Enter" and the screen flashed to one filled with icons. I wanted to scream, but bottled it for later fuel. Now was not the time to fall apart, and me causing a barely natural disaster in the warden's office wouldn't go unnoticed.

I swiped through what felt like thousands of icons, but didn't recognize a quarter of them. I did, however, recognize a stylized Medusae jellyfish. I selected it out of curiosity and found an interactive re-creation with measurements of its size and density. I couldn't decipher the chemical equations, but I assumed they were biological compounds. The next page was a list of lakes and rivers, with more equations. H_2O was the only one I knew.

I closed the tab and ran through another three pages of mystery apps before I found another familiar one. At the bottom of the page was an icon in the shape of the Commission ankh. I pressed it and the screen filled with pop-up photos, each labeled with a person's name. I thought it was a watch list, but couldn't find an entry on my father. I recognized Nagendra's real name, but this man had a beard, and dark hair that brushed his shoulders. I tapped it anyway.

The picture sprouted tabs along the right with labeled subfolders: medical tests, psych evaluations, genetic profile, background, aliases, and a tab for Brick Street. The top tab was for "Images," which I chose. The picture that opened was definitely Nagendra, tattoos, piercings, bald head, and all. Other images in the folder showed him in stages between the beard and the sideshow; the Commission had been tracking him for two decades, if not longer.

I went back to that first picture, but couldn't reconcile it with the man I knew, especially once I looked past the young face and realized Nagendra was wearing a black shirt embroidered with an ankh.

I started to scroll down and read the next tab, but I was out of time. Outside the door, someone was pressing buttons on a keypad. I dropped the tablet into the warden's bag and scurried to the underside of the table where I'd first landed. Hopefully, he'd leave again, soon, and in the meantime I could stay hidden and hope he said something that would tell me where I was, and better yet, how to get out.

CHAPTER 20

The warden was carrying a large wooden crate with the help of Evie's unnoticeable. They shoved several other boxes carelessly off the desk to make room for it; the one that landed nearest to me spilled out hundreds of photographs taken at The Show. My sisters. My father. Jermay. Me. Winnie, Birdie, and Klok. Some of them were years old.

"The men who crated these didn't realize what they had. They were misclassified. I'm sorry, sir," the unnoticeable said. "They look like the machines I saw before, and they're mostly intact, but—"

"Mostly?" The warden startled. He'd been staring, nearly salivating, at the crate, as though it concealed the wisdom of the ancients tied together with a bow of eternal life.

"They're heavy, but too small," the unnoticeable said.

Something clattered as the unnoticeable lifted it from the box. He stretched a mechanical wing to its limit, allowing the overhead lights to strike the rows of jeweled scales set into the underside.

Bijou?

No, no, no, no, no. He couldn't have Bijou. Bijou was with Klok, and Klok should have been with Jermay.

The only way the warden could have him was if the others had been caught, and they wouldn't have been taken without a fight—especially not Klok. Yet there was no question that it was my father's dragon.

"This has to be a builder's model," the unnoticeable said.

The tension in the warden's face eased, and he began to nod his head as he tested the joints of Bijou's wing. The golem was inert, but I didn't know if it was damaged or if Klok had pulled his power source before capture.

It had to be a capture; I refused to entertain the alternative.

"And the other one was larger, barely fitting in the tents," the unnoticeable continued.

Hope fluttered—a damp flint not quite able to spark a fire. Very few golems were larger than Bijou, and I doubted the warden would be making a fuss over a giant scorpion. He lifted Xerxes from the crate and set him on the desk.

"Many things concerning Magnus Roma seem one way, when they are, in fact, another. Change your perspective, and the impossible becomes rather ordinary."

The warden brushed his gloved hand along Xerxes' head until he found the switch that would activate him. Xerxes came to life snapping and shaking his wings. Golems always returned to the same mood they powered down from; the fight must have been vicious before he was deactivated.

The unnoticeable leapt back, and Xerxes turned his fury on the warden.

I knew what was coming. I may have even smiled a bit. Xerxes hated to be handled, and when he was unhappy with someone or something, he'd make that displeasure known by chomping off a chunk of whatever it was and spitting it out.

The warden had Xerxes in both hands, at arm's length. Xerxes reared his head back and struck, clamping his beak down on the man's wrist.

The warden didn't so much as flinch.

"None of that, now," he scolded. *Scolded!* He plopped the gryphon back on the desk, and gave his hand a cursory check. The glove was ripped, but there was no wound or blood to be seen. "Forgot who you were dealing with, didn't you?"

He patted Xerxes' head, with that same near-conspiring smirk he'd worn in the Caravan, and Xerxes, in turn, screeched and shook his wings.

"If there's some trick to returning them to their former size, I can't find it," the unnoticeable said. "And they both seem to have fallen off their peak, power-wise."

"The girl said she landed in the river. No doubt these were damaged at the same time as Magnus's coat, otherwise our encounter in the woods would have gone quite differently."

"Our specialists say they had to stop dissection on the train units when they realized they couldn't reassemble them."

Dissection?

My stomach sank. They were methodically destroying everything my father had built: my family, The Show, and now his golems. Chopping them into pieces small enough for their cramped, clouded minds to understand.

But there *was* hope. There was Xerxes.

If I could get to him, then I might not have to risk my father's traveling calamity sending me somewhere worse. If Xerxes could fly, so could I.

I needed a distraction.

"But how?" I whispered, barely breathing the words into the fibers of the sofa I had leaned against.

I closed my fist around Sister Mary Alban's medallion. That's all I had: my wits and my hands and a broken medallion.

"What do I do?" The words were a breath I couldn't hold anymore.

I worried the necklace like the protective talisman I wished it was, tracing the edges with my thumb—only it didn't feel like my medallion. The shape was wrong. I opened my fist.

Bless that nameless scavenger and his sister, Lizzie, too.

The stringing spider I'd hung around my neck was waking up in response to the words I'd whispered, trying to interpret my musings as a command it could follow. I clamped my other hand on top of it and tucked it closer to my body so it couldn't jump.

Stringers were notoriously skittish, and if startled, one could cause a ruckus big enough to stop traffic. When Nim was bored she used to hide them in Vesper's wigs so the poor things would come alive during rehearsals, causing Vesper to flail about screaming until she'd managed to disentangle them.

All I had to do was wait for my shot.

"That's the Roma girl?" the unnoticeable asked. He'd lost interest in the golems and was staring at the holographic image of my electric wings. It occurred to me that he must have been the warden's personal assistant to ask questions so casually in his presence. "Can they all do that?"

"It's entirely possible that 'all,' in this case, is a singular designation." The warden stretched a hand toward my wingtip.

"Surely she's not the last one." My heart clinched. He couldn't mean I was the last Roma girl. I refused to accept that.

"I'm more concerned with the prospect of her being the first," the warden said, nodding to the recording. "This is something I've never seen before."

"Are they evolving?"

"I think this may be more nurture than nature." Now both men were occupied with my doppelganger.

I opened my hands to find the stringer in a ball. Two taps on its back, and it flipped open. The spider dropped from my palm to the floor, its tiny legs in constant motion, even when it was standing in one place.

"Get Xerxes," I said.

It tiptoed across the floor on pinpoint legs, then scaled the desk. Xerxes spied it, and slunk down into an extended crouch. He slid one paw out.

"Don't pounce," I whispered, fingers crossed. "Don't—"

The spider jumped; Xerxes swatted it. It leapt onto his shoulder, and Xerxes went berserk, clawing at his own head to get it off. He crashed across the desk in a frenzy, ramming headfirst into the warden's back.

"What—"

My distraction was lost.

The warden reached over and slapped the switch on Xerxes' neck, ignoring what should have been another bone-crushing bite. The man had absolutely no reaction to pain. He also had no blood. His wrist should have been gushing beneath his glove.

The warden slid his hand beneath Xerxes' inert head, emerging with the spider pinched by one leg. Another leg stretched up and gave a tiny jolt to the warden's thumb, so he'd let go. Once it landed, it made a beeline for me, only to run past and slip out beneath the door. I'd officially *lost* the element of surprise.

My only chance was to take advantage of the shock on both men's faces when they glanced back and forth from me to the recording behind them, as though they weren't quite sure which of us was real.

I scrambled in reverse on my hands and knees, through the muslin cover and out the back.

"Go, go, go," I whispered to the coat. "Get me out of here."

It cinched in and kept shrinking, worse than every binding Evie had ever used on me. My ribs finally gave.

I screamed from the sudden sharpness, expelling most of my air while another pair of ribs tottered on the decision to snap or not.

Overhead lights exploded. The recording of my time in the prison yard turned into a chaotic spin of motion, going backward and forward at ridiculous speeds. The audio returned at top volume in one long, aggravating whine.

And then a pair of shoes stood in front of me.

"Can't breathe." Two syllables were all I had left in me. The warden's face—and his empty, colorless eyes—would be the last thing I ever saw . . .

The coat shuddered, ticking closed with the turn of an unseen winch, but this time, I was the only one who heard my screams. Somewhere, a printer erupted, spitting paper into the air. A dozen clocks chimed a dozen different hours, and a tea tray exploded into a fountain of water and burst glass. My hologram was replaced by pictures of other people appearing and disappearing at slide-show intervals. Each came with a name and random bits of information in a pattern of female, then male.

One of them was Winnie.

Her face became a globe with hundreds of glowing strings that tied together points on opposite sides: Sister Mary Alban's antipodes. More faces appeared at each location, tagged by names that tumbled into gibberish. The globe started spinning and wouldn't stop.

"Greyor!" The warden's face pinched, as though he were thinking too hard. "It's crushing her! Get a knife!"

The unnoticeable ran to do as he was told.

Furrows appeared on the warden's forehead. He lurched forward, with the ill-timed grace of someone caught by surprise, and his hands at his sides jerked up in a way that didn't look natural at all.

"Close your eyes, pet. This foul machination will likely throw sparks."

I knew his hand was on my arm, but couldn't feel it. I was rising, so lightheaded from lack of air that I was floating. And then—impossibly—the sound of ripping. The warden tore my coat at the kick split; he didn't manage to pull it completely apart, but I was no longer its prisoner.

I winced when he pressed his fingers into my side.

"Definitely broken. One, two . . . I can't tell about the third."

"I'll call for a medic from—" the unnoticeable said as he returned.

"No, just cut the fasteners so we can see the damage." The warden cut him off. "I don't want anyone knowing she's here. Not while Arcineaux's still tasting blood from the wounds she inflicted. Summon Iva."

Even half-dead, my mother's name was enough to bring me back.

"Don't worry. I'm not conjuring ghosts," he said when he caught me staring. "Iva's someone you can trust. I do."

He changed position, so that his weight rested on the balls of his feet, while his arms crossed on his knees and we were at eye level with each other. I flinched when he touched my face, a move we both regretted. He stopped his hand, but I still felt the churn of broken bones.

He flipped the hem of my coat up for a look at the torn underside. "I can't believe Magnus gave this to you. Transport routines are alien tech; so's the neural relay for the targeting system. He usually won't touch them. Was he really this desperate? Or were you?"

"I'm not telling you anything," I spat. I didn't mean to spit blood with it.

"Good girl," he said, and wiped my mouth with the cuff of his sleeve. "We'll get you patched up, and then—"

Then I stopped listening.

I wasn't planning to stay in his presence long enough for the patching, much less what came after.

"Get me out of here," I begged the coat.

There wasn't much that could be called worse than my present state. Even if the coat deposited me into a wall, or dropped me from a mountain peak, it would be a better ending than whatever drawn-out torture this man hid behind his phony smile.

"Please," I pleaded. The pain from my ribs had already caused my eyes to tear; despair did nothing to dry them. "Take me as far as you can. Take me somewhere safe."

I couldn't focus on a location, but the coat crackled. Sparks jumped from one side of the tear the warden had made to the other.

My nerves responded with a small seizure that froze my eyes in the open position and locked my muscles.

"You have to listen, pet. Stop the coat. Tell it to stop," the warden demanded.

As if I could—or *would*.

I felt the coat preparing for a move, but it was sluggish, a broken door unable to close. In my head I chanted "safe, sanctuary, refuge," to ensure that the coat didn't change its mind about where to send me.

"Penelope, please. You don't understand, I—" The warden stood up, leaving me on the floor. "Greyor! Sever the circuits! She's—"

Gone.

CHAPTER 21

I'd never had a broken bone, but I'd seen a few. In my imagination, it was the equivalent of a sour stomach—an uncomfortable flutter that would pass with dry crackers and hot tea.

I was an idiot.

This pain was a fire baton blazing along my side, and my insides ached with the need to purge themselves of things I'd only ever dreamed of eating. All I could do was lie on my side and wonder if the pressure was going to collapse my entire rib cage.

Every second languidly paced itself into hours while the coat continued to tighten so that my head felt ready to burst off my neck. But at the point I was ready to go searching for my mother on the other side of death, something changed. The combination of the strain and the compromised condition of the coat finally split it along the seams.

I slapped the ground with the one hand I could move while gasping, unable to stop. I never knew air had so many flavors, but I could taste every molecule down to the base notes of more flowers than I knew existed. So many, I would have sworn I was in a garden, if not for the lack of birdsongs and breeze. The rush of oxygen was so intoxicating that the euphoria nearly numbed me.

White light replaced the darkness, but there was no mistaking it for natural sun. This was brighter and as false as a creeper light. The ground was cold metal, grooved with holes. A polished pole stood bolted to the side—one of many that formed a guardrail around the walkway I'd been deposited on. I recognized the seal scored into the metal; this was a Commission facility.

Not quite the safe haven I'd been hoping for.

With a click, the clasps of my father's coat unfastened themselves, leaving the front open. I struggled to pull it off; wherever I was, I was staying. It had to be better than another directionless skip.

I used the pole as leverage to turn over so I could see my new resting place. It was a massive enclosure with several levels above and below mine. Floor after floor was nothing but trees and bushes and flowers; it really *did* look like a magnificent garden.

Was I in a greenhouse?

"Are you all right?"

The walkway was empty, so who was speaking?

Maybe I'd dreamed that the coat released me, and I was still hallucinating. Maybe this was what it was like to die slowly from lack of air.

"I'm over here," the voice said, but "over" was on the other side of the guardrail.

"Talking trees?" I asked.

I sat up, squinting across the room. The circular track continued on the other side.

"Too far."

The voice triggered movement in the leaves, where a boy perched in the topmost branches swept them out of the way with his arm. Our eyes met, and somehow the confusion and shock I felt transferred to his face. He leaned forward, mouth agape.

"Penelope?" he asked.

The trees shifted at the trunk, in a way that no person could shake them and no tree should turn. They bent, and when they were close enough, the boy slid off the branches and onto the metal floor beside me. He was my age, with brown hair and green eyes open wide.

"Are you Penelope Roma?"

He offered me a hand up, but I wasn't ready to accept help from unknown boys who somehow knew me—especially those who could be found inside Commission greenhouses. The last two men who called me by name were an unnoticeable and a warden, and given this boy's clothes, he was likely in training to become one of those things himself.

I launched backward, out of his reach, crying out when my ribs reminded me why I was sitting still in the first place.

"You're real, aren't you?" he asked, stepping forward as though I hadn't just wounded myself to get away from him. "You *really are* here?"

He flicked his wrist.

Something soft pushed at my back, nudging me onto my feet. I twisted to see who or what had snuck up on me, but there was nothing there besides a wall of green made from a single overlarge leaf.

My next breath was stolen by another shock from my ribs—this time, so severe, the pain threw me into the momentum of my turn; I landed on the leaf face-first. It held my weight.

"Penelope?"

The boy moved silently and too quickly. He placed his hand on my arm. I shook it off, and winced again.

"I won't hurt you," he said.

"It's not you," I growled. Keeping my voice low and controlled meant I needed less air, so my chest didn't have to expand as far. "My ribs are busted."

Stars were shattering into needles against my skin. I could feel the fire in my blood, and see the shine in my fingers. Hopscotching over the countryside had agitated the Celestine. She was awake and demanding freedom in retribution for my misery. I was losing control.

"Move back," I begged the boy.

I eased myself to the ground, lying with my knees bent so I could breathe easier. The boy crouched beside me. Who was he? Why did the coat send me to him?

"Are you sure they're broken?" he asked.

"I felt them snap."

Best not to mention the warden's diagnosis, just yet.

The boy sat down with one leg dangling over the side of the walkway.

"What are you doing here?" he asked. "Someone would have mentioned your capture, if they knew. Did you hide aboard a transport? No, that would mean passing security. But then how did you get past the rings? And how did you get from the rings inside without being seen?"

He fired questions with barely a breath between them, glancing around frantically every time his head moved. And it moved a lot, trying to see all parts of the room at once. He was more afraid than I was.

"Why would you come here?" he asked.

"It wasn't exactly a choice."

"No, I guess it wouldn't be. That might be a good thing. They'll never think to look for you here, but you've still got to be careful. The system tracks everyone." He held out his hand, glancing down, horrified, at a ring with a small red stone in it, then hid it behind his back. "Not being seen can be as dangerous as being in plain sight."

He couldn't possibly have understood the irony of his words, and it was precisely something he'd tried to hide that caught my attention. I sat up, leaning against the leaves like chair cushions, and reached for his closest hand. Metal bands circled his wrists.

"These are hounds' dampers," I said.

He was male. Dampers were useless on mundanes.

There had been men and boys in the prison yard I'd destroyed—was this another prison? Did the coat bring me here to destroy it, too?

I just wanted to go home.

"Who are you?" I asked, still holding the boy's wrist. "Why are you wearing these?"

He opened his mouth, ready to either answer or lie, but lost the chance when a set of double doors opened several yards down the walkway.

"Get out of sight," he ordered.

I glanced over his shoulder.

"Is it a guard?" I asked.

"Keep back and keep quiet. I'll try to get rid of him."

Before I could ask where he expected me to go or how he expected me to get there, the leaf that had been my lean-to lashed out, sweeping me into the foliage. I watched, awestruck, while thorny vines sprouted and grew, braiding themselves into a matted wall. It connected to another wall on each side until I was caged and left crouching at an awkward angle. The boy kicked my discarded coat in after me.

The guard was close enough now that I could hear his radio as well as the sound of his boots on the metal walk. I didn't want to scream, but the pain in my side was unbearable. Without some kind of relief, something bad was going to happen. I pressed my hand to the throbbing ribs and started to ask the boy for help, but one of those oversize leaves repositioned itself over my mouth so I couldn't.

It says something for living inside The Show that it took me so long to put the odd behavior of the local greenery together with the dampers and realize why this boy was in custody. I was used to the unusual, and I was used to tricks. When it came to something genuinely out of the ordinary, I accepted it without question, until it hit me that this boy was impossible. He wasn't mundane. Was he an aberration like me, or had the Commission done something to him to give him an artificial touch?

Why would anyone want that?

He looked at me again, mouthed *trust me*, and turned away, pretending to be engrossed in something near the ground.

"Hey!" the guard shouted to get the boy's attention. "Hey! Don't you move!"

The boy straightened up, feigning surprise. He ducked his head, moving in reverse until his back was against the railing. The guard stopped between us.

"He's here," the guard snarled into his radio. "Yes, I'm sure. I'm looking right at him." A pause, then, "*You* try finding a garden gnome in the woods."

He snapped the switch off, with an overdramatic flourish.

"Where've you been, *Petunia*?"

There was a slight hitch in the boy's posture at the name; it must have been a familiar taunt he'd taught himself not to respond to.

"Right here," he answered.

The guard scanned the area. I held my breath when his attention passed over my hiding spot.

"What've you been doing *right here*?" he asked. The boy finally looked up.

"Working with pineapples."

"Pineapples?"

The boy retrieved a potted plant from the greenhouse floor, holding it out, toward the guard.

"An experiment in crossbreeding. I've got an odd little flower with no scent, and seeing as the warden is obliging Commissioner Winnet's wife for the dedication ceremony, he asked for something unique to impress her, so I thought I'd make the flower smell like pineapples. But—"

The boy had to pause for a breath. From the expression on the guard's face, I'd have to say the ramble was uncharacteristic. It was the sort of thing that came from crafting a story on the fly. He was lying as fast as he could find words.

"Where's your tracker?" the guard demanded, cutting the boy off.

"Here. Why?"

He held out his hand, and the guard seized it.

"It's turned off. How—"

The radio strapped to the guard's shoulder came on. "What's your status? You said you found the brat, so what's the problem?"

"No problem," the guard said. "Just . . . *pineapples*."

"Say again?"

"No problem at all!" The boy directed his answer to the guard's radio. "I probably got water in the tracker's casing from the sprinklers. It must have ruined the circuitry, or something."

"Or something, I'm sure," the guard said.

"Get back to the dock doors. We're due company." The radio shut off.

"I'm taking this for repairs," the guard told the boy, pulling the red ring from his hand. "You stay in plain sight until you have a replacement."

The boy nodded. That was the only move he made until the guard left us, but once we were alone, he went to work removing the door from my hutch. I fell forward and landed hard on my knees, gasping once the greenery covering my mouth moved.

"I'm sorry," the boy said. His voice rang with a sincerity it would have been impossible to fabricate. "If he'd seen you—"

"I get it." Speaking was becoming a game of strategy, weighing length and syllables against each other to find the shortest combinations. I fit a few sentences together in my head, but barely managed to utter an "ugh."

"Let me help you."

The boy took my outstretched arm from the rail post I was using as a brace, and wound his own arm around it. Instead of pulling me up, which was my intended direction, he sat me down with my back against the post.

He disappeared into the cover of leaves and blooms, so that I could only track him by watching his feet, and when he came back, he was carrying a small metal pot. He set it down, then squatted in front of it, reaching inside to turn the soil with his hands.

The scene felt like one of the staged environments that The Show built to display automated figures.

"You need to put something on your skin before those burns get worse. I'm surprised they haven't thrown you into shock," he said.

"Burns?"

I glanced down, surprised to see that my blouse's sleeves had charred. The lace had melted, and my arms were lined with the circuit path from the coat. I'd been so occupied with my ribs that memories of the coat's searing my skin had dulled to background noise. The burns looked awful, though the damage was only cosmetic. I had no tingling in my fingers to suggest a more severe situation.

"It's not exactly modern medicine, but it can help," the boy said.

Once the dirt inside the pot was to his satisfaction, he raised his hands above it and held them there. Bits of topsoil began to bounce, first forming a tiny peak, then rolling down its sides. Something green split the peak, and in less than a minute, that empty pot was home to a spiky plant with spindly arms.

The boy snapped off one of the tips and reached for my hand.

"It'll help," he said. "I promise."

Tentatively, I stretched my hand out so that he could dab the piece of broken plant against the burnt patches above my wrist. It wept some sort of clear gel that cooled the burns.

"Better?" he asked, before trying to proceed up my arm.

I nodded, and he took that as approval.

"You grew that," I said.

"I grow everything." He shrugged and snapped off another bit of plant.

I straightened up as best I could to get another look at the room in its entirety. Nearly every inch was covered in layers of green. In some places, there were plants hanging from the ceiling mingled with others pushing up off the rails. Vibrant ivies trailed the opposite wall, and while I couldn't see to the bottom of the greenhouse from my vantage point, I could see how close the trees in the center came to scraping the ceiling. They had to have a massive root system, and I wondered if there was even a real floor down there, or if this space was built on flat dirt to allow the plants easy access.

"You did all of this?"

"It's what I do—and it's safe. Between the humidity and the leaf cover, they've pretty much given up on trying to watch what goes on in here. Even the warden leaves me alone."

"There's a warden here?"

"Warden Nye." The boy nodded, adding another bit of leaf to his pile of discards. "This center is his new post."

Right . . . new post . . . pineapples . . . a party . . . a commissioner's wife with her nose in how things are run . . .

This was not good.

"The warden's the one who collared you?" I asked.

"No collar—he doesn't like them. Says they're abominations that stunt a person's natural progression. I couldn't have built half of this collared. Most of it was experiment, and the rest was accident."

"But the dampers—" The restriction bands on his wrists shouldn't allow him to grow a weed, much less create an indoor Eden all his own. "Don't they work?"

"These?" He twisted his wrists so that his sleeves fell back to expose the bands around them. "They're more annoyance than anything. So long as I don't act out, they leave me be. All finished."

Both of my arms were now shiny with the gel from his plant.

"Thank you," I said. "I haven't crossed paths with many people who were willing to help me, lately." And it was amazing how much weight dropped off my shoulders just from knowing there was a single person willing to try.

The boy looked embarrassed, and unused to compliments. He turned away, taking the used remnants of his plant into his hand. I thought he was going to drop them into the dirt, to use for fertilizer as they decomposed, but his intent was nothing so usual. He took each shard and pressed it back to the leaf from which it had come. A thin line of gel formed, sealing the piece back to the whole, and by the time he was done with the last one, there was barely a ripple in the leaf's surface to hint at what had happened.

I'd never seen anyone like him who could take such miraculous things in stride.

"I can wrap your ribs well enough to help them heal." He wiped his hands on his jeans as he spoke, then tried to brush the jeans clean, too. "But, your clothes . . . I mean—" His entire face flushed red, all the way to the tops of his ears. "I don't mean . . . Your clothes are too thick to wrap over. Are you wearing anything else?"

A prisoner with the manners of a sheltered, high-town richie?

"I wear underwear."

"Oh good," he said, now looking at the floor with a spreading grin that still showed his embarrassment. "I'd have tried it with my eyes closed, but I'd probably end up wrapping your head."

"Don't make me laugh; it hurts," I said, fumbling with the bustle blouse.

"Sorry. I was trying to distract you," he said.

"Maybe you should keep trying, because there's no way I can reach the zipper with my ribs pulling every time I raise my arm halfway."

"Oh. Do you want me to . . . er . . ."

"Just pretend we're at a beach or something. It's nothing but a bikini."

It wasn't like I'd never faced possible humiliation in front of a stranger before. And I *did* need the ribs wrapped.

Maybe I could pretend he was Jermay.

"Besides, if you were feeling this pain, you wouldn't care about the clothes," I told him.

He choked on a breath and made a terribly unconvincing cough out of it.

"Arms up and stand still," he warned. "Some of the bigger ones don't always behave."

The boy stood up, looking toward the upper levels; he pulled his bottom lip into his teeth to give a shrill whistle that had all manner of green things overhead jumping at the call. Vines as thick as my leg uncurled, dropping into reach in long loops that never let go of their perch above us. Each one was strung with leaves a bit wider than the wrapping tape Evie used on me during performances. The vines circled snugly around my ribs, finally bringing relief to the ache.

"Will you tell me your name?" I asked.

"Birch," he said, with another shallow shrug. "But I don't think it's my original name. The warden says I grew birch bark on everything when I was small. It stuck."

He'd been like this since he was small?

"People call me Penn," I told him, though I didn't give him the reasons why. The last leaf tied itself off, and he released the vines back to their resting place.

He helped me fix my shirt and trousers, though they wouldn't zip all the way.

"The warden never called you anything other than Penelope," he said.

I gasped again, which he took for a cry of pain and adjusted his hands. There were very few people who knew the name Penelope Roma, and all of them were family *except for one*: the warden whose offices I had just escaped. If this facility was his to supervise, then the coat hadn't taken me far at all.

"How's it feel?" Birch asked.

"Better," I said, and the ribs were, but everything else . . . "Ugh."

Birch reached down to peel a strip of bark off a short tree that hadn't been growing beside him a moment before.

"Try chewing this," he said, offering me the bark.

"What is it?"

Self-protective paranoia was making a comeback, now that I wasn't so focused on pain. If this boy was on good enough terms with the warden that he was allowed free rein, then his helpfulness could be a farce. And I wasn't in the habit of gnawing bits of wood on a stranger's urging.

"It helps with pain," he explained.

"I'll manage," I said, pulling up on the rail to stand. I didn't get far before the limitations of having wrapped ribs became clear and I was back on my butt.

Birch stripped off another piece of bark and stuck it in his own mouth.

"It's not poison," he said. "Try it."

I put a tiny bit between my front teeth and nibbled on it. It tasted exactly like I thought wood bark would taste.

"Not like that." He laughed at me. "Chew."

He bumped my hand with his, forcing more of the bark into my mouth. I used my back teeth to grind the wood into a pulpy mess. Once the initial woodiness was gone, it tasted like strangely textured gum.

"It takes a while to feel the difference, but you'll know when it's working."

Birch stood and approached the hutch I'd used to hide from the guard. He flicked his wrist, and the walls pushed out, extending the interior. He jerked his thumb upward, and the roof rose. Other bits of greenery closed in around it to hide the shape from anyone who took only a casual glance.

"What are you doing?" I asked.

"You can't stay out in the open." The metal bottom of the box turned green, fluffing up with grass and moss for a mat. "The greenhouse is mine, but the patrols will still pop their heads in the door."

"I'll be long gone before they have a chance," I said.

"You can't leave. You can't even walk."

I could tell he was trying to sound reasonable, but he came closer to pouting. The idea that I couldn't walk was ridiculous. The presence of pain didn't equate to weakness. Of course, Birch wouldn't know that. He might know my name, but that didn't mean his warden had told him what I was.

"I can't go out the way I came in," I amended, "but I'll find a way."

"You can't just stroll out the door," he insisted.

"The voice on the radio told the guard he was due at the dock. All I have to do is get to the water."

Nim would help me as Anise and Evie had. I was certain of it.

"How can you not know?" Birch's entire posture changed, becoming more wary. He'd been toying with the piece of bark he'd used to prove the tree wasn't poison, but now he tossed it aside.

"Know what?"

"Where we are."

"A Commission facility, same as any other. I've already escaped one."

"Oh, Penelope, you couldn't be more wrong."

It was an apologetic sort of statement, as though I'd bungled some basic skill with my ignorance.

A bell rang through an intercom system mounted on the walls. There was one on every level of the greenhouse, giving the sound a peculiar depth. Birch's mood changed again, turning darker.

"Dinner bell," he said. "Don't leave. Promise you'll be here when I get back. The dock isn't what you think. Give me a chance to explain before you do anything foolish."

It was a lot to ask, no matter how much he'd helped me. Even if he was right, and staying here was best for me, what about my sisters and friends? What about Jermay? Birch didn't know I had people counting on me.

I must have stayed quiet too long because he shook my shoulders hard enough that I yelped.

"I'm sorry," he said. "But you *have* to promise me. It's important."

"Fine, I promise."

He didn't know me well enough to wonder if I meant it.

"Good. I shouldn't be more than a couple of hours. The trees block the viewing lenses, but if you hear footsteps or an opening door, get back inside and pull the door shut behind you." He jogged a few feet before turning to add, "If you're hungry, there are some fruit trees behind the hutch, and the berry bushes are coming in." Another few feet, and I heard: "I'm glad to finally meet you, Penelope Roma. I was beginning to think they'd invented you to torment me."

CHAPTER 22

Birch was right about the tree bark. Nearly an hour after he left me, the pain tapered off until I could breathe without having to hold the rail for leverage. I even managed to get myself into a better position, with my legs hanging off the walkway so I could peer into the abyss, or count the levels above my head.

There were nine.

The facility was unlike anything I'd seen, even in my father's sketches of things to come. I recognized some of his elements, but the construction lacked his stylistic markings. Whimsy had been replaced with steel and curves that looked like the cutting edge of a farmer's scythe.

Birch had been right about the fruit, too. I hadn't checked the trees, because I didn't fancy a climb through the hedge to get at them, but shiny clustered berries hung near my perch, close enough to pick at without moving. I ate them slowly, spacing them into a rudimentary clock. One that told me Birch had been gone too long for dinner.

He could have been sidetracked—or worse, caught. At that very moment, it was possible that he was facing punishment for his transparent pineapple ruse. Or Birch's ability to conceal his movements could have been a façade fostered by the resident warden to discourage Birch from taking precautions.

If he'd been caught, then I was on my own, and so I was left with the unpleasant conundrum: honor my promise, or try to escape.

I didn't want to outright lie, but I'd left flexibility in my phrasing. I hadn't said I wouldn't *plan* an escape or leave the greenhouse at all. If I left, and got back quickly, everything would be fine.

Besides, he'd promised to come back. If he didn't keep his word, then why should I fret over mine?

I pulled myself to my feet, bracing for the shift in my ribs, but while I could definitely feel pressure with every breath, it barely edged into pain.

The double doors were each composed of a single beveled piece of metal, similar to the casting blanks my father used to shape the exoskeletons of his golems. They had no handles. I pressed against one, but it didn't move. I placed my fingers near the outer edge of the door, feeling for the hinges, but there weren't any.

There had to be a hidden latch release or button.

"I don't suppose saying 'please' would make a difference?" I asked. "How about 'open sesame'? I bet you'd open for my father, you stupid hunk of steel."

I hit the panel, and a jolt leapt from it to my palm before both doors opened along a track of rolling casters. This was getting very weird. I might believe that my father's coat and the medallion he made for his sister could recognize me as Magnus Roma's blood, but why would that matter to Commission technology?

Outside, the hall was clear. The open levels stopped in favor of a single floor with bare walls marked by even gray lines that ran top to bottom. New panels had been tacked in place, but not yet painted. They were accompanied by blocked numbers, making the hall a ruler with too many marks. Number thirty-one belonged to the greenhouse.

I headed toward the descending numbers, on the assumption that the count had begun at an external doorway. It seemed likely that the higher numbers would be in more sensitive areas, which would require the most personnel.

On the other side of number fourteen, the walls turned uniform beige, and the rest of the tacking lines disappeared. New-paint vapors hung heavy in the air, mixed with the scent of cut wood. Workmen's stations made of ladders and scaffolds lined both sides of the hall to the next corner, and on around it. Open tool containers sat neatly out of the way where the men using them had stopped their work to go to supper and home for the night. Hibernating creeper lights sat beside the tools, waiting to be activated when work resumed.

In the distance, I heard voices from another hall. They weren't close, and I couldn't make out any of the words, but they blew my illusion that it was safe to be out on my own.

I didn't belong here. There was nothing uniform or beige about me, and I had no way to disguise my appearance. I was a carnie girl, full of color and glitter that couldn't go unnoticed for long.

"Four to the dock." One of the intercoms crackled with a transmission. "Repeat: four to the dock. High-wind certified, only." It sounded ridiculously loud in the empty hall.

I turned around and took one carefully placed step on my toes, tensing with every crinkle of the papers that had been spread on the floor to catch dripping paint. This time, the churning in my stomach had nothing to do with broken bones.

I heard a door slam just around the corner, and another voice. Unlike the others, this one was coming my way.

"It's too high for gear," the man said.

My only course of escape was on the scaffolds. I dragged myself up the metal frame and onto the boards that the workmen had set out. I lay on my back, close enough to the ceiling that I put my hands flat against it, and held my muscles so tight they distracted me from the fact that my ribs were starting to thaw now that I'd left Birch's magic tree bark behind.

"Do you copy?" asked the man I hid from.

"Passing nineteen, and headed your way," came the answer from a crackling radio. "Warden says *she* can handle the winds."

She?

The man said the word derisively, so she wasn't someone of high standing, like a commissioner's wife, or an officer or unnoticeable. But it was possible that she was someone considered less than nothing, like a hound. Possibly like my sisters . . .

I slid sideways, taking advantage of the angles created by the scaffolding. I could look down, but it wasn't likely that anyone looking up would see me. Whoever had spoken was directly underneath me.

More footsteps signaled that whoever he was waiting on had arrived, but that person was shielded by the board's edge as well.

"Where's the thing?" the first man asked as someone else approached.

"She's debugging the mixing room, and she's not deaf, so watch the insults." It was the man from the radio.

Curious, I followed their voices on my hands and knees. We turned the corner, and I found I'd made another mistake. Tracking descending wall numbers hadn't taken me toward the exit; I'd stumbled into a central hub.

The corridor widened into a breezeway, with railings that protected panels full of curved glass windows. The one directly across from me stretched along the contour of the main room. Behind it, crude versions of my father's creations toiled as automated personnel beneath a half-installed tangle of climber lights. Every few moments a conveyor moved. Heavy mixers turned inside clear, empty vats. Someone was testing the robots in preparation for whatever task they'd been designed to do.

Several of them didn't have legs, but operated as the top half of a body welded into a facsimile of a laboratory. They were dressed in lab coats and useless safety goggles, and one by one they glanced up and out their window to the hall, taking a look at nothing in particular with eyes that could never pass for human. Their mouths opened and closed in off-time breathing patterns, or silent, phony conversations. The back wall was emblazoned with the words *Bring the Rain.*

The rest of the machines could move from station to station, but even these existed in varying degrees of completion. They were functional, but they didn't have all their casings in place. Some had flesh on their arms, but it hung ragged at the shoulders, without clothing to cover the joints. One had a head that had been outfitted down to the hairs in its beard, but that was all it had. The rest of its body was exposed wires and framing. The entire layout had obviously been taken from my father's schematics, but whoever assembled the pieces had taken no care with the intricacies necessary for them to function with any sort of fluidity or grace. It was more of a freak show than our circus had ever been.

"We're here," said one of the men I'd followed, finally stepping out of the scaffolding's shadow, with a hand on the control for his radio.

A welded-torso machine shuddered and slumped at its station, like it had just had a heart attack. When the conveyor next moved, its lifeless head bumped along for the ride. A figure stood from behind the station, holding a soldering wand in one hand, and I had to catch myself before I fell off the scaffold from the shock.

It was my mother, back from the grave.

CHAPTER 23

When I was a child, I dreamed of finding my mother alive and well. She'd be beautiful and young, exactly as she was in my father's stories. I couldn't imagine her any other way.

When I got older, and understood what death was, I stopped dreaming of that day.

The woman behind that glass was perfect in the way only a child's imagination could be. Beyond that, there was something about her eyes . . .

I knew my mother's eyes. They were Anise's eyes, and Vesper's, and Nim's. They were the darkness of strong coffee and sparked like the last embers in a campfire. They didn't reflect the dull, glassy emptiness of a golem's stare. Whoever she was, she couldn't be my mother. My mother wouldn't be dressed in the silver uniform of a Commission drone. My mother was dead.

Her hair stuck to her face, but she didn't seem to notice. Water beaded on her forehead and cheeks, but she never wiped it away. As she moved closer, opening a door to the side of the viewing window, I understood why the one man had said "she," while the other called her "the thing." There was a wooden cadence to her movement, and an unnatural stillness when she stopped and forgot to blink.

She wasn't human.

"What do you require?" she asked the men waiting for her.

"Warden says you're to help on the rings. Winds are too high for the usual crew."

The woman clasped her hands behind her back and turned to follow them. Even her hair moved with a pendulum's precision.

She was a copy. *A machine.*

Somehow, the Commission had created their robotic soldier, but why pattern her after my mother?

Once they were gone, I climbed down for a better look at the hub. If the whole thing was like the tech room, then my knowledge of my father's designs would be an asset, but there was no equipment below the scaffolds where I'd been hiding. Instead, it was a window to the outside.

The window bubbled out, like a bug's eye, letting me see above and below. Everything was below, except the sun.

The facility was bumping the ozone layer and was held up by enormous whooshing turbines. There was an entire aerial flotilla moored to the ends of different walkways, which swayed in and out of wispy clouds as though they were in the midst of constant fog. At each end were rings. This was the "dock," and it had nothing to do with the sea.

Birch's "center" was a floating fortress the size of a small city.

I leaned out as far as I dared, holding the guardrail and turning over for a better look at what was above us. There was a dome that reflected the waning daylight. Beyond that was the outer shell of the atmosphere itself, close enough to space to see the curve of the Earth.

Escape was going to mean more than simply getting out the door, unless I wanted to jump.

Horrified, I ran back the way I'd come, not considering it a stupid move until I was inside the greenhouse and stuck between sobbing and gagging.

I was hyperventilating. I paced the floor near the doors, holding my head, then holding my sides, unable to decide which position did the most good. The pain in my ribs was back, and it had garnered sympathy from a dozen other body parts that began to ache in time. I needed more of that infernal bark.

I made my way to my hutch. The door was standing open, and Birch was inside.

He came back.

"Okay, think this through. She can't have been taken, there would be signs. No one's sounded an alert, so she's not caught; she's just not here. Which means she's out there, and that's not good." I got the impression he spent a lot of time talking to himself.

"Birch?"

He raised his head.

"Penelope!"

He turned and pounced on me.

"Ribs," I choked out, and he sprang back as suddenly as he'd grabbed me.

"Sorry," he said. "I don't get much company." He passed me a strip of bark from the pile I'd made. "Here."

"*I'm* fine," I said, but took the bark. "*You* look half-panicked."

"More than half. When you weren't here, I thought . . ."

"That I'd been found?"

"And taken," he said, nodding.

"And since I was in your space, the warden would have known who helped me." My focus had been singular and selfish. Birch had put himself in danger, and how did I repay him? I made it worse. "I'm sorry."

We both sat down on the metal floor.

"I thought all that was left of you was your coat," he said.

One of the traveling coat's sleeves poked out from under the grass mat on the floor.

"They never would have left it behind. It's too valuable," I noted. Warden Nye knew exactly what that coat was. I should have been more careful with it.

"I hadn't thought of that, but you're right. The warden's quite fond of the things your father builds."

That was a horrifying thought.

The golems were dangerous enough, but if the warden could fine-tune something like the mechanism in that coat, there'd be no need for holographic unnoticeables. He'd be able to skip anywhere in the world. That, combined with this center and the things he'd stolen from the train, would make him the most powerful man in existence.

"Should I bury it?" Birch asked. "I know it's a memento, but—"

"I'll do it," I told him. And then I'd bury whatever I buried it under.

"I'm sorry I made you wait, but I went back to my room for these."

He unbuttoned his silver jacket. Beneath it was another, though this one was tight enough to strain the buttons. He took that one off, too, revealing a black Commission shirt and jeans wrapped around his waist. I was surprised he could walk at all.

"These are my old ones; they're a size down, and this way, if anyone sees you, you won't stand out. The Center's swarming with silver jackets most of the day, and the assembly crews wear denim. I couldn't hide shoes, though." He kept pausing, and then finding new things to say when I didn't pick up the conversation. "I know you might not like to wear the ankh, but—"

"They're perfect," I said. "Thank you."

I hauled the clothes into the hutch, wedging the door into a dressing screen. Now I had a costume, and a role to play. I could venture out and not worry about anyone seeing Penelope Roma. All they'd see was one of their own who'd likely never been to a place as grand as this island in the clouds, and so any awkwardness or confusion from me was to be expected.

Birch had handed me a lifeline, so why did I feel like I was betraying everyone I'd ever cared for?

I found myself slowing down as I dressed. I'd worn so many disguises, but this one intimidated me. I didn't want it to infect me, sink through my skin and my bones, and change me because I'd worn it too long.

"Um . . . do you need . . . er . . . with your ribs the way they are, should I . . . I mean . . . Do you need help?" Birch asked, knocking lightly against the side of the hutch.

"I can manage," I told him.

"Oh." He seemed disappointed. "Good. I mean, I would have helped you, but—"

"I play five different roles in The Show, when I'm not acting as ringmaster, and have about two minutes to change costumes between them. I'm not that shy."

The sound he made in response didn't actually qualify as words.

"Besides, I'm wrapped with leaves to my hips. There's not much to see." Needling Birch was nearly as fun as doing it to Jermay, only Jermay gave back as good as he got.

I worked the shirt over my shoulders, wishing I had a mirror to make sure things were sitting straight.

"The Show's a circus, right?" he asked, seizing on a chance to change the subject.

"It's my family."

"I've seen pictures. Animals. Acrobats. You. The warden has cases full. I liked the movies, but you were only about seven or eight in them."

"He has movies that old?"

I'd seen the pictures, but the idea of Warden Nye replaying my childhood at will was worse.

"I wish I could have seen it in person, but . . . Sorry. I guess I shouldn't talk about it."

"No, it's fine," I said. "Talking keeps them breathing."

I left the jacket hanging open and pushed the hutch's door out of my way to join him again. I held my arms out as well as I was able, hoping for an impression of a dresser's dummy.

"How do I look?"

This would have been the point when Jermay and Birdie began making jokes at my expense, while Klok straightened my seams and Winnie rolled her eyes at them. Of course, that was before we knew she could speak. I wasn't sure about her real sense of humor. All I knew was that Birch had none.

"Be careful with your hair," he said, giving me a serious glance-over. He took a rolled-up cloth cap from his pocket and stuck it on my head. "Either hide it, or figure out a way to make it regulation. And try not to wince when you walk, or you'll get yourself escorted to medical." He pushed my shoulders back, gently. "Let's hear your voice."

I coughed into my fist to clear my throat.

"What should I say?"

Birch's face finally brightened at the sound of my altered accent. I'd combined my Caravan usher's voice with the sound of the men I'd heard in the hall.

"The warden's right, you *are* a brilliant mimic."

If this warden had spoken of me in those terms, and by a name no one had a right to know, then why had he waited so long to come for me? He'd obviously been watching me since I was a child. He knew what I was—had he been waiting to get rid of my father first?

"Does he talk about me a lot?"

"Sometimes. He's been wanting to collect you for a long time, but it wasn't safe before he moved up here," Birch said.

"Safe for who?"

"I don't think he wanted anyone on the ground to know. Especially Warden Arcineaux."

Arcineaux was what Nye had called the gargoyle. I wouldn't want him in my business, either.

"He's quite a collector," Birch was saying.

"Arcineaux?"

"No!" The word came accompanied by the immediate wilting of several plants on all sides. Birch grabbed his wrist with his other hand, dropping to his knees beneath a wave of pain he bit his tongue to contain.

"Birch!"

"Don't," he said, struggling to control his breathing. "Don't touch me. It'll pass, just don't touch me. Don't . . ."

"But what—"

"It's the restriction bands." His face shifted from red to pale and back again, and he reached out to touch the blooms he'd just destroyed. They sprang back to life. "I got angry, but I shouldn't have. I wasn't prepared for you mentioning him like that."

"Arci—I mean, the other warden?"

"You can say his name—or call him Arsenic, like the rest of us."

"I'm sorry," I said. "I tuned out, and he was the last one I heard you talking about. Who's the collector?"

"Warden Nye. He covets rare and unusual artifacts, including people who fall into either category."

"Unusual like a fortress in the stratosphere?" I asked.

"You made it all the way to the wheel?" Birch sounded impressed. "The warden said his great mistake has been underestimating you."

"I got to a window."

"Most of our windows are in the wheel. The hallways are laid out like spokes around it. You really are one of a kind."

Like my father's golems, and the copy of my mother . . .

I wasn't a weapon; I was a trophy, and if the warden was snapping up everything valuable to my father, I wasn't the only person who fit that description.

"I think one of my sisters is here," I said. I thought I felt Anise's grounding presence nearby, but it could have been my imagination. "Was anyone brought in off the road? Can I see them?"

Birch looked uncomfortable. "After the fiasco with the train, and the other attacks—"

"Attacks? We defended ourselves!"

"Even the run at Arsenic?" he asked.

"That was different. I was trapped, and I couldn't leave that boy behind—he needed help."

It felt good to be on the other side of that need for once.

"The way I've heard it, you left the Ground Center a wasteland, and nearly killed Arsenic on top of it. It's all the workers have been talking about for a week."

"Unintended consequence. I haven't used my abilities very often, and I wasn't prepared for them to take over the way they did."

"Whatever you did, Arsenic didn't like it. He's trying to convince the Commission that allowing Nye to control this facility makes him too powerful. If Arsenic figures out you're here, things will get worse. They'll want Nye to relinquish something, but he won't let go of the Center, and he won't lose you. I'd guess he'd hand out any other acquisitions at the dedication to solidify their confidence in him."

"My friends and family are not party favors!"

"He's got no alternative, and you won't be able to find them; they're somewhere out of sight. The prison level, most likely. That's where he hides people."

Warden Nye sounded like he was socking away emergency currency for a rainy day, not handling live people who might not agree that they needed to be hidden in a prison.

"You should have told me all of this first thing," I said.

"I wasn't sure you'd believe me."

"Well, I do, so tell me everything."

"Unless you're able to bounce when dropped from extreme heights, all you need to know is that there's no way out of here."

"There are supply ships coming from the ground; I saw them unloading cargo. *They're* the way off. Show me—"

"You'd never make it out the door, and if you found a way, you'd never make it to a ship unseen. Let your people worry about their own fates."

"I don't believe in fate. You said it was impossible for me to be here, but I am."

"Because of a device that no longer functions." He toed my discarded coat.

"But others do," I said. A plan was forming in my mind. It was far-fetched and possibly insane, but my father had made an art form out of both, and I had mimicked him long enough to pick up the skill. "The warden has something of my father's. A machine capable of flight. The last I saw, it was in a room full of holograms and packing boxes. It looked like an office. If you know where—"

"No," Birch said, backing away, suddenly terrified.

"You *do* know. Where is it?"

He turned and ran.

"Birch!" There should have been an echo when I called after him, but the greenery muffled it. Even my footsteps against the metal were stifled. "Birch!"

I caught up with him at the doors.

"What's the matter with you?" I asked.

"I should be in my room." He tried waving me off. "I'll be lucky if no one's looking for me."

"That didn't bother you ten seconds ago," I said. He leaned away from me, like even breathing the same air was a danger. "I don't expect you to come with me. You've already risked more than your share; it's my turn. And if you're afraid I'll leave you behind when I find a way out—I won't. I promise. I'll—"

"There *is no way out!*" he shouted. An expression sculpted by some buried trauma surfaced for a moment before he barricaded it behind his usual manners. "I'm sorry, but I can't."

He touched the doors, hand trembling as they opened, and bolted before I could make another argument.

I'd pressed too hard.

I had no idea how long Birch had been the warden's prisoner, or what he had endured, but I'd seen Winnie's scars, and I'd heard Nagendra's stories of the years following Brick Street, when those who claimed to remember the riots were forced to forget by means too terrible to repeat. Birch was hiding a fugitive under Nye's nose; the penalties for lesser infractions were unthinkable. Nye was a man even the other wardens wanted to keep on a short leash—of course Birch panicked.

But me? I was more determined than ever. Perhaps this was why the coat brought me to this place, first to that office, and then to Birch. It showed me what I needed. I wasn't brought here to stay safe; I was here to save as many as possible.

This flying atrocity wasn't solely my father's design, but his fingerprints were everywhere. The Celestine daughter of Magnus Roma might be the only one qualified to dismantle the Center and wrest it from the clouds. And if Warden Nye was keeping tabs on all of his contemporaries the way he was Arcineaux, then that office was the key to finding my family.

If Birch returned, which I was sure he would, I would pull as much information from him as possible at whatever rate he was willing to provide it. Until then, I'd make use of the uniform he'd given me and acquaint myself with the layout of the Center. I'd hone the gift I'd been taught to suppress, and when I was ready, I would repay Warden Nye for the destruction of my home by taking his.

CHAPTER 24

I barely slept that night. I spent hours inside my hutch composing lists with a stick for a pencil and spilled dirt for paper. I made myself walk through the trip to the wheel and back over and over to pull out every detail I could remember, and marked it down. I chewed a lot of bark to shore myself up, and when the bell chimed for breakfast, I was ready.

This time, I went toward the ascending numbers. Enormous glass tanks had been placed against the walls, tall enough to reach my chin. Someone was stenciling letters above them, but all I could make out was the word "RAIN."

After ten minutes, I turned back. So long as I went in short bursts, I could create a decent map in my head. Then I could add the new details to my dirt drawing.

"You're going the wrong way."

My plan did not include unexpected intrusions. The voice was behind me, and definitely not Birch or Warden Nye. I was certain that it was the less caustic of the men I'd overheard the night before.

I turned around.

"What?" I asked, maybe with a bit too much of his own voice in my mimic because he looked startled.

"If you're answering the call for extra hands on the rings, you're going the wrong way," he said. "You're headed for the wheel, not the exit."

"Oh." I set my expression to something that was hopefully more confusion than fear. "All these halls look alike."

"I've been here three weeks, and still get turned around. Blame the painters," he said, with a laugh and a smile that clashed horribly with his choice of profession. "What's your name?"

"Jermay Baán," I lied, speaking Jermay's name for luck, then tried to get his attention onto something else. "When do they put in the fish?" I nodded to the tanks.

"How long have you been here?" the man asked suspiciously.

I was past the twenty minutes I'd allotted for this excursion, and the desire to panic was sitting heavy on my chest. I ducked my head a little. It was easy to pass for male at a distance, but up close, sometimes too many of the features I shared with Vesper bled through. I should have used a girl's name.

"I came on board yesterday."

The man pointed down the hall I'd just walked. "Find the first crossway and go left, then do the same again. Signs should take you the rest of the way."

He moved aside so I could follow his instructions.

"Thank you," I said, mentally kicking myself.

"And Baán—" the man called.

I stopped.

"Yes, sir?"

"We don't call them fish up here."

"Sorry, sir," I choked, throat suddenly dry.

I hurried off down the hall at an imitation march, but stopped at a juncture, and waited for a two-minute count before I risked trying to get back to the greenhouse. I'd have no plausible excuse if I ran into that man again, which would mean a reprimand or being asked who my direct superior was. As the only name I knew was Nye's, that wasn't a pleasant thought. Thankfully, the man was gone when I returned.

I never imagined that all my years as guide for The Show would be necessary training to survive outside it, but they had just saved my life.

I made my way back to the greenhouse, unstopped. Once safely inside, I leaned against the nearest wall, pressing my head into the ivy cascade that covered it. Everything sounded strange, mixed with my frantic breathing and too-fast thoughts. Rustling leaves blown about by the ventilation system clacked together in mumbled voices that whispered about me behind my back. The air was too thick and too damp, coated in perfume as though a shop had spilled its inventory.

"You went out, again."

"Hello, Birch," I said, still with my head in the ivy. "Did you have a nice breakfast?"

He shoved a squashed croissant under my nose. Half a piece of bacon stuck out of the side.

"Is being overly reckless a habit from living with wild animals?" he asked. "Because I don't see how you survive it."

"Is being overly cautious a habit from living under a warden's thumb? Because I *know* I couldn't survive that." I tore off a piece of breakfast with my teeth and found that Birch had stashed some banana in it, too. Very odd combination. "I refuse to stay in here and rot like a mulched leaf. And you can stop worrying—the disguise worked."

"You were seen?"

"Jermay Baán was seen. Penn kept hidden. I'm fairly good at it." I took another bite. Still odd, but not unpalatable. "What are those tanks for?"

I started walking; Birch fell in step beside me, and together we followed the guardrail's curve around the room while we both stewed for different reasons. The rest of my bacon-and-banana sandwich gave me a good excuse not to talk for a while.

"Those are the kinds of questions I don't ask," he said at the quarter-point. "But the tanks make the technicians nervous. Two days ago, we received an entire shipment of extra safety equipment attached to them. Another's due soon."

"So they're dangerous."

"To be hidden up here, they'd have to be."

We were at the halfway point.

"Who's Jermay Baán?" he asked.

"A boy I grew up with. His name was the only one I could think of besides yours."

"Is he one of the people you lost?"

"Only until I find him."

And I *would* find him.

We walked another quarter round, with Birch skimming leaves over the rail as we went. The vines wrapped around the railing bloomed with red and orange trumpets at the touch of his hand.

"You're not even doing that on purpose, are you?" I asked him.

He glanced at his hand and pulled it away. No more flowers grew.

"Force of habit," he said. "I like color."

"I can tell. This doesn't look like a government facility at all—secret or otherwise."

It looked like the hidden garden from a storybook. All it needed were a few sculptures from a forgotten pantheon and a fountain or two. Birds would have been nice.

"Why no scary tanks in here?" I asked.

"I told the warden I don't like them. He's not as bad as you think," Birch said.

So much for the fantasy . . .

"He pointed a gun at my face, destroyed my home, and threatened to murder a girl half our age, so I'd say he's exactly as bad as I think."

"It's for show."

"Then his act needs work."

The leaves nearest to us started to curl and wither.

"You don't know—"

"I know he put those bands on you, and that he wants to do the same to me. You're his prisoner, and the only reason to build a place like this is so no one down below knows they should protest its existence. How can you say he's not bad?"

"Because he *didn't* put these on me. And because I used to have a collar that matched them before he took it off. He's protected me every day of my life, and he's the closest thing I've ever had to a father. If I hadn't been given to him—"

"You were *given* to Warden Nye? Like a reward?"

"Harvested," he said bitterly. Tiny thorns popped up along the rail. Nettle plants sprang up on the bottom edge. "Not all of us had the luxury of being raised outside a center."

"That other place—the one on the ground that I sort of took apart. People were there, regular people. Were you an experiment like them?"

The thorns popped up on the floor now, appearing in uncurling vines that stretched into our path.

"My parents were caught after their daughter was born. The baby had a nightmare or something, and set the house on fire. A neighbor saw it. They tried to relocate, but the Commission was waiting for them. All three were taken."

"They kept your parents?" I asked, not mentioning that he never once referred to the girl he spoke of as his own sister. She was a stranger. A story.

"How do you think they breed so many hounds?" he asked. "It's hit-or-miss, unless you know that the base pair both carry touched genes."

"They made them have more kids?"

"Them and others like them. It's mix and match, all done in a lab for optimum results. After enough tries, the Commission ended up with me. I'm a twin. My sister's like you. That makes me interesting to certain people."

Birch squinted, wincing at a pain I didn't mean to cause.

He hopped onto the top of the rail, arms out like it was a tightrope and he was one of the Jesek boys practicing a new routine.

"Want to see a magic trick?" he asked, then dropped into the center of the room.

"Birch!" I shouted, grabbing for him, but he was already out of reach.

A second later, he came zooming back into view, sitting astride the branches of a tall tree that hadn't been there before. He was laughing—*the creep*. Trying to catch him had hurt!

"Don't do that!"

"Sorry," he said, still laughing.

"*Why* did you do that?"

"Because I can." He shrugged.

I tried to storm off, but Birch kept up easily, moving treetop to treetop, strolling along as though we'd never stopped our trip around the room. More trees popped up under his feet, the way Anise ran pistons in her act.

"You're insane," I told him. "Being locked up all this time has scrambled your brains, or you've been chewing on the wrong plants."

"I said I was sorry."

"Which was a lie."

"Not anymore. I thought it would make you laugh, not get angry." He and Jermay looked nothing alike, but they could both make the same pitiful face. I hated that face; I had no defense against it. "I only wanted to show you something."

He held his hand out, offering to help me over the rail.

"And let you drop me on my head?"

"Never," he said.

Birch kept his hand exactly where it was—more olive branch than arm. He stood balanced at the top of the palm tree, and it was tempting to see how long he'd hold out, but his expression had too much Jermay in it for me to make him suffer. I took his hand and climbed onto the rail. When I stepped across, Birch's tree leaned in closer.

"Hang on," he said, then we were shooting toward the ceiling, where tiny bubble protrusions poked out from the wall. We came to a stop in front of one. "Take a look."

This section of the facility was taller than the wheel and provided a more expansive view. The complex operated as a gargantuan gyroscope, balanced on nothing but hope, and we were at the center point of a series of great rings. Ships pulled straight out of a sci-fi movie floated at the edge, moored to the outermost ring. The front of one opened, and a small army of men tromped out in formation, headed for the facility's main entrance. The walkway swayed beneath them, but they never broke stride.

"They look like military," I murmured. What was the Commission doing with an army?

"Sent in advance of the wardens and Commission reps," Birch said. "The rings can't support more than two large carriers at a time. They have to unload in shifts, and they have been unloading for over a week. See? You have to stay here. There are too many."

"Is that why you wanted me to see this? So I'd get scared and stay put?"

Seeing the odds as people in my way, rather than numbers in my head, was daunting, but not impossible. *I* was impossible, and that made me the greater force.

"They'll be at every door. I'm not letting you get caught because you think being special makes you invincible. I couldn't protect my family, but I can keep you from sharing their fate. Either listen to reason, or I'll make you."

He stepped sideways, off our palm tree and onto another, which shrank down by several feet. All of the trees nearby did the same. The ivies slithered away from the walls.

"Birch!"

I tried to go after him, but his tree leaned away, out of reach unless I wanted to hop the gap, and with my ribs the way they were, I couldn't.

"Get back here, Root-rot!"

"Promise me you'll stay put."

"I can't."

"Then I can't let you down."

"Birch!"

"It's for your own safety, Penelope. You'll thank me later."

No, I was going to *kill* him later. The only question was whether it would be death by stinging nettle or by hanging with a sumac noose.

"He's turned me into a coconut," I said to no one.

I thought by now I'd seen every surreal thing imaginable, but nothing had prepared me for being stranded atop a giant palm tree that stretched over the greenhouse like an umbrella. I peeked over the edge to find fruit and pine trees growing dwarfed in the shadow of my settee.

Birch was smart. He'd picked a tree with only top branches, so there were no foot- or handholds for me to grasp and climb down. There were gaps between the trees, each a dark abyss among the green that made it impossible to see the floor. Straight brown trunks created a funnel effect, pulling my attention down to nothing and nowhere.

The lunch chimes sounded, and still I was left to myself. I passed the time by tearing off bits of frond and pretending they were Birch until they caught fire. When the flames reached my fingers, I asked the irrigation system to put them out, and a thin mist doused the flames from an overhead nozzle. The more control I gained, the more elaborate an end I planned for Birch.

Why would he do this to me?

If he knew what I could do—what Xerxes could do at full power—he'd be helping me, but all he knew was the tainted reality of a life in custody. If I could make him see . . .

Wait. Why couldn't I?

I stood up on the treetop and brushed the soot from my fingers. If Anise's gift was willing to oblige another use—

"Dirt," I said into the chasm. "I need dirt."

I thought of Arcineaux's facility, and the mound that overran the fence. I needed the same beneath my palm tree.

"Dirt. Rocks. Come on—pile up!" Hopefully the world had gone haywire enough for this to work.

A sound like rain drummed against the palm's trunk.

I crouched, hanging on to the stem of a large frond for balance. A tide of grainy bits slammed into the side of my perch and washed over every guardrail in a waterfall torrent, but the power didn't come as easily as I'd expected. I felt the weight like the ghost pains of imaginary muscles that were unused to being flexed. Sandbags heavy enough to drag me down, whether I wanted to go or not. How did Anise live with this during performances? She never said a word.

The pile-on stopped several feet short of what I needed, but I was out of raw materials. I was going to have to jump, or, since I couldn't manage that—drop.

I let my legs dangle, shifting my weight from the tree to my hands, but as soon as I lost the support under my ribs, I couldn't hang on. Down I went, onto my back, hard enough to knock a tirade of Nagendra's forbidden, unladylike words right out of me.

My body took lying on the heap as permission to shut down. My eyes grew heavy. Who was I to argue?

CHAPTER 25

I woke to the sound of chiming shift bells. I was disoriented, and in pain, and still on my back, and seriously tired of conking out every time I tried to use my abilities. None of my sisters had that problem.

The mound had shifted while I was unconscious, putting me near the main floor. It was a miracle I wasn't buried alive.

"Move," I snarled, slinging my hand; the dirtslide nudged me toward the guardrail.

If only Birch had been able to see it.

I turned to congratulate myself, basking in the proof of my control, and cringed. Hundreds of thousands of pounds of soil filled the lower levels in towering columns that would require heavy equipment to move.

Leaving a mess would have served Birch right, but it would mean his explaining how it happened to anyone who saw it. I was going to have to put every grain back where it belonged.

I honestly didn't know how to do that.

With simple machines, the trick was to use short, clear commands. Maybe that would work here.

"Go away," I said, shooing at the mound. "Out of sight, and off the floor."

The whole thing rose, hovering in a loose-packed ball. Dirt and rock threw themselves over the railings, diving for cover beneath leaves and filling empty containers. When I was finished, there was no dust to settle; the greenhouse was spotless as an operating room.

My arms and legs felt weak, though I hadn't physically lifted a thing. My ribs had reached the point of healing where they felt worse than when they were first broken. All my aches and pains conspired to steal my strength so that I could barely manage a crawl. I retreated to my hutch and pulled the door shut behind me.

I'd faced two wardens and lived, but one awkward boy was well on his way to putting me in a coma. I should have stayed in the palm tree.

"How did you dig your way off the top of a tree?"

I blinked awake to find a shadow at my door.

A few facts leached into my mind. I smelled grass because I was lying on it. I was lying on it because I was in my hutch. Hiding in the greenhouse. Hiding from the warden.

The shadow stooped forward to grab my arm.

Warden Nye.

"Get back!" I screeched.

A sharp blast of wind blew the shadow out of my hutch in a burst of shredded grass. He landed on the metal walk.

"Penelope isn't an early riser—duly noted," Birch groaned.

My plan to be angry with him evaporated.

"Are you hurt?" I asked.

"I think I broke my omelet." He was covered in the eggs that were likely intended to be my breakfast. "I should have smuggled toast."

He sat up, picking bits of white and green from his clothes.

"I thought you were the warden," I said.

"No, but he's the reason I couldn't come back yesterday. He had me decorating guest rooms. He wants to make sure a certain someone develops hives. But seriously—how did you dig out of a tree? Your hands are dirty."

Yesterday? How long was I unconscious?

"I didn't dig. I dropped."

Birch glanced at the palm tree, then at the rail, as if to ask if I'd fallen all the way, but he shook his head. No one could survive that.

"I suppose I have you to thank for mixing up my planters?" he asked.

"Thank yourself. *You* stranded me."

"I didn't have a choice."

"Yes, you did! And you made the wrong one! You're no better than the Commission drones who run this place."

"I am nothing like them!" Birch shouted, jumping to his feet. "I'm . . . I'm . . . I'm sorry, but you wouldn't listen. It's dangerous down here."

"Danger doesn't follow a floor plan, Birch," I said. "*It follows me.* You can't fix that, but I wouldn't mind having you fix my ribs again. The bandages came loose in the drop."

"Come on," he said, and we both tried to leave it at that.

We returned to the area with the vines he'd used for wrappings.

"Arms up," he instructed, and an unexpected pang hit me.

I wanted to call it hunger from missing a day of meals, but it was a pang of familiarity. For a moment it was as if I were getting ready for The Show. I lifted my arms and hoped Birch would believe me if I said my eyes were watering from the pain.

"Potatoes won't grow in pebbles, you know," he said, filling in the silence I couldn't break myself.

"What?"

"You put my potatoes in pebbles. They won't grow that way. I'll have to replant them. And a few other *everythings*."

He grinned; I didn't.

"Collateral damage," I said.

"Plants are easier to fix than people."

"And you think I'll need to be fixed if I leave your greenhouse?"

"I think you want your old life back so badly that you're willing to get yourself killed for the idea of it, but around here, killed isn't as bad as it gets."

"I'm careful."

"You've been lucky, and the more people who fill this place, the less likely *lucky* is going to be. What if Warden Nye had been the one to see you? What do you think he'll do if the man you lied to gives your friend's name in his daily report? How common is Jermay or Baán that it will be overlooked, especially to a man who knows your circus inside and out?"

They weren't common names at all, and if the warden had seen me, busted ribs would be the least of my problems.

"The Commission isn't sending people up here for tea, Penelope. They're going to be looking for anything out of place, and if they find you, they'll put you somewhere that won't be nearly as easy to escape as that tree. You can put your arms down now."

Breathing wasn't easy, but I felt better. The wrappings weren't only holding my sides, they were holding me together.

"Why won't you just tell me why you're so afraid of Arcineaux and the others?"

"Doesn't everyone fear the devil?" Birch turned away. "I can't get you any more breakfast. You'll have to make do with tree fruit until lunch. There's no point in my telling you to stay here until then." He walked off without bidding the wrapping vines to return to the ceiling, and left the greenhouse.

I made up my mind to prove him wrong.

The vines he'd left behind seemed sturdy, so I sat on the widest. It swayed back and forth and side to side like a child's swing. I spun the vines into a spiral, and let them uncoil. Motion had always helped me to think; sitting still never did.

A stray breeze caught my swing, throwing the rhythm off and introducing the scent of machines and coolant. I was near a vent that had kicked on to churn fresh air through the room. Birch had overgrown the vent, covering it with vines and trellises like everything else, but it wasn't hard to trace the current.

The grate spanned from the floor to above my head. Openings this size allowed for quick access to the air circulators, but they were a pain to keep clear. The technicians had only turned the bolts enough to make sure the grate wouldn't fall, and Birch's ivy had done what ivy does best, forcing itself into every crack and crevice. It had pried up a corner, leaving the bolt loose enough to remove, so I could crawl inside.

Surely it was safe to venture out if I couldn't be seen.

A three-rung ladder bolted to the inside wall led to the crawl space between this floor and the one above. At the top, there was room enough to walk at a stoop. Crawling was easier. Thankfully, Birch's pain-killer plant still had plenty of bark on it.

Every few feet came a grate that opened through the ceiling of the main hall, allowing light to shine in. Several creeper lights milled in the corridors below, assisting technicians with their work; ceiling-mounted climbers bent up toward me, curious at my passing.

"Go back to work," I snapped, afraid they'd alert someone to my presence.

Birch was right about the crowd. The halls were overflowing as people jostled around and through other groups that were painting the walls and installing the final touches before the dedication. A man and woman wearing protective gear carried a huge bucket between them on a pole. They lifted it to a man at the top of a ladder who was wearing the same suit, and helped tip the contents into one of the tanks. It looked like sand. Plain, boring, and pink, but not dangerous sand.

I crawled farther and hit a dead end, forcing me to turn back, but when I did, I found I wasn't alone. A small spindly creeper light had ventured into the crawl space. It raised one of its legs and waved.

"Go away!"

It put its leg down and sat like a defiant puppy.

"Fine, stay there, but don't shine. You'll get me caught!"

It shuttered its lamp while I leaned near the closest vent to see if I could learn any names or faces that might come in handy later. Hardly anyone slowed down long enough for me to assess their features— until, finally, a singular individual appeared.

People in the hall reacted to her presence before I saw her, stiffening and hushing their voices. They were no more comfortable around the false Iva Roma than I was. She speared through the throng at a quick clip. I followed, struggling to keep up without clanging against the sides of the shaft, while the creeper rolled along behind me.

We went back the way I'd come, passed the greenhouse, and continued on; I moved just fast enough to keep her in sight. Iva turned once. There was a bit of an incline, and I was no longer in a section of airway over the main hall. I was above an office with its own view of the outside, but in this part of the Center, that view was blocked by one of the gyro-rings. Most of the window was taken up by a riveted plate the size of my head.

Iva glanced around, but didn't find what she wanted. She turned without entering the office completely and left.

I stayed put. This wasn't the office I'd escaped from, and there weren't any high-tech holographic projectors, but there was something potentially better. A computer sat on the desk, shiny and new, and unlike the warden's, this one had been hooked up.

I slid out of the grate and onto a shelf, then down to the desk. The routine wouldn't have me flying with the Jeseks, but Bruno and Birdie would have approved. The creeper light poked its face into the hole, but had no way to climb down.

"Shh," I warned it. "I'll be right back."

Like the warden's tablet, the computer had a password, but it wasn't *Celestine*. It wasn't any of the words I'd tried before. This wasn't a personal computer; it had to have a password with a broader meaning, but what? The room didn't even look like it was occupied yet. Everything was generic, from the equipment to the framed posters with that same "Bring the Rain" slogan I'd seen elsewhere here.

No, not elsewhere—everywhere.

I clicked the password box and typed it in; retrying without the spaces actually worked. It led to a basic start screen, with no icons for security feeds that might show me the prison level or its residents. There was no ankh here to let me pick up where I'd left off in Nagendra's file. I tried the Medusae jellyfish, but that only went to more biological studies. Lots of DNA references, but no answers for me.

I was about to log off and return to the greenhouse when a single word caught my attention: *Gemini*. Above it was an icon in the shape of the astrological sign for "the twins." Twins like me and Birch and all those footnotes in the warden's notebook.

Maybe this wasn't a bust after all. Maybe I could find out what happened to Birch's family and start to make up for the trouble I'd caused him. He'd have to agree that was worth taking a few risks.

The Gemini file contained subfolders, each of which held another two—one boy and one girl—so these were all fraternal twins, but I didn't know Birch's name. Birch didn't even know Birch's name. I opened the main project document and skimmed through it, hoping for a photograph or two that would narrow my search. I never expected it to widen my world.

The Commission called us Level-Fives.

There'd never been a fifth girl born to a touched family without a male counterpart, and the males were all marked as "outliers." The mention of chromosomal tripling I'd seen in the warden's notebook meant boys like this, like Birch. They had the requisite double-X that allowed them to be gifted, but they had a Y chromosome that made them male, and that difference was enough that their gifts couldn't be anticipated or regulated. Male levels of testosterone were some kind of wild card.

The strange thing was that in all the records of these fifth-birth pairs, and there were hundreds, there wasn't a single mention of a gifted girl. The female twins almost always died, and the handful that didn't were completely human.

So what had happened to me?

I heard voices in the hall, and knew I had to get out of there. I logged off and climbed back onto the shelf as fast as I could, then slipped back into the vent with the curious creeper light.

Iva came into the room, this time accompanied by Warden Nye. He was toting Xerxes under his arm, and set him on the edge of the desk. Xerxes was wearing a ridiculous pink ribbon for a collar.

"Arcineaux's men aren't careful how they speak," Iva said.

"And?" Warden Nye asked.

"They have the impression that the girl's lack of recent appearance is proof that she was operating under your orders."

"If Penelope had been there on my order, she would have flattened him before the building, or at least taken the one with the other. Whatever happened at his facility was unplanned. The girl was terrified."

Iva nodded, but not in the usual manner. Her head tipped forward like it might roll off, then snapped back.

"He's accepted your invitation, as have several others, but I doubt they have plans to celebrate."

"They're coming for the Roma girls, and Arcineaux will be searching out his test subject. Make sure she's hard to find." Nye made another failed attempt to pet Xerxes. He knocked against the gryphon's wing with his gloved knuckle, giving off a metal clang.

I had only until the wardens arrived to find my sisters and get them out of the Center. What did that give me? A week? Less?

Iva touched a glowing button on her ear that resembled the communication system we used in the Caravan.

"Another ship's arrived," she said.

"Tell them our sardine can is already full of dead fish." Nye sighed.

"Yes, sir."

"No, don't—Never mind, just listen for chatter about our wayward Celestine."

"Yes, sir," she said, and left the room.

"I know you sent her my way because she was defective," Nye said to Xerxes, "but you could have made her a tad less literal."

Xerxes turned his back on the warden and lay down with his head on his front paws, refusing to humor him with further conversation.

"And now I see where Penelope learned her social skills."

Xerxes flicked his tail. Nye went to the window.

"Where are you, pet?" he whispered, leaning an arm against the glass.

I scrambled back to the greenhouse at double time, and took the creeper with me so it couldn't cause any mischief that might necessitate maintenance in the shaft. I dropped the ivy back in place against the vent. Birch was standing outside my hutch.

"They're here," I said, running in his direction as well as I was able; the creeper light skittered, trying to keep up. "My sisters are here. I heard the warden myself!"

Birch looked stunned, and a bit guilty.

"Don't worry, I was careful. He said—"

"Penelope?"

My body shut down on the spot, hearing Greyor's voice inside my hutch. He emerged holding my father's red coat, which I hadn't gotten around to burying deeper than the underside of my mat.

"I can explain," Birch said.

"Traitor!"

My temper rose too quickly. All I could see was red, everywhere. The coat, and spilled blood, the embarrassment on Evie's face when Greyor cornered her before our last performance. Even the light suddenly beaming from the creeper's face seemed to be tinted scarlet. I ran at Greyor, unsure how I wanted to strike out. As long as it hurt him, I didn't care.

"Penelope, listen," he said, but listening to liars was a waste of time.

"My name is Penn!"

I set my sights on the coat. The broken circuits spit sparks, as the electric fence had at the gargoyle's facility, and like the unfortunates who had flung themselves into the current there, Greyor found himself with fingers that would not let go. The shock paralyzed him.

All I needed was water. It could electrocute him completely.

"Penn, stop!"

My rage was so singularly pointed at Greyor that I'd lost track of Birch. Warden Nye could have walked into the room and I wouldn't have noticed.

"I don't want to hurt you," Birch said.

"I *do* want to hurt him," I snarled, and raised my head toward the sprinklers.

"I'm sorry for this."

Birch tackled me. He took advantage of the weakness he knew I had, and used my broken ribs to put me down. I crashed to the floor, still watching Greyor as the coat died in his hands—he flung it away, on his knees and breathing heavy.

"Let me go!" I ordered, kicking out against the pain.

Somewhere between breaths, the tears from the searing in my bones turned to tears for having my vengeance snatched away by someone I thought had as much reason to hate the Commission as I did.

"He's not your enemy, Penn." Birch was still leaning on me, so I couldn't garner enough control to strike again.

"He was there!" I cried. "My sister—"

"Wouldn't listen to me," Greyor gasped. "I thought you were smarter."

"He's my friend," Birch insisted, easing up enough that I could shove him off, but I still couldn't get up.

"Not mine," I said. "And neither are you!"

The coat jumped and popped from another electric burst, though no one was close enough to feel it.

"The night you interrupted Nieva and me, I was trying to warn her about the raid," Greyor said. "That's why I was there."

"You can trust him," Birch said.

"Based on what?" I demanded. "The fact that he knew and did nothing to stop the raid?"

"I told her as soon as I knew it was coming. That's all I could do without jeopardizing the trust I've built with Warden Nye. He had over a hundred of us there that night—I couldn't have stopped it if I tried."

"I guess we'll never know, will we?"

"You can trust him based on the fact that I do," Birch said.

"I don't trust you, either."

Birch had done nothing but blindside me since he put me up that tree, and I was done with him.

"He can go places we can't," Birch said.

"Then maybe he should," I said. "And he can take you with him."

"Penn—"

"GO AWAY!" A small gust knocked him back once, then again.

"Penn, please . . ."

The coat crackled again. A line of current jumped from it to my hand, leaving my fingers shining blue with flaming peaks. I hadn't even tried that time.

Birch and Greyor both took a step back, the latter with a protective arm in front of the former. I was too angry to question why he'd do that.

"Get out, or you can see how well your precious potatoes grow in ashes," I said, holding my hand out toward the hutch. "I'll burn the whole place, me included."

"Go," Greyor said, nudging Birch toward the doors.

"I don't understand. What did I do wrong?" Birch said sadly, but he ran.

"If the heat reaches the fire-detection equipment, an alarm will sound," Greyor said with remarkable calm. He followed Birch out.

I shook my hand furiously to dislodge the energy contained there, then retreated into my hutch. If Greyor told the warden I was there, hiding wouldn't help.

I'd spent sixteen years whining because I thought our train was a prison I'd never escape, but without it, my world was smaller and lonelier than ever.

CHAPTER 26

I incinerated the coat, then sat vigil in my hutch, jumping at every noise, expecting every moment to be the one when the door was ripped away by Warden Nye. My new creeper-light friend elected itself my sentry, patrolling the greenhouse's walkway. But the night passed. The chimes sounded for breakfast, and I was still alone and uncaptured.

Had I been wrong?

Was it possible that Greyor was the asset Birch claimed?

And Birch . . . Oh, what I'd done to Birch. I'd threatened to annihilate the only place he felt safe. I deserved a foul fate.

There had to be a way to fix this. I couldn't survive on my own for long, and I had a suspicion that Birch couldn't, either. I needed to find him, but I nearly lost my nerve once I opened the greenhouse doors. There was so much movement and sound in the hall that finding anyone seemed impossible.

Greyor seemed to know I needed time to collect my thoughts. I hoped that would mean that he or Birch would be close enough to spot quickly. I picked a direction and headed out—straight into someone going the opposite way.

"'Scuse me," the man said. "Didn't see you there, brother."

"Sorry," I replied in one of the dozen voices I'd acquired in The Show. "Still not used to the layout."

"Map's on the wall now," the man called back over his shoulder as he carried on, lugging an official-looking messenger bag.

I saw it. A few feet away, there was a frame bolted to the wall between two of those massive tanks, which now sparkled with water.

"You shouldn't have any trouble now, but mind your feet before you get where you're going," the man with the bag said. "Report for duty in those, and you'll be cited."

I glanced down at my boots, then nodded another nervous thanks before turning back to the wall.

A wide glass case contained several official bulletins, which I ignored. Right in the middle someone had tacked a floor-by-floor schematic of the Center. The scale nearly took my breath away, but I could come back and marvel in horror later in the night. For now, all I needed was very specific information. Luckily, the map was color-coded, and my new creeper-light buddy was there to shine a light on it.

The dining hall was blocked in green. A yellow section denoted guests' quarters, and blue was for permanent residents. That's where Birch would live, so that's where I went, head down, and careful not to shuffle my feet.

"Thanks for the help," I whispered to the creeper light. "You should go join the rest of your friends, before you're missed at whatever station you're assigned to. I'll be fine."

The light blinked good-bye and rolled away into the scattering herd of identical units that were assisting on the floor.

No one else noticed me at all.

I was tall for a girl, but here, I was barely above average. I was thin, with jutting angles for knees and elbows, but so was everyone I passed.

"Hey," someone called. "You there, in the silvers."

"Me?" I asked. A man on a ladder was staring down. He was fixing a metal lid to the tanks.

"Yeah, you. Toss me that filer plate, would you?" he asked. "Up and down's an awful pain."

His toolbox was sitting open, with a stack of metal files on top, so I grabbed the first one and handed it up.

"Thanks," he said. "Wouldn't want these spilling over on folks, would we, little brother?"

I tried not to shiver at the endearment. It made the place sound like a cult.

"You're welcome," I said, and hurried off.

I passed the first junction and went to the second, which according to the map was where I'd find the living areas. Only whoever pasted up the map had put it backward. I was in the guests' section. The uniforms here were a rainbow of trouble, all guarded by Commission-approved men in body armor at the head of the hall.

"Keep walking, little brother," one said gruffly. "Not your hall."

"Which way's the dock?" I asked, with feigned confusion.

"One back and take a left," he said. "You'll get used to it."

"If I'm around that long," I grumbled, and the guard chuckled.

This wasn't going to work. I was never going to find Birch on my own.

I reversed my track, and headed back for the greenhouse, passing through an official's contingent as it headed in.

"Take some silvers for the hauling," I heard someone say, and nearly fainted dead when a hand latched on to my jacket.

"Where you headed?" its owner asked. He had one of the maroon patches belonging to that gargoyle Arcineaux on his shoulder.

"To the dock."

"Welcome committee?"

"They don't tell me until I get there."

"Then consider yourself told. Get some help, and take this to the dock jockey. You're collecting for Warden Arcineaux."

All that practice inside the Caravan saved me again. I knew how to keep my face blank.

"What's this?" I asked, staring at the card that the man stuffed into my hand.

"Clearance card for the warden's ship. You need it to verify possession of his things. Four bags, six boxes. Bring them straight to room forty-one. Understood?"

"Yes, sir," I said. "Four, six, forty-one."

Anything to get away from there before the warden showed up.

"What's your name?" the man asked.

"Jermay Baán," I said automatically, and hardly kept from cringing.

"I'll tell the warden. He remembers those who do a good job."

That's what I was afraid of.

"Thank you, sir," I said, surprised I had enough breath to speak. "I'll be quick."

"Even better." He let me go.

I wanted to run, but I managed a decent walk. I'd nearly reached the bend in the hall when—

"Baán," the man called me back, but Arcineaux could have been beside him now. Maybe he wanted to meet the person in charge of his things, and I couldn't risk the warden recognizing me.

I sped up, as though I hadn't heard him.

"Baán!" he called again.

The gargoyle's voice added, "I want to speak to you, young man."

I threw his card down and ran, charging through the workmen's stations as the sound of feet closed in behind me.

"Stop!" Arcineaux called.

"Baán!" the aide added.

I sprinted into the main hall, but couldn't stop in the greenhouse. They'd come in after me, and if Birch was in there, or they found evidence that he'd been helping me, then he'd be on the hook, too. I ran to the wheel.

More people milled through here, but at a less frantic pace. Some shouted "Hey!" when I flew by, upsetting their routines. I passed into the hall beyond it, but as I neared the first junction there, I heard another familiar voice in the mix—the other man who thought I was Jermay.

I needed a distraction, but they were in short supply. None of the personnel was going to help me evade a warden, especially not a warden as feared as Arsenic—unless the personnel in question weren't human.

I glanced at the mixing room. The tangle of climber lights was now properly installed and waiting to be activated. Hopefully, they were as accommodating as my other friend.

"Hey!" I tapped on the glass. Every light swiveled toward me. I was never going to get used to that. "Keep them busy. Make a mess."

They understood me as easily as the ones who'd saved me from the warehouse. The lights whipped themselves into a flagellating storm, flinging fixtures around the mixing room to create havoc. The three nearest the glass began to beat against it like they were trying to break free. That triggered an alarm and created a convenient bottleneck to give me cover.

"Thank you," I told the lights, then headed for the biggest doors, hoping they went outside so I could lose Arcineaux and his aide for good in the shuffle of ships being unloaded.

After I passed through, a security gate slammed down, and the doors shut behind me. Gears moved inside the walls, shaking the room slightly; the sudden force of upward acceleration threw me to the ground. I'd walked into an elevator lift, and I had no idea where it was taking me.

CHAPTER 27

I was stuck to the floor until the ride ended. The recoil of a sudden stop threw me again.

The gate rose behind a set of etched glass doors to reveal a curved room. It was empty and silent, save for the sound of moving air. Then I heard thump, thump, thump.

I ventured out, surprised to find that rather than being set into a wall, as it had been on the primary floor, the lift was now in a center column. The thumping sound came from its other side.

Thump, thump, thump.

There wasn't much furniture, nothing hung on the walls except a control panel of some sort, and like the spaces below, there were no windows. The lights were set to a low burn, allowing the reflection of the metal surfaces to carry the glow all the way around the column. It was like being inside an oven—an idea I cast out of my mind quickly, before the horror of it could take root and fill my thoughts with the agony of roasting alive.

Thump, thump, thump.

The sound came again, still in the same tight burst of three. I swallowed my fear and kept walking. It wasn't a machine, I was certain, as there was no true rhythm to it, and it didn't come at a set interval the way cycling ventilation might. As I passed around the last quarter of the domed room, dread edged in, prying my nerves loose.

Thump.

A brilliantly shined piece of silver streaked past my face and lodged in the column.

Thump.

Another matched it perfectly, nearly sharing the same space.

Thump.

The third wasn't so precise. I heard the rip when a hole opened in my sleeve at the shoulder. A slim dagger had left a swatch of material pinned to a target against the back of the lift.

"Penelope?"

I turned toward the voice, and found myself facing the warden who had plagued my every step since the train was destroyed.

"You came back." Nye moved slowly, in a dreamlike daze, approaching at an angle, the way one might a butterfly they didn't want to startle. He stopped a few feet away. "Or did you never leave?"

The fury that had fueled my attack on Greyor roared back to life, stoked higher and hotter until the burn threatened to sing the stars down on both our heads. But that was too easy. I wanted to hurt him, and I wanted him to see me do it. Blood for blood.

I reached for the dagger that had ripped my jacket, pulling it free of the target with the piece of material still skewered on its tip, and lunged for Warden Nye. All he did was step sideways and let my momentum carry me past him.

"Keep your eyes open, pet, or you'll never hit your mark," he mocked, fully returned to the arrogant man I'd met before.

"I'm *not* your pet!" I pivoted on my heel and took another arcing slash at him.

"I wondered how long it would take to get your temper up." He caught my hands and pinned my arms beneath his own.

I tried to speak, but it came out a wordless growl.

Nye released me, shoving me away. I scrambled sideways, expecting an attack, but he hadn't moved—and didn't, until I tried to skewer him again.

"And don't close your eyes in anticipation of contact," he said as he dodged. "You'll never make a clean kill."

I ended up colliding with the column. My stomach turned instantly sour; my knees buckled. I landed hard and couldn't get up.

"Still tender, are they?" the warden asked. "Very little hurts worse than broken ribs."

"I dealt with them," I rasped, no longer facing him with the silence of a slaughterhouse animal awaiting death.

"So I see." I flinched when he reached down. He picked off a bit of wilting green where one of the leaves Birch used to wrap my ribs had drooped from under my shirt. "I think this is the first time Birch has ever deliberately misled me. Are you rubbing off on him?"

"I stole the coat. I don't know anything about birch trees."

Nye tsked at me. "Terrible performance. I expect better from you."

He thumped my side with two fingers. I spasmed, screaming, with my knees drawn up.

I kicked at him when he pulled me off the ground, even tried to bite him, but he was always just a little faster and just a little more agile than he had a right to be.

"Rage is a good thing. Now you just have to learn what to do with it."

The knife was now under his control; he began to walk me backward with the dagger's edge against my throat. I felt the solid surface of the lift's column behind me. The other two knives glinted at the corner of my eye, just out of reach when I stretched my arm to take one.

"What you lack is the skill necessary to follow through." His voice had become a near whisper. "You weren't even aiming for my heart, pet—it's here."

He used one arm to hold me to the wall, displaying strength no man his age or size should have possessed. With the other, he flipped the knife so that the handle was to me and the point was nearer his own chest.

"Stop calling me that!"

He nudged the handle into my hand, leaning in until the tip dented his shirt. I didn't move.

"If you're this easy to tame, I'll be disappointed, *pet.*"

With no choice but to look directly at him, I could tell that the lines on his face were scars more than years of life. Hair I would have called silver or gray at a distance was neither, but rather very white blond, and the eyes I had labeled devoid of color and soul were blue as Jermay's, and sharper than the edge of the knife in my hand.

"What are you doing?" I demanded.

"Lesson one. There's a look a man gets when he knows he's about to die. The whole of his life gathers to a point. You can see everything he ever was, every dream he ever had, and all the things he'll never be because *you've* decided his life is over. You have to be close to see it—"

Warden Nye leaned in, driving the tip of the blade into himself until he bled.

"—close enough to breathe in his final breath. You have to be willing to see his face every time you close your eyes, because it will *never* leave you. There's no other feeling like it, and—"

I wrenched the knife from between us and threw it clattering into the distance. He stepped back, laughing.

"You really are your father's daughter," he said. "And *don't* think that's a compliment."

Nye crossed the room, bending to retrieve the dagger.

"Never lay aside your weapon, unless you mean to surrender, and never squander an offered opportunity to best your opponent. Another may not present itself."

The jovial façade went back into place as he shook the blade at me like a scolding finger.

"And I wasn't trying to hit you, so you know. Throwing keeps my hands limber." He worked the last two daggers loose from the lift column and returned all three to his pocket. "It's not in my interest to let anyone harm you, after today."

"After?"

The back of his hand slammed against the side of my skull so hard, I would have sworn I heard metal clanging. My sight went black, covered with a bursting lace of lights. All that remained as I drained away was Nye's voice:

"Iva, ready room six, and fetch the boy."

I'm sorry, Birch. I'm so, so sorry.

CHAPTER 28

I woke in my room on the train, and there was something in my eyes. I sat up; hair fell around my face and over my arms, down my back in a cascade of dark waves. My ribs no longer ached. I had to be dreaming.

My mirror was hung on the door of my armoire, so I ran to it, excited by the feel of my hair as it swept behind me like Vesper's magnificent wig. The girl looking back at me was more exciting still: she was Penelope proper, and every vapid wish I'd ever wished.

Sister Mary Alban's medallion dangled to my waist on its long chain. Clips kept my hair in place at each side of my face. My fingers had been painted with the polish that Penn had never been allowed. A deep red ring sat on my middle finger, a perfect fit to match the gown I'd somehow acquired. It, too, was red, with cut-out spaces that showed gold lace and underpinning. So what if the ring looked like Birch's tracker. In my dream it was nothing but a bit of shine with an inconvenient shape.

And it felt so real . . .

The replica of my room was perfect, right down to the flowered wallpaper I had covered with torn-up comic books in real life. I heard a purring sound and found Xerxes curled up asleep in a basket, still wearing the pink ribbon Warden Nye had put on him. When I laughed, he opened his eyes, scowled at me for the interruption, turned his head away, and went back to sleep.

Eager to get my bearings, I headed for a set of heavy curtains that scraped the floor—behind them was a blank wall. I trembled as I reached for the next cord. There was no window there, either. I ran to the room's opposite side and found the same, searching along the wall with my hands in case there was something more than I could see.

Frantic, I settled my sights on the door with its crystal handle. If it opened into a wall, I was sealed in.

I rested my hand against the doorknob; it turned from the other side.

"It's a dream," I said as the door opened. "*My* dream."

And as my dream, it should have been under my control. I willed the person on the other side of the door to be Jermay.

"Xerxes, come," I ordered. I didn't feel in control at all. "Xerxes, I need you!"

My dream. My dream. Mine . . .

Xerxes trotted over, leaning against my leg just as the person who had opened the door entered.

"I'm sorry," Birch said, shuffling into the room. "At least they fixed your ribs."

The mechanical imitation of Iva Roma came behind him.

"Of course he did! What sort of commander would he be if he allowed her to remain injured?" she asked, before addressing me. "Hello, Penelope. Do you like your room?"

"Wake up," I told myself. "I don't want you here. Wake up!"

I pinched myself, pressed my hand into my ribs, bit down on my tongue—anything to cause enough pain that I'd snap out of this cursed sleep.

"Silly girl," Iva said. Her grin turned nearly manic as it widened across her too-stiff face. "You *are* awake. The warden let me pick your clothes after I mended your ribs."

"*You* mended them?"

"Medical training is part of my programming," she said proudly, reaching for a strand of my newly grown hair. "It lets me fix all sorts of things. I may have gotten a bit carried away prettying you up, but I'm told you didn't like your previous hairstyle, and spoiling her youngest is a mother's right, isn't it?"

No! It was a dream! There were no machines that could mend bones or lengthen hair. Nye hit me hard enough to knock me out, and this was the result.

I glanced at Birch. He must have guessed my thoughts, because he shook his head solemnly.

"What do you want?" I demanded of the robot.

"The warden asked me to visit. Do you like your room?"

Her programming needed a tweak. She was stuck in a loop.

"It's nice enough, for a cage."

"They're your quarters," Iva said, shaking her head with a plastic pout.

"Where are my sisters? My friends? Where's my father?"

"Inconsequential." Her expression soured, but not smoothly enough to be considered a frown. "You have no need for remnants of an old life. You'll adapt to your new one. You have no alternative."

I had as many alternatives as there were windows or doors to leap from.

"I'll kill myself."

"That's Magnus talking," she said, heaving a forced sigh. "He's warped all your perceptions of us, hasn't he?"

"He *protected* me from you," I said, refusing to humor her. "He loves me. Where is he? Is he a prisoner, too?"

"You can have a good life here, Penelope. You can also have a bad one. Which do you want?"

I liked her better when she was dead. This false mother had done more than steal the only concrete image I had of the real Iva Roma. I couldn't even mourn my mother anymore—I wanted to destroy her with my bare hands.

Hands that began burning as my temper rose.

I called out with that inner sound of music that had brought the stars careening down upon Arcineaux's facility, but instead of the crash of burning rock against the building, a searing pain shot through my wrists. The more I tried to sing down the stars, the more intense the burn, until I pried up the lace gloves to see what was below them.

Restriction bands.

I grabbed my throat, but there was no collar.

"I told you he doesn't use them," Birch said.

"I *want* to leave," I said. When I stopped trying to use my abilities, the pain lessened. "My real mother would let me."

Iva opened the door wide.

"You're welcome to wander any space not closed by security protocol, darling. Birch can help you sort them out. Please be prompt when you're summoned. We don't want to give our guests a bad impression."

She left me and Birch alone.

"There wasn't anything I could do once the warden saw you," he said.

"I know." That was on me, and me alone. "I told him you didn't help me, but . . . Was it . . . was it awful, whatever he did to you because of me?"

"He didn't do anything," Birch said. "It's not like the centers on the ground. It's better here."

Birch laid his palm against the wall, causing the flowers painted on it to bloom. Real and fragrant roses trellised up the walls and across the ceiling and floor until he'd made me my own greenhouse, with only the furniture to hint that we were indoors.

"Making it look nice doesn't set windows in the walls or let me out the front door. Put it back the way it was."

He touched the wall again and the blossoms wilted into the paper, leaving them more muted than they'd been before. Birch was in the same condition.

"Why won't you let me make things better?" he asked. "I want to make you happy—and believe it or not, so does Warden Nye."

He pointed to the ceiling. At the very top of the room, a security camera's red light blinked from inside a vent grate. Nye was watching us.

"By turning me into a living doll he can trot out for guests to gawk at? That's not the kind of show I put on."

I flounced onto the floor in front of the sofa, determined not to let myself be comfortable in my cell.

"He gave you back your cat. All I had to do was ask," Birch said.

"You? You got him to part with Xerxes?"

"He says it's broken, so you can keep it. I'm supposed to tell you he hopes that seeing it will give you a dose of perspective."

It gave me a lot more than that. Hope was tempting me with the promise of possibilities again. It offered a hand up out of despair. I leapt for it.

"Can you put those flowers back on my wall?" I asked.

I raised my medallion, going through the motions of Zavel's sleight-of-hand lessons to make it appear and disappear and warm up my fingers.

"Why do I get the feeling I'm going to live to regret this?"

"If it works, we'll both live to celebrate. Put them back."

"I don't like that glint in your eye."

Still, he put his hand back to the wall, and at his touch, it bloomed.

"Better?" he asked.

"Keep going," I told him, giddiness bubbling up. "Show off. I'm not in the mood for an audience."

I flicked my eyes to the camera above us.

Flowers spilled across the tables while moss turned the carpet green to the door. Vines crisscrossed their way to the ceiling. I'd never seen anything like it. Creepers made of blooming jasmine spun and curled onto the furniture. One of these had the misfortune of catching Xerxes' attention. He pounced on it, only to be lifted into the air as the vine rose. The poor confused thing grabbed on with all four paws, terrified, before he remembered he had wings. He let go and coasted into my lap.

"Does the camera pick up sound?"

"I don't think so," Birch said. "I can make them believe a leaf strayed over the lens for a minute or so, but any longer and someone will come in person."

"A minute's enough," I said.

Like all illusions, this required staging and timing. Birch had provided the former, so that if anyone was looking in, it would appear that he was trying to cheer me up by turning my cell into a fairy-tale grotto of ivy and roses. The timing came from Jermay. He'd taught me tricks over the years so we could steal sweets from Mother Jesek, but now those lessons were more than childhood mischief.

I tested my skills, attempting to flick the casing of the medallion open discreetly. It passed through my cupped palm, and was open and shut by the time it reached the other side. Plucking out the control circuit wouldn't be difficult at all.

"Is that magic?" Birch asked.

"It might be," I said. Hopefully it would make us disappear right under the warden's nose.

I set Xerxes off my lap, petting his head as I pulled up to my knees.

"If this works, I expect you to lose the ribbon," I told him, palming the control circuit from the medallion.

Sing Down the Stars

He obliged in scratching it off.

I took a page from my father's book and didn't bother to hide my hands when I fiddled with Xerxes' access panel. I ran through motions that anyone with a basic understanding of mechanics would recognize as pointless, while using the wardrobe's mirror to make sure my face looked frustrated.

Birch squatted down for a closer look at what I was doing.

With one quick swipe of my fingers, I extracted the faulty cartridge and replaced it with the one from the medallion. I let out an exaggerated sigh and closed Xerxes' panel again.

Failure and success in a single breath—I had to force myself not to smile.

I burned out the medallion by shielding myself and my friends from Warden Nye on the road, but the circuitry was still intact. Xerxes had plenty of power, but his command circuit wouldn't hold; that's why he was stuck small. My father's components were usually interchangeable.

Xerxes trilled beneath my hand. His eyes glowed, losing the glassy quality that overtook them when he was powered down. I could see my father in him again.

"Welcome back," I told him. "Play dead and stupid, kitty."

He rolled onto his back, kicking his feet in the air, then scampered over to his basket to play with the trumpet vines.

"What was all that for?" Birch asked.

"Do you remember the flying machine Nye stole from my father?" He nodded.

"Meet Xerxes." I jerked my head toward his basket.

Xerxes was taking my "play stupid" command to the extreme. He'd completely ensnared himself in a tangle of greens.

"That's what you've laid your hopes on?"

"Assuming the cartridge isn't too old, he'll be much more formidable when I need him."

"If you say so."

That might have been a sensible response from anyone else at any other time, but Birch followed his profession of disbelief by turning a wastebasket into a grapevine chair so he could sit down. In his hands, the wire mesh transformed. Vines knotted together into legs and a back, while the upended basket itself became the seat. Arms twisted up, lacing together at the seams, and leaves matted to form a cushion; there were even clusters of grapes hanging from the sides like ornaments.

He made no sense to me. He had power, yet he wasted it on decoration and party tricks. He treated the outside world like some dreamland he'd never see, and maybe that's what it was for him.

How could anyone accept that fate so easily?

"Will they really let us leave here?" I asked, unwilling to sit stagnant another second.

"Where do you want to go?"

"Anywhere they'll let you take me."

CHAPTER 29

We returned to the wheel. Most of the hallways now had identifying signs above them, but not the doors to the elevator. It said "Aerie—Off Limits."

Across from the wheel's outer window, the room of automatic personnel was more complete, with a quarter of the machines completely outfitted with skin and clothes. The mixing vat was now filled with something clear, like thickening agar used to grow bacteria in petri dishes. Every half minute or so, one of the lab-coat robots would press a button and send a shock through the vat. A few inches of the gel would drain into tubes that siphoned it off to parts unknown, then a funnel above the vat would release more to be mixed. I still had no idea what the setup was meant to accomplish.

I stared out the window for what felt like hours. It was busy, being the day's rush; small ships came and went, and I spent twenty minutes watching a technician fish for floating weather instruments with a long, hooked pole. Docked ships swayed with the currents of cloud-level winds strong enough to pull against the clamps holding them in place along the stationary outer ring of the Center's gyro. Men on tethers, wearing magnetic suits so they could scale the hulls, saw to repairs on the vessels' sides while others climbed rappelling lines to check for weak spots.

Most of the personnel I encountered avoided me, except the few I caught staring when my back was turned. They didn't know I could see them in the glass, and I didn't know if their looks were due to my ridiculous doll clothes or stories of my role in protecting the train and destroying Arcineaux's facility.

"Why do you look down when they pass?" I asked Birch.

"Protocol," he said. "We make them nervous."

"If anyone's nervous, it's you."

"Too much metal makes me queasy. Would you mind if we went somewhere else?"

I didn't, and I knew exactly where he wanted to go.

We took up our habit of walking the circuit around the greenhouse, only he was moving unusually fast, with his arms stiff at his sides.

"They didn't have a choice, you know," he said after a while.

"Who?"

"My family. Just because my parents couldn't buy my freedom, it doesn't mean I wasn't loved."

"That wasn't what I meant," I said. "But that thing—*Iva*—she's made to look like my mother. Every time I see her, my better judgment goes out the window."

"Warden Nye gave me a letter from them, when I was little. He wasn't supposed to, but he even let me keep it."

Our conversation became parallel confessions of our childhoods.

"I had a twin. He was taken at birth, too," I told him, without mentioning that mine was as dead as his. I wouldn't be the one to tell him his sister was dead. "Were you raised in a center?"

"On the ground." He nodded. "It wasn't so bad until Arsenic came. I actually had friends, but then there was an escape from the girls' side. I miss the ground. No roots in the air."

I knew how he felt. It was the way I felt about being near Anise. Now that Nye had confirmed my sisters were on board, our circle had a center again. If I could get close enough to her, I was sure I could use that feeling to pinpoint where she was being held and get her out. Together we'd be able to rescue everyone.

"Will you tell me where the prison is now?" I asked. "I'm not hiding anymore, and once Xerxes is ready to go, I'm not—"

Birch threw his arm out in front of me, and went still. I assumed he was composing an answer so he could dodge my request, but he ducked his head, moving in reverse until his back was against the rail. In the hall, it had been habit. This time, Birch was actually afraid. The hand that still held mine tightened painfully as he slipped his fingers between my own.

"Wha—"

He yanked me into the spot beside him. A door had opened at the end of the walkway, and a figure was headed toward us.

"Good afternoon, Warden Arcineaux," Birch said mechanically, never raising his eyes.

"What are you doing running loose?" the gargoyle growled. "Aren't there leash laws up here?"

Directed at me or not, I imagined retorts to give him, but fury choked them off in my throat. The restriction bands made my fist shake at my side.

"I'm helping her acclimate," Birch said quickly. "She doesn't know her way around."

Warden Arcineaux turned to me. His dark eyes hardened, and he took my face in hand, pinching my chin between his thumb and forefinger.

"So this is the Level-Five aberration? A freak's freak, eh?"

"Get off me!" I pulled back, attempting to free myself.

The planting ledges around us began to rumble, vomiting up their soil. Arcineaux flicked it from his sleeve. Vindication made me calmer, lessening the burn.

"That trick was more impressive the first time." He glanced from me to Birch and back again.

I spat on him.

It was something Jermay had taught me, and a habit Evie had tried to break me of for years. Jermay had said that any boy worth his trousers could spit at least three feet straight out; Warden Arcineaux was a lot closer.

"Penelope, no," Birch whispered.

Arcineaux wiped his face with his sleeve, then grabbed my hair, bending my neck backward.

"So close to the stars, and unable to call them down. You must be miserable," he said.

I started to lunge, only to feel a thin vine wind around my ankles, holding me flush to the rail. Birch patted my side, but I wasn't the loyal lapdog the wardens had turned him into. My hand came up and slashed Arcineaux across the face.

"I guess this fancy shellac is good for more than looking pretty," I said, wiggling my fingernails at him as he wiped the blood from his face. "You can thank your friend Nye for that."

I willed myself to stand tall, prepared for him to strike me. Instead, he turned to Birch.

"Speed up your lessons, boy, before *that* wanders into the path of someone with less restraint."

"Yes, sir," Birch choked out.

He held his position, not releasing his hold on my waist, or the vines on my ankles, until Warden Arcineaux had continued on past us and out the door.

"Are you all right?" Birch asked, once he'd determined it was safe to move.

"How dare you," I fumed, pushing him off when he tried to check my face. I was furious and humiliated, and I couldn't stand to look at him anymore. I wanted out.

"Wait . . ."

"Stay away from me!"

A knot of leaves appeared in my path; Birch slipped around them.

"Arsenic's poison, Penelope. He can hurt you. I've *seen* him hurt people—*my friends*. This girl . . . my best friend . . . she was a lot like you. Stubborn. Fearless. She refused to follow protocol, and he made her pay for it in blood."

"I'm not willing to become a sniveling spaniel to spare myself a few licks," I said.

"It's more than a few licks." Birch stopped to make sure there was no one in the room with us. Then he turned his head, and brushed the longest pieces of his hair away from his collar to show rows of jagged scars that had healed thick and ugly over the back of his neck. I could see the hint of more down his back, like the ones Winnie had. "I was lucky. Nye protected me when he could, but the others—"

"G-get out of my way."

This wasn't happening. I wasn't going to spend my life in a place where scars were proof of mercy. I forced my way into the jungle Birch had created, prying apart leaves half as wide as I was tall. There was nothing but green on every side—stalks as thick as my arm.

"Birch! Let me out!"

"Not until you listen to me."

The stalks bent outward, forming an archway to allow him through.

"You've ignored every single thing I've tried to make you under-stand, but you *will* listen to this. The scars on my neck are nothing. I've got others that are too humiliating to show you—that's thanks to the man you just spit on. Nye and Arcineaux were *both* in line for command here. Arcineaux thought he had the position locked, and he should have. He's a legacy warden with an uncle in the Commission office, but *you* cost him this post."

"I'd think it was more Warden Nye, considering he's in command and I'm under guard."

"Nye's nobody. After you wrecked the Ground Center, he was given provisional control here. Arsenic will hurt you for that, if he can."

"He's welcome to try."

"This isn't a game, Penelope! It's not a performance or a practice run. You don't get to go again if you make a mistake." Birch took my face in his hands and leaned in close. It was such a similar pose to the one adopted by both wardens when they were trying to intimidate me, and yet completely opposite. "Maybe the version of you I expected is a fantasy built off photographs, but like it or not, you've been my bright light for a long time, and I don't want to go back into the dark. I certainly don't want Arcineaux to put you there."

"I don't want to be here. I want—"

"Forget it! Forget your sisters like I've forgotten mine. Forget whatever life you had before here. Be Penelope, and lock Penn inside so they can't touch her. He can take things from you that you don't even know you have to lose."

He had tears in his eyes. He tried to scrub them out, but I saw them before he turned away and bid the plants recede to their former size and place.

"Come on," he said, taking my arm by the elbow again. "I'll get you back to your room."

No matter what Iva or the wardens, or even I, had assumed, Birch wasn't quite as docile as he made himself appear. He'd hidden his true self away, but maybe there was a way to help him find it. Then we'd both be free.

CHAPTER 30

Alone in my room, with only Xerxes and whoever was on the other side of that red light for company, I tried to rid myself of every trace of Warden Nye's pet creation. I wanted Penn back, but I was stuck. The dress wouldn't rip, and the scarlet nail polish wouldn't chip.

In the end, I ran around the room, screaming and tearing at anything I could, while Xerxes joined in the mayhem and tried to shred the rug with his claws. He was cycling through his programming more quickly now, progressing away from the tabby's temperament toward the gryphon's. It didn't make him big, but he'd already destroyed two pillows and unknit his basket's weaving, and I was fairly certain that the furniture was next on his agenda. The training routine triggered by resetting his power source was almost complete, and I was more than happy to share my tantrum with him.

Had I been back on the train, Anise would have told me to be sensible and stop caterwauling, and Vesper would have shown me how to throw a proper tantrum, whipping up tiny whirlwinds to do her bidding.

"I grew out of crying jags when I was seven," she would have reminded me. "That's when I put Papa's hats out the window because he wouldn't buy me a hyena."

She would've sent the coverlet spinning off to the ceiling and flung the pillows to create a blizzard of feather-down until we were three inches deep in winter white. The tea trolley would've been a victim, no doubt, because it would've made the most spectacular noise.

Taking a cue from my melancholy, the trolley began to rattle on its casters. The dish covers clanged, and the sugar spoon tinked against the bowl. The kettle spilled over, drip, drip, dripping into a puddle. And then the entire contraption raised itself off the floor, slamming against the back wall. The pillows flung themselves from the couch to land on opposite sides of the room, and the fibers Xerxes had scratched out of the rug took flight.

Vesper's powers had finally made their appearance, to match her face in the mirror.

Warden Nye had done worse than hurt me physically; he'd destroyed my dreams. I had my mother back, and she was a monster. I had my real face and a costume that was as beautiful as Vesper's, but I hated it. I was literally in the clouds, but I felt like I'd been buried under tons of stone.

I broke down sobbing on the floor.

There'd never been a time I didn't have someone to turn to. Someone always had the answers I needed. Now all I knew for certain was that I was on my own, in enemy territory, over which continent or ocean I had no idea, and someone was knocking on my door.

My pulse lodged in the notch behind my ear, beating harder as the room's light grew bright in time to the rhythm. I glanced at Xerxes; he was completely tangled in ribbons. He snapped his wings out, shredding the ribbons to confetti, braced his legs, and growled with as much menace as his miniaturized self could muster.

"Don't go showing off until we're ready to give them everything," I told him.

We might only get one shot. I didn't want him tipping our hand.

Xerxes fell over and meowed.

Another knock, and the knob turned. The man who entered was neither the warden nor my false mother, but he was no more welcome.

"What do you want?" I asked Greyor.

"I know you don't trust me, and I'm not going to tell you that you should, but if you want to see Nieva, you need to come with me. We have less than an hour."

I was at the door in an instant. Worst-case scenario, this was a lie and he was exactly what I assumed him to be, but if Evie really was here, and I didn't take this chance to see her, I'd never forgive myself.

"Even think of calling me Penelope again, and I swear I'll find a way to cut your throat," I warned. "Where's Nye?"

"I'll choose my words carefully, and Nye's playing host to some new arrivals. They'll keep him busy for a while, but you have to be back in your room before he sees you're gone."

In The Show, we combated fear by strangling it with a woven tale; in my head I did the same as we entered an elevator lift and dropped through the floor. I was Orpheus. Greyor was my guide, taking me into the underworld to bring my sister to the surface.

"What if someone sees us? I'm not exactly hard to spot in this ridiculous dress."

I looked like a storybook princess done up for a ball.

"None of Warden Nye's men would lay a hand on you, but stick close if you see anyone wearing Arcineaux's patches."

"I don't need a guard."

"Most here would agree," Greyor said. "They've all heard what happened at the train, and then the church. By the time it came to the raid on Arcineaux's compound, you'd become a legend in your own right, and legends are powerful things. There's nothing Arcineaux loves more than power."

"Don't you all?"

The lift bounced to a stop, but Greyor turned toward me before we got off.

"I've had to do things that left me sick for days while keeping a smile on my face, Penn, but I did them," he said. "Others do more; I can't complain."

As he left the lift, it sounded like he added something under his breath:

"If I do, I'm not the only one who pays for it."

Greyor steered me down a hall guarded by two men flanking a gate at the far end. Warning signs and regulations were etched on plates so numerous and close together that they became metal wallpaper. There were no water tanks on this level.

The guard on the left stepped forward, glancing between me and my escort. He was either naturally pale or Greyor hadn't exaggerated my reputation.

"Warden thinks she needs to see her alternative lodging choices," Greyor said.

The guard nodded, waving to his counterpart, who opened the gate with a key. I watched the mechanism on the back of the doors roll shut once we were on the other side, ending with the sound of heavy pins to hold them in place. One more impossibility between me and the outside world.

"The locks are magnetized," Greyor whispered. "Try to open a secure door without proper clearance, and it won't budge."

He pressed his hand to a plate on the wall, igniting lines of lights in the ceiling. The room was nothing but doors. They were metal, and mostly opaque, save for a viewing window that was round like you'd see on a ship, and arranged with the same tiered structure as the greenhouse. Was this the prison?

"I don't know when they'll move your people, but they won't be here much longer. We have to hurry."

We passed dozens of cells full of pitiable people. Old and young, male and female, all filthy with a crazed and starved look about them. One, I think was dead and not yet discovered, and another I refused to believe looked as much like Sister Mary Alban as a quick glance said she did. Halfway down, we boarded what looked like an open chariot that lifted us to a higher level.

"Why is everyone rocking like that?" I asked.

"The cells are filled with the sound of a ticking clock. The rhythm gets so ingrained that some forget to breathe when it's gone."

I stopped at another cell for a closer look, and couldn't decide if it would be better to find someone I knew, or to see a stranger and hope my family was somewhere better. The man inside stood tall, wearing his hat as though he were offended to be there. At his side, his hand twitched in a steady rhythm against his leg.

People didn't exist inside those walls; they were buried alive until they were dead.

"Where did they come from?" I asked.

"Places no one gets missed—streets and shelters, public hospitals and asylums. People are held here until they're needed elsewhere, and the more pliable their minds are when they get there, the better. The ticking's meant to break down each subject's mental faculties so they're easier to control. One stop, then Nieva. This won't be a happy reunion."

Before I could ask more questions, he waved me over to one of the porthole doors, and I ran to the window.

"Winnie!"

She was in a ball on the floor, with her face tucked into her knees and her hands over her ears, but it was Winnie, no doubt. She was still wearing the school dress that Sister Mary Alban had given her.

"We can't open it," Greyor said, as I slid my fingers over the door, searching for a handle.

I slapped the window and called Winnie's name again. When that didn't rouse her, I beat against the glass as hard as I could.

She turned around, cocking her head to the side, listening. When she stood, a new horror revealed itself. Like some twisted dream, the faceplate from her Siren costume had been fitted to her mouth. The skin around its edges had blistered, fusing to the metal.

Winnie tore at the plate with bruised hands that said she'd already failed to remove it several times. Her eyes were wild, unfocused as she tried to find the source of my knocking.

"Winnie . . ."

Her name became a tear-choked sob. She'd been so strong, and now she was this *thing*.

"The glass only shows through from this side," Greyor said. "I'm amazed she could hear you."

"Why is she wearing the rebreather on dry land?"

"Arsenic has a sick sense of humor."

"I don't—"

"Do you think your father granted mercy to random strangers?" Greyor asked in an accusing tone.

"She was an orphan," I said, but Greyor shook his head.

"And how many other orphans did he pass by? Why her? Why the little girl who was at the church with you, or the boy the hummers attacked who has them all on tenterhooks? Did you never ask?"

I'd never questioned my father on anything. Why would he lie?

"They're touched, Penn. They needed his protection. He promised it to them, and he failed them."

Winnie had made it to the door and was patting the surface with her torn hands. She tried again to remove the rebreather, but the plate over her mouth wouldn't budge without causing her to bleed.

"Winnie, don't! You'll hurt yourself."

But she was in a frenzy.

"You have to help her," I begged, keeping my hand against the glass.

"I don't know how." Greyor twitched his head and took my sleeve. "We have to go."

He towed me back to the chariot lift while Winnie fell to pieces on the other side of the viewing window.

"Your father has a flair for dramatic irony. He's never denied what his children are, save for you. It was no different for anyone else under his protection."

The simplicity of that explanation was startling. My father had built my sisters' act around their gifts, and he'd built a tail for Winnie. He put false fins on a real Siren. One who could make a man retreat with a few words, and one Arcineaux feared enough to gag. And Birdie? Maybe her gift was more than a knack for hiding. Maybe Mother Jesek was right and the little bird could really disappear. But what kind of touch was that?

I needed another crack at one of the Center's computers. Maybe I'd ask Birch to take me there next.

"Is Klok here?" I asked. "Or Jermay?"

Klok, they might think they needed to lock away, but Jermay wasn't threatening or violent, and he had no special gift unless peculiar eyes counted.

"Please, tell me what's happened to Jermay. Is he still alive? I know my sisters are here. What about my father?"

"Keep your voice down," Greyor said, opening the chariot. I trailed behind him as we emerged on a lower catwalk. "Your father is currently the most wanted man on the planet. He's not here, but I don't know

L. J. Hatton

about the others. I only found your friend because I knew what to look for."

"Why were you looking for Winnie?"

He didn't answer.

We passed into the deepest parts of the prison, and Greyor stopped at one of the largest doors. Unlike the others, this one was cold to the touch; extra locks lined its seam.

"She won't be able to hear you . . . and I had nothing to do with this."

Greyor's dreary mood soaked through my skin like winter's chill intent on striking bone. Foolishly I had hoped he brought me to Evie last because it would cheer me up, or even because it was in order of convenience, but somewhere in the part of me where I locked the things I didn't wish to think about, I knew better. Once I'd actually peeked inside, I knew that if I dreamed that night, it would be a nightmare come to haunt me with the image of my broken sister.

She sat crumpled at an uncomfortable angle, like a puppet with its strings severed. Her legs were bent in front of her; her arms hung limp. Her head, half-hidden by her unkempt hair, was oddly set atop her neck, with unblinking eyes and an open mouth. She was wearing a hound's collar.

"She's dead!" I screamed, scratching at the door.

There was an odd groaning in the metal—the sound of someone forcing a lock with an ill-fitting key. I felt the searing heat in my wrists, but didn't care. If I fought the cuffs long enough, they would burn through my arms and I'd be free, then I could knock the Center from the sky, and all its evil with it.

"Penn, stop!" Greyor's arms wrapped around my shoulders while his leg corralled my own. His head came down to press against mine with his chin until I was cocooned by his body with no way to move.

"Murderer!"

Everything became a blinding wall of white fire from the lamps overhead, surging to match the furious rush of blood through my veins. This was all a cruel trick. He'd brought me here to see them suffer. Somewhere down the hall, doors banged open to slam against the walls.

"Nieva's not dead," Greyor said desperately.

"Liar!"

He shook me until I stopped fighting him. The light receded, taking the pain in my wrists with it.

"Penn, listen to me," he said, now stern. "Your sister is *not* dead; she's breathing."

He shoved me at the window. Evie hadn't moved, but every slight exhale blew the hair nearest her face.

I couldn't stand up anymore. The adrenaline rush that hit when I first saw Evie through that window burned away and turned my muscles to mush; Greyor was the only thing keeping me from falling.

"Calm down," he murmured. "She's okay."

"No she's not!"

"She's alive," he argued.

His restraining arms turned into an unexpected embrace of reassurances to still the chaos in my blood. But I was vibrating with the same buzzing terror that accompanied the sounds of monsters in my room when I was a child. The lights flicked on and off. Doors along the corridor slammed open and shut, always in step with my racing heart.

"Rein it in," Greyor whispered. "Make it stop before it spreads farther than the prison and the wrong people see it."

Why? I wondered. All those nightmares, all those monsters. My father had come so quickly when I cried in the night—he must have known the only monster was me. So why rein it in, when I could let it run wild and destroy everything?

"Penn, stop!" Greyor ordered.

"No! I'll shake this place apart!" I barely felt the burn in my wrists over the hateful fire burning the rest of me. The ringing in my ears became the most glorious song I'd ever heard. It was the sound of the Celestine rejoicing as she was set completely free.

BRING THE RAIN declared all of those signs and posters nailed up in every hall. I could do that. I could fill the sky with dark clouds and burning debris. I could rattle the clouds with a sound more terrible than thunder, and make the Center rain down on the Earth below.

"She's alive, Penn," Greyor pleaded. "It's the collar. You're alive and so are your sisters. If you do this, it won't be the Commission that killed them, it will be you!"

Greyor's warning had the same effect my father's voice did when I was little. The doors along the corridor clicked shut, and the lights evened out. The Celestine's song fell silent.

"You're okay," Greyor said as I wept against his arms. I could see his face reflected beside mine in Evie's window. "I should have prepared you, but there were no words sufficient for this."

"Is she in pain?" I asked.

"I hope not."

"Why did you bring me down here?" I turned around, wiping my eyes. "I don't want to see this."

"Birch told me what happened with Arsenic in the greenhouse—it can't happen again. And what you just did, that can't happen, either. If you don't care about pain or death brought on your own head, they'll choose another target, and they will show no mercy until you break or they're out of alternatives."

"Would they release her if I gave up? If I went to Warden Nye and said I'd do or be whatever he wanted, then maybe—"

"No. I simply want you to understand—Nieva didn't. There's no middle ground, no compromise. You either lose your will to theirs, or you fight them any way you can, knowing you may lose everything anyway. You're strong enough to fight. If you didn't believe that before, surely you have to, now."

"Is that what you do?"

"I do what I have to," he said, cryptically. "Despite what you may think of me, I *did* try to warn her. She wouldn't listen."

"You should've gone to Anise. She would have."

When I followed Greyor out of the prison, I didn't glance at the guards, but kept my eyes on my feet, letting Greyor decide the route we'd take. I didn't have to feign the somber air that had replaced my earlier hopes.

CHAPTER 31

Back in my cell, someone had cleared the tea trolley and replaced it with a tray of magazines and books. The paper kind. They'd trimmed back the greenery on the ceiling, leaving everything else the way Birch created it—a pointed reminder that they intended to keep an eye on me through that red light above my head. A blue dress, identical to my red one, was hanging on the back of my door with a note reminding me that civilized people didn't wear the same clothes every day. I thought of burning the note, and the dress along with it, but then I thought of Greyor's words about doing unpleasant things for a better payoff in the end. Changing clothes was a small compromise; all it cost me was my pride.

Xerxes had hit a training routine; he kept running at the wall, jumping higher and higher with each pass, knocking flowers off their stems. I'm sure my ceiling-watcher thought he'd slipped a cog.

How did Birch stand this? I knew he thought monotony was "better than" his previous life, but that was a measurement too easily moved. If "better than pain and torture" was the only guideline for an acceptable existence, there wasn't much hope.

I flopped onto my couch and reached for the first book off the stack beside it. It was nothing special, and didn't even have a dust cover. It looked and smelled like someone had taken it from a high school library. I flipped the pages with my thumb until a sheet of paper fell out, but all it said was "A more appropriate pastime than pitching fits."

I hurled the book straight up at the blinking red light, but missed by two feet. The lights in my room flared. Metal devices groaned through the walls with my frustrations, creating another quandary. All it took was allowing my thoughts to stray back to Evie's broken-doll appearance in her cell, or a flash of Winnie's face and the deformity created by her rebreather, and an invisible vise clamped down on my wrists.

I focused on the books and let the sound of Vesper's laugh shift my thoughts into more pleasant territory. I thought of her owls looping through the air and breathed out my irritation in one slow, controlled stream. The pages rustled.

It was a start.

I took another breath, trying to maintain that rustling sound in my ears. This time, when I breathed out, a warm breeze moved leaves all over my room.

Better, but I needed something more spectacular. I needed wings.

I stared at the stack of books to get the pages moving, then imagined air slipping between them, flat as a sheet of paper. The book on top wiggled. I concentrated harder, picturing Vesper's feet walking up a flight of stairs. She could support her full weight with a thought; I should at least be able to manage a book.

The wiggle became a wobble, and then a jerk. One corner tipped up, and the cover flew open.

I stood up and leaned closer . . .

Knock. Knock. Knock.

That topmost book exploded into dust, creating a paper snow-storm in my room. Xerxes was unimpressed. He crossed his wings over his head to keep the flakes off while I went to the door.

"So close," I said, slinging my hand to curb the sting brought on by the thought of what I'd like to do to whoever had interrupted me.

I set my hand on the knob, suddenly terrified of the possibility that someone might be able to peek in on me the same way I had with Winnie and Evie. The red light was bad enough; having someone gawk at me like a chimpanzee at the zoo was worse. Was I destined to be a stop on some sightseeing tour for the warden's guests? The star in a real sideshow?

"I don't want to go back to the greenhouse, Birch," I said when I found he was the one at my door.

Greyor was behind him, dour and guarded. There was something familiar in his silence. The tones of brown that made up his hair and skin and eyes were set in a combination I'd seen before, like seeing a stranger walk in wearing a friend's clothes. It was the same and differ-ent all at once. Mainly it was his eyes. The way they were shaped, and how the creases at the corners held all the words he wasn't speaking. He looked away, and I realized I'd been staring.

"We've been asked to supper," Birch said, managing to make it sound like another apology. He definitely noticed the paper snow sift-ing out of the air, but didn't mention it.

"I'm not hungry," I said.

"Warden Nye won't like it if you don't come."

"Promise me he'll choke on a chicken bone, and I'll do the carving and fold the napkins."

"Penelope, please—it's important. All of the guests are here. They want to see you, and he can't say no. Neither can we."

His jeans and Commission-silver jacket had been replaced with finer things: a crisp blue shirt to match the patches of the men who answered to Warden Nye, and a tie with the Commission's ankh embroidered on it. It also matched the dress that I'd been given.

I wanted to tell Birch that the idea of sitting at a table anywhere near Warden Nye tied my digestive tract in so many knots I might never eat again. But as much as I loathed the idea of coming when called, enduring a meal meant fuel every bit as much as choking down Klok's charred fish-on-a-stick. Fuel now meant strength later.

I could do this. It was just another part to play. All I had to do was choose a voice, and I could be Nye's wind-up toy for the night.

I thought of that charred fish, remembered the smell and texture, and focused on the few bits of white still floating in my room. Each one sparked with a tiny fire and turned to ash.

"On with the show."

Twenty people sat in a dining room at a single table; Birch and I were directed to the far end. A lone tank of water matching the ones in the hall had been installed against the wall. Greyor became my shadow, playing the part demanded of him.

There were men and women, each in the dress uniform of a Commission official, each wearing their own patch and their own colors. No one looked directly at anyone else, but kept their heads at an upward tilt, so conversation required looking down. Other than that, it looked more like a dinner party at some fancy restaurant than a clandestine meeting being held miles above the Earth's surface. And I was the only one wearing a dress. I really, really missed my ringmaster's pants, ugly stripes and all.

Warden Nye's seat was at the head of the table, where my father had sat when we ate on the train, but he was up and walking around the room. The fake Iva Roma stood at attention behind his chair.

Birch reached for a water pitcher on the table to fill my glass.

"I can serve myself," I snapped, taking it from him.

He shrank in a bit.

"I'm sorry," I said. "I'm used to doing things for myself."

It was so difficult to remember he was innocent in all of this. He spoke and moved like one of them, but he was a prisoner, too.

"Did you dress them up for our benefit? Or is this how you usually keep house?" A man with a silver moustache and tightly trimmed beard spoke from a seat at the center of the table. He, like the other guests, had someone behind him in the position Iva held with Warden Nye.

"Ignore them," Birch said when I started to respond.

"Nye's just showing off his new acquisition," one of the female wardens offered.

"Oh, will she be showing off?" Warden Arcineaux asked snidely. "I do love a trick."

"I'll juggle knives if you want to volunteer as target," I said. "I'll even tell your future, if you don't mind bad news."

The woman down the table choked on her drink trying not to laugh.

"Manners, pet." Warden Nye pressed me down into my seat by the shoulders, half-warning and half-amused. "Arcineaux, play with your own toys."

I clenched my fingers around the arms of my chair.

"Isn't it customary to gift a guest the thing he admires most about your home?" Arcineaux asked.

"Keep clear of what's mine, or you will be admiring my home from its exterior, on your way down."

"You can't blame us for being the tiniest bit jealous. Your timing was impeccable," the silver-haired man said, smiling, though there was nothing joyous about his expression, or friendly in his voice.

"Near choreographed," Arcineaux added.

There was a storm brewing between the three of them, so close I could almost hear the crack of thunder. The moment turned so intense and concentrated in the triangle that the whole table jumped when another woman yelped, twisting in her seat.

"Is there a leak?" she asked, wiping at her forehead. Another drop of water splattered against her plate. She scooted her chair sideways. Warden Nye leaned toward Iva. "Get a technician to adjust the fire control systems."

She nodded and stalked out.

Warden Arcineaux was laughing, Nye was scowling, and the grayhaired man was surveying everything, as though a few drips had settled their argument.

"I think we've delayed dinner long enough," Warden Nye said. He reached over me and removed my dinner knife, then slipped it into his pocket. "Can't have you making good on the threat to throw this, can I?" He turned to Greyor. "No knives at her seat, or the boy's. He's housebroken; I'd hate to see you ruin him," he told me.

Nye's meaning was clear. He wasn't amused by my tricks. And my actions had consequences for Birch, too. Greyor reached down and took Birch's knife.

"And how are we supposed to cut our food?" I asked.

Half a chicken sat on my plate with roast potatoes and asparagus.

"I thought you traveling sort just dug in with your fingers and teeth," Arcineaux said. The others at the table snickered.

I twisted my napkin in my hands beneath the table, grinding my teeth when the burn from the restriction bands hit my wrists.

Even so, the chandeliers rattled.

All of the laughter and muted gossip stopped. Attention shifted from me to the shaking crystals that hung from the lights. Birch's hand slipped around mine in my lap.

Warden Nye discreetly pulled my hair as he left my seat. He raised his other hand, flicking two fingers.

"Check the stabilization system," he hissed.

Another guard hurried out.

"Two issues in one day," the silver-haired man tsked as he cut his food. "Not the best impression, under the circumstances. I'm tempted to change my vote."

"Trouble certainly does have a way of piling on when you least need it," added a bald man who looked more like a serpent than Nagendra ever could.

"Maybe it was a bird flying into the engines," I suggested, stealing the smirk off his face. If I ever made it to another computer, I was going after the personnel files. I didn't like not knowing my enemy.

Birch's grip changed, allowing his thumb to graze the back of my hand.

Warden Nye cleared his throat and plucked a wineglass off the table.

"Back on task, if you please," he said, and dipped the glass into the water tank. The others raised their glasses in response. "Today we stand looking down from the shoulders of those who came before, and they would be proud. Soon, the rain will fall."

He poured the water back into the tank.

"Bring the rain," the rest of the table chanted.

"What's that mean?" I asked Birch. He looked away to his dinner, smashing his asparagus to paste with his spoon.

"Bring the rain," Warden Nye said.

"Bring the rain," the others repeated, louder.

"Seriously, what's it mean?"

Birch mashed his potatoes.

"Bring the rain!"

Every repetition made those three words more chilling, like this was some dark litany in a sanctuary very unlike the one in that old stone church.

In the back of my mind churned Evie's words from before our final show: *You are Celestine, and they cannot hurt you.* I wanted to prove the point, but I wasn't sure who needed the reminder most.

I pushed a little harder, biting my tongue and squeezing Birch's hand. It felt like a hot blade had sliced through the bones in my wrist. My reward was every glass shattering in time. Water and wine flew out, flooding over the sides of the table and staining the white cloth the color of blood. The tank cracked, but its walls were thick enough to hold.

The officials' attention snapped back to me, their jaws tight and twitching as they leapt up.

"Must have been a really *big* bird," I said.

If I'd had a glass in my hand, I would have tipped it at them, but I made do with tearing the leg off my dinner and taking a bite.

"Not as fresh as what you catch on the run, but it'll do."

"Get her out of here," Warden Nye ordered.

I was still chewing when Greyor hoisted me out of my seat.

CHAPTER 32

"Are you actually *trying* to get us killed?" Greyor growled beside my ear. "Because I honestly can't tell."

He dragged me from the dining hall so quickly and so roughly that my feet caught in the hem of my dress.

"You're the one who told me to fight," I argued.

"Only because I made the mistake of thinking there's more than air between your ears."

The people we passed, guards and workmen alike, moved out of our way. Each face held a mixture of awe for Greyor's temper and fear for what they thought I might do in retaliation.

"You're not the first to overpower the restriction bands, Penn, but you're the only one stupid enough to show off in front of a room full of wardens and commissioners."

"But you heard them—"

"They were baiting you—*Arcineaux* is trying to prove that Nye isn't worthy of command here by showing he can't control one girl, much less a full roster. You *embarrassed* Nye."

We'd reached the doors to the Aerie lift, and Greyor still didn't release my arm.

"Why should I care?" I asked.

"Because whoever gets the Center gets *you*. You don't want it to be Arsenic and the men who stand behind him. They'd do worse than lock you in a room with ticking clocks and too much air conditioning."

The etched glass doors split, allowing us into the Aerie.

"If she ever regains use of her tongue, ask your friend what her life was like with Arsenic directing it."

"Winnie was Arcineaux's prisoner?"

"More like his crowning achievement. Ask her how she managed to escape and take half the girls' dorm with her. *She* cost Arcineaux his first post with that escape, and you cost him this one with your performance at the Ground Center. He wants it back."

If Winnie had been a part of the girls' escape that Birch spoke of, then they were in the same center. He was there when the horrors Winnie never spoke of were inflicted upon her. Birch was so obviously terrified of Arcineaux . . . Was that the source of his scars?

"Do you think they've done something to Birch?" I asked. "Because of me?"

"That's a question you should have considered before you opened your mouth." Greyor began to pace the room. "You really have no idea what's happening here, do you?"

"No," I said. "What'd they mean by 'Bring the rain'? What are all those tanks for?"

"They're what made you. You, and your sisters, and Birch, and every other person ever touched. Sit down." Greyor took a spot on the floor. "We need to talk."

They were breeding Medusae, or at least hoping they could. The tanks weren't only filled with water. Combined with what I'd thought was pink sand on the bottom, the water Nye had used for a toast would create an alien primordial ooze—some kind of plasma reconstructed from all the samples and tests done after the Medusae left.

Bring the rain . . .

It sounded so simple, but *simple* was like *impossible*—it meant nothing anymore.

When the Medusae pressed themselves into our atmosphere, it rained. It's a background detail in every story told about them, something added because it's habit, but not really important, and yet it mattered more than anything else.

That rain carried fragments of the Medusae themselves. It soaked into the ground and fell into the water, and for those with the right genetic makeup, it changed them. But unlike Sister Mary Alban, who encountered the Medusae as sentient light, for most the changes weren't immediate. For those who stood beneath the rain, the changes came in the next generation. The children were touched, but not the parents.

At first, the Commission had tried to cover it up, but there were too many. Then they tried to contain the special ones, fearing that they were harbingers of a second invasion—or worse, that the genetic sloughing was a form of reproductive branching. Maybe the Medusae had grafted their DNA into the touched, and these children weren't human at all. In fact, they could be sleeper agents.

It was decided that Earth needed an offensive force comparable to the Medusae's legacy. Gifted individuals that would be loyal to the Commission and humanity, not an alien force. And for that, the Commission needed a way to create touched children of their own.

More elementals were born every day, leading to the assumption that they were the norm. Level-Fives were outliers, and that's what the Commission wanted. They built the Center in the sky, trying to replicate the precise conditions of the Great Illusion. If they could crack the secret to what happened in the twin sets, they could create people like Birch, with abilities no one could predict. People like me, who shouldn't exist. They would have the power to defend the world, or change it. But into what?

That question, no one could answer, so people like my father created refuges to save the ones like Winnie who escaped the Commission's experiments, but had nowhere else to go. People like Greyor and Beryl found ways to watch from the inside and help those of us they could. I'd almost ruined that with my fit at dinner.

Warden Nye didn't join us immediately, or even soon. He made me wait. And maybe it was my imagination, but I would have sworn I heard the endless ticking of a distant clock.

Finally, the etched glass doors opened.

"When I told you to mind your manners," Warden Nye said, "you could have warned me that you aren't possessed of any."

"Did you really expect me to sit and listen demurely while they compared me to a trained chimp?" I backed away from him, leery of whatever he had in the hand he kept at his back. He followed, never granting me more than an arm's span of space. "You should be happy I obliged them in showing off a few tricks."

The hand he kept in the open lashed out, and the next thing I knew, I was on the floor with a throbbing cheek, marveling again at how much stronger he was than he looked. I glanced at Greyor, but he had assumed his "at attention" stance and kept it.

"I could show you a trick or two." Nye leaned over me.

"What are you going to do? Lock me up? Fuse my mouth shut like you did Winnie? I don't care! I'd rather be in prison than here with you!"

"And I'd like to know how you know about that."

"Then it's my pleasure to disappoint you—was that polite enough?"

Warden Nye dragged me up with one hand until my feet were no longer touching the floor.

"One of Arcineaux's ghouls muzzled your friend. I've not yet found a way to remove the plate without ripping her mouth open."

He dropped me back to the floor.

"You turned my sister into a hound!"

"*Warden Files*, of the Midlands, not me. And for that you can thank your father. If he'd kept his promise, she wouldn't even be here. You can also thank him for this."

He brought his hand out from behind his back, allowing me to see an open circlet of glass and metal—a hound collar.

"I think a dose of reality will do you good."

"No, please . . . Please, Greyor. Please don't let—"

"Silence," Nye ordered, snapping the collar around my neck.

It fit my throat perfectly, and in the instant the circuits on it closed, my voice stopped. The words continued in my head, screaming until I went hoarse from the inside out, but no sound ever made it to my lips. Invisible fingers held my mouth so tight my jaw wouldn't open.

"Come along, pet."

Warden Nye took my hand, and I trotted after him to the other side of the lift column. Chairs and a small table were waiting as though there had been an earlier gathering that no one had bothered to clean up after. The same tablet I'd snooped through lay on the table.

"Have a seat."

My legs bent and placed me in the nearest chair.

I thought I'd felt pain from the restriction bands, but the collar was nothing but needles turned inward. Every time I tried to disobey, they plunged deeper into my throat, sending a shock to the tips of my fingers and toes. The only way to stop the pain was to do exactly as I was told and not even consider another option.

"Let me tell you a few things while I have your attention."

Nye removed his coat and set it over one of the other chairs. He unbuttoned his sleeves and began rolling them up.

"I met your father on Brick Street, during my trial by fire—did he ever tell you that? No. Of course he didn't."

What I knew of Brick Street was that it had been a thoroughfare of restaurants and shops that people traveled hundreds of miles to visit. No matter what you wanted, or where it came from, chances were it could be found there.

But that was before.

Now, nothing was left. It was there that anger and desperation had boiled into the streets as blood and violence, seven years after the Medusae appeared in the sky. Most people said it was a riot that flashed into existence due to mass hysteria and mistaken assumptions. A crowd had organized a protest in hopes that it could force the Commission to release all of its findings on the Medusae. Whatever started it, it ended in fire, and it was remembered only in a children's rhyme set to a cloverleaf.

Brick Street was where Nagendra began to hide himself inside tattoos and piercings so he couldn't be known on sight. And officially, it never existed as anything other than the scorched and rubble-filled husk it became.

"I know my superiors like to play at forgetting what happened there, but my reminders are a bit more difficult to shove into a closet."

Warden Nye peeled off his gloves, revealing his hands. Wires dipped into the skin near his wrists. Where use and repeated motion had worn away the coverings, tiny pistons showed through at the joints on his fingers. One palm was a mass of exposed optical line.

He crouched in front of my chair, wiping the tears I couldn't blink out of my eyes. They'd started to burn, but I couldn't close them; he hadn't given me permission.

"You know there's only one man capable of producing something this intricate." He flexed his fingers.

An immediate rebuttal formed in my mind, and was just as quickly demolished by the plunge of those infinite needles into my neck and the shower of splintered ice along my nerves. That was all it took for the version of Magnus Roma I had known to warp.

"Stop fighting it. It'll only get worse until you do." Warden Nye thumbed another tear away, then stood and paced to the wall. "I was young, and foolish enough to think that I could make a difference. I actually thought we were there to help. If not for your father, it would have been my final mistake."

He turned back to me with a cryptic half smile.

"And if not for me, you would have been born in a center, like your new friend with the green thumb."

Even denial of his words brought a wave of nausea. Something warm and wet ran from my nose. I was certain it was blood, but couldn't look down to check.

Warden Nye twitched his head at Greyor, who came to wipe my face with a handkerchief. When there was no way for Nye to see the shared look between us, Greyor's eyes turned heavy with regret.

Be strong, he mouthed.

"I was part of an information dispatch sent to placate the crowd. My partner and I were expecting hundreds, but there were thousands. And neither of us anticipated the children."

The warden kept talking in a distant drone, spilling the forbidden details of a day that had been erased. He reached toward the table beside my chair and picked up his tablet, swiping through images he didn't let me see. When he found the ones he wanted, he turned the screen toward me, showing me images of the day the world forgot.

"So many of them had children by the hand or on their hip— *touched* children. They'd come looking for answers, you see. Hoping we'd provide more than a few diagrams and a lot of double-talk. It was sweltering that day. Tempers flared, and the screaming didn't help. The little ones started to cry."

He found another image on his tablet and turned it back to me. I could see him as his younger self, scared and unsure on the verge of chaos. Young Nagendra stood beside him in matching uniform.

"They went off . . . We thought it was bombs at first, terrorists, but it was the kids. Fires erupted. Water pipes burst. The ground shook, and then the wind . . . We had no idea the mutations were that powerful. By the time I caught my breath, the street was a crater and I was half-buried in the remains of the building I'd been standing in front of. *All from kids.* None of them over seven. But I knew from that moment, my superiors wouldn't consider them anything but biological weapons."

He shivered. I would have sworn I saw tears, if I'd believed him capable of them.

I tried again to turn my head, searching for Greyor in the room, but it was still no use. I couldn't even move my eyes. He forced me to sit through frame after frame of devastation and loss.

"In the middle of it all was Magnus doing what he does best, every bit as careless with it as you are. He and my partner were among the few who had the foresight not to bring their children to the gathering. If your sisters had been there, I'm sure he would have been preoccupied with getting them to safety. Alone, he could focus on the crowd. He took trash in his hands and made excavators to find those lost in the rubble. He created devices that could set bones and seal split flesh, his fingers moving so fast I couldn't follow the motion. I'd never seen an adult with such abilities before—or a male. I should have reported him, but my thoughts were elsewhere."

The warden brought his hands up from behind his back and examined them. He pumped his fists and turned them over as though this were the first time he'd ever seen them.

"They were crushed and burned beyond use, and I was in so much pain I could hardly see. Your father noticed me shortly after I did him.

I've often wondered why he didn't just kill me rather than risk exposure. It's what I would have done."

That statement I had no problem agreeing with, and a rush of cool relief washed over my body; the collar had registered my response as obedience. Warden Nye placed his tablet back on the table.

"For my silence, he offered me new hands, but accepting such an arrangement would have meant compromising the few principles I'd managed to salvage, so I proposed a different one. He'd cooperate with the Commission, tell us how he gained his unique mutation, and use it for us; that would buy his safety and my future. In return for using my new position to protect his family, all I wanted was one small favor."

I was sobbing on the inside. This was my father's tale turned sideways. Warden Nye painted my father as someone groveling for the chance to breathe free air and begging the Commission to take his inventions instead of his children.

"I've known who you were since the day you were born, and I've protected you longer than that. You see, *you* were the favor he owed me. His machines bought him time; my silence bought me a Celestine."

No! Nye was a liar, and if he wasn't, then the promise had to have been a ruse. My father's every move had been to protect me and my sisters. He wouldn't have willingly handed me over to be used by the Commission, especially not to this man.

New pain exploded down my spine for the argument. It was so intense I would have blacked out, but the collar kept me conscious. Warden Nye returned to my chair. His intent was a mystery I couldn't figure out, not when I couldn't focus on a single thought before it was driven out of me like a hammer hitting a nail.

"When it came time for him to honor our arrangement, Magnus chose the coward's end. Had he followed through, your sisters would still be tucked safely in their beds on board your train. Your friend with the golden voice would still be swimming in her tank. He could have kept them all, but he was a greedy fool, and now you're suffering for it. And if Arcineaux convinces those who've gathered here to speak on his behalf when they return to the ground, your suffering is only beginning."

He wrapped his hand around my throat, over the collar, and lifted me from my seat. I could feel myself strangling from the pressure, but only managed to raise my arms a few inches before the pain was too much. They fell limp at my sides while Nye headed for the control panel on the wall.

"You need a new perspective, pet," he said.

With his free hand, he pressed his thumb to the controls, and the room began to move. Wall panels turned to shutters, flipping out to stack on top of one another. They retracted first around the ceiling, then the main sphere of the room, revealing nothing but clear glass behind. The entire structure was a bubble floating above the Center.

"They stopped right up there," he said, looking to the sky. "That's why this spot was chosen. To replicate the rain, conditions have to be as close as possible."

One of the glass panels slid back, creating an open-air platform; he walked us to the edge, forcing my legs to dangle over the side.

"Take a look around," he said, and at his words, I could.

The world spun beneath my feet in a maelstrom intent on dragging me to the depths.

"To the men and women you just went out of your way to insult, you're a control specimen, and nothing more. Any one of them would have you collared and locked in a lab for study."

Warden Nye's tone turned dark and somber as a new ship docked. A retractable metal arm clamped down, keeping it securely in position.

"I can send you back to Earth right now—call it euthanasia. It would certainly be a kinder end than allowing Arcineaux to have you."

My attention split between the pain of fighting the collar and the fear that Nye really would drop me. Over his shoulder, I could see Greyor twitching nervously, but he couldn't risk helping me.

"Where's your fire, pet? Where's your spirit? Go ahead—speak your piece."

"Please don't . . . Let me go. No! Don't let go. Don't drop me . . . please."

All my anger and ranting, none of it mattered. I had promised myself that I would curse him with my first free breath, and instead, all I could do was beg. My threats to kill myself lost all their weight.

I wanted to live.

"So easily broken," he said, shaking his head.

He stepped forward, so my feet were now as far beyond the edge of the platform as his reach. I closed my eyes, wondering how long the fall would take, and if I'd feel it when I hit the ground.

As my mind spun with the possibilities, I took notice of the wind. It was howling now, making my dress flap. The more attention I gave the wind, the stronger it became. I opened my eyes. The men who had left the new ship ran back to it, grasping at each other's hands to stay upright. The ship pitched against its clamp and broke free, tumbling toward Earth until someone inside got its engines running.

Vesper, I thought. *Help me.*

A gust picked up, as solid as a hand shoving my shoulders, so that I fell toward the Aerie and Warden Nye toppled with me.

We landed in a heap, with me on my side. Greyor ran forward, now that he had the excuse of helping the warden. Nye reached for me. I felt his hand on my throat again and anticipated a sharp snap that would stop me forever, but instead, my arms and legs began to thaw.

"Is this the life you want? Will it make you feel less guilty for doing as you're told? If so, I'll put the collar back on."

I turned my head and saw the collar, open in Nye's hand as he stood over me.

"N-no." I shook my head, but my whole body was trembling while I tried to get enough control over my own limbs to prop myself up. In those few minutes under the collar's influence, my reflexes had been rerouted, and everything took longer to accomplish.

"Never force me to use this *abomination* to make you reasonable again. If it goes back on, it doesn't come off. Take her to her room," he said to Greyor.

Nye clicked the collar shut and went to close the Aerie's dome, while Greyor scooped me off the floor and carried me out.

CHAPTER 33

I was so relieved to be leaving the Aerie alive that I didn't notice Greyor wasn't taking me to my room. Our destination didn't fully register until I saw the jungle's worth of plants on the other side of the door.

This was Birch's room.

He jumped off the couch.

"I can give you ten minutes," Greyor said, pushing me farther into the room, while he stayed outside. "You need a friend right now, not a flying toy cat in an empty room."

I ran to Birch. After Warden Nye rewrote my history and nearly took my future, I needed to know someone cared what happened to me. Xerxes would have made me feel better, but it wasn't the same as having a pair of human arms wrapped around me as if they would shield me from the world.

Birch was so surprised when I grabbed him that he rocked back, but he held on.

"I was going to wait in your room, but the warden forbade it," he said.

He was warm and solid, and I breathed him in with every sob against his neck. No residue of exploding powder like with Jermay, but a rustic scent of bitter leaves mixed with flowers and berries still on the vine. In my time at the Center, the wardens had very nearly succeeded in making me feel less than a real person; Greyor's detour gave me a chance to remind myself they were wrong.

"He collared you, didn't he?" Birch asked.

I'd never been comfortable around any boy besides Jermay, but it seemed impossible that I hadn't known Birch just as long. I grasped him harder.

"I crumpled," I said. "The second he took it off, I crumpled."

"Everyone does."

Birch tightened his arms, and I let him. He spoke into my skin, turning each word into a stolen kiss.

"I thought he was going to kill me. He said he'd rather see me dead than under Arcineaux's command."

"Arsenic's taking command?" The comfort in his voice turned to pure panic.

"They haven't decided yet . . . Birch, what did he do to you?"

"Nothing you'll ever hear me explain," he said. "No need to spread the nightmares around."

Something happened each time his mood shifted. Every plant bloomed when Greyor first opened the door. When Birch was apologetic, they wilted in sympathy. But at the mention of Arcineaux, and the possibility that he would become master of the Center in the sky, thorns as thick as railroad spikes burst out. The comforting jungle became a dragon with too many teeth.

"How did you do that without triggering these?" I asked and raised my wrist.

Birch shot a look at the door to make sure it was shut. We were still near the couch, so it was easy to maneuver back to it. He blew a puff of air toward the ceiling, and one of the plants unfurled a new leaf, covering the red light.

"They hardly ever watch me anymore, but if someone notices, I'll tell them I was trying to impress you and got carried away."

He grinned as he snapped off one of the giant thorns and held it out.

"Stab me," Birch said.

"What?"

"You want to learn? Stab me."

I recognized the confidence in his voice, so I wrapped my hand around the thorn and jabbed it into his thigh. He winced in pain, swallowing the yelp.

"I'm sorry! I thought you'd stop me."

"And *I* thought you'd go for my hand." He batted away my best attempts at triage.

"Your leg was a bigger target. Why didn't you stop me?"

"I couldn't," he said. "And that's the point. None of us can use our abilities to protect ourselves; it's how the restriction protocol is designed. That's why they think they have the upper hand."

"You could have just told me that! Are you okay?"

He laughed at me.

"You're adorable when you're worried," he said, and all my concern drained away.

"I still have the thorn, Root-rot."

"I surrender," he said, teasing. "I'm better than most. For some, the protocols stay in place even if the bands are removed. Arsenic found a way to embed them permanently."

"On the girls?" I asked.

"On my friends." Birch rubbed the back of his neck. A cluster of thorny spikes fell from the ceiling, sticking fast in the floor, and a new crop of short, white flowers appeared along the rug. They looked suspiciously like hemlock.

Now it made sense why Winnie hadn't saved herself from Tuck and Bull—she couldn't. All she could do was tell them to walk away, and that wouldn't even work on Tuck because of his bad ear.

"Try again." Birch changed the subject, laying his palm against the table. "You won't be able to, I promise."

Reluctantly, I slashed the thorn toward Birch's palm. Halfway there, it morphed, and wrapped around my wrist as a delicate flowered chain.

"What—"

"I can't stop you from stabbing me, but I *can* decide to make you a bracelet from a thorn," he said, very pleased with himself. "These"—he raised his wrists—"register emotion. Control what they can see, and they're not much of a deterrent without the collar." Birch laid his hand over my wrist, turning the bracelet back into a thorn, which he threw aside. He waved his hand and the leaf curled away from the surveillance light in his ceiling. "Unfortunately, it doesn't work on the restriction bands. I've tried."

"But there are other ways," I insisted. "Fill the engines with chrysanthemums, and you could bring this whole place down."

"And then what?" Birch got off the couch and started collecting the wilted leaves and thorns that had formed and fallen during his lesson, dumping them in his wastebasket. "Everyone dies—including us. What good is that?"

"Then do something less drastic: Fill their clothes with poison oak. Run pollen through the vents and leave them sneezing. Anything to prove you're a real person, and not some robot that can only do what he's told!"

"I *can* only do what they tell me." I saw that raw spark in him, again, but it faded quickly. "I'm *afraid* not to. I'm *afraid* of the pain, Penelope."

This time, I was the one following him. It was a circular game of chase that never ended as we moved around the room.

"Please don't hate me," he said sadly. "I can't stand it."

"I don't hate you, Birch, but I can't sit here pretending this is okay—it's not. Nothing you do or say can change that."

"What if it could?"

"Birch—"

He shushed me, biting his lip as he glanced around the room. He placed his face beside my ear, so close I thought that he might really kiss me this time, and whispered: "I know where they're keeping your brother."

CHAPTER 34

Greyor's promised ten minutes ended too soon, and he refused to spare me even a second longer. I had no chance to explain to Birch that my brother was dead.

"If Nye checks, you have to be in your room," Greyor said. "Another show of defiance would be a disaster."

So the good little prisoner returned to her cell, and Birch promised to come and get me when it was safe, despite Greyor's warning that we shouldn't be prowling around when he wasn't on shift. Hopefully Birch didn't mean some point in the distant future when Arcineaux was no longer underfoot.

Greyor escorted me to my own room, but the empty hall was too easy to fill with unpleasant scenarios of what could go wrong. I had to speak to distract myself.

"Was Nye lying about who put Evie in that cell?"

"People like your sisters could end droughts and stop floods. They could clean the air around factories, or raise new farmland, but people like Warden Files only see them for their destructive potential. Fear of fire is primal; he wants to wield that." He kept his eyes forward. It was a peculiar habit of people in the Center. They never looked at anyone when they spoke.

My poor Evie.

The gift that had brought squeals of delight to countless children who loved watching Samson jump and play would now be a curse drawing screams of agony.

"Warden Files was the bald fellow at the table," Greyor said. "I didn't know she'd been assigned to him."

My heart was breaking into smaller pieces each time some new horror smashed against it. If not for the stays inside my dress, my heart would have crumbled like powdered glass and landed at my feet. If I'd never known how close Evie was, losing her again wouldn't have hurt so much.

"What about Winnie?" I asked. "Will Arcineaux take her with him?"

"He'll try."

What I knew of Arcineaux made me just as certain, but there was a new determination in Greyor's face I hadn't seen before.

Life was so much simpler when the Commission was a single, massive monster, but on the inside, it was full of parasites chewing away at the whole.

Back in my cell, a lifetime passed for every minute I had to wait before Birch came. I tried distracting myself by helping Xerxes train, using random objects in the room for targets, but I couldn't concentrate well enough to keep them in the air. After I dropped the third book on his head, he stomped to his basket in a huff.

"Sorry," I offered, but he snapped his wings closed over his back and shut me out, stubborn as my father.

I was back to worrying that Birch might regret saying what he had, and that he'd lose his nerve or run confessing to Warden Nye. Could I trust him to keep his word when he said he wouldn't hurt me?

I clutched at my throat, imagining the collar back in place.

It was after midnight before Birch finally appeared. The guard who had replaced Greyor for the night tromped along behind us, not daring to say I wasn't allowed out of my room.

"Where are we going?" I asked.

"You'll see." Birch was like a kid in a strange school, doing something reckless to impress a new friend.

We took the path through the glassed walls of the wheel. The night was clear and bright, with the moon framed by the window. It had whittled down to a barely there sliver. Stars gathered, twinkling around it, and in the distance a tiny streak flared and died. I made a wish; Evie needed all the help she could get.

"You're prettier than your pictures," Birch said.

He'd stopped with me, while I gazed out the window into the endless blank of a sky with no upper limit, and no ground to be seen below. The moon's light made our skin glow. It caught his hair where red specks turned to gold near the ends and turned his eyes to the sort of glittering emeralds stolen from idols in adventure movies—every bit as green as Jermay's were blue. The golden flecks of lace that covered my hands and underpinned my gown glittered beneath the blue.

Illusion was becoming more real than reality.

"It's the dress mixed with lack of sleep," I told him. "Lime trousers and pinstripes don't flatter anyone."

I shook my head, took a deep breath, and started walking again. Penn wasn't beautiful; she looked like a boy. She was uncomfortable in dresses and blushed when Jermay said she looked pretty.

Penn hated Penelope.

"Keep moving, Root-rot," I said.

When we reached the greenhouse, the guard stayed outside. My reputation had grown since supper, and no one was certain of the protection afforded them by the restriction bands. The doors closed behind us, and Birch finally relaxed, letting out a breath.

"I was afraid he might try and come in," he said. "We'd have been sunk."

"What are we doing here? You said—"

Birch held a finger up, then pointed it sideways. One of the trees bent toward us; he stepped onto the closest branch and held out a hand for me.

"Private lift," he said with a grin.

"I've been on this ride before," I said. "It didn't end well."

"Would you believe that was a malfunction?"

"No."

"I think you proved there's no point in stranding you."

"Then what—"

"There are many reasons I love this room," he said. I let him pull me up beside him, and the tree began to move, shrinking down in a spiral until we were beside the catwalk of a lower level. "And you're the only one who knows them. They guard the elevators; no one cares about trees."

The floor we came out on was metal, like the others, but this one had a bluish tint to it, as though it had been exposed to high heat, or a chemical wash.

Birch ducked back against the wall before we crossed into a connecting hall, barely missing the pair of guards on patrol.

"Security's higher down here," he whispered when they'd passed. "Watch your step."

They'd created a paradox for him. The rules had to be obeyed, but the real Birch was fighting his way out of his own subservience.

"Birch . . ." I said cautiously. "Do you know your twin's name?"

"What's it matter? I'll never see her." His voice turned hard. "The warden told me they don't keep birth pairs together. It's too dangerous."

An oddly compassionate lie, kind of like giving a sad little boy a supposed letter from his parents.

"I never knew my brother's name, either. He died when I was born."

Birch stopped with a confused scowl on his face.

"He's dead? I must have misunderstood."

He plucked one of the clips out of my hair and laid it against the wall. Its teeth sprouted vines and leaves, snaking up the bare wall toward the ventilation shaft at the top.

"I heard them speaking about a Level-Five from the circus. I assumed they meant your brother."

A large trumpet blossom opened on the vines between us, and Birch pressed it toward my ear. Voices came through, grainy and distant like a degraded recording.

"That's Arcineaux!" I clapped a hand over my mouth and whispered, "Is that really him?"

"He must be in Warden Nye's private rooms. I listen in on him all the time," Birch preened. "No one knows it, of course."

The voices through the trumpet started again; I set my ear closer.

"Nye's been wrapped up in Roma's world for years! I don't believe he never noticed there was something off about that girl! He's up to something, and we'll all be worse off for it."

Arcineaux was furious.

"Let our host wager his life on his temperamental prize," a female voice added. I was pretty sure she was the woman who had sat beneath the leak when I lost my temper. "In the end, she'll cost him more than his position. The other assets on the table are far more stable."

"Agreed." That was the voice of the silver-haired man who had been so antagonistic. "I'd say lady's choice, but—"

"Not necessary," the woman cut in. "I've already secured the hydrokinetic. That leaves two. Any preferences, or does it come down to Rock, Paper, Scissors?"

They were handing out my sisters like cigars after drinks, and the mystery woman had taken Nim. I choked on a sob. Birch tried to take the trumpet from me, but I curled over it to keep it from him.

"Do you recognize the voices?" I asked softly, but he shook his head.

"Wardens don't bother to introduce themselves to me."

I needed Greyor. If the wardens left before I escaped, names would be the only way to find them.

"While it seems an odd idea to bring filth into one's home," the female warden continued, "I've seen terrakinetics find veins of precious metal in dead mountains—or level them. And the wind-walker? I've had men offer three months' pay for a look at mine."

"I want the Singh girl. She's a menace, but she's mine, and she was with the prisoners when they were captured; my man saw her. He was preparing to have her transferred into my custody when Nye hid her away. She was in active study; I want her back!"

"Take what's offered, Arcineaux," the silver-haired man warned him.

"Fine," Arcineaux spat. "I'll settle for the dust mite, and the next time Nye sets foot on solid ground it will be my pleasure to watch her bury him."

"Make it stop," I cried. "I don't want to hear any more."

The trumpet and its vine dissolved, leaving me with a clip of withered leaves.

"Arcineaux's taking Anise, but I don't know the other two. I'll never find them, Birch."

"I'm sorry. I wanted to help, and now I've made it worse."

With my worry over Anise and the others, I'd nearly forgotten Birch's mistake.

"Can we still get to him?" I asked.

Whoever he found wasn't my brother, but that didn't mean he wasn't someone worth finding. If Birch really heard the warden mention another Level-Five, that made whoever he found an asset.

"I'm going to regret this, aren't I?" he asked.

"If we're lucky."

CHAPTER 35

Birch truly had no idea how remarkable he was, and once he figured it out, I wouldn't be the one the wardens had to fear. The boy Arcineaux delighted in intimidating could move at will through the Center's securest areas by lifting himself into the ceiling vents. He did it too quickly and too easily—no way was this the first time.

We crossed a heavily secured floor inside the air system, watching through a grate as a trio of men hovered around a body with a view screen for a voice box.

"Birch! You're brilliant!" I wanted to laugh and cry at the same time. I kissed him on the cheek.

"You know him?"

"Klok's part of The Show." And definitely an asset.

He was in much the same state Evie had been, only clusters of hornet-shaped hummers stuck out of his body. I was quickly losing hope for Jermay and Birdie.

"Any progress?" Warden Nye demanded below us.

"If you'd allow us to remove the impediments—" a man in a white lab coat began.

"Not until we know its limitations. It's a machine; you're a mechanic. Figure it out!"

"It doesn't have systems like any machine I've ever encountered; they're nothing like Roma's others."

The man in the lab coat nodded toward a set of bins full of mechanical bits—apparent remnants of Scorpius and the Constrictus. The head of a dead-eyed unicorn sat on a back shelf with a hole where its horn should have been.

"There are no external ports, no visible sources of power. Its access panels, if they exist, are completely integrated. There are no seams."

"Then make some." Warden Nye reached for a small, round-bladed saw on the workstation.

"I can hardly believe it was made with human hands," said the second man in a lab coat. "The design is so complex . . . if I didn't know better, I'd swear it was *born* this way."

The saw fell from Nye's fingers to crash back onto the table. His face twisted in concentration, fixed on his own hand. It took several seconds before his fingers obliged him in flexing. He picked the saw up again and turned his wrist, testing it.

"He's worn them out," I breathed.

Birch shot me a confused look.

"Nye's hands are metal. He's worn them so long, they're wearing down." And without my father, he had no one to repair them.

Nye stalked into Lab Coat Two's space, stopping inches from the man's face.

"Roma's hardly human. He was protecting this thing for a reason, and I want to know what that reason is."

"But, sir . . ." Lab Coat One said nervously. "I think . . . I think it may be alive."

"Open it up, cut it apart, and give me a report on how it works, or I'll have someone open you and report that, instead!" He tossed the saw to them and stormed out.

His habit of throwing knives made more sense now. He was testing his hands, trying to maintain control even as they failed. A warden with wounds that severe wouldn't last a day past discovery, and now that he had Klok, he thought he had the means to repair himself.

"They meant my father, not Klok," I whispered, closer to Birch's ear. "He was the one you heard them discussing."

But I had no idea what Nye meant by his being "hardly human." Or why Birch would have heard him called a Level-Five. My father was a human man with a human sister. What else could he be?

"I'm sorry . . ." Birch said.

"Shh. I think they're leaving."

The two lab coats, now terrified, left the area without touching Klok's body. He was piled against a cabinet, half-sitting and half-falling over.

"Can you get me down there?" I asked.

Birch wrapped his hand around the grate, and it turned from steel to pliable bamboo that we were able to peel back far enough that I could pass through.

"I still don't understand why you stayed here, especially if things were so awful on the ground with Arcineaux."

There wouldn't have been a door or lock capable of holding him.

"I couldn't leave," he said seriously. "I was waiting for you."

He gave me a peck on the cheek, quickly, with a nervous blush, before another thin vine lowered me silently to the floor.

I crept over to Klok, turning his face so I could look in his still-open eyes. A stalled clicking sound came from his display, but I placed a hand over it to hide the light.

"Don't try to talk," I said. "Can you blink for yes?"

Blink.

He looked so helpless. His hair was a mess, his arms and hands lifeless at his sides. With his shirt open, all of the fused pieces of metal and wire were clearly visible across his torso. Brass bars traced his collarbone, joining in the center where glass tubes disappeared into his skin. More bars undergirded his ribs, but he'd lost so much color that his scars were barely visible.

"Are you in pain?"

He closed his eyes tight.

That was a relief. I'd never thought of Klok experiencing pain. He'd been as real *as* a person to me, in the same way Xerxes or Scorpius was real, but not *quite* human. Realizing I made that distinction was hard to face. I was no better than Warden Nye or Arsenic.

"Did you hear what they said about you?"

Blink.

"Are you scared?"

Tears burned my eyes as his blinked again.

"I have to get you out of here. They've got Winnie and Evie in cells, but I haven't seen Jermay or Birdie."

The vine beside me began to move, trying to get my attention.

"You have to go," Birch said from the vent. There was a sound in the corridor.

"I can't leave him!"

"It'll be worse for us all if you don't."

"I don't know what to do, Klok. What do I do?"

He rolled his eyes up, toward the vent, then turned them to the vine.

Tears were definitely coming. I took his face in my hands.

"You've never lied to me. Say you'll be okay, and I'll know it's true."

His eyes flicked down to the cluster of hummers in his chest. One melted into him. He was integrating them into his own construction.

"Penelope!" Birch jerked on the vine.

"I'm coming," I promised. "Be careful, Klok."

I kissed him on the forehead as the vine grew tired of waiting and folded me into a leaf. I slipped through the bamboo grate just as the men in lab coats returned; Birch turned it back to steel.

"Requesting special equipment will stall the warden for a week, but after that, we're sunk," said Lab Coat One.

"Destroy it." Lab Coat Two picked up the saw. "We can tell him Roma rigged it so no one could reverse-engineer another." He flipped the switch on the side, starting the saw spinning.

Birch had to pin me down to keep me from going back through the grate. My wrist was burning. There was no glass to break this time, but I shorted the overhead lights, causing them to flicker ominously. The power socket that the saw was attached to began to smoke and spark. Lab Coat Two dropped the saw and jumped away. We were too far from the windows to see falling stars, but I could hear them screaming out their song.

Lab Coat One reached for the saw and turned it off.

"Looks like we don't need an excuse," he said. "If the power systems need debugging, then we can't afford to risk running any kind of diagnostics. It might ruin the results, don't you think?"

"I think I don't want to try the warden's temper when it's already near its end, but I'd hate to waste something so spectacular."

"So we see what happens, and save the self-destruct as a fail-safe."

Lab Coat Two nodded. They powered down all of the machines in the room, leaving Klok in the dark, but unharmed. Another set of tiny glowing eyes went out, devoured by Klok's wiring.

My sisters always said I underestimated Klok. It seemed as though Nye and his minions were doing the same. Hopefully, it would be their ruin.

CHAPTER 36

We were back inside the greenhouse, chatting with our feet dangled off the catwalk, before anyone came to check on us. It seemed safer that way. If we'd rushed out, the guard might have been suspicious.

"I didn't know a person could live with that much metal in him," Birch said.

"Klok's unique."

I was beginning to loathe that word.

I concentrated all of my focus on a feather tree, until I'd created enough of a draft to send a plume of pink wisps skyward. Soon I'd try creating a golem of my own, something small, like Vesper's owls.

"I can't let him die, Birch. He's family, and I never even realized it." Inside, something started gnawing at me.

"Families are complicated."

"I miss them," I said. "Not just my father and sisters, but Nagendra, the Jeseks, Squint and Smolly—"

"Jermay?" he asked.

"Yeah, him, too. You'd like him; he can pull flowers out of thin air."

"He's like me?" Birch's face fell.

"He and his father do a magic act . . . *did* a magic act . . . for The Show." Thinking of The Show in the past tense made the gnawing worse.

"So it's not real?"

The way Jermay could make me laugh when I felt terrible was very real, as was the way he could make me feel better if things were too serious for laughter, just by taking my hand.

"Does this make me a magician, too?"

Birch reached behind his back and produced a bouquet that would have put Zavel's best efforts to shame, grinning as though he'd done something spectacular.

"You wouldn't understand," I said sourly, and the bouquet wilted. The branches around us began to rustle, pitching petals like an angry mob with rotten fruit. Birch yelped and grabbed his wrist. The noise died down, and he looked away, ashamed.

The Show was family, but Jermay was more. I *missed* my family; I *ached* thinking of the void left without Jermay's presence.

"I'm sorry," Birch said. "I'm not trying to make you upset. You're the first friend I've had since the Ground Center. There was a girl there, but I haven't seen her since the escape. I don't know if she's even still alive, and now you're here, and—I'm sorry."

The magnificent foliage around us drooped.

Light poured in from the hall. Our guard approached, looking frantic, then confused when he saw we were exactly where we were supposed to be.

"I've got her," he said, touching an earpiece. The guard nodded along to whoever was on the microphone end, saying "yes," then, "They've both been here for an hour."

"Is something wrong?" Birch asked.

"Back to your rooms." The guard pointed toward the doors with his weapon. "Curfew's in effect."

The guard took Birch to his room first. It was an unceremonious stop, with the guard practically shoving him inside and slamming the door.

"What were you two doing in there?" the guard asked me.

"Birch likes trees. He was trying to teach me their names, but I'm hopeless. I thought brown things on the floor were called palm cones."

"That's all?" the guard asked, suspicious of my airhead act. Maybe not my best choice.

"Sure. Why?"

"Keep quiet and keep moving."

He pushed me forward through the glassed-in breezeway. The moon was still shining, but the eerie serenity of it had been broken by motion. In the distance, streaks blazed across the sky, and closer up, men in high-altitude breathing gear swarmed the outer platforms, putting out fires from ruptured gas lines and tying down cables to stabilize pontoons and walkways. A gaping hole had appeared in one of the catwalks, nearly cutting it in half.

So I guess that's what happened when I thought the lab coats were going to dissect Klok.

"That bird from supper must have come back with its flock," I mumbled.

"Quiet," the guard said, and shoved me again.

One day, I wouldn't have to guess. Crippling the Commission wouldn't be an accident; it would be a surgical strike.

No one bothered me for two days; but Birch didn't visit, either, and my door stayed locked, only opening for food to be sent through. Each day, I'd get a new dress, identical to the previous ones except for the colors. After the blue dress, I put on a gold one, then I exchanged it for green, always feeling like a giant toddler was about to rip my ceiling open and reveal the Center's true identity as her dollhouse. Sometimes when I checked the clock, it seemed like we were going backward.

I'd felt the same shift in energy the night we lost The Show. It was the sense that some unstoppable and unavoidable change was on its way.

I dreaded each moment that passed, knowing it was one less chance to save myself and those I cared about. I didn't know if Winnie or Evie were still locked in darkness. I didn't know if Warden Nye had grown impatient and Klok had become nothing more than blood and wires heaped together for disposal. I had no idea how fast Klok could integrate the rest of the hummers, or how long before someone noticed there were fewer than there should have been.

Xerxes was my bright spot. The circuit from Sister Mary Alban's medallion was still functioning. I put on a show for whoever was watching through the burning red eye in the ceiling, but my games with my little golem did more than fill time. I tested Xerxes as far as I dared.

I tested myself, too.

I was one weapon who'd grown tired of misfiring; the problem was that fear and anger were my strongest fuel sources. I'd been striking back in retaliation, which is what the restrictors were calibrated to block. I tried to set fire to my pillows or call water down from the sprinklers, but it always ended in pain and frustration. The entire first day was a series of failure-induced shocks brought on by my planning unkind ends for the wardens. I had to stop thinking that way, or I'd remain my own worst enemy.

"Happy thoughts. Calm thoughts," I told myself as I took the water pitcher from my tea trolley and set it on the floor. "Think of home."

I sat cross-legged in front of the pitcher, placing my hands on either side, and pictured Samson lighting torches with his tail. He was leaping in the bonfire. Evie reached her blazing hand out to me; I took it and opened my eyes. Bubbles rose in the pitcher as the water inside began to boil beneath my gaze. It reminded me of how Nim's laughter burst like froth on a moving stream when she was happy.

Would she ever be happy again?

I wanted to destroy the Commission for what it did to us. . . .

The restriction bands stung, but eased off when I turned my thoughts away from revenge and back to The Show.

Beneath the bubbles, the water churned, defying its own nature to rise in a spinning column, rather than sink into a whirlpool. It launched into the shape of a shimmering sailfish with scales that caught the light.

Xerxes couldn't resist. He scattered the fish to drops that fell to the floor and soaked into the mossy carpet. It startled me into a fit of giggles.

I'd created a golem.

Trembling, I raised my hands as I'd seen Nim do every night during my tour when Winnie's part was over. The water beaded up, leaving the floor dry. I lifted my hands, and the water rose, creating an outline of the sailfish that quickly filled in with scales and fins. It tracked my hand, following my lead back to the pitcher, and poured itself inside.

I glanced up at that flashing red light and grinned with as much malice as I could find.

"Gotcha," I said snidely. Let the ceiling watcher see me—what did it matter? The stronger I became, the less likely the warden's people would be able to stop me.

A twitch of my wrist summoned the sailfish back into existence, launching it up to shatter nose-first into the ceiling. It stormed back down, accompanied by wind and lightning that formed right there in the middle of my room—the perfect weather to match my mood.

But wielding so much power was as exhausting as running a marathon in weights. Creating that sailfish left me too tired to even get off the floor; I fell asleep leaning against my wardrobe and woke in the same position to the sound of Xerxes growling at my door.

Someone was knocking. I heard the lock click and the door opened.

"Grey—?"

Greyor shook his head before I could finish, but it was only a slight move. Unvoiced panic chiseled into a stone face he couldn't allow to crack. Warden Nye was over his shoulder.

"Walk with me." Nye pulled me from my room, tucking my arm into his the way that Birch did. He flicked his fingers toward Greyor, who fell in step behind us.

The tanks lining the hall didn't look like they were filled with plain water anymore. The contents had a pale pink cast and were nearly gelatinous. The alien primordial plasma had fully formed.

"Are we going to breakfast?" I asked.

"With your table manners?" the warden said. "I don't think so."

We passed the dining hall. People in the corridors kept watching us, then turning away to whisper.

"Where's Birch?" I asked.

"Up a tree, I would imagine."

"I want to see him."

"And I wanted my Level-Five installed without alerting any of my contemporaries. Now we're both disappointed."

"I'm not *your* anything."

Except maybe his prisoner, which was exactly the fate I was afraid had befallen Birch. The word of one guard who had left us unobserved for over an hour wouldn't be enough to convince Nye I'd had no part in the damage done the night I found Klok. He'd obviously used the collar on Birch before. If he did it again, and asked what happened that night . . .

"You could be my greatest asset," the warden said. "And I could be your greatest ally. Both are hard to come by in this life."

"For someone who claims to disapprove of my father and his methods, you certainly sound a lot like him. He collected assets, too. Only he didn't need cages to keep them from running off."

"The fact that his prison ran on rails didn't make it less confining."

We turned a corner at precisely the right moment to see one of the tanks filled. A technician flipped a switch, and clear, pink liquid flowed in from a venting system. He was nowhere near it, but still wore a face mask and gloves.

"Interested in our aquatics?" Warden Nye asked.

"Not in the least."

"You're slipping, pet. The girl I used to know could weave words into a golden fleece."

"You don't know me—you knew Penn. Penn was a boy."

He opened a door I'd never tried. Behind it were halls I didn't know. They had no tanks and weren't the cold monochrome of the rest of the Center. Instead, they were wallpapered like a house, with rugs on the floor. Paintings filled the walls, alongside posters from The Show. Most startling was a family portrait of my mother and father with my sisters around them, and me as an infant wrapped in a blue blanket on my mother's lap.

"Why do you have this?" The picture was so perfect I knew that if I could touch their skin, I'd feel it soft and warm beneath my fingers.

"I collect the things that interest me," he said, twisting to look down at my face.

I pressed him away, hard as I could, but whatever defect existed in his mechanical hands proved intermittent at best; Nye was strong as ever.

"This was created by someone very much like your father. Someone who had to learn that his abilities had higher uses than his own."

Every step I took with Nye toward the painting, my mind ordered me to keep struggling, but this was a minor battle not worth fighting. His ways were indirect, and whatever this scene was, it was sure to prove only a lead-in to whatever grander scheme he had in mind. There was no sense exhausting myself when there was no real danger.

I reached out, allowing my fingers to hover just beyond the pigment.

"Touch it." Nye forced my fingers flat against the folds of my mother's painted dress, but rather than canvas, I felt lace. He slid my hand down to the end of my father's shoe, and I was touching leather. I brushed Evie's hand and felt a rush of warmth. Nim's hair brought the scent of salty sea breezes. Anise came with the scent of freshly turned earth, and Vesper was a breath of air.

"What sort of trick is this?"

"No trick," he rasped in my ear. "Just a man with a gift to paint his subjects' true natures."

I tried to pull back, curl my fingers into a fist so I could skip the image of my infant-self, but Nye pressed harder, and my hand covered the baby's entire face. An explosion went off against my skin. Fireworks underwater and fire below ground, air that carried ash up high to mingle with the rain. The clear sensations of my sisters' gifts muddied and mingled until I couldn't tell one from the other, and they all ended with a night sky that ignited along the horizon, backed by the distant clack of metal parts and grinding gears.

"Wondrous, isn't it?" Nye asked. He wouldn't let me move, and the strangeness of the painting kept shifting as though it couldn't make up its mind about me. "A body could stand here for hours and soak it in. In fact, I have. Before he was discovered, the boy who made this was creating trinkets to sell on roadsides for pennies. Now he has a priceless legacy."

"Which is it—priceless or worthless? We can't be both." I turned to face him, even more uncomfortable when I couldn't see him.

"The vessel's only value is in its contents. And *you* hold great value to me." I wished he would try to crush me, so I could stand my ground and bear it defiantly, but his fingers stayed loose around mine, merely lifting my face so I had to look at him. And I still felt drunk from whatever effect the painting had on me. "All this time, I had the answer to a question I never knew to ask."

The hall turned stifling. There were only walls and paintings and ceiling and floor. No doors or windows. No escape, and I knew Greyor couldn't help me, either.

Warden Nye removed his hand, and to my embarrassment I stumbled once I was free.

"Come along, pet. There's something you really must see." Nye clasped his hands behind his back and continued down the hall.

CHAPTER 37

The hall curved at the end, forming an alcove.

"I think you'll find this room familiar," Nye said, opening the door.

It was the office I'd been in when I first arrived, now unpacked. Set up like a library, the whole thing was a disturbing approximation of my father's office on the train.

Nye sat down in a large green chair. I stepped barely beyond the door, which shut once Greyor was clear of the threshold. Here the glass tanks had animals in them. Snakes in the first; I wouldn't indulge him by asking if they were Nagendra's. Next came a fish tank, with actual fish. Then mice, baby ducks, a tank full of scorpions, and an inert Bijou. He'd re-created the Caravan.

Nye wasn't a collector; he was obsessed.

The walls were decorated from the looting of our train and arranged to match different exhibits. In one case unpolished jewels and their shinier counterparts, all neatly labeled, lay in rows. These had been showcased as natural wonders of the world, taken as tokens from the various regions we had visited.

Noble crests and flags formed an arc around the door, gifts my father had been given by former hosts. Some were sent from overseas as enticements to visit. All stolen by Warden Nye.

In the spaces between, weapons filled the gaps—swords and daggers, balls of spikes chained to handles, whips with hooks on the ends. Every one was a testament to brutality that had no place among my family's memories.

"What do you think?" the warden asked.

"That you're a thief and a liar." Neither of those things surprised me.

"I'm a preservationist."

Greyor entered the room, so silent I could have believed he was a hologram again. He edged to the side of the office, settling in a spot beside the sofa and table where I'd snuck a look at the warden's tablet during my first visit.

"This is where I review security issues," the warden said. He flipped a switch, which turned on the screen I'd seen transform into a holographic projector before. It was divided into many parts, each with the image of a different room from the Center.

I recognized Birch's room from the plants, and my own, where Xerxes had his front half stuck under the wardrobe while his tail flicked in the air. In the dining hall, Birch sat alone, pushing his food around his plate and not eating. Arcineaux was either gone or out of frame, but the camera angle showed three other wardens at the table. None of the cameras showed the prison or the lab where Klok was being held.

"Can you show me my friends from here?" I don't know why I indulged the hope that the warden would help me, but I saw those screens, and all I could think was that they could show me Jermay and the others. "Let me see them, please."

"Would that make you happy?"

"Yes," I said honestly. "Show me they're alive, and I won't give you any more trouble."

"That's a promise you may regret," he said.

He keyed in a sequence of letters and numbers, and the squares on the screen changed. Birch's room was replaced with an image of Winnie in her cell. My room became Evie's. The dining hall turned to Vesper, who was in a cell, but unrestrained. She sat in the corner, shivering, with her wig pulled over her face.

"When our incoming guests began arriving, I was pulled away from my usual duties here. There were no reported incidents, so I thought everything had progressed smoothly."

He keyed in another sequence, and the image on the screen became my room alone.

"No! Where are the rest of them?" I demanded.

"If you want to know, remember your promise."

I glared at him, but clamped my mouth shut.

"Close enough. I'll give you two."

Anise and Nim appeared on screen; they were in the same state as Evie.

"Why are you doing this to them?" I demanded, reaching for the screen.

"Leverage has its uses," he said, and turned the screen back to my room. The recording began to move in reverse, faster and faster until lines formed between the frames.

"After considering your performance at supper and the surprise—"

"Bird attack?" I guessed when Nye paused and looked back at me to supply the answer.

"As you say. Then the incident that cost us three exterior mooring stations—"

"Three?" I'd only seen the one.

"The damage was quite extensive, and distinct. So I ran a trace on your tracker to see what you'd been up to." He glanced at the ring on my hand. "Care to see?"

He brought up a video feed of my room. The on-screen image slowed in the moments before Greyor came to take me to the prison.

The tea trolley that had flung itself against the wall turned upright, and the water from the kettle dripped up off the floor to leap back inside.

"This sequence kept me up for hours, going back and forth, back and forth, between this recording and that marvelous painting in my hall. I knew I was missing something obvious."

Nye stopped the recording during my fit, and started it forward through the flying trolley. He changed the view once more, so it was split between that recording and one taken of my success with the sailfish.

"You're getting stronger."

"I got angry, then I got bored, so what?"

"I had no doubt you were responsible for the exterior damage, but I'm more interested in what took place *inside*. You went exploring."

"You said I could."

Saying that was like eating sweets laced with poison. It was an acknowledgment that he had the authority to tell me where I could and couldn't go. Worse, it was an admission that I might *not* have gone against his orders.

"True," he said. "But you took an unconventional route."

One more command left us with a real-time view of that high-security lab and Klok. He was alive, but not moving.

"You've been keeping secrets, pet."

Nye's smile in the stark light of the recording screen was a grotesque thing, otherworldly and awful. I began tugging on my hair behind my back. I stepped away in the only direction not blocked by furniture and ended up colliding with Greyor.

"It's more than just the elements, isn't it? It's more than your being able to channel electricity." Nye took one of my hands and turned it over in his own. "You've got more than your sisters' touch—you have Magnus's, don't you?

He backed up the video feed of Klok to the night I snuck inside, and watched me kiss him good-bye. Thankfully, the camera angle didn't let him see the hummers being absorbed. A few seconds later, I was out of frame, the technicians were back in sight, and the power was going haywire.

"Whatever you did to that machine masquerading as a boy, my technicians can't unravel it. He's impenetrable. You altered your father's tech in two minutes with your hands, no tools, and a kiss on the forehead. That's a Level-Five skill, and it's one I intend to see put to use."

He flexed his fingers.

"But I didn't. I only talked to him. I can't fix your hands."

"And I thought we were past the lying stage." He smirked. "Or maybe you honestly don't realize what you can do."

At his command, the screens stopped receiving from inside the Center, and instead showed half a dozen shaky, amateur phone and tablet videos that had been uploaded online. Every one of them was a different angle of the table Winnie and I had shared with C. B. and Rye at the charity stop, and every one showed the creepers' strange actions that night as they all flocked to our part of the alleyway.

"Such a delicate vessel for so much power." The warden's thumb traced the lines on my hand as though he were reading my palm. He straightened my fingers from their natural curl, pressing all the way to the ends. "It seems like it should consume you from the inside out."

"What are you doing?" I asked.

"I should be able to break you as easily as glass, and yet you're what I need to save myself." His fingers circled my wrist, over the restriction band, and squeezed. "I couldn't imagine why your father would risk so much to keep you from me, but if he knew . . ."

The pressure on my wrist increased. His eyes twitched up, locking on to mine without a trace of the distant contemplation that had coated his voice in the previous breath.

"Let go," I said.

"Make me."

I tried to twist free, but he'd left me no room to move.

"Not like that. *Make me* release you."

He cued up an empty cell on-screen.

"Prison's no threat to me," I told him defiantly.

"It's not empty," the warden said. "You won't see the child, but she's there."

"Birdie?" I touched the screen. There was no outline or shadow, but I knew he wasn't lying. Birdie was doing what she did best—*hiding*.

"We've seen some interesting variations, but she's our first invisible girl. Do you think your Birdie would flap her wings if I had her thrown from the station's rim?" Nye asked.

"No . . . please . . . She's just a little girl."

At my back, Greyor's breathing sped up. I could feel his heart pulsing through the fabric of my dress, though he maintained his posture.

"The garbage has to be taken out once in a while, *Chey-chey*."

His baiting threats to my family and friends had taken me to the edge, but hearing him turn my family's endearment into a slow, mocking drawl forced me past my limits—and those of the restriction bands. Sand in the cases behind him started to churn.

Smash him! Hurt him! Break him!

The desire to inflict pain screamed inside me while spiraling tendrils of power reached for anything they could get a solid grip on. But rather than showing fear or caution, Nye was excited.

Smash! Break! Shatter . . .

The beat of blood against my ears turned to the sound of something pounding against glass and the rattle of metal.

"You can do better than that, *pet*." His thumb took up its path across my palm again. "You have the ability. You have the strength— make me." He wasn't even blinking. "Keep your promise, and do as you're told. Or I'll force it out of you."

One last time he reached for the screen's controls, and changed the image to Jermay. He was here! His face was bruised, and I could see the stains from his bleeding nose and lip, but he was alive!

"How strong are you, Celestine?" the warden asked. "Can you stop the flow of blood in someone's veins? Can you take the air from their lungs? Are bones close enough to rock for them to shatter on your say-so? Could you burn him with his own body heat?"

"Stop it!"

"What say I put that shiny collar back on and find out?"

Something tore loose inside me. I screamed from the pressure against my wrists, and then louder from a feeling like stones ripping through my body. When the moment passed, a rock the size of my fist had imbedded itself in the wall over the screen after shattering the reptile enclosure it came from. A jeweled necklace with stars made of diamonds sliced so close to my arm it ripped my sleeve before coming to a stop in Nye's chair. Greyor hit the floor beside me, face-first, to duck a hail of stones that had hurled themselves sideways at the blight of a man who held me prisoner.

"Look out!" Greyor cried, and covered his head.

Nye released me; I dodged as an ancient sword whose hilt was topped with a magnificent gem hurtled straight at his face. He caught the sword out of the air.

"Remarkable." He held the sword out before him, horizontal to the floor, as though testing its heft and balance. "Anger and instinct."

"Was that . . . was that me?"

I glanced from the sword in his hand to the screen, and back. Nye had an eager anticipation about him, unrestrained to the point that he was nearly hyperventilating. The maniac was smiling again—that same frozen mirth that had nothing to do with joy.

"It can't be." Greyor moved closer, staring in awe.

"I told you she was something new," Nye said. "The first viable Level-Five female. Let Arcineaux and the others scramble around trying to create power perfected. I've already found her."

"I won't help you," I insisted.

"Yes, you will. You'll do it for *him*."

Like he'd done with the film of my escape from Arcineaux's compound, Nye pulled the feed from Jermay's cell into the center of the room as a life-sized holographic projection.

"You'd let him go?" I asked, eyes blurring. I walked around the hologram so that Jermay and I were eye to eye. I reached for his face, but couldn't touch it.

Still, he raised his head as if he'd felt something.

"Safely to the ground, released anywhere you like. I'll even have Greyor escort him."

"Birdie, too. And Klok and Winnie."

"I'll give you the child, but the machine is too valuable. As for Winifred—" Nye's tone stayed conversational, bordering dismissive.

"She goes or you can forget it."

"It's not a negotiation."

"No, it's not." I forced myself to turn away from Jermay and face the warden. "I may be my father's daughter, but I am *not* him. I don't make deals with lives that aren't mine. All or none."

"Then you are definitely making deals with lives that aren't yours."

He didn't understand at all. Jermay would never agree to let someone else stay a prisoner so he could be free.

"This hologram, is it the same system you use to create the unnoticeables?" I asked.

"Same neural projection technology, different pathway."

"Neural projection like my father's traveling coat?"

"Similar, yes. Why?"

Because he was right about instinct triggering my abilities, and before it was destroyed, my father's coat could take me anywhere I wanted to go, if I could picture it in my mind. Every instinct I had wanted Jermay. I wanted to hear his voice and have him hear mine. I closed my eyes and imagined that we were only as far apart as we appeared in that office. All that separated me from him was a curtain thinner than the ones I pulled for The Show. I pulled it back and stepped across the threshold.

CHAPTER 38

A clock ticked softly in the background.

"Jermay?" I said carefully. "Can you hear me?"

Up close, his wounds were worse than on camera. He favored his left leg in a way that made me wonder if it had been broken.

"Penn?" He leaned toward me, but wasn't sure enough to follow through and take the step. "Are you real? You look fuzzy."

He tried to touch me, but our hands couldn't connect.

"I'm unnoticeable. It's the only way I could see you."

His eyes lingered on the bands around my wrists.

"Are you . . ."

"It's okay," I said, crossing my arms so my hands were out of sight. "I don't know exactly where you are, Jermay, but we're in the same facility."

Just in different kinds of prisons.

"Did they hurt you?" he asked.

"You're the one who's limping."

"You should have seen the other guy." He tried for a laugh that turned into a cough. "The fight was only about thirty against four." He got quiet, then asked, "What about everyone else?"

"My sisters aren't good. The warden wants to dissect Klok. Birdie's hiding, and Winnie . . ." I couldn't tell him about Winnie. He had enough dark thoughts without adding that image to them. "I can get you out. The warden promised that if I—"

"Don't you dare!"

Jermay jumped forward so fast that his leg wouldn't hold him. He grabbed for me as he stumbled, and I reached for him out of reflex. Our hands brushed each other as he crashed down, but I definitely felt him.

"Did you—?" he asked.

I lowered my hand with the pinkie out. He reached up and hooked it with his. Impossible or not, I could feel Jermay. I grabbed him in a hug more fiercely than I'd ever hugged anyone in my life.

"How?" Jermay asked.

"I don't care," I said, wondering if I could pull him out of the cell and into the room with me. "I'm getting you out of here."

"You can't make deals with him, Penn. You can't trust him."

"We're in the air, Jermay, miles and miles above the ground. We need help. You and Birdie reaching the Hollow is our best shot at getting it. You have to find my fath—"

My head spun. I couldn't even finish the word.

"Penn!"

I was on my hands and knees, unable to focus on him anymore. I'd held the connection too long; it was more than my body could handle.

"Penn!"

Jermay tried to get an arm around me to pull me up, but I was intangible again. His arm went through me. "No, Penn! Come back!"

The cell began to blur until I couldn't hear Jermay, only the clock ticking. I blinked and I was back in Warden Nye's office, collapsed on the rug, shaking and freezing cold. The hologram of Jermay was still soundlessly screaming my name.

I stretched out my hand, pinkie up, and held it inside his until my arm grew too weak to keep up. It crashed to the floor, and I blacked out. Again.

Losing consciousness wasn't like falling asleep. Sleep was a pause; losing and then regaining consciousness was being dragged into darkness against my will and restarting my own body. I woke gasping. My frozen thought process slammed into disorientation, trying to reconcile a room that looked like my father's office with the presence of Warden Nye and the still-broadcasting hologram of Jermay's cell.

Jermay was tucked into a ball in the corner and couldn't hear me when I called his name. I tried to stand up, but fell off the couch instead.

"Not so strong a vessel, after all," Nye said. He dropped me back on the couch where I'd started.

"Strong enough to save him," I said.

"Is that a 'yes,' then?" Nye asked.

He held his hands toward me. I took them, and reached out with the instincts I'd been raised to suppress to find the rhythm of the current flowing through his arms. I could hear the eroding circuits stutter and feel the groan of pathways on the verge of collapse. This was a lot more complex than getting a creeper light to mimic finger drumming. His components were as sluggish as muscles in atrophy; they didn't *want* to move. Wires and fiber bundles rolled like contrary veins evading a needle stick.

"Behave," I growled at the tech. "Get back in line."

The proper alignment appeared to me as a blueprint highlighting each malfunction.

I willed the fluid lines to bypass the burnouts, and realigned his joints by begging, all while trying to keep myself from slumping back into the abyss. Finally, the warden's hands matched up with the natural flow of blood through his body, and I let go.

"They still need replacing, but it's a patch. They'll work. Take Jermay home."

A spray of floating dots shuddered across my eyes; I closed them so I wouldn't fall on my face again.

"I imagine things like this get easier. You just need a pass through the fire, to harden your edges," he said. "And you're about to get it." He buttoned his sleeves back around his metal parts and turned off the hologram. "You should have taken the offer when I first made it."

So much for the man who refused to lie.

"I can tell them to never work again," I threatened, but the bands on my wrists disagreed. A white-hot flash of pain reminded me they were still there.

"Empty threat, pet, but mine wasn't an empty promise. I'll release the boy and the child when their safe transport can be assured. This is not that time."

The room spun again, shuddering wall to wall; the sofa tried to pitch me off. This wasn't me—something was wrong with the Center itself.

"We have a gyroscopic stabilization system," Nye offered.

"I've seen the rings."

"They've been disrupted."

The door opened, allowing Greyor back inside. He had his hand to his earpiece.

"Understood," he said. "Move three to the main doors. Quarantine the nonessentials and face-check each ID. Seal the vents; they're unsecure." He looked at me for that last part, like it was my fault their stupid installation was built with vents big enough for airplane props to spin inside. "Turbine seven's dead," he told Nye. "Eight's about to join it. Four through six are at seventy percent and falling fast. The rest are holding steady behind the secondary firewall."

"He's into the power systems, then. It's not physical damage—Iva can fix it."

I wasn't sure how long I'd been out, but it was long enough for something scary to have happened. The overcharged anticipation of doom I'd felt before the train was lost had settled in the air, and both Greyor and the warden had reached the tipping point of trying not to panic. They were about to fail.

"I could—" I started.

"You could do a lot more than exhaust yourself," Nye snapped. "Trying to handle something as complex as this facility could burn you out for good. You aren't strong enough yet, and I won't risk it without using up our other options first."

The room shook again, and Greyor reached for his earpiece.

"That was turbine six," he said. "We're coasting. Twenty minutes and we're in amateur radar range. If the under-shielding fails, we'll be visible before that."

"Stay with her."

Greyor nodded as Nye hurried toward the door.

"What about my friends?" I asked.

"One crisis at a time, pet," the warden said on his way out.

"What's happening?" I asked Greyor.

"The wardens weren't persuaded to change their votes in Arsenic's favor. This is his parting shot in retaliation. He's either trying to distract Nye to get a crack at you, or he really intends to destroy the Center to keep Nye from it."

"But there aren't enough transports on the rings to evacuate everyone."

Birch said that only two of the large vessels could dock at once. It would take at least ten to clear everyone.

"The other wardens are likely already fleeing with the transports, and there aren't nearly enough emergency vessels for everyone on board. If he damages the Center, we crash."

"He'll go down with the rest of us."

"Ahab always sinks alongside the whale," Greyor said, using the desk for an anchor against the next tremor. "Now would be a really good time to tell me you can walk on air."

Maybe if I tried I could get enough lift for myself, but that wouldn't do him or anyone else any good. Jermay and Birch, Winnie and Birdie, Klok—they'd all be helpless, and so would my sisters, in the shape they were in. I was stuck in that office, surrounded by the family mementos I'd thought I lost when the train was destroyed, and it was about to happen again.

I'd had one idea to save us that night; there was no reason it wouldn't work here, too. I ran for the other side of the room. "Maybe *I* don't need to fly." I snatched Bijou from his display. He was collapsed, but not fully, and currently about the size of Xerxes' house cat persona. "If you can get me to my room, I think I can get us out of here."

I flipped Bijou's power switch and said, "Hang on tight." He climbed onto my back and clung to my shoulders like a metal backpack. If his wings had been bigger, I could have used him for a glider.

"It's broken."

"And so were Nye's hands," I argued. "Two golems should be able to carry seven people."

Warden Nye could go down with his post.

"Fine," Greyor said. "But we're only stopping long enough for you to grab the cat. With Arsenic on the loose, Birch is probably hiding in the greenhouse."

"What did Arcineaux do to him?"

"He's twisted, Penn, and so are the people he supervises. Birch was one of the few Level-Fives we had at the Ground Center, and that meant everyone wanted him under their own microscope. Arsenic was happy to oblige, one piece at a time. If Warden Nye hadn't regained possession of him, I don't think Birch would have survived. Now come on, we can't linger here. If Arsenic is done with the power sector, he'll come here looking for Nye, or to watch his handiwork in real time."

Greyor headed for the door with me behind him. The alcove and hallway were clear, and when we passed Nye's prize painting, I couldn't resist the urge to skim my fingers across the surface one more time.

The warden was right; it *was* addictive, but it was more than nostalgia that guided my hand across my painted parents and sisters. When heat flared on Evie's fingers, I pulled it inside myself. I absorbed the ocean in Nim's eyes. My father instilled me with mechanical precision, and Anise's resolve left me unstoppable as a boulder crashing down a mountain. Vesper reminded me to breathe. Touching them made me stronger, and it reinforced who and what I was—not just Celestine, or Level-Five. Together, my family had nearly bested the full power of the Commission; I could certainly take care of one warden. Or two.

I reached for my mother's face, allowing myself to linger on the feel of her cheek and hair. A scent of faint perfume breezed into my nose.

"It's too big to carry, and we can't stay here," Greyor snapped.

I nodded, and took a final moment to shift my fingers to my mother's mouth and whisper: "I'm sorry, Mama." But ghosts can't grant absolution, and paintings don't mourn for the son missing from them.

I fell back in line with Greyor. Behind me, I could have sworn I heard Iva's voice say: "As am I, my darling. Now, watch."

The kinetic weight of the air became more hectic, molecules buzzing and bouncing off one another, knitting a daydream to drape over reality. In it, Warden Arcineaux skulked around corners, every bit the gargoyle he'd seemed when I first saw him. I gasped when I recognized the hallway he was walking, and pulled Greyor back.

"Wha—" he started, but he had his answer. Arcineaux turned the corner.

Most people's smiles brighten their faces, but Arsenic's made shadows.

"How convenient," he said. "Two birds. Now all I need is a stone."

CHAPTER 39

"Penn, get back." Greyor raised his gun.

We moved in reverse with Arsenic advancing, until we were back in the office, with nowhere else to go. The warden assessed the room, taking in the damage with a disgustingly approving leer.

"Your doing, was it?" he asked me. "This is more than a little desta-bilization would cause. But there aren't any bodies, so I don't suppose you solved either of our problems and killed him."

"I'm not a murderer," I said, feeling the need to defend myself.

"Not for lack of trying." He bent over, picking at the bits that had flown about the room. With his boot he nudged the sword that had hurtled at Nye's head. "Looks like you need to work on your aim."

"Stay there," Greyor ordered when Arsenic straightened up, but his words were weak and unsure. He shooed me behind him.

Arcineaux circled in front of the monitor, switching the images back on in turn. He barely reacted when the next hiccup in the stabi-lization system made the Center shimmy. When it passed, he was still grinning.

"I guess I know where our host went."

He continued around the office, skimming his fingers past a spiked ball on a chain, and straightened the blazons that had been knocked askew. One dagger in particular, which had been paired with the sword, gave him enough difficulty that he had to use both hands to pry it free. Greyor tensed.

"I remember you from the ground." Arsenic pointed the dagger at him. "I thought you looked familiar, but it was one of my people who made the connection. You transferred in immediately prior to the security breach that cost me most of my test subjects, then transferred out from the disgrace."

I took a step forward, wondering if I could muster the anger or control to overpower the restriction bands and send the room into flight again. There wasn't enough space to extend Bijou and ask him for help.

"And now you're here, responsible for Nye's prize possession." Arcineaux glared at me. "Am I to call that coincidence?"

"Shoot him," I told Greyor. He didn't have to kill him, all he had to do was wound him. With the damage Arsenic had done, surely Greyor was justified by Commission standards. The other wardens knew the man had lost it.

"If he was going to shoot, he would have," Arsenic said. "You see, the longer you threaten someone, the less likely you are to actually act." His hand dropped to his side, still holding the dagger, but no longer flaunting it.

"I was protecting Winifred," Greyor blurted. His voice was getting higher, more desperate. "You were torturing her . . . all of them. They're kids."

"Subhuman mongrels, and you released them on a population that doesn't have the sense to know they need protecting."

"My sister is *not* a mongrel!" Greyor shouted.

"You're Winnie's brother?" I asked, but it already made sense.

He was the reason they never knew how the girls escaped the Center, and he'd let them go at the precise moment that caused the most damage to the man who hurt her.

Winnie was in the twin database. Did that make Greyor the other half of the pair? If so, he had to have an ability, too, but I hadn't seen him do anything spectacular.

"I would have released them all, if I'd found a way," Greyor said defiantly.

Ignoring the gun, Arcineaux clasped Greyor on the shoulder.

"And now I see you are an honest man, as well as a brave one." His voice had turned deadly soft while his focus hardened. "Dumb, but honest."

The hand that had been slack at his side moved so quickly I didn't see it until Greyor pitched backward from the impact. His blood didn't show on the warden's gloved hands, but it ran over the hilt and the blade protruding from Greyor's abdomen. More trickled from his mouth.

"You really should have taken your shot," Arsenic whispered in Greyor's ear, then shoved him back. Greyor bent in half, his hands beneath the dagger's handle but not grasping. His voice had left him; all he could do was swallow over and over and over. And then he fell.

I was on my knees beside him when he hit the floor, trying to do . . . I didn't even know what. There was nothing to be done. Arsenic's strike had been brutal. Greyor was gone.

"See? Aim is critical."

Arsenic pulled the dagger from Greyor's body. The blade came free with the sickening suction of a filling void that soon brimmed with dark blood. He tossed the dagger into the heap of relics on the floor. I still hadn't gotten off my knees, or released Greyor's hand. I didn't even know when I'd taken his hand.

"You didn't have to do that!"

"I'm disappointed," Arsenic told me. "You didn't try to save him."

"You did this, not me!"

"*He* did this." Arsenic pointed at Greyor. "Ambition can be a deadly vice if you aren't the one holding the knife."

I cared less about knives than the sword that had nearly skewered Nye earlier. It was still on the floor, and completely out of Arcineaux's line of sight. My wrists were on fire, but that only reminded me that people like Arsenic were so afraid of me, they had to try to control me. He couldn't do that with pain. Pain was the ally telling me that I was still alive, and still dangerous.

"What are you doing?" he asked. From the look on his face, I was pretty sure he'd seen my eyes turn black and knew he was in trouble.

The sword clattered up off the ground, and this time no one caught it.

I was still shaking when I made it back to my cell. Birch was there, but I was in no shape to acknowledge him.

"Penelope! I've been going out of my head."

"Xerxes!" I blew straight past Birch to Xerxes' corner, but his basket was empty.

"Is that blood?" Birch was inspecting the door. My hand had left a red stain from pushing it open.

"Xerxes!"

My golem wasn't on the couch, or under it when I got down on my stomach to check. New fears branched off my existing terror. Had someone snuck in to take Xerxes while I was in Nye's office?

And how was I supposed to tell Winnie that her brother was dead?

"Did someone hurt you?" Birch asked.

I turned on a lamp, and left it spotted with evidence of Greyor's murder. Birch stared at my bloody dress.

"Penelope, stop!" Birch grabbed me by the shoulders. "Whose blood is this?"

"A dead man's."

"Did you—"

"Greyor." I raised my arms to push him off. "Arcineaux murdered him right in front of me. He's insane. I'm not staying here. I have a way out and I'm taking it!"

Something was bumping behind my wardrobe.

"You aren't making any sense," Birch said.

"It's *this place* that doesn't make sense. You act like this is normal."

"Do you think Greyor was the first person Arsenic has killed? He won't even be the last."

The bumping grew louder and more insistent. Xerxes' head poked out between the wardrobe and the wall. His wings had lodged while he was exploring, and now he was stuck. I dragged the wardrobe away from the wall.

"He's the last one I'll watch die," I said.

Memories of my first so-called conversation with Warden Nye came back to me, along with his words about how it felt to take another life. There was no feeling in the world that matched the bleak uselessness of being unable to stop death. I wouldn't watch the life fade from Evie's eyes or Jermay's, even Birch's.

"Stay close," I told Xerxes, and touched the metal coil around my throat. "I've got Bijou, and I know where the others are. We're getting out of here, even if it gets us killed."

There was no carefully formed plan at work. I'd simply come to the point that I couldn't abide any more of the madness that was the Center's everyday operation. I was running on instinct; fortunately for me, that was the root of my power.

The last thing the ceiling camera caught before its light went dark was me snapping my fingers to sever its circuits.

"Come with us," I said to Birch. He shrank away, eyes darting side to side.

"I can't . . . I mean, we—"

I took his face between my hands and held him still.

"You said you stayed to wait for me. I'm leaving—come with us. Xerxes can get us to the ground."

"The outer doors are on the docking level. There are at least forty men down there."

"Just get me into the room where they're keeping Klok."

"But—"

"*Trust me.* You don't have to be a prisoner anymore."

I moved to the door and held out my hand, waiting for him to take it.

"If you didn't need me to reach your friend, would you still want me to come?" he asked.

"I'm not leaving you behind," I said.

Birch glanced up at the dead light, then down to Xerxes, who had his ears up and nose out, searching for trouble. He brought his eyes back to me, and slowly took my hand.

"Let's go."

CHAPTER 40

We'd reached another dreadfully perfect moment where there were no close calls and no near misses. Every hall was empty, as though the men who should have been occupying them had been drawn away. It should have felt too convenient, but I accepted the easy road at face value; there was no time to waste worrying that I was wrong.

The area where Klok was being held was still dark. His body was no longer leaned against a floor cabinet, but laid out on the table. Instruments sat on a tray beside him, saws and solder, but also things that looked as though they'd come from a surgeon's stand.

"Klok, are you awake?"

A soft light shined in his palm. The rat-tat of his screen was the most beautiful sound in the world when he answered me with a glowing blue: `"Fully functional. I was worried about Penn."`

"Penn was worried about you." I hugged him as well as I could manage.

He sat up and another message blipped across the screen. `"He is Penn's friend?"`

Birch had followed me.

"He's going to help us get out of here," I said.

"Where are the hummers?" Birch asked.

Even inside the vent, he'd been able to see them before. Not a single one protruded from Klok's body any longer. Instead, a layer of armor covered his entire torso, bearing the same markings as a hummer's exoskeleton. He'd made it impossible for the technicians to dissect him like Nye wanted.

"You were protecting yourself," I said.

"I think they lost interest."

"No one's been back?"

"Moved me, then left."

"Have you heard anything?"

"A lot of noise. Something is wrong."

"There you are!"

Klok had a pronounced gift for understatement, and something was definitely wrong. Our escape was over before it began; Iva had caught us.

"It's not her fault." Birch put himself in front of me. "It was me. Please don't report us."

"I don't know what you're on about," she chirped, entering the room. "Quickly, dears, no time for feet-dragging. Warden Nye is quite insistent on our making haste. The stabilization system is beyond even my scope for repair."

Klok's display tapped out: **"That is not your mother."**

"I know," I said.

"Ghosts do not exist."

"She's not a ghost, Klok." She was something much more dangerous.

"Oh dear." Iva's attention settled on the drying blood, which had turned my moss-green dress nearly black in patches. "The warden warned me you might be in an awful state, but I never imagined it was this bad. I do wish I had something for you to change into. There isn't even time for repairs."

While she chattered, I knelt to stroke Xerxes' head, letting my fingers stray down his neck until I was able to reach the switch that would turn him from a toy into the creature that had made grown men flee from the Caravan tents. Klok nudged Birch backward, a warning that the room was about to get cramped.

"Darling, whatever is wrong with your kitten?"

Xerxes had been expanding, though slower than usual, which I expected from the age of the circuit I'd used to patch him. But now, he was stuck. He'd grow an inch, then shrink two, then bigger, then smaller. He cried out with a pained yelp.

"No . . ." I fought with his access panel, but it kept changing size along with him and wouldn't open. "Don't you do this to me, Xerxes. Don't you dare let me down, too. You have to hold. You have to—"

With one piercing screech and a chaotic fluttering of wings, Xerxes fell over, landing stiff on his side, legs twitching like an animal in the final moments of life. That piece of my father's soul flared in Xerxes' glass eyes, then faded away like smoke around a dimming bulb. His beak opened and stuck.

He was dead, and the last thing I wanted to feel was the lifeless touch of my mock-mother trying to wrap me in her arms.

"Oh darling, I'm so sorry. Is there anything I can do?"

Klok tapped Iva on the shoulder, grimacing.

`"Penn does not require a hug. She requires a control circuit to make her golem better."`

"Is that all?" Iva asked.

She pushed back to her feet, releasing me so she could cross the room to the bins that held the technicians' equipment and tools. I sat on the floor, with Xerxes half in my lap and my head on Birch's shoulder. He'd crouched beside me, and watched, stunned, as she foraged through the bins.

"What's she doing?" Birch asked.

"I don't know."

I thought I knew, but the thing I thought made no sense. Warden Nye's right-hand robot wouldn't be searching out new circuitry to restore Xerxes. She wouldn't be taking pieces from destroyed golems, and she wouldn't be bringing them back to me with a less phony smile on her face. Yet, that's exactly what Iva was doing.

"You made an awful lot of fuss for something as simple as a control circuit. Won't this one work?"

She handed me the unit that had once given life to Scorpius, and while I saw to installing it in Xerxes, Klok searched out what remained of the things the warden had stolen from us. Winnie's tail was still intact, though I doubted she'd want any part of her costume once the rebreather was removed.

"Find another circuit for Bijou," I called, coaxing the dragon down off my shoulders.

Birch appeared beside me with several in his hands.

"Will one of these do?" he asked. "They look the same as that one."

"Perfect," I said. I snapped one into Bijou. His wings flared out, shimmering with the layer of jeweled color on their undersides. Xerxes whirred back to life, and he was on his feet, as well.

One of the dismembered unicorn heads twitched on its shelf, then was suddenly knocked aside by the friendly creeper light that had served as my companion when I was in the greenhouse. It blinked nervously, almost timidly, if such a thing was possible for a machine, and joined us on the floor. It still couldn't talk, but I understood it well enough. It wanted to come with us.

"Such a marvel," Iva said, grinning at the creeper. "You really *are* your father's daughter. They can tell, you know. They recognize your voice."

"She's not acting right," Birch whispered.

The artificial quality had faded from her demeanor, along with the pallor from her cheeks; her movements were no longer stiff. When Iva spoke, it wasn't to warn me to watch how I behaved around the warden. She'd changed as drastically as the golems that fought for The Show to their deaths, and that couldn't be coincidence.

"Iva, for what purpose were you created?" I asked.

I stood directly in front of her, met her eyes, and was astounded to see the clouded glass had given way to something warm and deep. They held the dark warmth of strong coffee, intelligent and wary.

"I am the physical interpretation of Iva Roma," she said. "Wife of Magnus and mother to Nieva, Nimue, Anise, Vesper, Penelope, and my poor lost boy."

"For what purpose were you sent to Warden Nye? Because you were defective?"

"I am *not* defective. I was sent ahead of my daughter, in the event that she was acquired by Warden Nye. My primary function is to protect. Penelope Roma is in danger, therefore the primary function overrides the secondary functions implemented by the warden."

My father had sent her to help me, in case he wasn't able to.

"Never doubt that one of your father's creations will do exactly what it was designed to," Iva said.

The plan I'd not bothered to make before solidified in my mind. The snares and thorns blocking our escape shriveled and died as a new path opened up—one wide enough for many to share.

"Iva, do you have access to the prison level?"

CHAPTER 41

We walked briskly, with Iva in the lead and Klok at the back, carrying a satchel filled with one creeper light and a restless Xerxes and Bijou. Birch was in the middle with me. Klok had taken a technician's coat to hide his clothes, but no one would have noticed if we'd gone straight out the main doors and headed for a ship. The hall was pure anarchy.

Men were sprinting toward other areas of the facility. A row of round windows set into the wall showed fleeing personnel rushing to fill the few small vessels still moored to the outer rim. An explosion nearly threw us to the floor.

"This is ridiculous," Iva said. "The Commission won't tolerate this level of competition between wardens. It sets a bad example." She shook her head. "Sorry, secondary programming bled through."

All of this is because Arcineaux didn't get his way?

Iva pointed to a small ship through one of the breezeway's windows. "Those evac pods only deploy during catastrophic failure. Each one signals reinforcements from the ground."

We reached a set of lift doors; the men who bolted out didn't pay us any mind, other than to shove us out of their way.

Klok set the satchel on the elevator floor, allowing Xerxes and Bijou their freedom. Both golems took a position in front of the doors, ready for their first chance to really move since the fall of The Show. Their impatient growls were drowned by another, stronger explosion.

"What was that?" Birch asked.

Iva cocked her head to the side, listening.

"The primary ramp cables on the outer walkways just detached—unfortunate for anyone crossing them. Auxiliary paths will still allow access to the escape pods, but the regular vessels will be derelict."

The next explosion shook the entire lift, throwing me and Birch into Iva and Klok.

"And that's the support cables. We'll be in a bit of a bind if the pontoon braces go, but that shouldn't be an issue so long as there's power."

Our car stopped at the prison level. Bijou and Xerxes charged off the lift into the empty corridor. The guards had either fled or gone to help defend the Center.

Iva took a key from a chain around her neck and put it in the lock. When she turned it, nothing happened.

"The protocols have isolated the magnets," she said. "No one can access them."

"But what about the people inside?" *If the Center crashed . . .* "I'm not leaving my sisters behind!"

"The wardens fled; they likely took what was theirs," Birch said.

"Arcineaux's still here! If he's here, Anise is, too, and even if she wasn't, Jermay's in there with at least a hundred others! Break it open."

Xerxes and Bijou took the same stance that they had in the lift, only now they were butting the gate with their heads and leaving not so much as a dent.

"Please let this work," I whispered, and bent to switch the golems to full capacity. Both of them stretched back and out, reaching full size with a clink as their metal bits slid into place. They kept beating against the gate, making it shake.

"It's not enough," Birch said.

There was no more room for caution.

"Klok, I need a spark," I said.

He raised his hand, palm up, with the lantern in it glowing. The glass panel on his hand slid back, revealing the tiny electrical spark that fueled it. Hopefully, it would be enough to create a fire.

"Cross your fingers," I said.

"Vampires do not exist. They are like ghosts," Klok reminded me.

"Not that kind of cross, Klok. It's for good luck."

"Oh." He obliged in twisting all of his fingers into a tangle. **"Luck does not exist, either. Should I make you a list of things that do not exist?"**

"Maybe later. I need to concentrate," I told him.

I was about to stick *my* fingers into a live current, but without the anger I'd used to do it the last time.

"I don't need wings, just a feather," I whispered. "Feathers are light. Feathers are simple. Feathers—"

I held my breath, and grabbed fire. When I opened my eyes, a sparking blue flame danced in my palm.

There was heat, definitely, but no burn. I blew across my fingers, causing the flame I'd captured to drift into Bijou's snout. He reared back, rattled his wings, and sent a jet of liquid fire straight into the gate. Xerxes slashed a wing through the flames, and the weakened metal gave with a groaning crash. We scrambled through the opening.

"Give me two minutes to reach the master release," Iva said.

She ran across the prison ward faster than humanly possible, leaving us to hope the Center didn't fall out of the sky while we were waiting for her return.

"Excuse me." Birch tapped Klok on the shoulder.

Jermay would have laughed at his formality, but I was coming to appreciate the differences between them. Jermay could teach Birch about the outside world; Birch could teach Jermay a few things about patience and focus. They'd be good for each other, if Birch didn't mulch him into fertilizer on sight.

Klok's display flashed blue, a prompt for Birch to go ahead and ask his question.

"I was just wondering . . . since you *did* disable the hummers. Are they similar enough that you could maybe . . . Would it work on these?" Birch held his wrists in the air, showing off the restriction bands.

How had I not thought of that?

"Klok, can you get us out of these?" I asked.

He wrapped Birch's wrists in his hands. The braided metal wires and glass tubes uncurled from the bands to encase Klok's palms, leaving only the lantern and screen areas of his hands uncovered.

"You're keeping them?" I asked.

"Could be useful."

He absorbed my bands and used them to cover his fingers, so he had complete gloves. The Commission was slowly building their super-soldier, but he was on the opposing side of a war that no one should have been fighting.

"Thank you," Birch said, rubbing his wrists.

Something changed when Klok took the bands off my wrists. I was more alive than I had been before, as though I was fire made flesh. I could have blinked and batted down the moon.

If this was how it felt to me, I couldn't imagine the rush going through Birch after being chained so long. He leaned against the railing, blinking rapidly.

"Did you feel that?" he asked.

I nodded.

A metal clang started at the top of the prison level and traveled down, passing us on its way to the bottom floor. Birch and I exchanged glances, asking each other silently if this was somehow my doing or his, but the noise gave way to sliding doors and open cells. Iva had released the master switch.

Each door that opened came with the sound of a ticking clock, and no two were set to the same rhythm. People spilled out—some on the run, some more timid—not daring to believe it was safe to do more than poke their heads out for a look. One pair began waltzing in the aisle to music that didn't exist. Others chose the path of least resistance and leapt the rails.

I peeked into one cell and found its occupant still inside, huddled up and rocking, addled by the conflicting beats. Strangest of all was the man with the regal bearing I'd seen before. He'd located the chariot lift on his own floor and made it to the exit without a hitch—and he was still wearing his trilby hat.

"Hello, miss," he said, politely tipping it as he passed. He hurried out, hand twitching.

"Find Winnie and get the rebreather off of her," I said to Klok, refusing to consider that she'd become one of the empty-eyed horde around us. "Tell everyone you pass to get to the docking rings."

Hopefully the rush would overwhelm the Center's personnel. Some of them might even make it out alive.

"Keep an eye out for our family," I told Xerxes and Bijou. "I'm going after my sisters." I knew at least three of them were immobile and couldn't escape without help.

Xerxes and Bijou lifted off, landing on separate walkways, each with a heavy clink.

"I'm coming with you," Birch said.

We ran for the chariot lift; on our way down we passed levels teeming with prisoners, but none looked familiar.

"Which one?" Birch was out of the lift first, scanning the identical doors. This level appeared to be vacant, save for the remains of those who had thrown themselves from the higher walks. I tried not to look, afraid that they might not be dead; I couldn't bear the thought of passing them by if they weren't.

"Look for bigger doors with extra locks. Evie's is cold to the touch." All pyrokinetics hated the cold, and Warden Files would have known that.

Maybe it *would* have been better if my father had simply given the Commission what they wanted. If I'd grown up like Birch, Evie and the others would have been free. I couldn't have regretted the loss of my freedom if I'd only known captivity. The whole thing was my fault.

"Here!" Birch shouted.

The shadows looked different mixed with the motion from other levels, but it was Evie's cell, sure enough, and it was empty. I placed my hands against the floor, searching for a hint of warmth to say the miraculous had happened and she'd walked out recently, but not even a trace remained to show she'd ever been there at all.

We'd started back for the lift when a flash of unsteady movement caught my eye. I wasn't going to look, fearful that what I'd seen was a dying twitch from one of those who had jumped, but my conscience wouldn't let me pass by knowing we'd left someone behind.

"There's someone down here." I stopped, turning around for a better view of the level. "Listen."

The endless ticking from above was still there, but softer, and at a distance. Now a strong and steady tempo was coming from somewhere close, and with it came the familiar calming wave I only felt when I was near Anise.

"Check the cells!" I made for the nearest door; Birch started down the opposite side of the aisle.

The first two were empty, except for Vesper's wig, but in the third, a figure stumbled from wall to wall at an uneasy lurch. Her back was to me as she patted her way around the perimeter of the small square, seeking the door. When she made it all the way around, she put her hand through the opening and kept going. She was still wearing the cropped shirt and dust coat she'd had on during The Show's last performance. Her goggles had fallen from her head.

"Anise!"

At the sound of my voice, she turned feral, clawing her throat to tear the collar off.

"Birch! Help me!"

It took both of us to keep her stable on her feet. She pitched with each step, closer to me, then away toward Birch. Her eyes were glazed over, unfocused.

"It's the collar," he said, struggling against her resistance. "It's trying to force her back into the cell."

I tried not to remember the agony that made me wish my spine would break just to stop the pain when Nye collared me. It had set my nerves on fire, twisting the muscles so far out of shape I wanted to tear off my skin to pull them out. No wonder my sister looked like a madwoman.

"Anise, stop," I begged. "We'll get you upstairs; Klok can take the collar off."

But she kept tugging on the collar. I grasped it, hoping I could work my fingers between the wires and her skin to give her some relief. A slight buzz started in my fingertips as they touched the collar's edge . . . Maybe I didn't need to wait for Klok.

"Open," I whispered.

Open. I am the daughter of Magnus Roma. I am Celestine. I order you to open!

A spark zipped along the wires, and at the point where the collar's two sides joined, the latch popped open. The collar fell to the ground, and Anise collapsed beside it.

CHAPTER 42

The dancing couple was still spinning up and down the aisle of the main floor. A siren wailed through the intercom, replacing the ticking. Hopefully due to the breakout, rather than a warning that the Center was at terminal descent.

The copy of my mother was waiting for us at the door.

"You found one!" she cheered. "And now you've brought me another darling daughter to brighten my day."

"Anise was the only one left," I said.

"Should I take her? She seems a bit more than you can carry."

Birch and I rolled Anise's weight from our shoulders onto hers. Anise's head lolled sideways; she opened her eyes a crack.

"Mother?" She groaned. "Oh good . . . I'm dead." Her head fell back again.

"Her collar came apart in my hands," I said, still trying to believe the words were true.

"I knew you were meant for great things," Iva said.

"Did you see Sister Mary Alban with the escapees?"

"Who, dear?"

"Your sister-in-law. My aunt. Papa helped her hide away. She helped us escape before, but she was caught. Did you see her?"

"I don't know about any aunt, but the only special prisoners were the ones brought in with your group. Magnus likely omitted a few details in my history banks, especially the ones he didn't want the warden to know about. I'm afraid we can't take much time to search. If the others—"

"Penn?"

I whirled around.

Jermay stared from the other end of the walkway. It was like no time had passed at all. He ran my way, dragging his leg; I ran his, and we met in an embrace that seemed determined to break us both so neither could escape.

"Are you another dream?" he asked.

I tried to shake my head, but I couldn't move.

"I found Anise, but Evie's gone," I said in a rush. "A warden took her."

He looked past me, without letting go, to Iva holding Anise. Then his blue eyes moved to Birch, and he pulled me behind him.

"Get back," Jermay warned.

"No, it's okay," I said. "I know what he looks like, but they're the only clothes he has. Birch helped us save you, Jermay."

He kept watching Birch, but stepped aside. I took his hand and pulled him with me, determined never to drop it again.

"We should go," Iva said. "Klok and Winnie returned ages ago. Oh, and that poor little girl. The darling child's positively exhausted."

For the last few words, her voice reverted to a mechanical monotone. Every syllable grated on my nerves.

She shuddered, disgusted at the sound herself. "I *really* am trying to curb that. Your father would be livid."

"You can take it up with him when we get out of here," I said.

It was just another topic in what was bound to be a very long and detailed conversation. The more of us he had to answer to, the better.

I put my fingers to my mouth, blowing out a long, high whistle. Bijou and Xerxes leapt from the upper floors they'd been patrolling. The walkway rumbled with the impact, and a new vibration rippled through for every step Xerxes took as he followed us back through the prison gate and into the hall.

Klok was there, and so was Winnie. He was carrying Birdie, who was unconscious.

"Birch?" Winnie blinked at us.

He ran over and hugged her as fiercely as Jermay had hugged me.

"I thought I'd never see you again," he said. "I wasn't even sure you made it out of the Ground Center. They split us from the girls who fell behind, and refused to tell us anything."

"We barely made it. We were cut off before we could get to your side," she said. "I tried to get to you, I swear."

"What happened to you?" He touched her face where it was blistered red from having the rebreather fused to her skin.

"It doesn't matter. This time, we both go," she said.

"Winnie's the friend you lost at the Ground Center?" I asked.

I knew Winnie had been in Commission custody before. Where would they have kept her, if not a center? And Birch trusted Greyor completely. Of course it was because Greyor had defied a warden to try to free him.

"She's the best friend I've ever had," Birch said.

"Are you all right?" I asked Winnie once they'd stepped apart. Her eyes were hard, and in them I found my answer. How could anyone be all right after what she'd endured?

"Klok says we can trust that machine. Is he right?" she asked bitterly.

"My father sent Iva to help us. The warden never knew."

Winnie scoffed. "At least one of his contingency plans finally worked." She glanced at my dress. "That's not your blood, is it?"

"It's not, but—"

"Good. You'd have a hard time keeping up if you're wounded." Her voice was coarse and strained after so long without use. "Where's Greyor?"

"Winnie—" Birch started, but the words wouldn't come.

"He wanted to save you," I told her. "But Arcineaux recognized him. He—He—"

She read the truth within my stammering and cut me off.

"Then there's no one else to wait on." She anchored herself to Birch with an arm around his waist, and his around hers.

"Winnie . . . I'm sorry," I said. "I didn't know who he was until—"

"Let's go, before we all die with him."

Klok stepped onto the lift first. He stood in the center, stretching his arms from wall to wall.

"The lift's dimensions are insufficient to accommodate the golems," he said.

That much was obvious as soon as Xerxes tried to fit his shoulders through the door.

"Collapse them," Winnie said.

Xerxes hissed at the suggestion; Bijou flicked his tail. Neither of them liked the idea of being shrunk. Iva's control circuits were holding so far, but taking them from large to small and back again would be a strain.

"It's too big a risk," I said.

"Then how do we get off this floor?" Winnie asked.

Birch lit up.

"How are you at climbing trees?"

CHAPTER 43

The greenhouse should have been a clear shot, but it was chaos, and that was my fault. When we'd turned out the prisoners, I was naïve enough to think they'd head for the escape routes. Most of them had no idea where they were, much less how to evacuate the Center. They were able to make it out of the prison through the hole that Bijou and Xerxes made in the doors, then they flooded into every available space. Since the greenhouse wasn't kept locked, getting inside was easy.

People had jammed the walkways; others were using the trellises to get to higher floors.

"Make a path," I told Xerxes. He screeched loud enough to shake leaves from the nearest trees and vines. Terrified by the sound, and more so by what had made it, the throng split.

"Up the sides," I told the golems. "We'll meet you on the docking level."

"We should go with the golems," Klok spit out. "We are too heavy for trees."

He wrapped an arm around Bijou's neck, while keeping the other on Birdie; my friendly creeper light peeked out from the satchel on his shoulder. Bijou sprang onto the wall and used his claws to slither up the side. Iva and a semiconscious Anise made the same trip with Xerxes.

"Tree taxi," Birch called, with a poorly timed laugh. He summoned us a ride, and stepped onto it with Winnie.

"Ready?" I asked Jermay.

"You and me, like always." He tightened his grip on my arm, and we jumped over the rail, landing in the leaves.

"Stay to the inside," Birch warned. "I've seen mobs before. This won't be fun."

Faceless groups grabbed at us as we passed, snatching at our clothes with frantic hands, but rustling leaves and eruptions of thorny clusters made sure no one could find a handhold until we'd stopped.

"Nice trick," Jermay said, stepping off the branches.

"I'm not a magician," Birch said. "My tricks are real."

Bijou dropped down in front of us on the docking level, while Xerxes brought up the rear, following us out of the greenhouse. We made it to the hall, on our way to the exterior doors, but unlike the prison level or the greenhouse, the sounds of personnel were everywhere. There were shouts and running feet, flashing alarm lights, and a distant popping that could only be gunfire. The whole place was awash in pink sludge, but no one had time for protective gear.

"There's trouble up ahead," Iva said. "Tread carefully."

"What sort of trouble?" I asked, assuming she meant the sludge around our ankles.

Instead of an answer, she threw her arm out to stop us from rounding the corner.

As chaotic as the greenhouse had been, the area surrounding the external doors was worse. The hall widened into several spaces large enough to accommodate units from arriving or departing transports. Each of those spaces sat at the mouth of an airlock with oversized double doors to the outside. Beyond the doors, more pods had joined the exodus, and the gyro-rings were spinning out of control.

Security assigned to the Center stood on one side, blocking the exits, while others from Arcineaux's group faced them, trying to force their way through.

"What are they doing?" I asked. "They should all be leaving."

"They blame Arcineaux," Iva said. "His people are guilty by association."

"That's insane," I said.

The guards involved had declared war on each other for no reason besides the erratic whims of two lunatics who had lined them up like a collection of toy soldiers. The area's close quarters ensured high casualties, and unlike toys, these men could bleed, and they weren't so easily melted back together.

"Nye's people are terrified of me," I said. "They'll let me pass."

"And what about Arsenic's men?" Winnie snapped. "Do you think they'll do the same?"

"Xerxes and Bijou would catch them off guard. We'll have time to make a run for it."

"They'll kill you as soon as you're in the open," Jermay said. "They'll kill us all."

"We've escaped before," I said.

"And then we got caught," Winnie cried, as she touched the blisters on her face. "Look at me! And these scars are nothing compared to what they did before! This is the only level open to the outside, and those are the only doors. There's no way out of this!"

She wrapped her arms around herself and slid to the floor, shielded between Xerxes' front legs. Her head bumped against his feathers, while her fingers picked at the raw patches around her mouth. She was a wreck, and Anise was barely alive. We'd found their bodies, but I was no longer certain we'd saved them.

"This isn't the *only* open floor," Birch said.

He glanced at the ceiling, then to me.

"You mean the Aerie?"

"What's that?" Jermay asked.

"Nye's inner sanctum," Iva said. "The whole top retracts into open air."

"It's isolated," Birch said. "The greenhouse doesn't extend that far, so I can't reach it, but *they* can."

He nodded to Bijou and Xerxes.

"All we have to do is get the doors open. If they can scale the inside of the lift shaft the way they did the greenhouse's walls, they'll fit one at a time."

"A sound plan," Iva said, looking at me. "Your father—"

She choked.

I'd heard so much gunfire so often that one more pop didn't seem important. All the explosions were things happening elsewhere to other people until Iva's voice stopped.

"Your father . . . your father . . . your father . . ." Her head jerked, stuck on those two words. "Your father . . . your father . . . Good-bye, my darling girls. I'm so sorry to be leaving you ag—"

Iva froze. Her face static, mouth open. The light in her eyes went out before she crashed to her knees, taking Anise with her and revealing a stumbling and bleeding Warden Arcineaux behind her. He'd shot her in the back.

"I've always hated that thing." He spat at Iva. "But not as much as I hate every loathsome creature spawned by that traveling rat's nest you call a circus. I told you that your aim was atrocious," he sneered, pressing a hand to the gut wound I'd made with the sword.

Losing my mother so young had spared me the memory of her death, but now it didn't matter that this Iva was a copy. I couldn't look away.

Arcineaux smirked at Winnie and Jermay, but wasn't so bold with Bijou or Xerxes. They hissed at him, Bijou stretching his snout almost close enough to bite. Smoke from Bijou's nostrils curled up and around Arcineaux's head, making him cough.

"Call them off or I'll snap your neck," he ordered, taking my throat in the hand that wasn't trying to stanch his bleeding stomach. Arsenic was a mess—beaten, bloodied, his uniform torn—but the gargoyle was granite strong. Jermay tried to pry him off me; Arcineaux threw him.

I brought my knee up straight into the wound I'd given him, and he doubled over, but he never let go, even when my creeper light tumbled out of Klok's satchel to butt him in the leg. He kicked the poor thing across the corridor and pressed against me harder to regain his balance.

"It appears we're on the fast track to a fiery death, so I'd be interested in your other way out." He slammed my head against the wall.

Xerxes took a step forward, but Arcineaux forced my head into the wall with greater pressure until it felt like my skull might snap. I cried out; Xerxes backed down.

"I don't understand Nye's fascination with you. You're far too much trouble, but that's the risk you run taking in strays off the street."

Another glance at Winnie.

He'd restricted my airflow so long that the world began to disappear into the ether. Iva's sparks fizzled; even the gunshots died to a barely there crackle of weak fireworks.

Determined that Arsenic's toxic scowl wouldn't be the last thing I saw, I set my focus over his shoulder to Jermay and Birch and Winnie, all being held at bay by Arcineaux's men, and to Xerxes and Bijou.

Bijou's snout and the smoke still curling from it.

I closed my eyes and used the remainder of my strength to home in on one of those distant muted pops. When I found one, I snatched the burning flash from the end of whatever barrel spawned it and brought the flame into my hand, holding it at my side until Arcineaux had no choice but to notice.

"How—"

He recoiled from the sight, leaping backward, and the second I was free to draw a breath, I sent the embers off my fingers into Bijou's snout, diving for the floor as white-hot fire cleared the hall.

Klok grabbed Anise with the hand not holding Birdie; Jermay and Birch propped my arms up over theirs; and we were off with Winnie in the lead. I could hear my creeper light rattling along with us, but it was no longer alone. Our accidental mascot had attracted others, and they were joining us as a swarm. Creeper lights poured out of doorways. The ceiling clogged with climbers. They covered our retreat, leaving Arsenic without a clear shot.

"Stop them!" Arcineaux ordered, turning our escape into a mad chase, which became even more hectic when his men started shooting.

Bullets pinged off the metal walls, chipping plaster when they managed to hit that instead. Someone aimed far too high and an overhead light crashed down to the side, but we didn't miss a step.

One shot shattered a section of the plasma tanks that ran the length of the walls, spilling a tidal wave of pink sludge onto the floor, but the men chasing us kept coming, splashing through it as they ran. We lost our traction, and our advantage. Klok wiped out, and the rest of us didn't have time to slow down before we piled into him.

"Do something, Penn!" Winnie shouted.

I put my hands wrist-deep into the sludge. Plasma was a conductor; I could fry them.

"Get clear!" I warned our creeper light and its friends; they all scattered out of range.

I felt the surge, and the crackle of electric current, but it wasn't broadcasting the way I'd expected. The plasma bubbled up, and at first I thought it was boiling, but the bubbles didn't pop. They rose off the floor, growing frills around the edges, and delicate luminescent lines at their base that dropped into newly formed tentacles . . . *Medusae*. Adding current to the plasma was creating tiny Medusae.

"They're golems!"

I wasn't sure I'd said it out loud until Winnie and the others backed away from me.

"Oh my God," Anise breathed, leaning on the wall.

"What did you do?" Jermay shook me. "Penn, what did you do?"

"I-I don't know!"

I pulled my hands out and stared as the infant Medusae seeped into the sludge and lost their shape. The ones I'd made had been the size of baseballs, but the ones from the Great Illusion were the size of cities. Who—or what—could create a golem that big? And why would they?

I couldn't wrap my head around it. All I knew was that the failing Center had been built to duplicate the conditions from the Great Illusion. I'd just made myself part of the process, and Arcineaux had seen me do it.

Half the men chasing us ran when they saw the blobs of plasma start to transform, but Arcineaux came straight for me, yanking me up by my hair. It made sense to me now why Vesper had despised her wig so; every inch was another weakness to exploit.

"Aren't you full of surprises?" He dragged me up until I was directly in front of his horrid face. "Maybe you're worth keeping after all. You're certainly worth more than some."

This time when he tossed his condescending smirk at Winnie, she wasn't the shell of herself rocking on the ground. She was on her feet, and furious.

"I may have to spend some extra time on you once we're on the ground. I'm sure you're just full of interesting *secrets*."

His eyes left my face, skimming over the rest of me until I felt like I'd been stripped with my clothes still on.

"Let. Her. Go," Winnie ordered.

"I've warned you about using that mouth without permission." Arcineaux shoved me away, toward Birch. "Maybe this time," he said, advancing on Winnie, "I'll save myself the trouble and cut out your tongue so I can teach you to hold it."

"You'll never lay another hand on me or anyone," Winnie said.

"Something else you never learned, vermin: never bluff if you can't follow through. You can't hurt me."

Winnie didn't blink.

"Don't be stupid," she said; a chilling twitch tugged at her mouth. "Causing pain is *your* specialty."

Arcineaux started forward again, but Bijou coiled his neck around Winnie, warning him off. Winnie patted Bijou's scales.

"The protocols may keep me from protecting myself, but they can't stop me from protecting someone else. And I *don't* have to hurt you. It won't *hurt* at all." She twisted her wrists in the air, as though the scars encircling them were bracelets. "All I have to do is tell you to hold your breath, and never let it go."

Her eyes turned jet black, and her voice became a terrifying rasp that would have chilled anyone who'd seen her act over the years.

Arcineaux gaped like a fish thrown on land. He stumbled away, panicked into a sweat.

"My tongue works just fine where it is." Winnie stopped fighting the smile on her lips.

Arcineaux brought his hands to his throat, trying to force air into it.

"You made your point; let him go so we can leave," I said.

"He's stolen too many breaths from too many people. He deserves this."

"And more," Birch said beside me. "Let him choke."

"But you don't deserve to live with this because of him," I pleaded. I didn't say it, but I was actually relieved to see that he'd survived my attack in Nye's office. I'd lived with the weight of killing my brother; I didn't want to carry another soul on my shoulders.

"Guilt is only for those who regret what they've done," Winnie said. "I won't."

Arcineaux fell to the floor, trembling with convulsions. He was still writhing when we reached the doors.

CHAPTER 44

It was the Aerie or nothing.

Bijou and Xerxes forced a path through the clog of people on the main floor, but the crowd thinned quickly past the halfway point. No one unfamiliar with the Center's layout knew that the warden's private lift was anything other than the ornate dead end it appeared to be. Klok forced the doors open; the car was stopped above us.

"Cut it," I said.

A few people moved closer, either curious or desperate for the promise of possible escape, and I had no doubt that once word of Arcineaux's demise spread, there would be more. But anyone who wanted to follow us was going to have to find their own way up.

Xerxes slashed through the cables like scissors with twine, and the brass car clanged against the sides as it fell beyond our floor to the facility's lowest levels.

"All clear," Klok said, once he'd inspected the empty shaft.

I climbed on Xerxes' back with Jermay and Birch.

"Don't drop us," I whispered, and laid my head on the gryphon's neck to steady myself against the jolt when he stood vertical on his hind legs to grasp the inner wall and pull us up. The satchel that Klok had carried became a harness of sturdy vines in Birch's hands to help us hang on against gravity, while Klok kept a tight grip on Anise and Birdie, cradling them between himself and Bijou. Winnie held on to his neck.

Bijou blew out a warning blast to discourage the handful of Arcineaux's men who had shadowed us. He scuttled onto the opposite wall, as it shuddered.

It wasn't a smooth ride, but the worst of the explosions had ceased, and we made it without difficulty or delay—a triumph even the golems shared; Xerxes shattered the glass doors with his head, and I couldn't help but think there was a particular sort of satisfaction in the way he stood once he was inside the Aerie. Bijou stormed out of the shaft, curling around the lift column so that half of his body was on its other side.

The shutters that had been in place the first time I'd set foot there were still retracted, giving a panoramic view of the ships fleeing the Center. In the distance, official vessels were headed in to assess the damage. Grainy shouts crackled through a radio setup in the lift, demanding details and reports from anyone able to give them.

The Center was still sinking.

"I'll open the top," I said. "Be ready to lift off as soon as we're clear."

I launched from Xerxes' back, heading for the panel that controlled the Aerie's covering, but someone had ripped it out of the wall.

"I'm afraid you won't find much use in that, pet. I misjudged the source of the racket you and your merry band were making on your way up. I thought my less-than-worthy adversary had come to make his escape from on high. Improvisation has never been my strong suit."

Nye stepped out from behind the column, as far away from Bijou as the space inside the Aerie would allow. The heat-laden hiss of dragon's breath warmed the air around us. He had a squat glass in his hand, half full of amber liquid.

"Arcineaux's dead," I told him.

"I'll take Iva's absence to mean he wasn't the only casualty."

"He killed her," I said. "And Greyor."

"That must have been horrible for you. I'm sorry." The harsh cadence of Nye's voice was every bit as magnetic as the view. The more I told myself to avoid it, the harder it became to do so.

"Don't." Birch had followed, and grabbed me by the arm. "Stay away from him, Penelope. He's just trying to get his hooks in you again."

"I was never on his hook."

"Oh yes, you were," Nye said. "My mistake was in thinking you were there as the catch, rather than the bait." There was shouting in the lift shaft, then banging, as though people were trying to climb the remains of the cables, but not quite managing it. "You're stardust. I was a fool to try to bottle you."

"Penn!" Jermay shouted, craning his neck from atop Xerxes. The noises from inside the elevator shaft became more uniform, with tall shadows of men cast against the walls. "They're coming up."

Anise was awake now, clinging to Bijou's metal scales, her weight tipped forward. Her collar's daze seemed to have lifted.

"Forget the controls," Birch said. "I can get us out of here, but you have to be off the floor. It won't be there when I'm done." He turned to Nye. "*Run.* You're the only father I ever had, so for that you get a chance—use the lift cables to get to a lower floor."

"I knew you were a bad influence on him, pet," Nye said. "Bravo. He needed one."

He turned to the view outside the Aerie, staring at the space beyond, as if he were seeing things the rest of us couldn't fathom. His dreams were dropping out of sight, falling faster than the rest of us.

"Get back to Xerxes," I told Birch. He looked uneasy, but he did as I asked.

"They say in the old days, captains of great ships would stay with the wheelhouse if their vessels sank. Go out a gentleman, with brandy and cigars as a peace offering for Death." Nye swirled his glass. "Take your freedom, pet—you've earned it. I've earned *other* things."

"Penn!" Jermay cried again. "If those ships reach us before we leave, we won't be going anywhere."

He and the others were already hovering off the floor, and the Commission's response vessels were growing larger. I heard Klok's display running at double speed.

"Nieva says when Penn is reckless, I can be rude. Penn is being reckless."

That was my warning before he hoisted me up by the back of my dress to plunk me down on Xerxes.

"Stay near the column supports . . . please," Birch called out to Nye, waiting for him to retreat. "I don't want to watch you die."

Then Birch laid his hand against the Aerie's side, eyes closed in concentration. A delicate pattern of white started below his fingers on the glass sphere, spreading out like quick-spun lace. Birch opened his eyes and blew out a long breath, setting a giant cloud of fluff flying in all directions.

He'd turned the Aerie into a dandelion.

"It was a pleasure to meet you, Pe—*Penn*." Nye choked on the nickname. "You gave me hope, and for that I shall never forgive you."

In his own twisted way, Nye had an integrity unto himself. He'd sold every piece of his soul, save his love of the truth, without realizing the people he sold it to had nothing of value to offer in return.

Anise reached a weak hand across the space between Bijou and Xerxes, seeking mine. I gave it to her, relieved that she had the strength to squeeze it. And that gave me one last, crazy idea.

"Are we over land or sea?" I called to Nye.

"We're directly above the facility that deployed those ships," he answered with a knowing smile.

"What does it matter?" Birch asked.

"Because we need cover, and those ships can't fly in a dust storm without clogging their engines. Anise? Can you do this?"

She nodded, tightening her grip on my hand.

Good, because what I was about to do, I couldn't manage without her.

I dug down, imagining my hands in soil, and called back the sensations that had been imprinted on the painting of my family, allowing one to take precedence over the others. Air and earth—always touching at the horizon, yet separate—became a solid circle. That circle churned, spinning faster and faster until its momentum nearly pulled it from my grasp.

"What are you doing?" Winnie yelled into the storm.

"Finding my balance."

Earth can be scattered by the wind. My father's voice looped through my memory, chanting lessons I'd taken for granted. But Magnus Roma never said anything on a whim.

He hadn't been teaching me to cage the Celestine—he'd been teaching me to *harness* her. A forbidden truth hidden in plain sight.

Nye wrapped one arm in the lift cables to steady himself as the winds raked across the ruined Aerie.

"Do your worst, Penelope Roma. Bring the rain!" He tipped his glass toward me, then drank it down and smashed it on the floor.

I summoned a tempest spirit so much like Vesper's I thought I heard her laughter in the air, and sent it straight toward the ships bearing down on us. It whipped around the platform, gaining speed until I let it fly as fierce and sure as the stone in a slingshot. The lead ship began to fall.

I felt a nudge, heard a rumble. Rocks pinged off my legs and arms, swirling about my face until I managed to gain control and weave each tiny particle into the fabric of a solid wall of writhing dust that set itself between the approaching ships and the Center.

Anise shored me up with her strength and focus. I was the current; she was the circuit. Together, we were unstoppable. The vessels resigned themselves to a midair stop to avoid choking their engines; they bobbed in the gentlest part of the wind and did the only thing they could—wait.

"There you go, giving me hope again. Magnus would be proud." With an irreverent salute, Nye left us, using his metal hands for a brace as he dropped down the lift chute.

It was the kind of remark you'd make about the dead, but I wasn't ready to give up on my father. For sixteen years, I'd watched him blur the line between magic and machine. He'd found a way to evacuate The Show's family from a raid; he'd built Iva, bringing my mother back from the dead to protect me from the warden. He certainly wouldn't have left himself out of his equations. That was more than enough room for hope to settle in.

I was fighting spots in my vision and numbness in my hands and feet. Inside The Show, being Celestine had been a nuisance. Outside, it was painful, and I was already feeling the fatigue of using too much power for too long. The sand curtain began to thin as Anise succumbed to her own exhaustion. If it dissipated completely, the ships would be able to start up again.

I whipped the wind into a frenzy, pulling the bits of rock and soil along with the dandelion fluff from the Aerie into a whirlwind.

"Fall," I told the stars. *Fall. Break. Shatter and ruin.*

And so came the true test. Could I pull down heaven while holding up earth and sky?

I tasted blood in my mouth from the strain, but grasped that invisible line between me and the stars, and pulled it taut. The increase in power, which had manifested when Klok dissolved the restriction bands, was there and flowing, setting the sky ablaze as one burning stone after another broke through the higher clouds. Destruction dripped from my fingers.

I brought the rain.

The Commission ships never saw it coming.

The first hit was direct, smashing the lead vessel in the side and making my ears ring. Smaller stones caught the exoskin of another, turning it to cinders so the skeleton peeled away toward the Earth.

Another ship's engines stalled out, the fan blades spitting mulch like a lawn mower.

"I bet Circus Boy can't do that," Birch said, smirking at Jermay.

By now the remaining ships were retreating, but I didn't tell the stars to stop until my arms grew heavy and my head fell forward, dropping against the feathers on Xerxes' neck. Jermay caught me like I knew he would, because he'd never let me fall.

The Show was dead, but the legacy of Magnus Roma lived on. I could only hope I wouldn't come to regret it.

CHAPTER 45

If something goes wrong, get to the Hollow . . .

Things had definitely gone wrong, and there was nowhere else I could think to go.

The others scanned the area around us, confusion on their faces, but only Jermay spoke.

"I don't see any houses."

There were no houses, not even a hovel or a hole in the ground. Only someone who had been told what to look for could find it: three trees in a line that looked like burnt-out husks, with branches that tangled into an arch above them, and white rocks arranged in a star twenty long steps in the opposite direction.

My father had drawn what he called "the doorway" and made me memorize it as a child—then he threw the paper into the fire when I asked if I could keep it.

"We have to find the markers to know where the door is," Anise said. "They're farther in."

We had to shrink the golems so that they'd fit between the trees. A few paces into the woods, Jermay let go of my hand and started running.

"Oh no." The words came out a choking sob from my mouth, Anise's, and Winnie's all at once.

There was a pile of rock with stones carefully laid and fitted together into a low mound. A worn top hat sat at one end, waiting for its owner to reclaim it. Not the kind of marker any of us wanted to see.

"Zavel?" Birdie sniffled into Klok's side.

Jermay was on his hands and knees, head bowed and crying.

I knelt beside the grave and placed my hand against the stones.

"I guess it's not really a surprise, is it?" Jermay asked, after a few minutes.

"Yes, it is," I said, and cried with him.

How long had it been since we set out believing that the Hollow would keep us safe?

We did our part—we got here. We'd nearly *killed* ourselves to do it. We should have been safe. That was the promise my father made us all: So long as Magnus Roma lived, those counted as his would be protected.

He was either a failure, a liar, or a corpse, so what did that make his daughters?

Jermay sat back and crossed his legs, staring at the grave.

"Do you think he made it to my mother?" he asked. "He'll be heartbroken if he didn't."

"I'm sure he did," I said.

"We need to get inside," Winnie urged softly. "I'm sorry, but it's not safe out here."

Jermay nodded and stood up, taking my hand again.

No one touched the top hat.

Anise found the tree with our father's mark carved into the trunk. This was the door to the Hollow, covered in chipped wood laid a layer at a time, to match the pattern of the trees around it.

She slid her hand up into the branches to flip the lock latch; the trunk swung open, wide enough for us to squeeze inside. A narrow flight of stairs took us down into the Hollow itself. Jermay was still holding my hand.

The door slammed behind us, cutting off the light we'd had from the moon.

"I don't like it in here," Birdie said, crowding close. She'd picked Xerxes up like a teddy bear, and his beak was digging into my back.

I let my fingers skim the walls as we went down, just to make sure they hadn't vanished. Klok held up his hand so it shined like a lantern, but the darkness was as thick as a solid curtain.

"They've moved on," Anise said.

The place was deserted, and had been long enough for dust to collect on the tables and chairs. Someone had stayed to bury the dead, but they'd given up on us. Or they'd had to flee. Either way, there was no one left.

"Where are you going?" Anise asked when I walked away from everyone else, but I couldn't say.

I had thought I was going home, but this was another tomb.

I was born under an impossible sky.

It was only an eclipse, but my father called it impossible. He said my mother watched the night shake the sun from the middle of the day, and went into labor on the spot. She took it as an ill omen, and her hopes for me died before I drew breath. I believe that was the moment she began to die as well, though I never told my father. He would have denied it, but I always wondered if he would have secretly agreed with me.

Now I stood in front of an open, dusty wardrobe in what should have been my parents' room, trying to imagine how my mother had looked in the clothes still hanging from the pegs, and if she'd ever wanted more than the life my father had carved out of the ground to hide her and my sisters while he could. Would the woman who wore these T-shirts and jeans have approved of life aboard the train?

I pulled at my bloodstained gown, cutting the seams with a pocketknife I found on a shelf. Its weight had become unbearable.

I put on my mother's jeans, then reached for a shirt that had belonged to my father. There were only two; the first had succumbed to moths and time and came apart in my hands, so the yellow one it was. I clipped my hair up off my neck to feel a bit more like myself. Short-haired Penn in her father's clothes.

Sliding my hands into my pockets was something I'd done when I played my brother's part. It kept my hands hidden, so no one could tell how small they were. I did the same thing there in my parents' room, but my mother's pockets weren't empty. One had a folded-up card inside. My name was on the envelope.

I opened it to find a cheap "Happy Birthday" greeting with an embossed "16" and a glitter-covered cake. Inside was a note in my father's block handwriting:

HELLO, PENN . . . PENELOPE. I SWORE NEVER TO BURDEN YOU WITH THIS IF I WAS ABLE TO CONCEAL IT, SO IT'S A GIVEN THAT I'M NOT THERE WITH YOU AS YOU READ THIS.

Tears blurred my eyes, making me glad that I was alone as I read.

I'M BOTH HAPPY AND SAD TO KNOW YOU'VE MADE IT SAFELY HERE. SAD FOR KNOWING I HAVEN'T ACCOMPLISHED IN THE LAST SIXTEEN YEARS WHAT I SWORE I WOULD FIND A WAY TO DO, AND SAD THAT

MY REGRETS HAVE BECOME YOUR BURDENS. BUT THERE IS ALSO HOPE. YOU'RE STRONG ENOUGH TO SURVIVE WITHOUT ME.

My survival had less to do with my strength than it did with the good fortune of having made the trip with the others. I had less confidence in my abilities than my father did.

I HOPE YOUR SISTERS ARE WITH YOU, BUT I KNOW THAT ANY OR ALL OF THEM WOULD HAVE GIVEN EVERYTHING TO PROTECT YOU AND OUR FAMILY. DON'T MOURN THE SHOW, PENN. IT WAS ALWAYS AN ILLUSION ON THE VERGE OF COLLAPSE. ONLY THE PEOPLE WERE REAL. EVEN THE ONES WHO NEVER LOOKED HUMAN.

I flipped the paper over to read the other side, but there was no explanation of what he meant by that.

IF YOU'RE HERE, AND I AM NOT, THEN I'VE MISSED YOUR BIRTHDAY. I OWE YOU SO MUCH, MAINLY APOLOGIES, BUT THERE'S NO TIME TO GIVE YOU THOSE. SO INSTEAD, I LEAVE YOU THIS—THE GIFT OF TRUTH. USE IT WISELY.

LOVE, PAPA

Below that was a micro memory chip that I had no way to play, but I was fairly certain Klok could. I didn't know how long the envelope and card had been in that pocket, but the memory chip looked new, and the tape holding it on the paper was still sticky. If he placed the card here when he left us and the train, he'd been alive as recently as a month ago. That was the only truth I needed.

His voice had sounded somber in my head. I was afraid to open the files on that chip and find out why. If he meant to tell me about the dark deal he'd struck with Warden Nye, I was in no mood to hear it, so I put the card back in my pocket and began walking from one room to another, touching keepsakes I didn't remember.

367

There were carved wooden fish for Nim to make float and strands of wind chimes strung throughout a room for Vesper. Evie's dresses and playthings lay in drawers as though my parents had gathered up their children and fled, leaving it all behind as unimportant.

At the end of the hall, one door was partially closed. Curious, I pressed against the handle, and it swung open before I realized where I was standing. This was the nursery meant for me and the brother whose name had never been uttered because it was bad luck to speak of the dead.

That grave chill returned, but worse, forming a wall I would have to breach if I wanted to go inside. Toys and books occupied sparse shelves, not quite so neat as the other rooms. Something had dislodged them, and a few had fallen into a pile on the floor. I bent, meaning to stretch my hand through the doorway and take one. There had been no trace of a scent on the clothes in the other rooms, nothing to say that someone else had ever touched them. I hoped I'd find something to prove the Hollow hadn't always felt like a crypt.

"They called him Nico," Anise said. I hadn't heard her approach. Her dark eyes glinted in the light like the sharpened point of a knife, and they cut just as deep.

"I thought he died before they had a chance to name him."

My brother hadn't seemed quite real as an unnamed entity. He'd been more dream than ghost, but a name added weight. I'd killed a real person rather than the idea of one.

Penelope killed Nico. Penn killed Penelope. Now Nico had killed Penn. His face should have been below the top hat, not mine, and not another day would pass without me knowing that.

"Your names were picked out weeks before you were born," Anise said. "I'll take it as a technicality that Papa's unavailable to argue with me—you deserve to know."

She leaned into the door frame, not entering any farther than I had, arms crossed, but not in anger.

"It's just a room, Penn. One that's yours. This whole house is yours as much as it is mine. It's your—"

"Don't say home."

"It *is* your home."

"Which I destroyed."

Just like I destroyed The Show, which was the only home that mattered to me.

"You didn't," she said. "And Papa should never have let you think you did. I shouldn't have stayed quiet when I knew better." She braced my shoulders. "You were an infant, Penn. What happened, happened, but you can't take the blame for your born nature, nor are you responsible for dark deeds done by others in your name. What happened to the train is *not* your fault."

I shattered.

I'd held myself up so long without even realizing I wanted to hear someone say exactly that. I'd *needed* to hear someone say it; that was the only way it would ever be true.

Days' worth of exhaustion, and years' worth of guilt, churned up like the froth below a waterfall. I collapsed against my sister, hanging on with both hands. She'd managed to find soap enough for a shower, which mixed with the scent of earth that came from her skin and chased the darkness away.

"What's wrong with me?" I asked her.

"Nothing. All of the wrongs around you are coming from outside."

"But I raised Medusae, Anise. *Me.* By myself. No one did that to me or for me. It has to mean something."

"It means that you are exactly as singular as Papa believed you to be."

All of the questions about our father and what he knew of my true abilities rushed to my mouth, only to tangle at the back of my tongue with questions about what he knew of Winnie and Greyor and Birdie. What did he know about Nye or Nagendra's past with the Commission?

What did Anise know besides my brother's name? It should have been easy to ask her, but in the moment, it was more difficult than escaping the Center. So I let go of her and kept quiet, certain that she'd be there when I was ready to ask her everything.

"It's just a room, Penn," she said again. "There's no reason not to go inside, especially to avoid ghosts that do not haunt it."

Anise pushed off the door frame and left me to myself.

I stood at the door to my nursery for more long minutes and half-held breaths, putting my foot forward, only to draw it back and start over. Finally, I stepped across what had seemed an impenetrable barrier of open air.

The rug was full of dust, dulling the colors. Small clothes sat folded on wooden cabinets beside a music box. No blue or pink on either of the cribs, nothing to suggest male or female even in a place that should have been safe from the Commission's sight. When I opened the music box, it played a song I wished I could remember. There was a picture inside of a woman with long, dark hair and eyes like all of my sisters, except Evie. I tucked the photograph into my pocket and closed the door behind me when I left.

Eventually, I found my way back to the kitchen, and the others. Somebody had scavenged up something to eat. From the amount of greens, it was probably Birch. I took a seat on the bench beside Jermay, trying not to notice how the surface around his plate was old and scarred, gouged with deep lines, and blackened by fire. This was where my brother died. There'd been no ghosts in the nursery because they were all waiting for me in the kitchen.

I reached toward one of the marks, and an infant's wail filled my ears. The image of my mother's face twisted from the perfection of her photograph to anguished eyes and the death mask expression Iva took on when she shut down for good. I pulled my hand back just before my fingers grazed the table, sure that it would burn me if I touched it.

"Are you okay?" Jermay asked.

"I'm better off than most," I said. I had no right to complain when things could have been much worse.

How many of the recruits from the Center never made it out? How many had families who would be crying over their graves the way we were mourning Zavel? What had the Commission done to Sister Mary Alban?

I wished I had a candle to light. The Hollow needed more good thoughts to paint the ceiling with their smoke. I needed a few myself.

"What do we do now?" Birch asked. "They'll be looking for us."

"I want my papa," Birdie cried.

I wanted mine, too.

"We'll find him," Anise said.

"How?" Jermay asked. "Magnus said to come here, but he never told us what to do if here wasn't an option."

"I know a place," Winnie said. "I wouldn't call it safe, but the Commission won't be there."

Slowly, and without a spoken word, we all agreed. *Safe* had become more abstract in the last weeks. Maybe the safest place for us was one where the Commission was afraid to go—that possibility terrified me.

Winnie and Birch started packing our things while Klok saw to Xerxes and Bijou. Once I could get Klok alone, I'd ask him about the memory chip I'd found. Maybe I'd ask Anise, too, and see if their stories were the same. Klok wasn't capable of lying, as far as I knew, but I wasn't sure about anyone else, anymore.

"I'll clear the kitchen," I said.

"Do you want help?" Jermay asked, but I shook my head. As usual, he seemed to understand when I needed space, and he drifted off with Birdie.

I took out the photograph of my mother. Iva Roma smiled up at me, and in her eyes was the warmth I'd seen in my father's re-creation just before she was stolen from me. It was too painful. I let the paper fall into the flames and catch, crumbling away a piece at a time until there was nothing left but ash on the wind.

I lifted the kettle that Klok had used to fix our dinner and set it off the fire. I should have poured it out, let the water soak the flames into the dirt floor, but I stood there—just watching. The scent of simmered greens turned clean and crisp with the salted bite of sea air; the bubbles that had died away without heat began to boil again. My shimmering sailfish burst through the bubbles into the air.

I turned my attention to the ground; a tremor below the surface drummed out a timpani beat at my feet. Grains of sand formed a sturdy paw, with shards of broken stone for claws. Behind them a tufted wild-cat sprang up and slashed at the fish before a swirling breeze sent the golem sifting back to the earth that had birthed it.

I crouched and held my hand over the flames until I knew I should have felt them. Instead I closed my hand and drew the flames up off the logs so they shined from the ends of my fingers.

Strange as the idea seemed, the best advice had come from Warden Nye: *Do your worst.*

A flick of my wrist created a bird made entirely of fire that perched in my palm. I blew across it the way I'd seen Evie do a thousand times, and the flaming golem burst into embers, without a trace left behind.

"Ready?" Jermay asked, popping his head back into the kitchen.

I nodded.

For now, I'd go with the others. I'd find my sisters and my father. I'd get my answers. And then the Commission would burn.

ABOUT THE AUTHOR

L. J. Hatton is a Texan, born and raised. She sometimes refers to the towns she's lived in by the movies filmed in them, and if she wasn't working as a professional pretender, she'd likely be holed up in a lab somewhere doing genetics research.

12780008R00212

Printed in Great Britain
by Amazon.co.uk, Ltd.,
Marston Gate.